# SHADOW'S
# SURRENDER

## AN INSURGENTS MC ROMANCE

CHIAH WILDER

I love hearing from my readers. You can email me at chiahwilder@gmail.com.

Make sure you sign up for my newsletter so you can keep up with my new releases, special sales, free short stories, and other treats only available to newsletter readers. When you sign up, you will receive a FREE hot and steamy novella. Sign up at: http://eepurl.com/bACCL1.

Visit me on facebook at facebook.com/AuthorChiahWilder
Visit me on twitter at twitter.com/chiah_wilder
Visit me in Instagram at instagram.com/chiah803

## Insurgent MC Series:

Hawk's Property
Jax's Dilemma
Chas's Fervor
Axe's Fall
Banger's Ride
Jerry's Passion
Throttle's Seduction
Rock's Redemption
An Insurgent's Wedding
Outlaw Xmas
Wheelie's Challenge
Christmas Wish
Animal's Reformation
Insurgents MC Romance Series: Insurgents Motorcycle Club Box Set
(Books 1 – 4)
Insurgents MC Romance Series: Insurgents Motorcycle Club Box Set
(Books 5 – 8)

## Night Rebels MC Series:

STEEL
MUERTO
DIABLO
GOLDIE
PACO
SANGRE
ARMY
Night Rebels MC Romance Series: Night Rebels Motorcycle Club Box Set
(Book 1 – 4)

## Nomad Biker Romance Series:

Forgiveness
Retribution

## Steamy Contemporary Romance:

My Sexy Boss

# PROLOGUE

*Pinewood Springs*
*Nineteen years before*

STEVIE SAT UP with a jolt, blinking to focus his eyes in the darkness. The familiar *thud* of his father's footsteps on the stairs filled the boy's ears as fear burned in his veins like liquid fire. He glanced over at the nightstand and the red light from the clock radio his mother had given him for his birthday glowed 3:47 a.m. When his father hadn't come home after the bars had closed, the boy thought his dad wouldn't show up until the morning as was his routine more times than not. No such luck—and from the way he was walking, he was drunk … *again.*

"Dammit!" his father's voice bounced off the hallway walls. "Why doesn't that stupid brat keep his shit in *his* room?"

The knot in Stevie's stomach coiled tighter and his heart pounded as he listened to the Transformer Nemesis Pax figure break apart. He clutched the sheets and brought them up to his chin while he inched toward the edge of the bed, his gray eyes fixed on the doorknob.

The door burst open and the boy stared at the menacing form as it staggered toward him. Stevie slipped off the mattress and tried to crawl away, but his father rushed over to him, grabbed one of his arms, and yanked him toward him. The carpet on the bedroom floor burned the back of his leg.

"Lemme alone!" he cried out as his father jerked him up then tightened his grip on both underarms, thumbs digging between the muscles.

"What have I told you about leaving your shit in the hallway?" His breath stank of alcohol.

"I'm sorry," Stevie mumbled.

"You didn't think I was comin' home, did you?" His father's eyes narrowed.

The boy just stared into his dad's bloodshot eyes.

"Answer me!"

"Russ, leave him alone," his mother's voice filtered from across the darkened room.

"Stay outta this, Carmen, or you know what you'll get!" For a split second, Russ looked over his shoulder then back at his son. "I told you to answer me."

Stevie's arm ached and a surge of defiance pushed away his fear. Staring his father straight in the eyes, he lifted his chin. "No, and I'm sorry as hell you did." His mother's gasp echoed in his ears right before he was slammed against the wall with a *thud*. Pain ripped through his body.

"What did you say?" his dad gritted out.

Stevie hung his head to avoid his father's gaze and looked over at the box of Legos his mother had given him that morning for his eleventh birthday.

His dad grabbed his hair. "What the hell did you say?"

"Nothing," he muttered.

"Tell me what you said!"

"Russ, stop this now! Leave Stevie alone. You're drunk—just go to bed." His mother came over and tried to pull her husband off the boy.

Without even a sidelong glance, his father backhanded his mother and then slammed Stevie against the wall again.

Falling on the floor, the boy looked up and glared at his father. "I said, I'm sorry you came home. You wanna hear more? I wish you would never come home. Never!"

"You little shit!" His dad kicked him in the stomach, and the boy cried out and crawled away.

"Never! Never! Never!" Gasping between words, Stevie tried to make it to the closet, but his father followed alongside him. Then he bent down on his haunches, his elbows on his knees.

"You ungrateful bastard!"

"Russ! Stop it!"

Stevie saw his father's hand balling into a fist and he prepared for the blow that would land on his face.

All of a sudden his dad's face twisted in pain. "Fuck!" He jerked back and held his head between his hands as he slumped down on the carpet.

"Go downstairs and call the police," his mother said as she placed the desk lamp on the nightstand.

"What the hell did you do to me, Carmen?"

Stevie scrambled to his feet. "I'm not going unless you come with me." After years of watching his father slap his mother around he didn't want to take any chances, especially since this was the first time she'd fought back.

"I'll be fine, honey. Just go."

"Not unless you come downstairs too."

Nodding, she reached out and ran her fingers through his thick black hair. "You always look out for your mama, don't you? You're my shadow … always with me." She grasped her son's hand and they ambled out of the room, his father's groans growing fainter as they walked down the stairs.

# CHAPTER ONE

*Sixteen years ago*

IF HIS FATHER would've been locked up for a long time or had gone away, it would've been the perfect ending to an existence of fear, anger, and hurt, but life didn't work that way. At least it didn't seem to for Steve Basson. His father spent a few weeks in jail, then wooed his way back into his mother's heart. All was good for a while until his dad's old ways crept back in: chasing every skirt in town, getting drunk, and hitting on his wife and son.

At fourteen years old, *Steve* had grown much taller and had begun to fill out, and he'd also adopted the nickname his mother had given him a few years back—"Shadow." Now when his father hit on his mother, Shadow put up a battle, transferring his dad's wrath to him over his mother's protestations.

It was a cold winter night when the front doorbell rang at one in the morning. The chimes sounded odd at that hour in the quiet of the house. Shadow had reached the door first and grasped the knob. His mother shuffled toward him, her long fingers tying the sash around her robe.

"Who could it be?" she whispered.

Shadow looked through the peephole and saw two police officers. "Cops. Dad's probably gotten himself in trouble *again*." He pulled the door open.

"Mrs. Basson?" one of the cops asked, looking over Shadow's shoulder.

"Yes." She gripped her son's arm.

"May we come in?"

"Just say what you need to right where you're at," Shadow grumbled.

The older officer threw a hard look at the teenager. "Who are you?"

"Sha—Steve Basson. Why're you here?"

The younger cop fidgeted in place, glancing at Shadow then at his mom. "Is Russell Basson your husband?"

"Yes." Her fingers dug deeper into Shadow's skin.

The older uniform cleared his throat. "We're sorry to inform you, but your husband was killed this evening in an alley behind the Old Miner's Bar."

His mother sagged against Shadow, and he wrapped his arm around her. The only thing Shadow felt was relief upon learning of his father's death. It turned out that some guy had slit his father's throat—ear to ear—in a fight that had spilled out of the dive bar his dad had frequented every weekend for as long as Shadow could remember. The only thought that kept flitting through his brain was: *We're finally free of the sonofabitch.*

Losing his tyrannical father that day threw him and his mother into a financial tailspin, but for Shadow, the peace in the household was worth losing their family home and moving into a rusted trailer in the seedier part of Pinewood Springs. There was a five-year waitlist for government housing, so a friend of a friend of his mother's had hooked her up with a landlord who only cared about the rent, and they had moved in just before Shadow's fifteenth birthday.

It was hotter than hell in the trailer that night, and the three fans blowing the stagnant air around the tiny living room weren't doing shit to cool anything off. Beads of sweat rolled down Shadow's back as he walked over to the fridge and grabbed a Coke. He ran the cold can over his face and around his neck before popping it open and guzzling it down. He crushed the can and tossed it into the trashcan.

"Remember to stay inside," his mother said as she adjusted her stockings. "These damn things are clinging to my legs, it's so hot."

Shadow looked away. He hated that his mother had to work at a strip bar to pay the damn bills. Every time he brought up quitting school to work at Crossroad's Ranch in the valley, he and his mother would get into a fight, and it always ended the same—Shadow promising to stay in school until he graduated. The measly part-time job he had at Hanson's Barber Shop in town barely covered the electric bill.

"I'm gonna hang out for about an hour with Eli," he said, avoiding his mother's eyes.

"No, you're not. I don't want you running around at night when I'm not here or getting into any trouble. I couldn't stand it if anything happened to you."

*Fuck!* "It's just for an hour and we're gonna hang around here."

"I don't like the people who live here."

Shadow felt his mom's arms wrap around his waist; she was standing behind him, and he could smell the coconut perfume she always wore. She told him that it made her feel like she was on vacation at a beach resort. How he wished he could take her to one of those islands she was always talking about.

"Ma," he wriggled out of her grasp, "I'm almost sixteen. I can go to Eli's house—he lives in a nice neighborhood and you've met his parents before. I hate sitting around here all the time."

His mother blinked rapidly. *Fuck—she's gonna cry. Why the fuck don't I keep my big mouth shut?* "Okay, Ma, I'll stay here. You know, I worry about *you* when you're at work. There're a lot of creeps at Satin Dolls."

"I watch myself. Anyway, if all goes the way I think it will, I won't have to work there too much longer."

"What does that mean?"

"I may have a good prospect. I better go—I'll be late for work. Stay inside, okay?"

"Yeah," he mumbled as he watched her walk away.

Shadow never thought about his mother dancing—that would just be too weird, so instead, he pretended that she was a bartender at Satin Dolls and that seemed to work for the most part.

After an hour, Shadow called Eli and told him he was coming by in a half hour. For the past six months, Shadow had been going out at night even though he knew his mother would be livid. He always made sure to come back before she returned from work. He and his best buddy, Eli, usually hooked up with some other friends and they'd just hang out at the diner or the park. Sometimes they'd pick up chicks, graffiti some street signs and buildings, go to the movies—Eli always paid for him— or play pool at Cues. Dirk, the owner, let them come in after 10:00 p.m. even though they were underage. One of Dirk's friends, Banger, came around sometimes, and he had one of the coolest motorcycles Shadow had ever seen. Each time Banger set foot in the pool hall, he'd go over to Shadow and talk to him for a bit. Shadow looked up to him, and he admired how the biker commanded respect the minute he'd walk into Cues. When Shadow found out Banger was the president of the Insurgents MC—an outlaw club in town, he wasn't surprised. Banger spent time telling him about the ride and how motorcycles worked, and the more he talked, the more Shadow wanted to be part of the MC world someday.

Shadow kept the desire to own a Harley-Davidson and to check out the Insurgents' clubhouse when he turned eighteen—Banger's rule, not his—to himself, not even confiding in Eli. As far as his mother was concerned, he would graduate high school then go to Pinewood Community College for a couple of years and get a good-paying job. Shadow didn't have the heart to tell her that he wanted something more than to be tied down to a nine-to-five job.

Several weeks later, his mom started coming home with bags of new clothes for him, a new computer, and a new phone.

"Where're you getting all this money from?" Shadow asked before he shoved a forkful of hamburger casserole into his mouth.

"I've been saving all my tips." His mother put another scoop of green beans on his plate.

"Enough," he said, lightly pushing her hand away.

"You need to eat more vegetables to stay healthy," she replied as she put the spoon back into the serving bowl.

Shadow put his fork down and stared at his mom. "Now tell me the truth about where the money's coming from, and I don't believe for a minute it's from your tips."

Carmen touched the bottom of the sterling silver pendant with her fingers. Since he'd bought it for her birthday a few months before, his mother always wore it. He'd seen it at one of the booths selling Navajo jewelry at a biker rally Banger had invited him to. The minute Shadow had seen the pendant, he'd thought of his mother. The cross was sterling silver with red coral and turquoise inlaid in the intricate design. It dangled on a silver chain. The price for the necklace was out of his range, but Banger had offered to loan him the money, and Shadow had been paying the biker back a few dollars every week.

"Are you selling drugs?" He picked up his fork again and speared a couple of string beans.

His mother's eyes widened. "No! How could you ask me that?"

Shadow chewed slowly, his eyes never leaving his mom's. "I'm not judging you, Ma. There's nothing wrong with trying to make some extra money. We've been poor long enough."

"Don't ever have anything to do with"—she looked behind her at the broken-down screen door and lowered her voice—"drugs. They're evil and they'll destroy you. Have you tried them?" Her blue-gray eyes glistened.

"No, and stop changing the subject. Where you getting all this money?"

"I met a man," she whispered, looking down at her plate. "He's rich and he wants to help us."

"I'm sure he does. Did you meet him at the club?"

"I've seen him around town, but, yes, he comes to the club. We've known each other for a while. I was going to tell you, but I wanted to wait until the time was right. He's a very nice man who has a generous heart." A smile spread across her face.

"Are you gonna marry him?"

"I want to. He's in the middle of getting a divorce, so we have to keep our relationship low-key for a little bit." Carmen ran her fingers through her long hair. "Stop looking at me like that—I know what you're thinking. He *is* going through a divorce."

"Don't all married dudes say that?" Shadow stood up and took his plate to the sink. "Be careful, Ma, or the jerk's gonna break your heart."

"No, he's not. The only one in my heart is you, and there's no room for anyone else. I want you to have a better life." She stood up and came over to him. "I want to get outta this dump—you deserve a safer place to live and ... I want to stop dancing."

Shadow hugged his mother. "If he makes you happy, then I'm good, but the minute this rich dude gives you any trouble or pain, I'll bash his damn face in."

"Deal," she whispered.

A few months later, Shadow and his mother were living on the top floor of a luxurious apartment building overlooking the Rocky Mountains and the Colorado River. His bedroom was bigger than the whole trailer they'd lived in. His mother didn't dance anymore and she was always smiling.

Shadow hadn't met the new man in his mom's life—didn't even know his name, but several times in the past two weeks, she'd hinted that he may have a rich *stepfather* very soon.

It was a late summer's night and school was starting the following week. Shadow sat on the couch staring at the television screen when he heard the familiar click of his mother's heels on the hardwood floor.

"You know the rules about staying in, right?"

He tore his gaze away from the screen and glanced at his mother. "We're in a good neighborhood now."

"I know." She approached him and the scent of coconut swirled around him. "I just worry about you being out when I'm not home. You're not sixteen yet."

"Is that the age of freedom around here?" He rolled his eyes then switched his attention back to the screen.

"I know I'm being overprotective, but a young boy can get into a lot of trouble—even end up in jail."

"I'm not Dad, and I'm not gonna do anything stupid. You gotta trust me sometime, Ma."

She crossed over to him, then bent and kissed the top of his head. "I do trust you—it's all the others out there who I don't." She threaded her fingers through his hair. "I was so wild when I was your age and I made so many mistakes. I just don't want you to screw up your life. Learn from my experiences."

Shadow knew what she was talking about—falling in love with his dad and getting pregnant by him at seventeen. Her parents had thrown her out of the house, so she'd married his dad and spent fourteen years in hell. He grasped his mother's hand and squeezed it. "I don't plan on screwin' up my life, and I'll never be like Dad … *ever*."

"You never could be—you're a good person and he wasn't. It's just that I couldn't live if something happened to you."

He let go of her hand. "Nothing's gonna happen to me, Ma. Now go and have a good time with your rich boyfriend. I'm good with watching TV."

"Someday when you have your own kids, you'll understand," she said, walking toward the front door.

Shadow pushed up from the couch and followed her to the foyer, then he opened the door. "Don't worry about me, Ma."

"I can't help it." She walked down the hall toward the elevator.

He stood just outside the door watching her. When the metal doors opened, she stepped inside, smiled, then waved. He returned her smile, then went back inside and crossed over to the window facing the street. Shadow looked down and saw a chauffeur open the door to a black limousine and his mom disappeared inside it. The man then walked around to the driver's side and slid in, and in a few seconds, the car pulled away from the curb.

Shadow stood staring at the street long after the limo vanished from sight. The cellphone in his pocket vibrated, jarring him back to the present. He fished it out and smiled when he saw the text was from Maggie—the cute blonde he'd met the week before at the pool hall. She was twenty-two years old, stacked, and had a reputation of being fast, at least that was what Dirk had told him. Upon learning that piece of information, Shadow set up a date with her, and she was texting him at that moment to find out when he was going to come by her place.

A stab of guilt pulsed at the back of his skull, but he ignored it. Maggie was most definitely not the type of girl his mother would approve of for him, but what his mom didn't know wouldn't hurt.

After texting Maggie back he walked to his bedroom to change his clothes and then rushed out and strode briskly toward Main Street to hail a cab; he didn't want to keep Maggie waiting.

IT WAS LATE and he knew his mother would be angry and disappointed when he arrived home. The anger he could deal with, but the disappointed look on his mom's face crushed Shadow each and every time. He swore under his breath as he crossed the street—only six more blocks to go. He should've left Maggie's place two hours before, but the chick was such a wildcat that Shadow just couldn't tear himself away from her. She was nothing like the high school girls he'd fucked. Yeah … he'd be hooking up with her again real soon.

He glanced at his phone again, surprised his mother hadn't called to ball him out. The glowing numbers read 2:08 a.m. He shoved the phone back into the rear pocket of his jeans and walked past big houses with manicured lawns.

All of a sudden the scream of a police siren ripped through the night, shattering the quiet. Flashes of red and blue lights penetrated the darkness, and Shadow jumped back into the bushes and waited for them to stop in front of him. Curfew was 11:00 p.m., and he grimaced when he pictured his mother's face as she came down to the police station to take him home. But the cars sped past him, and he watched as they disappeared over the hill.

As Shadow approached he saw cop cars with flashing lights and an ambulance up ahead; they were stationed in front of his apartment building. His steps faltered, and then he began to run toward the chaos.

When he reached his building, he saw the yellow crime scene tape cordoning off the area. Several people gathered in front, and he recognized the man with the black and tan Pekingese, who lived on the second floor of the building.

"What's going on?" Shadow asked, his heart pounding.

The man shrugged his thin shoulders. "The cops aren't telling us anything." He looked at Shadow. The reflection of the flashing lights made the neighbor's eyes glow a weird reddish color.

"Somebody's been murdered," a woman whispered.

Shadow spun around and saw the old lady from next door standing behind him, her hair in curlers, her white robe held closed by one bony hand.

"Who is it?" he asked, panic tugging at the pit of his stomach.

"I don't know."

Shadow searched the small crowd for his mother, but she wasn't there. A bitter bile rose up the back of his throat. *Stop being a fuckin' wimp! Ma's just fine. She wouldn't come down with all these people. She's not a damn looky-loo. I just gotta get inside—get to her.*

He glanced around again and noticed that a lot of the residents hadn't come down. This fact should've reassured him, but he couldn't stop the dark fear creeping inside him, threatening to smother him. Shadow ducked under the police tape and bounced up the front steps.

"Whoa, kid. What the hell do you think you're doing?" a tall cop asked as he approached Shadow.

"I live here."

"You can't go inside."

"I'm pretty sure my mom's worried about me 'cause I'm late."

"I'm going to say it again—you can't go inside. Call her."

A smile spread across Shadow's face. Why the hell hadn't he thought of that? Of course, he'd call his mom and explain that he was stuck outside and would be upstairs when the cops let everyone back into the building. How fucking simple.

As he took out his phone he saw a man in a dark suit walk toward him.

"What's your name?" the man asked.

Shadow stopped tapping in the number and glanced up. "Steve Basson."

The man glanced at the doorway to the building then back to him. "Do you got something saying that?"

"My school ID." Shadow fished it out of his wallet and handed it to the man. "Who are you anyway?"

The man studied the card then handed it back to Shadow. "I'm Detective McCue." He motioned to one of the police vehicles. "Can you go over there for a minute?"

"No. I have to call my mother. She's going to be real worried why I'm not home." He forced himself to focus on tapping in the last four digits of his mom's phone number. Panic skittered up and down his spine, but he ignored it and held the phone to his ear.

Detective McCue reached out and gripped Shadow's wrist. "I need to talk to you, kid."

"About what?" Blood rushed to his temples, echoing in his ears, burning through his veins.

"Just come on over."

"No. I have to talk to my mother."

The chattering of the crowd subsided and Shadow looked over his shoulder and saw the paramedics wheeling a stretcher toward the ambulance. A body lay on it, covered with a white sheet.

"Take it to my office," a medium-built man said. The medics nodded and lifted the stretcher into the ambulance.

Shadow bolted toward the vehicle, but the detective's hands gripped his shoulders, pulling him back.

"Lemme go! I need to get to my mother." The fear he'd been trying to ignore overwhelmed him as cold sweat poured down his face. He turned around and stared at McCue. "Who's on that stretcher? Why do you wanna talk to me? Why didn't my mom call me to see where I was? Why!"

The detective's grip loosened and he fixed his gaze on Shadow. "It's never easy, but I'm going to tell it to you straight—your mother was murdered. I'm sorry, kid. I'm so fucking sorry to have to tell you. Do you have anyone you can call?"

The sirens, the flashing lights, the cop's voice grew dimmer, and he clutched his middle as pain clawed him from the inside out, his anguished cry catching on the breeze and carrying it away.

*Ma's dead. Murdered. Fuck! Ma …!*

In that moment, Shadow vowed that no matter how long it took, he would find the bastard who did this and make him pay.

# CHAPTER TWO

*Pinewood Springs*
*Present day*

THE CLUMP OF his boots bounced off the walls as Shadow reached the bottom of the stairs. He stopped just short of entering the main room, his forehead wrinkled, his lips flattened, as he struggled with the cuffs on his sky-blue collared dress shirt.

"Fuck this shit," he muttered as the buttons eluded him.

"Need some help, handsome?" Tania's voice washed over him and he glanced up.

"I can't get this damn thing to work."

The club girl laughed and walked over to him. She swatted his hand away, then quickly buttoned the starched cuffs and straightened his dark-blue patterned tie. She stepped back and her large brown eyes raked over him boldly.

"Damn, you dress up real good," she said as she reached out and ran a finger down the front of his tailored shirt. Tania then squeezed his sculpted biceps and licked her lips. "Real good, baby."

Shadow moved around her. "Thanks."

She cozied up beside him. "And you smell so good too."

He chuckled and stepped away from her. "That's good to know."

"You want a little something before you go?" Tania squeezed his tight ass.

"No time—maybe later." He winked at her then walked into the main room.

"Fuck, we got a *GQ* model who's been posing as a damn biker, dudes!" Helm's voice rose above the din of the room.

"Turn the damn TV down," Bones said. A huge grin spread across his face. "What the fuck, bro?" he asked Shadow, who took the shot of whiskey one of the prospects offered him.

"Don't you look *fancy*," Smokey said before breaking out into laughter.

The members in the room had now diverted their attention to Shadow, and he gritted his teeth.

"Fuck off," he said as he set down his empty glass.

"Are you having tea with the Queen?" Rags sniggered.

"Or the fuckin' president? We got a turncoat in our club—hobnobbing with the rich." Hubcap stretched his legs in front of him as the other brothers guffawed.

"Get a fuckin' life. I'm going to Eli's damn engagement party." Shadow fished his keys out of the side pocket of his dark-blue pants.

"Eli's getting married? His woman must be a rich bitch for you to be dressed like a pansy," Smokey said as he brought the bottle of beer to his mouth.

"For me, a party is barbecue, jeans, weed, and women who spread their legs easily. That would be my engagement shindig if I were ever fuckin' stupid enough to get saddled down with a chick," Blade said, and the other guys mumbled their agreement.

"It's Eli's fuckin' deal, not mine, and I'm wasting time talking about it with you losers. I gotta go." Shadow shrugged on his suit jacket and started walking toward the door.

"Maybe you'll get lucky—isn't that what happens at that kind of shit?" Bones asked.

"It's weddings that people fuck strangers, dude, not engagement parties," Rags replied.

"How the hell do you know that? Is there some damn rule book on that?" Bones scrunched his face.

"Maybe Shadow knows. What is it, dude?" Helm said.

Ignoring them, Shadow walked out into the blaring sunlight and crossed the parking lot to his Ford Ranger. Normally, he'd hop on his motorcycle, but he didn't want to arrive at the function dripping in sweat. Even though it was early evening, it was still hot as all hell, and there wasn't a cloud in the sky.

Shadow pulled himself into the driver's seat, switched on the engine, cranked up the air conditioner, and sped out of the parking lot. As he drove to the Pinewood Country Club, a few chuckles escaped his lips as the voices of the members flitted through his mind. He had to admit they'd let him off easy, and if he had been sitting there and one of them had come into the room looking like he did, Shadow would've ribbed him real good.

"I'm doing this for you, Eli," he muttered under his breath as he took a left on Willow Road. He'd decided that he'd talk to Eli for a few, be polite to the chick he was marrying—he never could remember her name—have a couple of drinks, and then get the hell out of there. The club was having a big party later that night with several of the brothers coming in from different chapters. Shadow didn't want to spend his night with a bunch of stuffy suits.

He pulled up to the front of the club and a guy in his early twenties rushed over to the truck and opened the door for him.

"Where do I park?" Shadow asked.

"Just leave your keys in the ignition, sir. What is your name?" The guy held a card and a pen in his hand.

"I'm not gonna let you drive my truck."

The man shook his head. "This is valet. I'll be careful with your vehicle, sir."

Shadow narrowed his gray eyes. "The first thing you need to do is stopping calling me *sir*, and the second is to step away and just point to where I need to park."

"But, sir—" The valet stopped short and looked down at the ground.

"Fuck, dude, this shouldn't be complicated."

"I … uh …" the young man began.

"What's the trouble?" a man in his thirties asked. He wore a red jacket with a name tag that said "Jay Paille – Supervisor."

"He doesn't want me to drive his truck," the younger man said in a low voice.

Streaks of anger shot through Shadow and he gripped the steering wheel and inhaled deeply, trying to calm the storm that was beginning to rage inside him. Ever since he could remember, he hated living by arbitrary and stupid rules, something his dad had imposed on their household for pure evil spite. Shadow also didn't go in for complications; he liked his life simple, his whiskey neat, and his women easy. Drama didn't do it for him, so his patience at this point was wearing thin. All he wanted to do was park his damn truck, and these two guys were making something so simple into a convoluted mess.

"Sir," the supervisor said. "We can't let you park your own car."

Shadow jerked his head at a space to the right. "Is that one free?"

"Yes, but—"

Shadow closed the door and pulled into the parking space. He shoved his keys into his pocket and glanced over at the two men as he walked by the valet station.

"We'll need your keys," the supervisor said.

"No, you won't. My truck's not blocking anything."

"This goes against the rules," the man replied.

"Rules are for breaking, isn't that the way the saying goes? I like to live dangerously—I'll keep my keys." Chuckling, he strode up the stone sidewalk, then walked inside the country club.

The sweet scent of roses wrapped around him when he entered the small ballroom, and he spotted several large vases filled with the flowers against the walls and on a small stage at the back of the room. Chandeliers hung from the coffered ceiling, glittering like crystal stalactites. Flickering candles shimmered on numerous round tables that dotted the room. Shadow made his way through a sea of crisp suits and summery cocktail dresses until he reached the bar. After throwing back a tumbler of whiskey, he placed the empty glass on the edge of the counter and walked away.

"Champagne, sir?"

Shadow looked sideways and saw a waiter carrying a large tray of flutes. He reached out and took one then jerked his head at the man, who scurried toward a cluster of people standing near the buffet table.

There were a lot more people at this party than Shadow had expected. From the looks of it, he surmised that the majority of partygoers were from the fiancée's side. He brought the champagne glass to his lips and glanced around the room in search of Eli.

"Fuck," Shadow muttered under his breath as his gaze fell on a woman standing across the room near one of the floor-to-ceiling windows. She was gorgeous. Tall and curvy in all the right places, her golden hair cascaded down her back in waves. His eyes slowly traveled over her body, admiring the way the tight pink dress hugged her so damn deliciously. A slit up the side of the dress revealed a shapely tanned leg that made his mouth go dry. *She's one fuckin' sexy woman.* Shadow knocked back what was left of the champagne, his gaze still fixed on the beauty across the room.

As if sensing his stare, the woman ran her hands over her bare arms then glanced over. Shadow whistled softly through his teeth as his gaze met hers. *Fuck, she's stunning.* The look on her face was rebellious and dangerous and beautiful all at once. Her gaze didn't waver from his and he liked that. There was something about her that captivated and held him.

"You came, dude. I thought you were going to be MIA." Eli's hand clasped his shoulder and Shadow dragged his eyes away from the blonde.

"Yeah. I've been here for a bit." He glanced over Eli's shoulder and saw the woman still looking at him, a small smile twitching on her full lips. *I gotta find out who she is.*

"You actually wore a jacket and tie—I'm impressed." Eli chuckled.

"You better be—I don't wear this pansy shit just for anyone." Shadow replaced his empty flute with a full one from another waiter's tray.

"I know, dude, that's why I'm feeling honored as fuck. Mom and Dad are here. They'd love to see you." Eli craned his neck as he looked around the room.

"I'd like to see them too—it's been a while."

Shadow owed a lot to Eli's parents: They opened their home to him after his mother's murder. Social Services wanted to send him to a foster home, but Patricia and Robert wouldn't hear of it, so he stayed with them for the next few years. After graduation, he made a beeline to the Insurgents and he never looked back. Eli's parents always extended an invitation to him for holidays and Sunday suppers, but as the years went by Shadow saw less and less of them, preferring to spend his time with his real family—the Insurgents.

"Brooke!" Eli yelled, and a pretty brunette in a short poufy dress turned around and then walked toward them.

*That's her name.* Shadow lifted his chin at her. "Hey ... nice party." He took a sip of the bubbly stuff.

"Thanks." Her eyes skimmed over him. "I never would've recognized you." She gave him a toothy smile.

He didn't answer and his gaze darted again toward the blonde who was now walking to the patio doors.

"Did you get any hors d'oeuvres?" Brooke asked.

"Not yet. I think I'll get another drink."

Brooke's eyes slid from the full flute back to Shadow's face. "You don't like champagne?"

"It's fine, but I'm more of a whiskey guy." He finished his drink and tipped his head at her and said, "I almost forgot to congratulate the both of you." Then Shadow clasped Eli's arm. "I'll catch up with you later." He set the empty glass on a table and walked toward the patio.

She stood by a tree, staring out at the pond in the distance. The flush on her cheeks was berry pink, and the sunlight filtering through the branches made her hair glisten like pale gold. All at once, she turned toward him and he was blown away again by her loveliness. *So damn sexy. I'd like to bury myself inside her.* The tight fit of her dress accentuated her perfectly rounded breasts, and his gaze lingered on them before slowly trailing up to her face and falling on her lips. Plump. Pouty. Hot.

Perfect for wrapping around his cock.

For a brief moment their eyes locked, and then she looked down, smiling slightly. Shadow shoved one of his hands in the front pocket of his pants and kept his gaze fixed on her. The woman looked back up at him from beneath her lashes, the tip of her tongue skimming the top of her lip.

*Fuck.* Shadow handed his glass to a passing waiter and started toward her. She turned away, her gaze returning to the distant pond and trees.

"Can I get you a drink?" he asked as he stood next to her.

"Excuse me?" She whirled around, feigning surprise.

*Yeah, baby, I'll play the game.* "I asked if you wanted a drink." He moved in closer, and the scent of spiced vanilla swirled around him.

"Yes, thanks."

"Yo," Shadow said, motioning a waiter over. "We need a couple of drinks here. A Jack for me." He cut his gaze to her. "What can I get you?"

"A vodka cran," she said to the waiter.

Her voice was soft, warm, and a little deeper than he expected. Sexy and damn arousing. He stepped closer until her bare arm brushed against his suit jacket. He tilted his head down, and her gaze flew up and met his as the corners of his mouth tugged up slightly.

"Are you friends with Brooke or Eli?" Shadow asked.

"Brooke—we went to college together. What about you?"

He made a mental note that she didn't move away from him.

"Eli. We've been buddies since high school. What's your name?"

"Scarlett. You?"

"Shadow."

Her forehead crinkled a little. "That's an unusual name."

"It's a nickname."

"A whiskey for you," the waiter said as he handed Shadow his drink, "and a vodka cranberry for the lady."

Shadow handed Scarlett the glass and his fingers purposely touched hers. He enjoyed the look of surprise that quickly crossed her face and he chuckled before taking a sip of his drink.

"Nothing like a shot of whiskey," he said.

"That's my father's favorite vice—drinking too much whiskey." She wrapped her lips around the tiny straw and held his gaze.

His jaw tightened and he cleared his throat as he ran a hand through his hair. *This chick is something else.*

"I needed this," Scarlett said as she stirred her drink, the ice cubes clinking against the glass.

He leaned in so close that his lips brushed against her ear. "Did you?" The scent of her perfume filled his lungs. He wanted nothing more than to bury his face in her neck and bite her sweet, soft flesh all the way down to her impressive tits.

Without moving an inch, she turned toward him. "Yes," she whispered. "It's hotter than hell out here."

"You're hotter than hell." Her skin was soft under his fingers as he trailed them up her bare arm and over her shoulder. A streak of satisfaction rode up Shadow's spine when he felt her flesh pebble beneath his touch and he looked to meet her gaze.

"Let's go inside," she said before wrapping those luscious lips around her straw again and draining the glass.

The coolness of the room was a welcomed relief from the stifling heat outside.

"I see you met Scarlett," Eli said as he approached them.

"Yeah … I did." Shadow smiled at her and a light pink flush crept up her neck.

"Jessica is looking for you," Brooke said to Scarlett.

Shadow turned his back and leaned in close to Eli. "Why the fuck didn't you ever mention this chick to me?"

Eli laughed. "You're so out of her league, dude."

"Not for a hookup." From the corner of his eye, he saw her watching him. "She's hot as shit."

"Take my advice, stick with the club girls." Eli popped a shrimp in his mouth.

Shadow chuckled, but he knew before he left the party that his cock would be buried in the sweet piece who was giving off all kinds of *fuck-me* signals.

"Are you having a good time?" Brooke said to him.

He darted his gaze to Scarlett then back to Brooke. "Sure am."

"The buffet is open if you want to eat. The music's going to start. Do you like to dance?"

"Yeah, if it's with the right woman." Again he glanced over and met Scarlett's green gaze.

The faint line across Brooke's forehead deepened as she cut her eyes to Scarlett. "You better go and find Jessica." Annoyance laced her voice.

Scarlett turned toward her friend. "That's right. See you around," she said to Eli. With a lingering look, she licked her lips. "Bye, Shadow."

He gave her a chin lift and watched her walk away; the sultry sway of her hips made his dick twitch and dirty thoughts flashed through his mind.

"Come with us and get something to eat." Brooke grabbed his hand and pulled him toward the buffet table.

After eating and chatting with Eli's parents, Shadow stood up from the table and roamed around the room, hoping to run into Scarlett again. The dancefloor in front of the makeshift deejay booth was packed with people gyrating to the beats of Jennifer Lopez's "On the Floor." The music was pounding in his ears and he was just about ready to walk away when he saw Scarlett, swaying those sexy hips, the slit in her dress parting all the way to reveal a few spectacular inches of her thigh. Shadow hissed through his teeth and threw back the rest of his drink.

Scarlett's head titled back, her eyes were closed, and her body moved so damn seductively to the music that before he could think about what he was doing, Shadow pushed through the crowd and crossed over to her. He stood behind her and wrapped his arms around her small waist and yanked her back against him.

"Keep dancing, baby," he said into her ear.

She glanced up at him and a wide smile spread across her face as she pushed back and rubbed her ass against his crotch. Shadow moved his hands over her flat stomach, then brushed his fingers along the bottom of her tits. Scarlett ground against him, her hands reaching behind and settling on his narrow hips.

"Fuck, baby," he said against her ear. "You're killing me."

Laughing, she wiggled her fine ass all over his hard-as-hell dick.

"You're asking for some trouble." He licked her earlobe.

"Maybe that's what I want," she answered then leaned back against him so her head rested against his shoulder.

"Then I'm all in, baby."

They moved against each other, and he hadn't wanted a woman like that in a long time.

"Just tell me when you wanna get out of here," he said. His hands slid back down to her hips.

The song blended into another one, and Scarlett swiveled around in his arms until she faced him. They were so close that her ragged breath caressed his face. They held each other's gaze as his hands dropped down to her rounded ass.

She licked her lips. "Let's go," she said.

Shadow dropped his hands from her ass and broke away, then grabbed her hand and pulled her behind him as he walked off the dance floor. He maneuvered them through the guests until they were out into the hallway. He glanced around until he found a closed door at the other end of the hall.

"Do you know this club?" he asked as they moved toward the room.

"Yes. I'm a member."

"What's behind the door?"

"Another ballroom."

Hoping that another party wasn't going on inside, Shadow pushed open the door revealing an empty space. *Perfect.* He pulled her inside then slammed her against the closed door. Shadow bent his head and pressed his lips against hers, teasing his tongue along her bottom lip until she parted them. When he plunged his tongue inside, Scarlett moaned deep in her throat and drew her body against him, her arms circling around his neck. Her fingers tangled in his hair and she yanked it hard.

"You like it rough, don't you?" he said against her lips.

Instead of answering, she dug her nails into his scalp.

"I like it rough too," he rasped as his hands cupped her tits. "I've been wanting to see these since I first laid eyes on you." Shadow pulled her away from the wall and fumbled for the zipper at the back of her dress. She chuckled. "Where the hell is the damn thing? If I don't find it, I'm gonna rip it off."

"This dress cost over two thousand dollars," she said as she reached behind her and guided his hands to the zipper.

Shadow tugged it down and she shimmied out of it. His gaze fixed on her tits, barely contained by the thin, lacey half-bra.

"Take it off," he said.

She reached behind herself, and the wisp of fabric fell to the floor.

"Your tits are fuckin' beautiful." Desire burned and crackled inside him, a voracious wildfire blurring everything but his lust for this sexy woman. Her breasts were perfect: round pink tips that were hard and erect. He reached out and brushed them with his thumb and she gasped, arching her back and pushing them farther out. Shadow bent down and swiped his tongue across the hard buds before sucking them into his mouth.

"Fuck." She moaned.

"You like that?" He nipped, licked, and sucked a bit harder.

She grabbed at his jacket, trying to pull it off. He shrugged out of it and let it pool on the floor beside her dress, her nipple still in his mouth. Shadow broke away as Scarlett loosened his tie then groped at the buttons on his shirt.

"I want to see you," she whispered.

He quickly undid his shirt and tie, and she ran her nails up and down his bare chest.

"You're magnificent. So hard. So sexy. You must work out all the time." She leaned over and trailed soft kisses over his taut skin. "And your tattoos are so dangerous," she murmured.

"Fuck, baby," he growled, filling his hands with her tits.

Scarlett raised her head and her lips met his in a fiery, deep kiss. He picked her up and she wrapped her legs around his waist as he carried her over to a counter against the side wall. He kissed the side of her neck, his cock straining against the zipper in his pants.

"You taste so fuckin' sweet." He placed her ass down on the counter, then fished a condom out of the pocket of his trousers and set it on the counter next to her. Shadow slid his hands lower and his fingers looped around the elastic of her thong. His gaze met Scarlett's as he slipped them down her legs. With his eyes still locked on hers, his finger climbed up her toned leg until he shoved it inside her heat.

"Oh, God!" she cried out, bucking against his digit.

"You're so fuckin' hot. So wet and tight." He kneaded her breast with his other hand while he nipped the soft flesh of her neck. The scent of her arousal and the way she was panting and arching into his touch drove him so crazy with lust that he was afraid he was going to blow before he got a chance to sink into her.

Shadow broke away and reached for the condom, then he unbuckled his belt and dropped his boxers and pants. He smirked when Scarlett's eyes widened as she took in his size, and he rubbed his thumb against the side of her hard nub. Her gaze snapped to his and her mouth fell open.

"You like that?" he asked.

She moaned her response as he continued to play with her clit. Their heavy breathing filled the room, and not able to hold out any longer, Shadow spread her legs wide and ran the head of his dick up and down her slick juices.

Scarlett placed one of her hands on his shoulders and the other grasped the edge of the counter.

"I need to be in you," he rasped.

"I want it so bad," she whispered.

As soon as he shoved inside her, hard and deep, groans escaped from both their mouths.

"Fuck, you feel good. So tight, baby." He grunted as he pummeled in and out of her in quick, deep strokes. She rocked her hips into his thrusts, and he held her gaze as he fucked her hard and rough.

Shadow bent his head down and placed his mouth on one of her tits, sucking and biting at the delicate skin hard enough to leave a mark. For some reason, he wanted Scarlett to remember him and what they had done when she was alone later.

He flicked his index finger across her sweet spot and she cried out.

"You're so fuckin good," he ground out as he pounded into her. "You like that?"

"Uh-huh." She panted as her hips kept beating against his with a demanding urgency. "I'm close … so close." Scarlett's nails raked his shoulder as his mouth found hers and their tongues intertwined.

His fingers picked up speed on her clit as the tension inside him rose to an all-time high.

"Oh, God. Yes!" she cried out as she came.

Shadow moved his hand away from her clit and gripped the back of her neck, pulling her into his thrusts as his balls retracted, and then the knot at the root of his cock dissolved in fire, melting.

A rumbling groan burst from deep in his chest. "Fuck." He rested his head against her chest for a few seconds, waiting for his breath to return to normal, then he pulled away. Shadow tossed the used condom into a nearby trashcan, then pulled up his pants and tucked himself back in. He was well aware that Scarlett was watching him as he scooped up his jacket. He picked up her dress and handed it to her.

"You need me to help you with that?" he said as he folded his tie and pushed it into the pocket of his dress pants.

"That'd be helpful." Scarlett avoided his eyes as she jumped down. She dressed in silence as he stood there checking his phone. "Zip me up, please."

"Sure."

Scarlett fluffed her hair and took out a tube of lipstick from a small evening bag and swiped the wand across her lips. "We shouldn't go back into the party together."

"Whatever," he said as he started toward the door.

The light from the hallway spilled into the room as he walked out and headed back to the party. Two women he recognized from the gathering passed by, checking him out, and he winked at them and continued on his way. From behind him, he heard one of the women say, "Scarlett, where have you been? Warren came about fifteen minutes ago, and he's been looking all over for you."

"I was feeling kind of sick. It must've been something I ate. I didn't think he'd make it."

"Well he did, and Melody's got her claws out for him. You better get back in there fast."

The voices grew fainter when he entered the room and walked over to Eli.

"Where the hell have you been?" Eli asked.

"Club business," he said knowing that would end all questioning. "I'm gonna grab one last drink and take off."

Eli nodded. "I'm surprised you stayed as long as you did."

"It's a good party," he said as he grabbed a glass of champagne from a passing waiter. "I can't believe you're gonna be hitched, dude."

"I can't believe how lucky I am to have found Brooke. It just happened. You'll find out when the right woman comes into your life."

Shadow drained his glass. "Not much chance of that happening. I like my life the way it is—uncomplicated. I can have all the chicks I want, so why settle for one?"

"When you meet the right one, she'll be the only one you'll want."

"Not for me, dude, but I'm happy for you."

Shadow saw Scarlett waltz into the room looking calm and collected. No one would've guessed that she'd just got her brains fucked out. She had poise, he had to give her that. And damn … the pretty socialite was one of his better fucks.

A tall man in an expensive-looking suit came over to her and slipped his arm around her small waist. She smiled warmly at him, but her gaze drifted to Shadow's and he lifted his chin at her. She then wrapped her arm around the dude's neck and kissed him. Shadow chuckled and turned toward Eli and Brooke.

"I'm outta here," he said.

"So soon?" Brooke said.

"Yeah—I got some stuff to do."

Shadow bumped fists with Eli, then he strode out of the room without a backward glance at Scarlett.

When he entered the clubhouse, the usual Saturday night party was in full swing. He strode over to the bar where Helm, Rags, and Bones were enmeshed in a conversation.

"How was Eli's deal?" Rags asked.

"Not bad. And for the record, people fuck strangers at engagement parties." He clasped Helm's shoulder then walked away, leaving his buddies dying for more information.

Shadow climbed the stairs to his room, anxious to get out of the pansy suit and join the party.

# CHAPTER THREE

SCARLETT SAT ON the large front porch cooling herself with a colorful Chinese fan; it had been a gift from her parents on one of their many trips to Hong Kong.

"I'm just melting here," Kiara said, running her fingers through her short hair. Kiara and Scarlett had been friends since their first day of high school, and had even gone to the same university back East. After graduation they'd both returned to Pinewood Springs, where Kiara secured a part-time job at her father's prestigious financial planning firm, CWP Wealth Management. "I wonder how long the outage is going to last."

"It's already been too long," Scarlett replied. Heat licked and coiled her limbs like a hot-blooded serpent, and perspiration surfaced on her forehead and the bridge of her nose. The sky blazed blue and the sun burned an intense yellow while the ground smoldered and sent up a disoriented haze. Even the birds were silent, and the grass stood still as if too hot to move.

"You seem restless since Brooke's engagement party. Jessica and Daisy have noticed it too." Kiara leaned forward and poured iced tea from an insulated pitcher into her glass. "What's going on?"

An image of herself perched on the counter with legs spread wide and Shadow thrusting and grunting made Scarlett shift in her seat. "I guess I'm just bored."

Kiara's eyes widened. "Of Warren?"

"Of the monotony of life. I want something other than fashion shows in Denver, tea at the club, committee meetings, and all the fundraisers and cocktail parties I have to go to." Scarlett pulled at a loose thread in her cotton sundress.

"That's the world we live in—high society," Kiara said as she ran the glass of iced tea over the side of her glistening face. "The people on the other side of the tracks think we got it made, but they have no idea how many obligations we have." She took a sip of tea.

Scarlett leaned back against the soft cushion. "There are so many damn rules I have to live by that they lace me in tighter than a corset. I'd love to throw caution to the wind and just have a wild summer." She picked up her glass of iced tea from the glass-top table.

Kiara giggled. "Me too." She glanced around and lowered her voice. "But I don't dare. Being respectable can be such a burden." She sighed. "If I'm being totally honest, I just want to plan dinner parties and wait for some big, handsome man to come home from work." She tilted her head up and stared at the non-moving ceiling fan. "I want to take kids to swim lessons, broil steak on the grill for my good-looking husband … and make love all night." She glanced sideways at Scarlett. "Why do you keep pushing Warren away? If you're not careful, some other woman's going to swoop in and take him from you—someone like Melody. You know she has her eyes on your man, right?"

Scarlett shrugged and watched the melting ice cubes in her glass. "My dad's the one obsessed with him, not me."

Kiara laughed. "I think you're right about that. You seem so much more at ease since your dad's been away on business. When's he coming back?"

"Tomorrow." Scarlett's mouth turned downward and her eyes narrowed. "And the forecast is storm and thunder."

"Your dad's always scared the hell out of me ever since the first day I met him," Kiara said.

"You and practically the whole town, and that's the way he likes it. He's not at all like your dad." Scarlett's stomach clenched at the thought of her father coming home and the end of the temporary peace that had descended on the house during his absence.

"He's pretty wonderful." A small smile spread across her friend's face as she rolled her eyes. "I'm totally a daddy's little girl."

Scarlett returned the smile. "That's okay, I wish I were. You even have a mom who's cool. Mine is too busy acquiescing to every fucking thing my dad wants. Do you know that my mom has *never* taken my side in any argument or disagreement I've had with him? And my two older brothers are just miniature versions of my father." Scarlett threw her head back and stared up at the ceiling. "Ugh … my family is such a fucking cliché—rich people who are miserable."

Kiara laughed. "That's the way most of the families are in our circle. I'm one of the lucky ones—mine is pretty normal. I think once you have your own house and are married to Warren, your life will improve."

"I'm terrified of being Mrs. Warren Huntington," she whispered.

"Getting married is scary as hell for women *and* for men, but I'd love to be in your position. I mean, Warren ticks all the boxes, right? He comes from a respectable family, has a degree from an Ivy League college, and treats you like a princess. What more can you ask for?"

"A spark between us. I mean, forget about love, but I'd like to feel something akin to desire or lust for him, but I don't. Let's face it, my dad's a big real estate developer and Warren's dad owns a ton of land in an area where my father wants to develop." Kiara's eyes widened as understanding crossed over her face. Scarlett snorted. "Yeah … our relationship is just one big fucking merger."

Her friend shook her head emphatically. "No, you're wrong. Warren cares about you—I see it in his eyes. All our friends wish they could be you."

"Yeah … Well, Warren isn't as great as you all think. He likes having me as arm candy, and he's not a very good kisser."

"He's not?" Kiara looked around as if she were afraid Warren would come out from the neatly trimmed bushes at the side of the porch.

"Nope." Shadow's lips on hers with their tongues twisting and dancing together flashed through her mind, and a moan escaped through her lips. *He didn't even ask for my phone number.* The thread of disappointment that had been weaving through her since that night, coiled tighter around her nerves.

"Wow, you never told me that. I hope he's making up for that in other ways."

"Nope." Warren's lack of foreplay and technique made their intimate time together less than exciting. Hooking up with Shadow at the party had turned out to be the most exciting and wild sex she'd ever had. She'd orgasmed *twice* and that was two times more than she had ever climaxed with Warren since they'd started sleeping together. Based on *that* alone, who could blame her for using the excuse of a migraine for the past several days to get out of making love with Warren? The fact that Scarlett hadn't told any of her friends about her hookup surprised her. She and her sorority sisters shared just about everything, but for reasons she couldn't articulate, she'd wanted to keep her encounter with Shadow to herself. *So silly.*

"One of my mom's friend's"—Kiara cut her gaze to the opened windows of the house—"Mrs. Fielding," she whispered, then gave another glance at the house, "has had lovers for the last several years, and the men are always in their thirties or younger." She sat back and clasped her hands in her lap.

"Well, Mr. Fielding has been cheating for years on her, so I guess she's decided to see what she's been missing out on." Scarlett laughed.

"You're so bad. Would you ever think of doing *that*?"

"Not if I were married. That's why it's so important to be sure about the guy beforehand, and I'm not sure at all about Warren."

"And here he comes," Kiara said, her head tilting toward the circular driveway.

Scarlett looked over her shoulder and saw Warren's cherry-red sports car slowly pulling up and then stopping in front of the house. A big smile showed off his brilliant white teeth, and he waved at the women as he walked up the brick sidewalk.

Warren Huntington always looked as though he were on a runway modeling clothes for Armani or another equally expensive designer. With his piercing blue eyes, short blond hair, and angular jaw, he was one of the most eligible men in Pinewood Springs society—something Scarlett's parents, brothers, and friends kept reminding her. Too bad he didn't do anything for her. He was too charming, too perfect, and Warren *always* said the right things at the right time in public. She swore he must have a script tucked away somewhere for every occasion. Even when they were together, he rarely let his charm … or his guard down.

"Hi, beautiful," he said as he leaned over and brushed a kiss across her cheeks. He pulled back, a slight frown creasing his brow. "You're sweaty, sweetheart."

"No shit—the AC's out." A jolt of satisfaction ran through her at the look of disapproval Warren threw her.

"Isn't the power out at your house?" Kiara said.

*Good ol' Kiara—always trying to keep the peace.*

Warren turned away from Scarlett and focused on her friend. "It is, that's why I came over. How about taking a ride in my car with some nice cool air? I'll treat you ladies for lunch in Aspen." He glanced over at Scarlett. "That is, if you don't still have your headache." A twinge of bitterness laced his voice.

"That sounds wonderful," Kiara said, looking over at Scarlett.

Her first inclination was to beg off, but the heat was oppressive and a cold glass of white wine in an air conditioned restaurant sounded like a slice of heaven.

"Let me freshen up a bit," she replied, rising to her feet.

Scarlett stood up and walked into the house, then made her way to the en suite bathroom in her bedroom and turned on the faucet. Cupping her hands, she let the cool water fill them before splashing her face several times. She glanced up at the mirror and watched as lines of water trailed down her face.

"What the fuck is wrong with you?" she said to her reflection. "Why can't you get *him* out of your head? You had amazing sex at a party with a stranger. Get over it. This is becoming pathetic."

She flung off the damp sundress and glanced again in the mirror. A tingle shivered through her and landed straight to her core as she stared at the purplish-red love bite on her breast. Scarlett's eyes moved downward to the small bruise marks on her hips where Shadow's hands had held them as he pounded into her, and she pressed her thighs together as the memory of their liaison invaded her mind.

"Stop it, right now. Stop," she said as her pulse raced.

"Scarlett?" her mother's voice called.

"Shit," she muttered under her breath as she grabbed a plush towel off the rack next to the sink and wrapped it around her.

"Who are you talking to?"

"Just thinking out loud, Mom. Warren and Kiara are waiting downstairs for me, so I have to go." She squeezed out a small amount of tinted sunscreen and rubbed it over her face and down her neck.

"Where are you going?" Beads of sweat pearled along her mother's hairline.

"Warren's taking us to Aspen for lunch." Scarlett applied pink gloss to her lips then looked at her mother. The older woman's face was more lined than usual and had a dove gray pallor. "Are you okay? You don't look so good."

"It's just the heat. I wish your father would've put in a generator like he said he would the last time the power went out."

Scarlett nodded, filled a glass with cold water then handed it to her mother. "Drink this—you need to stay hydrated. Why don't you come with us for lunch?"

Her mother put the glass down on the counter and wiped her mouth. "I don't think Warren would like me tagging along."

"I'm sure he wouldn't mind. Anyway, it's an oven inside the house. Go get your purse and let's get out of here." A bit of color had returned to her mom's cheeks.

"I'm feeling better. Anyway, your father might call. I'll have Clara make up a pitcher of lemonade and I'll sit on the back porch with the battery-operated fan your father bought last week at the hardware store. Have a good time." Her mother started to walk away but stopped and looked over her shoulder, catching Scarlett's gaze. "It's never good to keep your man waiting. You better get going." She turned away and shuffled out of the room.

Scarlett chose a pink and lavender sundress from her closet, slipped it on, then headed down the stairs.

"I'm ready." The wrought-iron screen door closed behind her.

Warren placed his phone in his pocket and pushed away from the white rail. "You look so pretty and cool." He held his hand out to her.

"Thanks." Scarlett scurried down the steps and over to the sports car, then opened the passenger door.

"This is going to be so much fun," Kiara said as she climbed into the back seat. "I hope when we get home the power's restored."

Warren switched on the ignition and cold air blasted from the vents.

"That feels so good," Kiara quipped.

He leaned over, grasped Scarlett's chin between his fingers, and forced her head back. Scarlett clenched her jaw as she looked up at him.

"I'm losing patience with you," he whispered in her ear.

Before she could reply, he kissed her hard, driving his tongue between her teeth. Anger shot through her and she pushed against his chest with her fists and pulled away.

Warren's eyes flashed, but he settled back into his seat. Scarlett knew he wouldn't have let her off so easily if her friend hadn't been in the car. To Warren, public appearance was *everything*. He jerked the car into drive, switched on the radio and cranked up the volume.

Scarlett pulled down the visor and reapplied her lip gloss, then swiveled in her seat and looked out the window. She brushed her fingertips across her lips trying to feel something, but her mind betrayed her. Warren's image blurred, and the memory of Shadow's kisses replaced it. Trees rushed past as they sped down the mountain pass, and she wondered if she'd ever see the rugged stranger again.

# CHAPTER FOUR

SWEAT RAN DOWN Shadow's back, making his T-shirt stick to his skin. He peeled it off then tossed the wet shirt on the floor near the closet. A knock on the door stopped him from going over to the desk in the corner of the room to rifle through the top drawer for extra batteries for the fan.

"Hey," he said to Smokey when he opened the door.

"Fuck, it's hot in here." Smokey stepped inside and pointed to the moving fan. "And that isn't doing jack shit."

"I know. It's hotter than hell in here. It reminds me of that broken-down trailer my ma and I used to live in after my old man died. It got so fuckin' hot in that metal box—even worse than it is in here now."

"I hear you. We didn't have AC when I was growing up either." He chuckled. "My brother and I used to hang out in the basement a lot during the summers."

"Have you heard from him lately?" Shadow asked as he switched off the fan.

A sad looked crossed over Smokey's face for a brief second. "Not for a while." He jerked his head toward the hallway. "A group of us are gonna ride over to Silverton. You in?"

"Fuck yeah. When's the dude supposed to show up to fix the damn generator we paid a fortune for?" Shadow asked as he slipped on his cut then grabbed the keys to his motorcycle.

"Soon. Banger just chewed his ass out and reminded him that the Insurgents take priority over everyone on his damn list."

Shadow laughed. "I'm sure the dude doesn't wanna piss off an outlaw MC." He followed Smokey down the stairs.

All the windows and the front door in the main room were open, and the steady hum of several fans filled the room. A large stack of batteries sat on the corner of the bar. Two of the prospects placed a couple of shots of Jack in front of Hubcap and Tank, who were leaning against the counter. Shadow perched on a stool next to them and picked up the shot of whiskey Skinless slid over to him. He threw it back, enjoying the hot burn down his throat, then set the glass back on the counter.

"You riding over to Silverton?" he asked the two members.

"Yeah," Tank said as he pushed away from the bar.

Hubcap shook his head. "Banger wants me over at the dispensary—we're short-handed today."

Shadow held up his hand when Skinless began to pour another shot of whiskey for him. "Is the generator working over there?"

"Yeah, so at least it'll be cool, but I'd still rather burn up with a ride than be stuck in an air conditioned building."

Tank and Shadow nodded in agreement: for a biker, the ride was *everything*.

Tania shuffled over to them, and the exposed skin in her tiny bikini glistened with perspiration. "Are you guys going out for a ride?" she asked, her gaze fixed on Shadow.

"Yeah," he replied as he motioned Skinless over. "Gimme a big-ass glass of cold water," he said to the prospect.

"I bet it'll be cooler with the breeze rushing around you," she said.

"Yeah." Shadow curled his fingers around the glass and guzzled the water down.

"Skinless, can you soak a few paper towels in cold water again for us?" Tania nodded toward the couch where Wendy and Rosie lay motionless.

"It's a hundred and six fuckin' degrees out there," Animal said as he and Blade walked into the club.

"We're just heading out for a ride to Silverton." Shadow put the empty glass on the bar.

"We're comin' too," Blade said. "I'm just gonna grab a long sleeved T-shirt. He walked out of the room.

"How're Olivia and Lucy?" Shadow asked Animal.

"Good. They and a group of old ladies drove to Grand Junction and are hanging out at the water park. That's why Chas, Rock, Jax, and Hawk are joining us."

"A water park sounds like a good idea," Tania said as she placed the cold paper towel on the back of her neck.

Shadow looked over at Skinless. "Take the club's SUV and drive the club girls to the water park in Grand Junction."

Tania squealed in delight, then rushed over to him and kissed him on the cheek. "You're sweet as hell, baby."

"Whoever wants to get the hell outta here and get their asses to a pool, this is your chance," Animal said.

Wendy and Rosie leapt up from the couch, their sheer bras and panties plastered to their skin.

"Give us a few minutes to change and get our stuff together," Rosie said as she scurried toward the stairway. "You guys, we're going swimming," she yelled as she bolted up the stairs, her footsteps growing fainter.

The club members chuckled as they watched Tania and Wendy rush after Rosie.

Tank clasped Shadow on the shoulder. "You made the girls happy, so they'll be extra willing to please later tonight."

"Yeah," he answered, not really feeling it. Since he'd fucked that sweet piece at Eli's party, he hadn't been up to banging any of the club women. For reasons that pissed him off to no end, the sexy blonde had been a permanent fixture in his head for the past several days.

"Let's ride," Animal said as he walked out the door into the parking lot.

After dousing his head and neck with cold water from the nearby hose, Shadow pulled off his cut and slipped on a long-sleeved T-shirt he grabbed from his saddlebag. Then, he threw on his cut, straddled his bike, and waited for Hawk to give the signal to pull out.

Soon twelve Harleys roared through the twisting back roads, and Shadow reveled in feeling the breeze against his face. Silverton was roughly sixty miles from Pinewood Springs, and for part of the trip, the two-lane road followed the path of a small river that ran along its border. Shadow glanced at the clear water as it glittered under the sun and cascaded over the rocks while the motorcycles descended the mountain. Around the next curve, the road cut through a valley nestled between the Rocky Mountains. The sweet smell of grass swirled around him as he took in the hundreds of cows grazing on the green and yellow pastures.

At the end of the valley, the group of bikes rode over a few hills until they entered the town's limits. Silverton looked like a town from the Old West with its two-story store fronts made of faded red brick and wood.

The brothers pulled into the parking lot of Coyote's Café and secured spaces near the front of the roadhouse. Chrome from other motorcycles gleamed under the strong sun, and Shadow switched off the engine and jumped off his bike. The scent of hickory and grilled meat tantalized him as he walked toward the wooden steps leading to the restaurant.

Coyote Café had been serving thirsty and hungry travelers for the past eighty years and was a popular road stop for both bikers and motorists traveling through the Colorado backroads. It sat in the shadow of the Rocky Mountains and was built from railroad ties and mortar from a nearby rail yard.

"That was an awesome ride," Chas said as he took off his sunglasses then started to clean the lenses on his T-shirt.

"An icy cold beer is calling my name," Smokey said as he walked in tandem with Shadow.

"Me too, bro," Shadow replied, hooking his shades to his damp T-shirt.

"It's time for us to cool the fuck off," Rags said, opening the front door.

A blast of chilled air rushed over them as they stepped into the busy eatery.

"Over there," Chas said, jerking his head toward the back where Hawk and Animal were pushing tables together.

"Good food, cold beer, and some real hot chicks at the bar," Smokey said.

Shadow glanced over and saw a curvy woman with long blonde hair leaning against it, her back to him. He sucked in a deep breath as he stood rooted to the spot and stared. As if sensing that someone was watching her, the woman turned around and he let out a breath. It wasn't *her*.

"How 'bout that blonde who's giving you the eye?" Smokey said as he nudged him. "She's a sweet piece." A low appreciative whistle came from the slight gap between his teeth.

"Yeah," Shadow replied, looking away from her. "Hawk's motioning us over." He turned around and made his way to the back of the roadhouse.

There was one thing that Shadow had had a lot of in his biker years and that was hookups with chicks. Some of his one-night stands were wild and fun, while others were just dull and plain bad, but he *never* thought about any chick the next day. So he couldn't figure out why the fuck he'd kept thinking about *her. She was just a one-time fuck. I've had tons of those.* But Scarlett was different, he grudgingly admitted to himself; she was a hookup, for sure, but she wasn't like the rest of them. There was something about her that made him want to see her again, and it wasn't just for sex, although he'd love another go with her. *Wait ... what the fuck am I thinking? I'd love to fuck her again ... that's all. Nothing more.* Shadow ignored the fact that he never met up again with one-nighters, but he'd become so good about pushing down any feelings or thoughts he didn't like, he was immune to them. His heart had turned to iron after his mother had been murdered.

"Fuck," he muttered under his breath as he pulled out the wooden chair then plopped down. The fact that he was still thinking about the pampered, rich chick pissed him the hell off. He and rich folks didn't mix too well, especially since he suspected that it was his mother's rich boyfriend who had offed her and, so far, had gotten away with it.

"You good?" Jax asked.

Startled, Shadow looked up and saw Jax, Animal, Smokey, and Helm staring at him, concern etching their faces. He hadn't realized that he'd clutched the water glass so tightly that it shattered in his hands. Drops of blood fell from his fingers and spotted the wood tabletop.

"Uh … yeah. Fuck," he said, taking the napkins Animal handed him. "I didn't know I was holding it so hard." He laughed dryly, but he knew his buddies didn't believe his bullshit.

"Here you go." Helm slid his full glass of water toward him.

"What did you do, honey?" the dark-haired waitress in jean shorts and a form-fitting tee asked him as she wiped the area in front of him with a rag.

"I broke the fuckin' glass," he said.

She laughed. "You ain't the first one to do it. You should come 'round here on a Saturday night when everyone's good and drunk. A lot of broken shit then. I'll get you an alcohol wipe and some Band-aids." She scurried away and Helm shook his head as he watched her disappear into the crowd.

"What a fine ass that one has," he said wistfully.

"I'm bleeding here and you're thinking about asses?" Shadow joked.

"He's *always* thinking 'bout asses," Animal replied.

Helm laughed and leaned back in his chair. "That's the truth, brother. I've never denied that I am an ass man."

Shadow, Jax, and Animal laughed, and as Rags and Smokey shared which female parts they were partial to, Shadow looked over at the bar and saw the waitress making her way back over to the table. *That's the type of women I'm attracted to—salt-of-the-earth women, not pampered princesses.*

"Gimme your hand, honey." The brunette took his hand and wiped it clean, then attached three Band-aids around his fingers.

"What's your name, sugar?" Helm asked.

She looked over her shoulder and smiled. "Brittany."

"Well, you're doing a real good job taking care of my buddy here," Helm said.

Smokey rolled his eyes as he brought the beer bottle to his mouth, and Jax sniggered.

"I aim to please," she said, winking at Shadow.

"I bet you do, sugar." Helm's gaze landed on her backside.

"That should do it," Brittany said as she straightened up.

"Thanks for giving a fuck," Shadow said.

The waitress threw him a big smile then proceeded to take the food and drink orders from the table.

When she rushed off again, Helm let out a loud sigh. "I gotta get some of her. Maybe I can take her for a spin on my bike."

"All chicks wanna ride on a Harley," Animal said.

Scarlett's body squeezed close to his, her golden hair flying all around her while she wrapped her arms tight around him flashed through his mind. *Fuck!* He wanted her out of his head, but he couldn't seem to forget the way her soft, curvy body felt, or the taste of her lips. It pissed him off that he was still thinking about her and wanted to seek her out. *Not gonna happen. No. Fuckin'. Way.*

"Pulled pork sandwich with slaw." Brittany's voice sliced through his thoughts, and he glanced up and took the dish from her. "Thanks, honey," she said, throwing another wink his way.

"I got the fried-shrimp basket," Smokey said, and the thin teenager helping Brittany put the food in front of the biker.

For the rest of the afternoon, Shadow forced his brain to focus on the conversation, the food, and the women who flirted with him. All he had to do was keep his mind busy, and in no time at all, the hookup at Eli's party would be forgotten—he had no doubt about *that.*

"Whatcha doing tomorrow?" Smokey asked him.

Shadow shrugged. "The usual—checking out the rentals." He owned three storage places—two in Pinewood Springs and one in a nearby town. His mother had used some of the money her rich sugar daddy had given her to take out a hefty life insurance policy, making Shadow the beneficiary. For a long time he didn't touch the pay out, viewing it as blood money, but Eli's parents convinced him that his mother would've wanted him to make something of his life and invest it. So he'd bought the properties, and their revenues gave him a very comfortable life.

"You up for helping me out? Pat and Carlos called off for tomorrow, and I got an on-going project that I gotta do," Smokey said. "It's just gonna be Guy, Manuel, and myself, so I could really use the extra hand."

"Sure, I'll help you, but you're gonna owe me big time." Shadow laughed.

"Whatever you want, bro."

"Just text me the address and I'll get there after I do my rounds."

"Will do, and if you want to make some extra money, I'll cut you in on a big project I got going next week that'll take several weeks to finish. Interested?" Smokey picked up his beer and took a long pull.

"Depends on how much we're talking about."

Smokey put the bottle on the table. "Around 15K."

A wide grin spread across his face. "I'm in."

Smokey lifted his chin. "Cool."

Sometimes Shadow helped out the brothers who owned businesses if they needed it. In the past, he'd lent a hand at Wheelie's carwash, Throttle and Rags' landscape company, and Hawk's motorcycle repair shop. He'd even helped Animal out a few times at his appliance repair business, even though he didn't know shit about fixing fridges and stoves. Shadow liked keeping busy, and he preferred being outdoors as much as he could. He figured it was a throw back to his childhood when he'd spend hours away from the house in order to avoid another beating from his dad.

Bile rose in his throat and he chugged down the rest of his beer. Thinking about his dad always made him pissed and anxious. *You were such a fuckin' bastard.*

"We ready to roll?" Hawk asked as he stood up. "Cara just texted me—the old ladies are back home, and the power's been restored."

The men with old ladies pushed back their chairs and jumped to their feet. The single ones lifted their chins at their buddies as they left the table, then returned to finishing their drinks and chow.

After another hour, Shadow pushed his empty plate away from him and drained the last bit of beer in his schooner.

"I'm gonna head back," he said.

"The club girls will be real happy to see us after having fun at the pool," Smokey said, his blue eyes shining.

"I'm ready for some fucking," Rags said as he pushed up from the chair.

"I think I'll hang around here and see if Brittany wants to have some fun after her shift ends." Helm stretched his legs in front of him.

"Dude, she was kissing the shit outta the bartender when I went to wash up," Shadow said. "Give it up."

"No fuckin' way," Helm said, straightening up.

"Charlotte's got a great ass," Smokey said.

"One of the best ones of all the club girls," Rags added.

"I can have Charlotte any time—I want Brittany." A wrinkle crossed his brow.

"Fuckin' pathetic," Smokey said as he put on his sunglasses.

"Now's your chance, bro—she's coming this way." Shadow fished out his mesh gloves from the pocket of his cut.

"You guys heading out?" she asked as she picked up the remaining empty plates.

"Yep," Rags said.

"Where you going?"

"Back to Pinewood Springs." Rags wrapped a bandana around his head.

"So you're not too far away." She smiled. "Have a good trip back home."

When Brittany started to walk away, Helm called out to her, "Hey, you got an ol' man or something?"

She laughed, her light brown eyes sparkling. "Yes, and he *is* something."

Helm scrunched his face. "You into having some fun on the side?"

"Shit, dude," Shadow said as he elbowed the biker in the ribs.

"What? It's a fair question since you saw her kissing a dude."

Shadow's gaze cut over to Brittany's. "Ignore him, he's fallen on his head one too many times."

She shook her head. "I guess bikers like gossiping just like anyone else." She put the dishes back on the table, then placed her hands on her hips and glared at Helm. "First off, I don't cheat on my husband; second"—Brittany looked over at Shadow—"the *dude* I was kissing was my old man and he's the bartender, and third"—she picked up the plates again –"mind your own business." She turned around and stomped away.

Helm took out his sunglasses. "It's too bad she's hitched 'cause she's got a mighty fine ass."

The men guffawed and swaggered out of the restaurant. They crossed the parking lot and jumped on their bikes. With a load roar, they sped away from the roadhouse and made their way back home.

When Shadow entered the clubhouse, cold air swirled around him at the same time Tania's fingers curled around his muscled forearm.

"I owe you a big thank you, baby. The pool was perfect." She leaned against him, her ample tits spilling out of her top. "I got some fun things planned for us."

Shadow smiled and gently pulled out of her grasp. "I'm glad you girls had fun. I'm beat, but if I get a second wind, you'll be the first one to know, okay?"

Disappointment spread across her face. "You don't wanna play?"

"Not right now. I got some shit I gotta do with the rentals. I have to look over the books."

"Can't you do that tomorrow?"

"No. I'm helping Smokey out at one of his jobs in the morning." Shadow squeezed her shoulder. "Another time, okay?"

"All right," she said, casting her gaze around the room. "It's your loss." Tania walked away and made a beeline for Hubcap, who sat on a bar stool with a bottle of beer in his hand.

As Shadow watched Tania wrap her arms around the biker's neck and then kiss him passionately, Scarlett's lips pressed against his own flashed through his mind. *Fuck!*

He walked up to the bar and told the prospect he wanted a bottle of Jack. Gripping the whiskey in his hand, he walked out of the room and trudged up the stairs.

# CHAPTER FIVE

"I NEVER KNOW what you want. You seem so restless, especially the last couple of weeks." Warren picked up his scotch. The ice cubes clinked against the glass.

"It's just been so hot outside," Scarlett said as she looked out at the golf course.

"What the hell does the weather have to do with it? Except for that one day last week when the power was out, you're always in air conditioned places."

She shrugged and fiddled with the napkin in her lap, avoiding his gaze. What she wanted to tell him was that she was at a crossroad—a junction—in her life. Up to this point, the road she'd traveled had been straight and planned, but the moment she laid eyes on the black-haired man with the stormy gray eyes, a desire to break loose seized her. After their torrid and urgent coupling, Scarlett knew Shadow was a sudden and dangerous detour diverting her from that orderly path.

"You're not pregnant, are you?" he asked while he motioned the waiter over for another drink. "Is that why you've avoided making love?"

She glanced up at him and put her fingers to her lips as a heavy sigh escaped from them. Her long hair swished around her shoulders as she shook her head *no*.

"Then why the hell are you freezing me out? Did I do something wrong that I don't know about?" He reached for her hand and pressed it to his lips.

"I'm just feeling out of sorts, that's all." She slipped her hand out of his grasp.

"Well, see a fucking doctor. A man can only take so much, *sweet-*

*heart.*"

The waiter put the drink in front of him, then began to clear the empty lunch plates. "Would you like anything else?" he asked, shifting his eyes between them.

"No, thank you." Scarlett reached down and grabbed her straw clutch purse and caught Warren's gaze. "I have to get going."

"I'm not ready—I just got my drink."

She patted the back of his hand. "You stay. I have a million things to do for the upcoming charity ball. We'll talk later."

"What about dinner tonight?"

"I can't—I have a committee meeting." She rose to her feet.

"I can come by later tonight and we can go to my place. Richard's in Denver on business for the rest of the week."

"That won't work. I promised Logan and Rhea I'd babysit."

Before she could dash away, Warren grabbed her wrist and held it tight … too tight.

"I don't know what the fuck's wrong with you, but you better get over it fast. I'm done playing your fucking game," he said in a voice so low, she barely heard him.

"You're hurting me," she said, yanking out of his hold. "And I'm not playing a game with you. I'm just out of sorts like I already told you. Thanks for lunch."

Scarlett hurried away, her heels tapping on the floor. She couldn't say she blamed Warren for being fed up with her; she'd been sulky and edgy ever since she let a stranger fuck her brains out. If she'd felt guilty about it, at least that would've been something, but she didn't. *Maybe I should go away for the summer. La Jolla or Malibu would be great.*

The valet guy pulled her midnight blue Mercedes in the front and she walked over, handing him a tip before sliding onto the cool leather seats.

When she turned into the driveway, Scarlett saw the indoor tennis court taking shape over to the far left of the house. Why her father was hellbent on building it was beyond her, especially since no one in the family played the game on a regular basis. Her mother would get together with her friends and play at the club, but the truth was that they spent most of the time inside at the bar getting sloshed. For some unknown reason, her dad liked the *idea* of having an indoor tennis court, so he decided to have one built. For the past two days, Scarlett had woken up to the sounds of drills, saws, and hammers, and she couldn't wait until the damn thing was finished.

"Did you have a nice lunch with Warren?" her mother asked as Scarlett walked into the sun room. Her mother was bent over one of her many plants, pruning it.

"It was okay." Scarlett kicked off her high-heeled sandals and wiggled her toes.

Her mother looked over her shoulder, a slight frown burrowing into the lines of her forehead.

"What does that mean?" she asked.

Bending down, Scarlett picked up her shoes. "It means it was *okay*." She knew where this conversation was going, so she started walking out of the room.

"Your father thinks Warren should've proposed to you by now. He's very angry about it and thinks that you're putting Warren off."

"Life doesn't run according to Dad's schedule. Anyway, I don't want to marry Warren." Scarlett looked over her shoulder and saw her mother cup a hand over her mouth as she gasped.

"What are you saying?" she whispered.

"I guess, that I'm not that interested in him. Dad's been the one pushing this, not me."

"Warren is a great catch and any woman would be proud to stand by his side."

"Then let 'any woman' do that."

"You ungrateful, spoiled brat! Your father does everything for you," her mother said through clenched teeth.

"I'm not getting sucked into this, Mom. I'm going to take a cool shower and try and read even though it sounds like a construction zone in here because of Dad's crazy-ass idea that we just had to have a damn indoor tennis court." She stalked out of the room and climbed up the stairway, blocking out her mother's crying. One thing she'd learned over the years was that her mom was quite the manipulative drama queen.

Scarlett quickly stepped out of her dress, hung it in the closet, and walked into her en suite bathroom for a refreshing shower. After she'd dried off and brushed her long golden hair, she padded over to the dresser and picked out something to wear. She threw on a pair of white shorts and a yellow tank top, then walked out of the bedroom. As she descended to the main floor, the high-pitched *whirring* of electric saws sliced through her head, and she pressed her fingertips to her throbbing temples.

"Are you all right, Miss Scarlett?"

She smiled weakly at Heddy. The head housekeeper had been with the family before Scarlett had been born. Barely over five feet tall, Heddy's pale blue eyes held concern in them as she looked up at Scarlett. She ran her hands over her crisp black uniform then touched the top of her tight gray bun.

"It's just all the noise from the construction," Scarlett said.

"Why don't you go into the family room and I'll bring you a cold towel to place over your forehead."

She shook her head slightly, the movement caused her to wince in pain. "You don't need to do that. I'll be fine."

"I'm going to the club to meet up with Maryann and Julie," her mother said, looking cool and sophisticated in a cream linen dress that skimmed over her slight figure. Her blonde hair was coiled at the nape of her neck, and a strand of South Sea pearls rested against her collarbone.

"Okay," Scarlett replied, thinking that the red lipstick her mother had on was a bit too much.

"Please try and be in a better mood when I get home. We aren't finished discussing your attitude toward your soon-to-be fiancé." She turned to Heddy. "I want you to bring some lemonade to the men working on the tennis house. Has it been made?"

The older woman bobbed her head. "Yes, Mrs. Mansfield."

With a curt tip of her head, Pamela Mansfield crossed over to the door and walked out.

"I can bring the lemonade over to the workers," Scarlett said as a thread of satisfaction wove through her. Just thinking about how appalled her mother would be about that made her smile.

A look of horror washed over Heddy's face. "Oh, no, Miss Scarlett. I'll have Clara and Jane go down there."

No matter how many times she'd told Heddy not to call her "Miss Scarlett," the house manager always did. One time when Scarlett's mother overheard her telling Heddy to drop the *Miss*, her mother had chastised Scarlett, telling her that it would be disrespectful for a servant to call anyone in the family by their proper name only. *"Heddy and the others know their place,"* her mother would say so often that it made Scarlett want to scream.

"That's crazy. They have enough to do and so do you. I'm not doing much of anything, so I'll go."

"But …" Heddy's mouth puckered and worry sank down deep into the lines of her face.

"Don't worry about my mother—I'm not going to say a word."

"Miss Scarlett, it just isn't proper." Heddy's gaze ran over her.

She laughed. "I'll be fine." Heddy could be so old-fashioned. "I'll have either Clara or Jane help me carry some of the pitchers."

Heddy looked unconvinced, and she kept shifting in place. Scarlett went over to her and hugged her lightly. "Please don't worry. It's all right. Anyway, I'm not in high school anymore. I'm twenty-five years old." She pulled away. "I'm all grown up now."

Heddy nodded, a strained smile on her lips. She slowly turned away and headed toward the kitchen.

As Scarlett ambled on the brick pathway toward the construction, she gripped a pitcher in each hand. Clara followed behind her at a slower pace, balancing three pitchers on a silver tray.

"Oh, shit," Scarlett mumbled as some of the lemonade spilled over her hands. She stopped and put the pitchers down then wiped off the sticky liquid and resumed her march.

An eerie hush followed them as she and Clara made their way toward the workers. The men stopped whatever it was they were doing to stare at them as they approached the construction zone.

A dark-haired man with piercing blue eyes walked over, meeting them halfway. Tattoos covered his muscular chest and arms, and Scarlett watched in fascination as the ink danced when he flexed his arm to wipe the sweat off his face.

"Hi," she said. Tilting her head to Clara, she said, "It's so hot that we thought you'd like some ice cold lemonade."

The man darted his eyes from her face to the two pitchers she carried in her hands. A slow smile broke out over his face, revealing a slight gap between his two front teeth.

"That's real nice of you," he said, his gaze slowly running up her body. "I'm Smokey—the contractor."

His stare made her self-conscious and she wished she would've changed into her jeans. Masking her discomfort, she put the two pitchers down, took the plastic cups from the tray, and poured lemonade into them.

She pointed over at a small wrought iron table. "Please put the tray down on that table, Clara."

Several men came over as Scarlett and Clara handed out the refreshments. Scarlett filled several more cups, and when she looked up to hand them out, her gaze locked with Shadow's. One corner of his mouth hitched up in a cocky smirk, and her heart skipped a beat as a rush of nerves flowed through her.

"Hey," he said.

"Your lemonade," she whispered.

His fingers brushed hers as he accepted the drink. Their gazes met and held. For a moment, neither of them moved.

Scarlett's stomach fluttered, clenched, and fluttered again. He drew his hand away from hers very slowly and took a sip from the plastic cup.

She watched as he swallowed, mesmerized by the way his Adam's apple moved up and down.

He wiped his full lips with the back of his hand and returned the empty cup to her. "That was *real* good. I'd even say it might be the best I've ever had." The deep timbre of his voice sent shivers along her spine. "Thanks." He winked and stepped back, and two workers quickly took his place in front of her.

"Clara, I'll fill the rest of the cups and you can hand them out, okay?" She hoped her voice didn't betray her nervousness.

"Yes, Miss Scarlett." Clara came around front and Scarlett took her place at the table.

After she finished pouring the lemonade into all the cups, Scarlett scanned the area looking for Shadow. She saw him standing next to a sawhorse, his dark hair shining under the sun like spilled ink. She couldn't believe he was here … at her house … so close to her.

He looked more rugged than he had at the party, but not any less handsome. Coarse stubble covered his chiseled jaw, and more tattoos than she'd seen that night decorated his arms. As Shadow picked up a wooden plank, she noticed the corded muscles in his chest strain. She tried to look away, but there was just something too magnetic about the man, and her eyes swept back to him. They traveled over his broad shoulders and chest to the tight lines of muscle that rippled like waves as he worked. Her gaze skipped down to a narrow waist and rock hard abs, and she groaned inwardly as she pictured her tongue running up and down the rigid dips of his magnificent body. A deep *V* of muscles disappeared beneath the waistband of his low-slung jeans, and knowing what was below them sent a frisson of excitement through her.

*He's so damn sexy.* Images of them together made Scarlett clench her thighs together and fan herself with her hand. Occasionally, Shadow would look over, his heated gaze lingering on hers before moving to her mouth and landing on her breasts. A few of the workers, including the contractor, seemed to notice that something was going on between the two of them. Smokey walked over to Shadow and it looked like they were talking about her because the dark-haired man would glance over at her from time to time.

*I hope Shadow's not telling him what we did. I'll die of embarrassment if he is.*

"The lemonade is gone, Miss Scarlett," Clara said as she picked up the silver tray.

Scarlett tore her gaze away from her hunky hookup then removed three of the empty pitchers from the tray. "Carrying them all is too heavy. Let's head back to the house."

Scarlett walked toward the house and could feel his eyes staring at her. She held open the back screen door for Clara, but before Scarlett went inside herself, she glanced back at Shadow, his eyes met and locked onto hers. For a long moment neither of them moved while desire wove between them like a sparking current. It was only when the contractor stepped in front of Shadow, blocking him from her sight, that Scarlett was able to turn away. She quickly entered the house and closed the door, then walked into the study and sat down. Scarlett leaned forward in her seat, placed her elbows on the desk and rested her chin on the back of her hands. She stared at the books lining the shelves of the custom-made cases and waited for her body to calm down. Seeing Shadow was a shock, but seeing him shirtless with his muscular chest and arms gleaming with sweat in the summer heat was a delicious treat. Of course she couldn't keep her eyes off him. And she knew *exactly* what he was packing between those muscular thighs of his. She had seen it, touched it, and … Shivers danced over her skin as the memory of him thrusting inside her flooded her mind.

"I have to stop thinking about him!" She leaned back and pounded her fist on the desk. But the truth was that as hard as she tried, Scarlett couldn't get the sexy man out of her thoughts. For the next few hours, she tried to concentrate on the upcoming fundraiser that she was chairing. It was to raise money for a charity that was dear to her: the Sheridan Center for Children. The organization's mission was to empower children who have experienced abuse or neglect or trauma in an effort to bravely and safely change their life's story. Much to her mother's chagrin, Scarlett had been active with the Sheridan Center for the past two years. Her mother had pushed her to be involved with the more prestigious charities like the Children's Hospital or the theater, but Scarlett had fallen in love with the work that the Sheridan Center was doing. She'd always felt blessed to have been born into a privileged family, and she never lost sight that so many people didn't have the same opportunities she'd had as a child. Scarlett just wanted to give back any way she could.

A knock on the door made her jump.

"Come in," she said. Her muscles tensed up as she stared at the door, hoping Shadow would be behind it. Her shoulders sagged when Heddy stood in the doorframe.

"Would you like anything else before the staff and I leave, Miss Scarlett?"

Scarlett took off her reading glasses and rubbed her eyes lightly. "Is it five thirty already?"

"Yes," she answered.

"I didn't realize the time had passed so quickly. Is my mother home?"

"No, Miss Scarlett."

*God, how I wish she'd just call me Scarlett.* "I'm fine, Heddy. Have a good night and I'll see you tomorrow."

"You have a good night too, Miss Scarlett." With a curt tip of her head, the house manager walked out of the room and closed the door behind her.

Scarlett switched off the computer and stretched, then moved her head from side to side, working out the kinks in her neck. She'd been sitting for several hours hunched over the keyboard. She pushed away from the desk and ambled to the kitchen in search of a snack.

The house was quiet and the construction noise that had been a constant since the morning was gone. A fruit bowl sat on the granite island, and Scarlett plucked out an apricot and went over to the sink to wash it. She glanced out the window and saw that the workers had already left. *He didn't even stop by to say goodbye.* Scarlett quickly pushed away any feelings of hurt. *I'm being ridiculous. Why would he stop by? It's not like we're friends or anything.* She dried the apricot with a paper towel, then bit into it. The sweet juice trickled down her chin, and she dabbed it away with the towel. Apricots were one of her favorite fruits, especially when they came from the farmers market.

Scarlett tossed the pit into the trash. She grabbed a bottle of water and sauntered over to the back door, unlocked the screen, and stepped out, determined to check out the tennis house that they didn't need.

"Hey," a deep voice said.

A small cry escaped from her lips as she stepped back toward the screen door. The scent of sawdust, leather, and sweat swirled around her.

"I didn't mean to freak you out." A deep chuckle rumbled from his chest, and Shadow came closer to her.

He was much too close. "I just didn't think anyone was here," she whispered. She breathed in deeply, and her body tingled at his dangerously potent male scent. Scarlett tried to take her eyes away from the tan skin stretched tight across his chest, glistening in the sun.

"You got one of those for me?" he asked. His gaze crawled over her then landed on her mouth. A whisper of a smile touched his sensuous lips.

A flutter started deep in her belly, and she felt the immediate hot and intense sizzle of current between them a little frightening.

"Are you gonna invite me in?" he asked in a low voice.

"Yeah ... sure ... okay." She turned away and breathed deeply a couple of times in order to regain her composure. "You must be real hot from working outside all day." She wiped her damp hands on her shorts then opened the screen door. "Come on in. I'll get you a bottle of water." Nervous excitement streaked through her as she shuffled over to the refrigerator. "How's the work coming along?" She bent down to grab the bottle from the bottom shelf.

"It's going. How've you been?" he asked.

"Good," she said, pretending to search for something in the fridge.

"You been thinking about me?" he asked.

"Uh … yeah … a little." *Like nonstop.* "What about you?" She gripped the bottle in her hand and closed the refrigerator.

Shadow brought his arms around her waist and tugged her back against him. "You know the answer to that," he murmured, his breath hot against her ear.

"Do I?" she asked weakly.

"Fuck yeah, baby." His tongue was warm against the lobe of her ear, causing her breath to catch. "I been thinking all kinds of dirty thoughts about you."

She shivered as his lips pressed against the sensitive skin just behind her ear. And when his hand moved higher on her waist she held her breath in anticipation.

"You're so sexy and beautiful," he whispered as his fingers teased her breast, cupping the weight while his thumb flicked over her nipple.

Scarlett moaned and leaned further back into him, grinding her ass against his erection. Shadow let out a low growl. "Fuck, babe." He kissed and bit her neck, then spun her around and claimed her lips.

Circling her arms around his neck, she buried her fingers into his thick hair and parted her lips, welcoming him inside. As they kissed, Shadow lightly touched the side of her face, and she panted and pulled him in closer. Then he was everywhere—up her back and over her arms, squeezing her ass and kissing her harder, deeper, more urgently. Scarlett's body responded, fervently urging him on, and suddenly she realized that no one had ever kissed her like that before and that she'd never have enough.

She clawed at his chest with an overwhelming desire to mark him. He pulled away and looked at her with lust-filled eyes. She moved in and bit him on the neck while she rubbed against his hard dick until he grabbed the hem of her top and yanked it over her head.

"Fuck, baby," he growled before tearing off her bra and lavishing kisses and bites to her breasts.

Scarlett threw her head back and groaned when his hot mouth slipped over her nipple. He sucked and nipped it hard, making it stiffen and ache. Burning desire consumed her: searing flames that melted her bones and scorched her skin.

"You like that?" he said against her skin as he pushed her shorts and panties down over her hips, past her thighs and knees.

She stepped out of them then pulled him close to her and felt the cold of his buckle against her skin. With trembling fingers, she fumbled to undo it, the palm of her hands skimming over his hardness.

A chuckle rolled from Shadow's chest, and he helped her undo his jeans. He took out a packet from one of the pockets before pushing down his pants and boxers. For a split second, Scarlett wondered why he had a condom with him while he was at work, but she quickly pushed the thought away as her eyes feasted on his thick, long dick.

She waited in anticipation as he ripped the foil packet with his teeth and deftly rolled on the sheath in one quick movement. Tugging her to him, Shadow kissed her deeply once more; then, he shoved her over to the table, turned her around, and bent her forward.

"Tits flat on the table, legs spread, ass in the air," he directed.

Shadow's command shivered down her body and landed at her core, and she readily obeyed him. The thought that her mother might walk in at any minute tugged at Scarlett, but the way his calloused hands electrified her made her feel daring and wanton. The only thing that mattered at that moment was having Shadow inside her. When he buried his finger between her wet folds, she jerked and cried out.

"Feels good, huh, baby," he rasped as his thumb played with her clit while he buried two fingers inside her, as deep as they would go.

"Yeah … fuck." Scarlett's voice was so hoarse, she didn't even recognize it herself.

"I fuckin' love the way your pussy's so damn wet and ready." He pulled his fingers out then shoved them back in.

She squirmed against his hand and a sharp crack on her ass made her cry out. *Holy shit!*

"No moving, got it?" Shadow's voice was stern and it turned her on in the worst way.

She pushed up a bit and looked over her shoulder at him. His heated gaze locked on to hers, and she watched as he leaned down and kissed her stinging butt cheek, his eyes never wavering from hers.

*That is so damn sexy. And the filthy things he says turn me on so much.*

Another smack on the behind. "Turn around and spread your legs wider. I want that pretty ass of yours up higher."

*If he keeps this up I'm going to orgasm. I've never felt this way with any man.*

He withdrew his fingers and before she could react, he thrust into her.

"Oh, shit," she cried out and gasped as she stretched her arms out and gripped the edge of the table.

Shadow let out a harsh groan, pushing into her two more times before his hands slid from their grip on her hips. Scarlett felt the weight of him against her as he leaned over and kissed her back and the nape of her neck. It was an intimate gesture she hadn't expected.

"You feel so good, baby," he said, his hands covered hers and their fingers entwined as he drove inside her.

"I want it harder." She moaned.

He moved his hands away and placed one on Scarlett's back, further flattening her against the table. She moved her hips, trying to push back to meet his thrusts. The collective sounds of pants and groans filled the room as Shadow pounded into her. The edge of the table rubbed against Scarlett's sweet spot with every thrust, and the pressure inside of her mounted until it exploded.

"Oh, shit!" she cried out as a fierce orgasm ripped through her. Her legs shook and she feared they were going to give out.

"Fuck!" Shadow's fingers dug painfully into her skin as he stiffened then collapsed against her. His labored pants told her that his climax was as volatile as her own.

After several minutes, he moved away and helped her up from the table; then, he drew her into his arms and kissed her tenderly. Scarlett wrapped her arms around his waist and leaned her head against his chest. Content to stay like that forever, panic quickly set in when she heard the garage door open.

"My mom's home. Shit!" Scarlett broke away from him and scrambled to throw on her clothes. When she glanced at him, an amused smile tugged at his lips. "This isn't funny. You have to pull up your jeans and get out of here ... like *now*."

Shadow shrugged and slowly raised his pants then buckled his belt. "Your hair's all messed up. You better comb it." He chuckled.

Panic spread across her face. "You don't know my parents. My mom will tell my dad and ... I don't even want to go there." She frantically searched through the drawers for a brush, and then finger-combed her hair when she couldn't find one. "How's that?" she asked.

"Not bad." He pulled her to him. "Damn, you're really stressed out about this, baby." He kissed her gently. "Better?"

The door to the house opened. Scarlett pulled away. "Not really."

"Scarlett? Who are you talking to?" Her mother stopped short in the doorway to the kitchen, and her eyes widened as they darted to Shadow and then back to Scarlett. "Who is *this*?" she asked in a tight voice.

Shadow took a couple of steps forward. "I'm working on the indoor tennis court."

"Oh." A frown replaced the surprise on her mom's face.

"He wanted a glass of water. It's been so hot today. The men enjoyed the lemonade. How was your lunch?" Scarlett rambled on.

"Fine. I bumped into Warren and he asked about you. He's going to come around in a little bit."

Scarlett folded her arms and shifted her weight from one leg to the other. "I'm meeting up with Kiara tonight."

"You can tell her that you'll be late." There was an edge to her mom's voice.

"I gotta get going," Shadow said as he moved toward the back door. Looking at Scarlett, his mouth quirked up on one side, then he pushed open the screen.

Through the mesh, she watched him stroll down the walkway with that rolling swagger that made her want to chase him down, tackle him to the ground, and pepper kisses all over his hard, sexy body.

"Scarlett! Close the door—you're letting all the hot air in here," her mother said.

After she turned the lock, she swiveled around. Her mother's blue eyes were dark with worry in her pinched face.

"That was foolish to let a worker into the house, especially since you were all alone. Who knows what was going through his mind."

"You always think the worst of everyone, Mom. He's fine."

"You don't know that. He's not from your class and you have no idea what people like him think." She ran her hands up and down her arms. "I do," she whispered.

"There are plenty of guys from *my class* who I wouldn't trust to be alone with." Scarlett laughed.

"It's not funny. You can joke about these things because you had an easy life."

Scarlett shook her head. "You're not going to tell me again how you fought to get to where you are today, are you?"

"You really are a spoiled princess." Bitterness laced her mother's voice. "Just don't invite any of the workers into *my* home again." She turned around and stalked out of the room.

Scarlett heard the clack of her mom's heels on the stairs. She crossed over to the window and watched the butterflies flit from flower to flower as thoughts of Shadow filled her mind.

Scarlett was inexplicably drawn to him, and she felt this tremendous sense of chemistry she'd never experienced before with any man. Scarlett knew all the reasons she should stay away from Shadow, but she wasn't able to do it.

"I'm playing with fire, but I'm so attracted to him, just like a damn moth to a flame," she muttered under her breath.

And if she wasn't careful, her desire for him would destroy her.

# CHAPTER SIX

T HE ROOM REEKED of cleaning products despite the *whirring* from the iron fan set on top of the filing cabinets. Shadow sat on a faux leather chair, his legs stretched out in front of him, and watched the second hand of the wall clock.

"Sorry to keep you waiting," Detective McCue said, then sank down into the chair behind the desk. "It's been crazy all day today. It must be the weather. Heat makes people angry and on edge." He picked up a scratched-up decanter and poured some water into a coffee mug. "You want something to drink?"

Shadow shook his head and crossed his arms over his chest. "Is my mom's case still open?"

McCue grabbed a wad of tissues and mopped his forehead and neck, then threw it in the trash can. "It's so damn hot in here."

"Is it open or what?" Shadow straightened up and leaned forward. "What the fuck are you"—he waved his hand—"or this damn department doing about finding the sonofabitch who murdered my mother?"

The detective took a gulp of water then wiped his mouth with the back of his hand. "It's still open, but not active. We got our hands full here and we haven't gotten a new lead in over a year."

"Is the rich bastard paying someone off?" Shadow narrowed his eyes. "Maybe *you*?"

"No one's paying me shit. I thought you and I had come to an understanding over all these years."

"Find the rich fucker she was dating and you've got your killer. It's so damn simple."

McCue sighed and fixed his gaze on Shadow's. "I don't know if he's who killed her and neither do you. We've had a lot of crazies in Pinewood. Just a while back we had that nutcase who was stalking women on that dating app." He splayed his hands on the desk. "Look, I know how hard this is for you. I wish I could tell you that we'll find whoever did this, but I can't. All I can tell you is that I'll keep working the case until I retire. A lot of cold cases get solved, more than you think."

"There're only three in the county and you fuckin' badges haven't solved any of them."

Shadow jumped to his feet and stormed out, blocking out whatever it was McCue was saying.

A tornado of rage swirled around inside him, and he kicked the front of the building. "Fuckin' assholes!" he yelled, slamming his fist into the brickwork with a painful force.

Blood trickled down his hand and dripped onto the pavement. He leaned against the wall, glaring at the people passing by. Pulsating and throbbing anger mixed with guilt. *I should've been home that night. I could've stopped the fuckin' bastard.* The memories were always there, as if lying in wait.

After several minutes, he stalked over to his bike and hopped on. A fast ride would calm him down—it usually did. The motorcycle roared to life, and he revved the engine to the maximum and sped off, leaving a trail of exhaust fumes and deafening noise.

ONE EVENING THE following week when Smokey entered the clubhouse, Shadow lifted his chin and saw the way his buddy glared at him. He didn't blame Smokey one bit for being mad as hell at him. That day, he'd dropped the ball and never showed up to work on the damn tennis house.

"What the fuck?" Smokey said when he came over to the table. "Where the hell were you today, asshole?" He gripped the top of a chair and pushed it hard. It toppled over and Smokey kicked it aside, a string of cuss words spilling out of his mouth.

"I fucked up, man. Sorry," Shadow said as he picked up his beer bottle and took a long drink.

"*Sorry*? That shit doesn't cut it. If you don't want the job, man the fuck up and tell me, but don't pull pussy bullshit on me. If you were any of the other workers, I'd throw your ass out."

Shadow didn't respond. He just sat there drinking his beer, pissed at himself that he let a brother down because he couldn't get his shit together. The truth was that for the past several days, he and Scarlett had been going at it whenever they could: during his lunch break, in the guest house after work, even a couple of times in the kitchen when her bitchy mom wasn't around. A headache inched its way up his neck and he pressed his thumbs against his temples.

"So, do you want the fuckin' job or not?" Smokey's voice sliced into his thoughts.

Shadow looked up and nodded.

"Then take this as your one and only chance. Next time you pull that shit, you're out." He kicked the fallen chair, then stomped over to Charlotte and yanked her to him.

Shadow turned away and rested his elbows on his knees then placed his throbbing head in his hands. He had to stay away from Scarlett. She was doing shit to him that he didn't understand or want. Each time he pushed inside her, inch by inch, he became more mesmerized by her. For some damn reason, the intensity of being with *her* jolted his senses like a power surge; he was hooked and it fucking pissed him off.

There was a scrape of chair legs across the floor.

"Did Smokey kick your ass?" Rags asked.

Shadow raised his head just as the biker plopped down.

"He was so fuckin' pissed at you. He came in during the day looking for you."

"I went for a ride," Shadow said as he leaned back, snapped his fingers, then stretched out his legs.

Wendy rushed over. "What is it, honey? You need some loving?" She inadvertently glanced over at Smokey, then back at Shadow.

"I need three aspirin, please."

She ran her nails through his hair and lightly massaged his temples. "Okay, honey." She sashayed away.

"What's going on with you?" Rags asked.

"He's got the hots for the rich bitch in the castle," Helm said as he swung his leg over the chair and sat down.

Shadow narrowed his eyes. "I'm not in the mood to kick your ass, so keep your fuckin' thoughts to yourself."

A low whistle escaped through Rags' teeth. "Damn. You hate those rich assholes. I never figured you'd go for one of the princesses."

"You want a problem with me too?" Shadow growled as he tossed the aspirin in his mouth and took the glass of water from Wendy. "Thanks." He winked at her and she leaned down and kissed his cheek.

"Anytime you need me, you got me." She squeezed his bicep. "But you already know that." Giggling, she smiled at the men and walked slowly away.

"The way her hips sway and her ass bounces when she walks gives me a fuckin' hard-on," Rags said.

"Everything gives you a hard-on," Throttle said as he joined the group. Shadow and Helm laughed.

"Fuck off," Rags said, a tinge of amusement lacing his voice.

"How was work today?" Helm asked as he scooped up a handful of nuts from the bowl on the table.

"Brutal. It's too fuckin' hot out there. We sent two of our guys home today 'cause they looked like they were gonna pass out or something," Throttle replied.

"Heat stroke is a real serious thing. There are a number of symptoms you can look out for to tell if it's that or maybe heat exhaustion," Helm said.

"Did you watch a documentary on this?" Rags asked.

"I just know shit," Helm said before popping some more nuts into his mouth.

"It may have been something like that, but I didn't wanna take any chances, so I sent them home and told them to see a doctor or something." Throttle looked over at Shadow. "Smokey's madder than fuck at you, dude. He said you blew off work."

"I guess everyone in the damn club knows about it, huh?" Shadow replied.

"Yep, pretty much," Helm answered.

"That's not cool, dude." Throttle took a swig of his beer.

"Smokey and me already sorted it out, so it's old news now." Shadow folded his arms across his chest.

"He says you're acting like a fuckin' asshole with"—Throttle snapped his fingers—"Some chick who lives there. Hell, I don't remember what the fuck he told me."

"Then you shouldn't be opening your fuckin' mouth," Shadow gritted.

Throttle pushed the table forward and jumped out of his chair. "You wanna do something about that?" His body was as rigid as an arrow.

Searing pain sliced through Shadow's head when he stood up. "I'm ready if you are."

"Both of you sit the fuck down," Rags said. "You"—he pointed at Throttle—"didn't know what the fuck you were saying, so you shouldn't have said shit, and"—he glanced over at Shadow—"you either like this rich chick more than you want to admit, or you're just in a fuckin' bad mood today. So both of you sit your asses down."

Throttle laughed as he sank back down. "That's it—Smokey said you had a hard cock for the chick who lives there. She's Mr. Mansfield's daughter. Damn, dude, you of all people? You hate rich folks."

Shadow resumed his seat and motioned for the prospect to bring him another glass of water. "I do, so you can see why the shit Smokey's saying is fuckin' ridiculous."

"Isn't a Mrs. Mansfield giving us a hard time with building the strip mall in West Pinewood Springs?" Helm asked.

"Yeah, the bitch and her committee of uptight prudes," Throttle answered. "Don't even mention her name to Banger or Hawk—they'll go ape shit." The men laughed.

"She's a total bitch," Shadow said. "Even though I don't go in for hitting a woman, the way she looks at us makes me want to punch her right in her sour face."

"I get that," Rags said. "She's just against the strip mall because *we're* the ones that wanna build it. She probably hasn't fucked her old man since he sold the club the land a year ago."

"I bet she hasn't fucked her old man even longer than that," Shadow said. "She strikes me as one frigid lady." *But her daughter is just the opposite. Scarlett is one sexy wildcat. Fuck! I'm thinking about her again.* He slammed his fist on the table and the three men looked at him in confusion. "Just thinking about her pisses me off." It was true, but the guys didn't have to know which *her* he was referring to.

"The old man probably has a young cutie he's supporting to take care of his needs," Throttle said.

"He does," Smokey said as he dragged over a chair.

"You done with Charlotte already?" Helm asked.

"Yeah—I just wanted a quick fuck," Smokey replied. "The old man keeps a chick half his age in one of the luxury condos on Larkspur Lane. I did some work on the place for him."

As the men asked questions about the man's mistress, the mention of Larkspur Lane threw Shadow back to the first day he and his mother had moved into the penthouse apartment on that very street. She had been so happy that day, and he was relieved that his mother could stop taking her clothes off for a living. If only he'd known that the move would turn out to be the biggest mistake of their lives, he would've held his mother close and never let her go.

"You still with us, dude?" Throttle's voice, faint at first, became more audible, and Shadow jerked his head back.

"I was just thinking about something." He threw a warning stare at Rags and Helm. "Did you ask me something?"

"No, your phone's been buzzing like a damn bee. I'm pretty sure it's

Hawk asking if you can work tonight at Dream House. He's already hit up all of us," Throttle said.

"You should be well-rested since you had a day off." A deep frown etched into Smokey's rugged face.

"I told Hawk it's a go for me," Helm said. "It seems like there's gonna be a frat reunion or some kind of shit like that, and he wants extra help and security."

Shadow nodded as he read Hawk's text. "It's a go for me too," he muttered as he tapped in his response to the vice president.

"Honeysuckle will be happy to see you," Rags said. "Last time I was there, she was asking 'bout you."

"How's she doing with her dancing? She was pretty stiff when Hawk hired her a couple of months ago," Smokey said.

"She's figured out that the better you move, the bigger the tips. Crystal's been working with her and she's getting real good. A lot of guys like Honeysuckle 'cause she's super friendly and she's got a great pair of tits." Rags laughed.

"The tits always do it," Throttle said as he pushed away from the table. "I gotta pick up Kimber. We're going to Silverton for dinner."

"You both riding?" Smokey asked.

A big grin split his face. "Nope—my old lady wants to ride with me."

"Yeah, even when a chick has her own bike, she still wants to hold her old man tight," Smokey said.

Throttle chuckled. "It doesn't happen very often, but I do like my old lady pressed against me. See you guys later."

"You gonna help out at Dream House?" Helm asked Smokey.

"Fuck no. I *worked* all day, so I'm gonna go on a long ride, then come back here and chill."

Shadow ignored the dig. "You guys wanna grab some chow at Ruthie's?" The diner was one of the favorite spots for the Insurgents.

Smokey shook his head and stood up. "I'll pass—I wanna get on my bike and hit the back roads."

"I'm in," Helm said at the same time Rags voiced his agreement.

"Then let's get our asses in gear," Shadow said.

The three men walked out of the clubhouse, jumped on their bikes, and made their way to the diner.

THE PARKING LOT of Dream House was packed with everything from dated pickup trucks to the newest Mercedes AMG GT, which ran over a hundred thousand dollars. Music from the club spilled out into the lot each time the door opened. At the far end of it, Shadow heard a girl giggle and he watched as she staggered to her feet from the passenger seat of a Porsche, wiping her mouth. She wore stilettos, a mini skirt, and a thin strip of fabric that substituted for a top.

"I'll meet you inside," Shadow said to Helm as he walked toward the tipsy woman.

A man in his late twenties stepped out from the car and stared at Shadow. The biker instinctively placed his hand on the Glock in his pocket and continued walking. The woman stopped and looked at him with unfocused eyes.

"You okay?" he asked her, his gaze still on the man.

"Yeah, just a little drunk." She put her hand over her mouth and giggled.

"You with this dude?" Shadow pointed at the man standing by the luxury car.

"I was," she slurred.

"She *is*," the man said. "She's my girlfriend." He stretched out his arm. "Come here, baby."

The girl teetered on her heels, confusion marking her face. "You want to go for another round? Can you get it up that fast?"

He turned to Shadow and shook his head. "She's totally wasted. She was feeling sick in the club so we came out for some fresh air, and I thought it would be better if she rested in the car."

"That's a load of bullshit. She just finished giving you a blow job that you paid for. We don't allow that shit on our property." Shadow looked at the woman again, who was now sitting on the ground with her head between her legs. He didn't recognize her; she wasn't one of the dancers. "You got a way to get home?" he asked.

She shook her head.

"Where'd he pick you up?"

"Over on Penn."

Penn Street was the red-light district in Pinewood Springs. It was where the street hookers hung out, offering much lower rates than the call girls who worked for a couple of the escort services in town.

Shadow narrowed his eyes and took a couple of steps toward the man in the expensive silk shirt and dress pants. "Are you going inside the club?"

"Yes, I'm meeting friends there."

"I'm gonna let it slide this one time, but you're on notice. You don't bring hookers here; you don't touch any of the dancers, and you don't offer money to fuck any of the dancers. If you obey the rules, you and me are gonna get along okay, but if you don't … well, you won't be walking so good for the next week. You got that?"

A flicker of panic crossed the man's face and he nodded. "I didn't mean to disrespect you or the club. I thought it was cool since this is a gentlemen's club."

"Hookers aren't allowed. Now get your ass inside and the only time you come out is when you leave."

"Okay … okay," he muttered as he walked toward the front entrance.

Shadow walked over to the young woman and helped her up. "You got a place to stay?"

"I'm at the Wildflower Motel," she answered.

Despite the name, the motel was a seedy dump that catered to drug deals, prostitution, and other elements from the underground world.

"Are you staying there alone?"

"My boyfriend's there, but he'll be mad if I go back now. I need to make a bit more money." She looked up at him and smiled. Black smudges from where her mascara had run formed half-moons under her eyes. "Do you want a blowjob? I'm real good at it."

"How much do you have to bring home to the asshole who you think is your 'boyfriend'?"

Her smiled faded. "Roy is good to me. We're just low on cash, that's all."

"Why doesn't he get his ass out and work?"

"He's got a bad back. He told me the condition he has but I can't remember it."

"How much do you need to make tonight?"

"He'd be good with a couple hundred bucks, but I only got a hundred and twenty."

Shadow took out his wallet and handed her a hundred dollars. "Take it and go home. I'll have one of the bartenders drop you at the motel."

Her eyes widened. "Thanks, mister. Why're you being so nice to me? Are you sure you don't want a quickie or something?"

"I'm sure. Hang on a sec." He sent a text to Gary, and a few minutes later the bartender came outside. Shadow jerked his head at the woman. "Give her a lift back to the Wildflower Motel. I'll cover for you behind the bar."

Gary nodded and Shadow helped the woman to the bartender's car. "Keep your head out the window 'cause you don't wanna puke in his car."

"That's for fucking sure," Gary said as he closed the passenger door. "I'll be back in a few minutes."

"You got your piece on you?" Shadow asked.

"Yeah. Am I going to have to use it?"

"I don't think so, but she's got a pimp so be careful. You need one of us to go with you?"

"I should be fine." Gary slipped into the car and drove away.

The woman's head hung out the window like a dog, and she kept looking at Shadow until the car turned the corner and disappeared. The hollow feeling that had haunted him since the day he'd first learned his mother worked as a dancer was amplified at that moment. Concern for the young woman tightened his chest.

"You coming in to pick up the slack behind the bar?" Klutch asked.

"Yeah," Shadow said as he approached the front door.

"It's fuckin' crazy in there. We got three of the big tables full of frat jerks who love to spend daddy's money." Klutch laughed. "The dancers are loving it."

"We gotta make sure those pricks keep in line. I don't want any of the women feeling uncomfortable or cheap."

The Insurgents were adamant that the dancers be respected by the patrons, but Shadow was particularly obsessed with it, and he knew the brothers thought he was a bit wacko when it came to them. Only his good friends knew the reason why, but they kept it to themselves. He didn't want the whole club to know that his mother used to dance. When he was younger, he'd heard her and her friend, Flo, talk about the way the men pawed them and how they hated that the owner and manager didn't protect them.

Shadow clenched his jaw so tightly that a muscle jumped in his cheeks, and molten anger rolled through him when he thought about what his mom had to endure to make ends meet. And it was all because his bastard father used every cent he made to drink and fuck other women.

Shadow lifted his chin at Hubcap and Wheelie who were searching patrons on their way in. When he entered the gentlemen's club, he was surprised at how many people were packed inside. He glanced over and saw a few people perched on stools that surrounded the big wooden bar, but most of the patrons were standing, crammed around it like sardines in a can.

Bones, Cruiser, and Blade were rushing back and forth trying to keep up with all the orders, and Shadow dashed over to give a helping hand.

"Glad to see you, bro. It's fuckin' nuts in here tonight," Blade said as he poured tequila in several shot glasses.

"Tell me what you need," Shadow said.

"Ten rum and Cokes. Stella will be by to get them."

Shadow glanced over the sea of people and noticed Honeysuckle gyrating on stage in a glow of yellow and blue lights. He grabbed the soda gun and squirted Coke into the glasses with one hand while adding shots of rum with the other one.

The whole time he worked, he kept his eye on the guy who was with the hooker in the parking lot. He sat with a group of frat boys who'd reserved several tables for a reunion. Blade had brought him up to speed on the different groups of guys at the club that night. The bikers' job was to make sure everything ran smoothly at the place and that the men didn't get out of line.

The Insurgents only employed three citizens at the club: Gary, the bartender, and two bouncers—Bane and Eddie. The rest of the staff were club members. Cruiser, Blade, and Bear were the ones who worked at Dream House most of the time, and Emma, an old lady of one of the bikers, managed the place. Hawk did the books, and the other members helped out when needed. It made the business run like a well-oiled machine.

A half hour later, Gary came behind the bar and nudged Shadow.

"Everything go okay?" Shadow asked.

"Yeah. I waited for a bit just to make sure." Gary grabbed a bar towel and wiped the counter.

"I'd have taken her back, but I know I would've ended up beating the shit outta her pimp or worse." He pressed his lips into a thin line. "And the fucked up thing is, if I'd done that, she'd be all over me, screaming and kicking to defend her piece of shit."

Gary nodded to one of the waitresses when she recited an order. "We're fuckin' slammed tonight."

"Yeah," Shadow muttered, his mind still on the woman at the motel. When he and his mom used to live in the trailer park, there were two women who always sported black eyes or busted lips. They'd service a few of the lowlifes in the park, but what he remembered the most was their "boyfriends" yelling and punching them when they didn't bring back enough money. He'd always wanted to run over and help them, but his mother had made him promise never to get involved with any of the personal shit that went on in their neighborhood.

"You can't save them all, dude," Gary said, clasping his hand on Shadow's shoulder. "It's just the way it is sometimes."

Gary's voice dragged him back from the past, and he looked at the bartender and nodded slowly. "Yeah … you're right about that. Life can really throw a bunch of shit in your face. Do you need me back here?"

"No—four of us is the limit, otherwise we just get in each other's way."

"Okay. If you need a break or anything, find me." Shadow walked out from behind the bar and strolled over to Helm, who stood against the left wall, his eyes scanning the room.

"Hey, bro. You're not needed at the bar anymore?"

"Gary's back. How're things on the floor?" Shadow zeroed in on the group of suits who had tables in the front and were throwing money on the stage.

"So far, so good. The girls are pulling in a lot of dough with private dances and tips. A good night for all." He motioned Tiffany over. "A generous glass of Jack for me and Shadow."

"Sure, honey." She winked then disappeared into the crowd. "Honeysuckle's already asked about you." Helm's eyes kept scanning.

"She's dancing real good now," Shadow replied.

"She and Diamond seem to be popular with the rich frats. We gotta make sure the fuckers behave, you know."

"Yeah." Shadow kept his gaze on the dude from the parking lot, who was currently leaning over the stage and trying to hand Diamond some money. Shadow jerked his head toward the dancer. "I gotta stop that shit right now."

Helm's eyes fixed on the dude who was practically climbing on stage. "Go for it. When you get back, your Jack will be waiting."

Shadow put his hand up when he saw Jax stalking toward the guy. He gestured that he had this one and Jax stopped in his tracks.

With one fluid movement, Shadow grabbed the guy by the back of his neck and dragged him back.

"What the fuck are you doing?" he yelled as he tried to break away.

"Leave him alone, asshole!" another man shouted.

Protests in agreement resounded around the table, but Shadow ignored them and plopped the guy down on an empty chair.

"Stay the fuck off the stage. You can't touch the dancers and they can't take the money from you when they're dancing." His eyes narrowed dangerously.

"You gonna let him talk shit to you, Jonah?" one of the frat boys asked in a slurred voice.

Jonah's gaze locked with Shadow's, then recognition spread over his face. He looked down at the table. "I was outta line. Sorry," he said.

"Fuck that! The bitches are strippers and we're paying money to do what the hell we want," a guy with short brown hair and an expensive dress shirt said.

Shadow gripped the big mouth's shoulders and pulled him out of his seat. "You're outta here."

The man struggled to get away and several of his buddies stood up. Jax, Helm, and Rock rushed over, and the men sunk back down in their chairs.

"This asshole doesn't know how to respect the club, the dancers, or me." Shadow shoved him toward Rock. "His ass is outta here."

One of the men stood up and smiled at the glaring bikers. "My buddy's drunk as hell, so he doesn't know what he's saying." He took out his wallet. "I'm Warren Huntington, and I'm prepared to make this right." The guy glanced around the table. "We'll make sure he doesn't make trouble." Warren opened his wallet and withdrew several hundred-dollar bills.

*The dude looks familiar.* Shadow racked his brain trying to remember where he'd seen this asshole, but it escaped him.

"Your call," Rock said, looking at him.

Shadow glanced over at Jonah, who had his gaze fixed on his drink, and then he took in Warren, who thought money was the answer to everything. "Fuck that," he muttered under his breath as he shook his head *no*. "Your fuckin' buddy's outta here."

Before Warren could reply, Rock dragged his friend away.

"You better make sure the asshole's got a way to get home," Shadow said.

Two of the men jumped up and dashed toward the front door.

"Did you *really* have to do that? I mean, we know you're an Insurgent and this club is owned by you guys, but you don't have to be all badass about it," Warren said as he slipped his wallet in his back pocket.

Anger pricked at Shadow's skin. "That was your only chance for the night. Next time you say or do something stupid, you'll be joining your buddy." He turned around and stalked away, heading to the area behind the stage. He pushed the black curtain aside and squinted against the bright florescent lights.

"Hey, sexy," Kitty said as she adjusted her sequined bra.

"Hey. Are all the girls back here?"

"I think so. What's up?"

"I just want everyone to know that if any of those fuckin' frat assholes say rude shit to any of you, come find me or any of the other Insurgents."

Kitty ran her hand over her thigh-high stockings. "Uh … okay. Are my seams straight, sexy?"

She turned around and he glanced at the back of her legs. "They look fine. I meant what I said."

"What's going on?" Destiny wrapped a flimsy robe around her nakedness.

"Shadow's just tellin' us not to take any shit from the frat boys. Can I borrow your garter belt—the silver one. I forgot to bring mine tonight."

"Sure—second drawer in my dressing table." Destiny turned to

Shadow. "Those guys are generous as hell. I've already made some good money from them, and Honeysuckle and Diamond have several private dances lined up with them."

"Just don't let them disrespect you. I'll be watching, but the place is jammed tonight, so I can't see everything—none of us can."

"I can handle them. I got a dance with one of them now, so I gotta get my outfit on." Destiny ran her hand over his. "You're so sweet with the way you worry about us. I mean, all you guys make us feel safe and respected, but you go the extra mile. We all notice that and appreciate it a lot."

Shadow stepped away. "Yeah … well, just pass the word along to the other dancers."

The night passed quickly, and an hour before closing, Jax came over to Shadow and told him that his old lady called and their kid wasn't feeling very good so he had to leave. Shadow took over Jax's duty of watching the monitor in the private rooms to make sure the men behaved during their lap dance.

"Any problems?" he asked Danny, who was also watching the cameras. On busy nights, two people were needed to monitor the rooms since they always stayed full.

"Not really. Emma's telling me the dancers are making a small fortune tonight." Emma was Danny's old lady, and she used to be a dancer until the club promoted her to manager several years ago.

"Here you go," Honeysuckle said as she gave Shadow a bottle of beer. "I thought you'd be thirsty." She looked down then back up until she caught his gaze. "How've you been?"

"Good." He picked up the bottle and tipped it toward her. "And thanks for this."

"You're welcome. Maybe we can talk some after the place closes? I've got to do a private right now, but you're sticking around 'til the end, right?"

"Yeah." He took a few swigs of beer and watched as she left the small room.

"She's got the hots for you, dude." Danny chuckled. "Too bad Banger and Hawk have this 'no fuckin' the dancers' rule. I'd kill to fuck Destiny and Kitty at the same time."

Danny and Emma had an understanding that he could fuck any of the club girls at the club parties a couple of times of month, but hang-arounds and other citizen women were strictly off limits. It'd worked for them for over fifteen years.

"It's a good rule because business and fucking don't mix." Shadow stared at the monitor and watched Honeysuckle walk inside the Boudoir Room with Warren Huntington following behind her. As Honeysuckle did her thing, Warren watched in fascination and everything seemed to be okay until Shadow spotted the dude pulling his cock out. Honeysuckle shook her head and said something, but Warren just laughed and yanked her to him.

"That's it," Shadow muttered.

"You want me to buzz Rock?" Danny asked as he craned his neck to see Shadow's monitor.

"Nope—I'll take care of this one myself." He jumped up and stormed down the hallway.

When he burst inside the room, Warren had his dick against Honeysuckle's thigh and his one arm wrapped around her waist, holding her tight.

"What the fuck are you doing?" he said as he advanced toward the couple.

"What? What's wrong?" Warren asked as his erection went limp.

"You can't be taking out your cock and touching the dancers. You fuckin' *know* this."

Warren zipped up his pants and Honeysuckle stood off to the side. "I didn't know that, dude."

"Bullshit." Shadow pointed to a sign that stated the rules for the private room. "You can read, can't you, college boy?" He glanced over at Honeysuckle. "The dance is over. Did you get the money up front?" She shook her head *no*. "Then I'll take care of the money."

"Okay," she said as she walked out of the room.

"You expect me to pay for a dance that was interrupted?" Warren rose to his feet and zipped up his pants.

"That's right, unless you want your fuckin' face rearranged." Shadow crossed his arms over his chest. "It's your choice."

"You're threatening me." Redness flushed across Warren's face.

"Nope. I'm just stating a fact—if you don't pay, I'll beat your ass. You got choices here, man."

Warren glowered at him as took out his wallet then took out a fifty-dollar bill.

Shadow jammed the bill in his jeans pocket. "No tip for Honeysuckle? I mean, you were groping her and shoving your cock against her."

Warren opened his mouth as if to say something and Shadow crossed over to him, his face inches from Warren's. "Don't even fuckin' say it. The dancers aren't hookers—they're honest women who are doing their job."

Warren snapped his mouth shut and dug out forty bucks. "This is the last time you'll see me in this dump."

"No worries 'cause you're gonna be put on the 'banned list' anyway." He gestured for Warren to leave the room.

"It's trash like you who give bikers a bad name," Warren muttered as he walked out of the room.

Before he made it down the hallway Shadow was on top of him, wrestling the frat boy to the ground.

"I guess you missed the fuckin' class on respect," he said, then turned Warren over on his back and punched him in the face. All of a sudden it came to him where he'd seen the asshole. *Eli and Brooke's party.* The image of Warren kissing Scarlett stirred up dark feelings inside him … feelings he had to reluctantly admit were jealousy. *What the fuck?* Shadow punched Warren once more in the face for good measure and jumped up.

Warren pushed up to his feet, his hand cupping the side of his jaw. "You'll be hearing from my lawyer." He huffed as he walked away.

"I look forward to that." Shadow clenched his teeth. *Asswipe.*

He walked to the women's area and handed Honeysuckle her tip. She circled her arms around his neck and kissed him on the lips.

"Thank you," she said breathlessly.

He smiled as he gently pushed her away. "No worries."

"Can we talk for a bit?" she asked.

"Is it about work?"

"Not really."

"Then I'm gonna have to pass. Why don't you take off? It's almost closing time. Rock will walk you to your car."

"Okay." The dancer's voice was flat.

Shadow patted her on the shoulder then strode over to the back door and went outside, smiling wryly at the colored lights the women had strung around the back fence. He leaned against the brick wall, lit a joint, then inhaled deeply. He exhaled smoke into the air and watched the wisps curl and dissipate. A light, warm breeze blew in from the east, carrying the perfume of roses, and he let it wash over him. The scent took him back in time to a vivid evocation of summers past. Roses had always been his mother's favorite flower, and even though the trailer park they'd lived in was rundown, dirty, and smelly, his mother had planted two rose bushes at each side of the steps leading up to their front door. How she'd loved them and taken pride in those bushes.

"'*Beacons of hope,*' Ma used to say," Shadow whispered.

A soft rustling of the leaves as crickets chirped brought a smile to his face. As a kid he used to catch crickets and fireflies, but his mother always made him let them go so they could live like *"God intended them to."* His mother's voice was as clear as day in his mind.

The screen door squeaked behind him and he glanced over and saw Bones coming toward him.

"You got an extra one?" his buddy asked, pointing to the joint between Shadow's teeth.

He handed one to Bones, and the two stood in silence, smoking and looking at the swaying branches of the oak trees in the yard.

"Honeysuckle's singing your praises," Bones said.

Shadow grunted as he tried to push down the jealousy he'd felt when he recognized the douchebag. The feeling had surprised the hell out of him because he'd never experienced that before when it came to a chick. *What the hell is she doing to me?* He didn't know the answer, but all he knew was that he wished Scarlett were here with him now, watching the strings of colored lights swing slowly back and forth in the soft breeze.

Brows knitted into a frown as he realized that she had burrowed in his brain nice and tight. No woman had ever affected him this way before, and it angered and intrigued him at the same time.

Yeah … there was no doubt about it: she was getting to him.

He took another long drag then dropped the roach on the ground; he stubbed it out under his boot heel and went back inside.

# CHAPTER SEVEN

SCARLETT STOOD AT the corner of the window in the second-floor study, watching Shadow as he lifted the sledgehammer over his shoulders and then slammed it onto a wooden post. The defined muscles that ran between his shoulder blades and down his arms flexed and bunched, their contours glistening with sweat in the bright sunlight. He was magnificent … hypnotic.

The now familiar clench between her legs made her shift in place as she continued to watch him and remember their stolen times together. For the past week or so, her whole focus had been on Shadow, and it frightened and excited her at the same time. Scarlett knew she should give him up, but she craved the rush she got from him. She'd been hooked from the start, and she laughed dryly at her foolishness in thinking that just one quick hookup with him would ever be enough. She was just like an addict now, jittery and unfocused until the next fix.

Scarlett pressed her forehead against the glass pane and wondered how she would ever get off the carousel. Shadow did things to her no man had ever done, and she felt free and alive when she was wrapped in his arms or moving in sync with his powerful body as he thrust inside her. The crazy thing was, she knew very little about him besides what a wonderfully delicious lover he was, and she wanted to *know* him outside of their sexual encounters.

As if he sensed her, Shadow looked up at the window and she turned away quickly. Scarlett hated that he'd caught her spying on him, especially since he'd been keeping his distance from her for the past few days. Her rational mind told her it was for the best, but her body wildly yearned for him: his touch, his lips, his taste. She never imagined herself capable of such ferocious passion, such desire to open herself up wholly to a man to do with her as he liked.

Scarlett balled her hand into a fist and pounded it lightly on the wall. He was so damn good that she was sure he ruined her for all other men. "Damn you," she mumbled under her breath. Against her better judgment, she peeked out the window again and saw him disappear behind the wall that the men were building. Why was he pushing her away? Was he already tired of her?

"Damn you," she said again, only this time louder.

The sound of her phone ringing pulled her away from the window, and she hustled over to the end table and picked it up.

"Whatcha up to?" Kiara asked.

"Nothing much," Scarlett replied as she sank down on the leather wingback chair. "How about you?"

"Waiting for my lunch break. Do you want to come over and we can go to the French Bistro. I'm craving paté for some reason." A small chuckle came through the phone.

"I can meet you there. It'll give me an excuse to get out of the house. I've been going crazy with this upcoming fundraiser."

"Is that why you've been so distracted for the past week or so?"

Scarlett stiffened. "Yeah. So what time is good to meet?"

"One. I like taking lunch after the crowd goes back to work. I guess that's one of the perks of working for my dad."

"I can't even imagine working for mine—it'd be a disaster. I'll meet you at the bistro at one."

Scarlett gripped the phone and glanced over at the window. As tempting as it was to stand there and watch Shadow all day, she had to stop acting like a pathetic girl with a crush. The whole thing was ridiculous anyway and totally unsustainable. *I guess Shadow figured that out too.* An empty feeling wrapped around the thought, but she quickly pushed it away, stood up, and made her way to her bedroom to change her clothes.

When Scarlett walked into the dining room, she was surprised to see her father sitting at the head of the table and eating a sandwich while reading a document. He glanced up and a small smile skipped across his lips.

"Hi, Dad," she said as she crossed the room to retrieve the briefcase she'd left in the corner the night before. After lunch, she'd planned to stop by the Palace Hotel to talk to the chef about the food for the gala.

"How are you?" His gaze skimmed over her face as if he were trying to discern something in her features.

"Fine. What are you doing home for lunch?" Her father rarely came home during the work day.

"I was in the area, so I thought I'd grab some peace and quiet while I went over this contract." He pointed to the document on the table. "Your mother's worried about you." His eyes kept her gaze.

Scarlett shrugged. "I don't know why—I'm fine."

"She thinks you've got something on your mind that's keeping you from committing to Warren."

*Here we go. Shit.* "I don't. I'm meeting Kiara for lunch, so I have to run."

"You stay right where you are. How long have you and Warren been dating?"

"I don't know."

"A year," he said.

"Why did you ask if you already knew?" She sighed and looked down at her phone. "I really do have to go."

"A year is long enough to get to know someone. I expected a ring on your finger by now. What's the problem?"

Scarlett inhaled deeply then exhaled. "I guess I don't like him. No … as a matter of fact, I *know* I don't like him."

"Why not? He comes from a good family, the women seem to take to him, he went to a good college, he's personable … What don't you like about him?"

"He's a snob, a phony, and I don't think he's very sincere. He plays whatever part a situation demands. And if I'm going to marry a man, I want to be in love with him."

"Love is over-rated. You need a solid foundation to build a family and a life."

*And have young mistresses to scratch your itch or make you feel loved? God, how I wish I could say that.* "I don't agree. I really have to go, Dad."

Her father stared at her with pursed lips, then nodded. "We'll talk later, and stop upsetting your mother." He picked up his sandwich and took a big bite as his eyes wandered down to the contract. Their talk was over—she'd been dismissed.

As Scarlett sped down the hill, anger sparked through her. The last thing she wanted was a marriage like her parents. Her mother filled her time with luncheons, golf games, and the occasional committee, and business preoccupied her father. Her mother found solace in a bottle of gin, and her dad found it in the arms of his latest girlfriend. The only time her parents went out together was when protocol demanded it. Occasionally her mother would go on one of her dad's business trips, and she always seemed to choose the cities that had the best shopping. Scarlett couldn't remember the last time she saw her parents kiss or hold hands—they lived a marriage of convenience.

Scarlett waved at Kiara, who sat at a round table in the corner of the eatery by the large window looking out on Spruce Street. She maneuvered her way through the small bistro until she reached the table, then plopped down on the blue paisley cushion on the white wrought-iron chair.

"Sorry I'm late. My dad was home for lunch and wanted to talk about his favorite subject—Warren." Scarlett rolled her eyes and picked up the menu.

"What's going on with you and him? I saw Warren at the club the other day, and he said that you've been avoiding him."

"I have." She motioned the waitress over. "Can I please have a glass of water with two slices of lemon?"

The young waitress smiled. "Sure. Have you decided on what you'd like to eat?" They gave her their orders then she dashed away.

"Why have you been avoiding him?" Kiara asked as she broke off a piece of bread.

"Because I'm done with him. I know I have to tell him, but I really haven't been in the mood for *that* talk. I figured he would just get bored and move on." Scarlett looked down at the blue-checked tablecloth then glanced back up. "I know—it's a coward's way."

"I don't get why you don't like Warren. He was so funny at the club, and Melody was pushing her boobs into his face. She's shameless, really." Kiara spread butter on her bread then took a bite.

"She can have him. Oh, Kiara, I want something *completely* different for my life. I don't want to be going to lunches at the club or playing fucking golf or waiting home to please my man after he's had a hard day at the office. I mean, don't you feel like we're stuck in the damn 1950s or something?"

Kiara cocked her head. "Not really. We go on trips to wherever we want. I have a good job. I can do what I please. And if I don't marry, it's no big deal." She wiped the corners of her mouth with her napkin. "I do want to get married and have a family, but the important thing is that it's *my* choice."

"Is it really? You know your parents want you to settle down and have a family. It's—"

"They want my brother to marry and have kids too. I think it's just a parent thing, regardless of the time and place in which we live. Parents want to make sure their kids aren't alone after they're gone."

Scarlett squeezed one of the lemon slices into her water then took a sip. "Okay, I agree with you but I'll bet the daughters in most households get pushed more into marrying and having a family than the sons do, especially when they're in their twenties. Look at us—we're still living at home. We go to the club, we do our charity fundraisers, we date men who say all the right things. Aren't you bored out of your fucking mind?"

"Not really. Why don't you find some stud and have a fling? That would perk up your summer. Flirt with one of those guys who are working on the tennis house at your place. Oh God, that would be such a classic stereotype—rich woman with a hired hand." Kiara giggled.

A thread of guilt wove through Scarlett. *Maybe I should tell Kiara about Shadow.* Then she reminded herself that he was dissing her, so her summer fling may very well have burned up before the summer had ended.

"You've got such a serious look on your face. What're you thinking about?" Her friend's eyes sparkled when the waitress set down a Gruyère and paté baguette in front of her.

Scarlett picked up her fork and picked at her spinach and mushroom quiche. "That I'm going to tell Warren it's over, and that I want to get an apartment and a job."

Kiara froze in mid-bite and looked over the top of her sandwich at her. "Wow," was all she said, then she sank her teeth into the crusty bread.

"I've been thinking about it for a long time. I just feel stifled at home. I want my own place, and I want to earn money instead of having an allowance."

"What kind of a job and where would you live?"

"I'd love to do something in marketing or event planning at a hotel or marketing firm. For the past year I've been looking at places on Larkspur Lane. My dad has several apartments over there that he rents. He's had a few of them for years."

"Would you rent from your dad?"

"No. I want to do everything on my own. I have money in the trust fund my grandparents set up for me before they died."

Kiara smiled. "This is exciting. Can I go with you to look at places? You should go for it. It's scary, but you should do it." She covered her mouth with her hand. "What are your parents going to say?"

"I know my mom won't be happy. In some weird way she gets comfort from me being there, even though we're not close and we never *really* talk. Oh … she tells me what I should be doing or how I'm screwing up my life, but that's about it. Strangely, I think my dad will be cool with it." She pushed the half-eaten quiche away from her. "I could be wrong. With my family, you never know."

"We could have parties at your place instead of Daisy's, where her mom is always trying to pretend she's one of the girls. I feel so sorry for Daisy when her mom does that."

Scarlett nodded. "Especially when she does it with her boyfriends. Once, when Warren and I were at a party at Daisy's house, Mrs. Miller hit on Warren so bad." She giggled. "He overreacted and talked about it for like a month. I felt so sorry for Daisy as she watched her mom make a fool out of herself."

Kiara placed her knife and fork across her empty plate and leaned back. "I agree. I can't imagine how hard that must be for her. I'd die if my mom acted like that. When we start partying at your apartment, I bet Daisy won't be so uptight."

"I'm positive you'd win that one. You know, I'm going to do this. I'll call Trudy at my dad's office and have her line up some places for us to see this week. I'll swear her to secrecy. I really want to do this." Excitement streaked thought Scarlett.

"Let me know. This will be so much fun." Kiara pulled out a credit card. "I have to get back to work."

"I have to go too. I'm meeting with the chef at the Palace." Scarlett put a twenty-dollar bill on the bill tray.

After paying their tab, the two women walked out of the eatery and into the heat of the day. Scarlett waved to her friend as she opened the door to her Mercedes sports car and headed over to the hotel.

WHEN SCARLETT RETURNED home it was nearly five o'clock, and her heart sank when she didn't hear any construction noises coming from the north side of the house. She rushed into the house and walked into the den, which happened to face in that direction, and relief washed over her when she saw the workers still milling about. Shadow came into her view and her breath hitched just like it did most times when she saw him. She dashed up the stairs to her room, kicked off her heels, and quickly changed into a simple sundress.

When she reached the bottom of the stairs, she heard her mother rustling about in the sun room, and Scarlett crossed the foyer and went into the kitchen.

"Would you like something, Miss Scarlett?" Clara asked as she looked up from the ball of dough she was kneading.

"Do we have any sweet tea?" she asked, opening the refrigerator.

"We have a pitcher of it and another one of unsweetened tea."

"Perfect." Scarlett grabbed the two pitchers. "Can you grab me that stack of plastic cups," she said, jerking her head toward the butler's pantry.

Clara wiped her hands on her apron and scurried away to fetch them.

"Do you want me to help you?" she asked.

"I've got it, thanks." Scarlett stood in front of the back door and chuckled. "I guess I need you to open the door for me, Clara."

"Be careful, Miss Scarlett. The pavement is real hot and you don't have your shoes on."

She looked over her shoulder and smiled. "No worries. Thanks again."

Scarlett hurried off the pathway and made her way toward the construction area, enjoying the late afternoon sun on her shoulders and the soft grass under her bare feet. One of her favorite things to do as a young girl had been to stroll barefoot in the grass in the early morning dew. The cool softness had felt wonderful beneath Scarlett's feet, and she wondered why she'd stopped doing that just because she was older.

"Hey," Smokey yelled out to her.

"Hiya," she answered as she put the two pitchers on a small patio table and took the stack of cups from under the crook of her arm. Scarlett untwisted the tie and took out about ten of them. "I thought you guys would like something cold to drink. I brought sweetened and unsweetened iced tea."

"That's real good of you," Smokey said, winking at her. "I'll let my crew know." He turned around and whistled, then yelled out, "Iced tea if you want it."

Scarlett scanned the crowd of men, looking for the only face she wanted to see, but Shadow wasn't among them.

As she poured the tea, she kept hoping that he would come out from the partially-built structure, but he didn't.

"Thank you for the drinks," Smokey said as he put his empty cup down and wiped his mouth.

"You're welcome. How's the construction going?" she asked.

"Good, considering that it's been hotter than hell the whole time we've been working."

"When do you think it'll be finished?" She held her breath as she waited for his answer.

"We probably got another ten days or two weeks left. I have some other small jobs we're doing too, so it's taking us a bit more time than I planned."

"I don't think there's a big rush for you to finish. Just between us, my dad will probably use it a total of four times before he gets bored and the novelty of it wears off."

Smokey laughed. "I take it you don't play?"

"I know how, but I don't like it."

"I've never played the game, but it doesn't seem like much fun hitting a ball with a racket. I'd rather use all my free time riding my bike."

"Hey," Shadow said from behind.

She whirled around and held herself back from falling into his arms. "Hi. I was just giving out iced tea. Do you want some?"

He cut his eyes over to Smokey. "Don't you have some shit you gotta do?"

Smokey narrowed his gaze. "You and me both." He turned back to Scarlett and smiled. "Thanks again." Then he lumbered away.

"How've you been?" she asked, pouring him a cup of tea.

"Good. What were you and Smokey talkin' about?"

"The construction."

Shadow grunted and took the cup from her. His fingers brushed along Scarlett's and a current of desire flashed through her—it was brief, but her body responded to him as if he'd touched her intimately. Scarlett looked up and when their eyes met, an unspoken feeling of want passed between them. He downed the tea and handed the cup to her, his gaze never leaving hers.

"Thanks," he said thickly.

"You're welcome." She bent down and brushed away some ants that were crawling over the top of her feet. "Am I going to see you later?" she whispered as she straightened up.

"I got some stuff to do right after work."

"What?"

He shrugged. "Stuff."

"Don't you want to be with me anymore?" The minute the question spilled out of Scarlett's mouth, she wanted to take it back. She sounded so weak and needy. How she hated that.

"It's just that we had a good time, you know. I mean, you're rich and I'm—"

"Common," she interrupted.

"*Different* is what I was gonna say."

"Common suits you better." She knew it was a cruel blow, but he'd wounded her pride. She picked up the empty pitchers and cups, and tucked the bag full of unused ones back under her arm.

"Don't get pissed off, baby. It's the way it goes. We had a lot of fun."

"I'm not pissed. I agree with you—it's time to move on."

"You're acting pissed."

"Don't flatter yourself. You were this summer's diversion, that's all." Scarlett turned to leave when he gripped her arm.

"I'm not buying your bullshit."

She smiled sweetly at him. "I don't give a damn if you believe me or not." She tipped her head toward the work zone. "You better get back there, after all, my father's paying a lot of money." She turned away from him with a sharp little jerk, pulling free from his hand, and walked back to the house.

"Here, let me help you, Miss Scarlett," Jane said as she grabbed the pitchers from her hands.

"Thank you," she said.

She placed the unused cups on the counter in the butler's pantry, threw the empty ones away, then scrambled up the back stairs. Tears trailed down her face as she locked the door to her room. She lay across her bed and cried.

# CHAPTER EIGHT

FLO KARAS PUSHED open the door to her favorite coffee house and looked around the room, trying to find the perfect spot to make the phone call. She settled on a low table in the corner by a window and headed toward it, her heels clacking on the wooden floor.

Flo—her birth name was Florence—had been coming to A Perfect Cup ever since it opened ten years before. She sank into a plush leather chair and crossed her legs as her kohl-lined eyes glanced over at the wall clock: 2:32 p.m. She ran her slender fingers through her russet tresses and smiled when the young lady set down a mocha café latte with extra whipped cream in front of her.

"Thank you," she said. Flo leaned forward and curled her fingers around her daily indulgence, the bracelets on her arm clinking together like wind chimes. The tip of her tongue lapped up some of the whipped cream, then her bright red lips puckered when she blew slightly before taking a sip. She sighed and leaned back against the chair's cushion and looked out the window at the tree-lined street. Tourists strolled along sidewalks bordered by quaint shops and several carts selling ice cream and cold drinks. A group of children ran down the pavement and dodged a couple with a baby carriage before they raced into a candy store.

*You've come a long way from the trailer park.* It seemed like a lifetime ago since she'd lived in the dirty, smelly dump she'd called home for almost twelve years. But Flo never wanted to forget how bad her life had been back then so she could appreciate how good it was now. When she'd met Carmen and her teenage son, Shadow—she never could figure out why a mother would give her son that name—she'd just thrown out her third husband. Of course, he'd been a charmer before he put the ring on her finger, but afterward, he'd turned into a cheating bastard just like the other two before him. If it hadn't been for Carmen, who'd told her to try and get a job at Satin Dolls, she probably would've ended up on the streets. Her loser husband had taken all her money and spent it on his cheapies.

Flo took another sip of coffee. Those years at Satin Dolls paid the bills, but she hated the way the men leered at her like she was some cheap hooker. Carmen felt the same way, but she'd tell Flo she'd do anything to keep her boy in school and give him a better chance in life than she'd had.

*Poor Carmen. She didn't deserve to die like that.* Flo rubbed her lids that were shadowed too much with gleaming pink. She knew she was probably too old for all the sparkly makeup she wore, but it made her feel young and sexy, and she didn't give a damn what anyone thought.

Flo took one more sip of her drink, then fished around in her designer handbag for the burner phone she'd bought the day before. Each time she made the calls, she'd buy a new burner phone. With the dangerous game Flo was playing, she was very much aware of staying one step ahead of the killer.

Her hazel eyes looked around the area, but no one was even remotely close to her. Relaxing a bit, she tapped in the number and waited.

"What do you want?" the voice said in a strained whisper.

"You're getting better at guessing that it's me." Flo laughed nervously. Even though her friend's murderer didn't know where she was, Flo always felt that she was being watched when they spoke on the phone.

No reply. Only heavy breathing.

"I need some more money."

"You already got your money for the month." Tightness mixed with anger laced the killer's voice.

"Some unexpected expenses came up." Flo tapped her fingers against her lavender linen skirt. "I rarely ask for extra." The truth was, she and a few of her friends were going to Denver that weekend on a shopping trip.

"I've given you plenty over the years. Like I told you two weeks ago, this is going to stop at the end of the summer."

Flo clucked her tongue. "I don't think you want to do that, but of course, it's your choice. You do what you need to … and I'll do what I need to."

"How much extra?"

"Five thousand by Friday."

"I can't get that much that soon."

Flo took out a tissue and dabbed the sweat from her face then tucked the crumpled Kleenex inside her purse.

"You can get it … You always do."

"I should've killed you that night!"

"But you didn't. Drop it off at the usual place."

Flo clicked off the phone, and her hands trembled slightly as she ordered a Lyft. It was much too hot to walk the few blocks back to her luxury condo on Larkspur Lane. In less than a minute, a white Buick La Crosse pulled up to the curb in front of the coffee house. Flo pushed up from the chair and hurried to the door.

Once Flo opened the door to her home, relief washed over her; she felt safe inside with her advanced alarm system. Slipping off her shoes, she smiled when she saw the Rocky Mountains in the distance; she'd never tire of the spectacular view from her condominium.

The thought of losing her only source of income scared Flo, but she doubted that would happen. *But what if it does … or what if something happens to me? I should try and find Carmen's son and let him know what really happened to his mother, just in case.* She realized she had no clue if he was still in Pinewood Springs. In all those years, she'd never bumped into him, so it made her think he must've left the area after Carmen's murder.

Deciding she'd think about it another day, Flo went into her gourmet kitchen and poured herself a glass of white wine. She padded back to the living room, leaned against the floor-to-ceiling window, and brought the glass to her lips. Looking up, she spotted an eagle soaring high in the cloudless blue sky, and at that moment, she wished she could be free and fly away … far, far away.

# Chapter Nine

"W HY ARE WE eating here?" Scarlett asked when Daisy turned into the parking lot of Big Rocky's Barbecue.

"I've been told they have the best ribs in town, and they make a real mean martini." Daisy switched off the ignition and checked out her makeup in the rearview mirror.

"Okay. Aren't Ashley and Shelby coming?" Scarlett slid out of the car. She wore a short yellow flounce skirt that showed off her long legs, an ivory off-the-shoulder top that molded around her upper body nicely, and strappy sandals that showcased her morning pedicure.

"They're coming with Kiara. Let's go," Daisy avoided Scarlett's eyes and forged ahead. She kept pulling down her micro miniskirt as she walked.

"Maybe you should've splurged for a bit more fabric." Scarlett joked as she sidled up next to her friend.

As they neared the entrance, she saw two rows of motorcycles lined up, the sun reflecting off the shiny chrome.

"Look at these," Scarlett said, pausing to admire a metallic yellow bike with skulls painted on it. "This one is so cool." She was running her hand across the black leather seat when a man wearing a leather vest and blue jeans came over.

"Don't touch the bikes," he said gruffly.

Scarlett shook her head slightly and gave a small laugh. "Are you serious?"

"Are you the bike-keeper?" Daisy added. The two women giggled.

The man stared at them stone-faced. "Keep. The. Fuck. Away. From. The. Bikes." He narrowed his eyes.

"Chill, okay?" Scarlett said as she tugged Daisy away.

The man turned around and she noticed the back of his vest read *Prospect* on the bottom. "What does that mean?" she asked Daisy, pointing at the guy's back.

Daisy shrugged. "Who knows? These men who ride motorcycles think they're so bad," she whispered. She looped her arm through Scarlett's and walked away.

When they entered the restaurant, the aroma of tangy hickory swirled around them, and Daisy strode up to the hostess desk and gave her name. Within minutes, the two women were following the slim brunette to a table by a window.

"This is so beautiful," Scarlett said, looking out the window.

The restaurant was nestled among the evergreens on Aspen Lake, and rays of sunlight shimmered and danced across the blue water.

"Looking at the lake reminds me that we have to plan our pool party," Daisy said.

"Wait until the gala is over—I'm too swamped right now with that," Scarlett replied.

"I forgot about that, but I do have it marked on my calendar. I asked Connor to go with me." Daisy smiled. "He's real cute, don't you think?"

Scarlett nodded. "He is, and he seems like a nice guy. Are things moving from the friends stage?"

Daisy rolled her eyes and picked up a biscuit and broke it in half. "Who knows? Dating is so much more complicated now than it used to be in our parents' day."

"Isn't that the truth." Scarlett gazed out at the water again.

"Hi, beautiful," Warren said.

She snapped her eyes to him just as he pulled out a chair and sank down next to her. *What the hell is* he *doing here?* Her gaze cut over to Ashley, Shelby, and Kiara, who wore guilty expressions on their faces as they approached the table.

"I didn't know you were joining us," Scarlett said, scooting her chair closer to the wall.

"The girls called me and I thought, why not? I haven't seen my girl in a while. I'm glad to be here." He clutched her hand and squeezed it before leaning in for a kiss.

She turned away so that his lips landed on her cheek, then she glared at Kiara as she slipped into one of the chairs.

"Brent and Jeremy are coming too, right, Warren?" Kiara said, as if *that* would appease Scarlett.

"Yeah, they should be here any minute," Warren replied as he craned his neck and looked at the front of the restaurant.

Ashley and Shelby sat down, leaving an empty seat between them. Licks of anger burned inside Scarlett as she fumed from the deceit of her friends.

"Did you know about this?" Scarlett mouthed to Daisy, who shook her head *no,* then crossed her heart with her index finger.

Scarlett huffed and leaned back against the chair, deciding that she'd hurry through dinner then cut out of there fast. She was more than pissed at her meddling friends, who seemed hellbent to keep Warren in her life. *Why can't they just butt the fuck out?* After a long week of committee meetings, listening to her parents lecture her on what she should do, *and* Shadow's rejection of her—which was, hands down, the worst part of the week—she yearned for a girls' night out, and here was *Warren* sitting beside her. Yeah … feeling betrayed at that moment by her friends didn't even describe it.

Soon the whole gang was there, and as Warren and his buddies talked about business and sports, and her friends planned the next pool party, Scarlett sipped martini after martini. She had to give credit to Warren for catching on that she wasn't exactly thrilled to see him, so he'd backed off with the touchy-feely crap and pretty much ignored her once Brent and Jeremy arrived.

The waiter put down four platters of ribs on the table along with mounds of mashed potatoes, corn, and coleslaw.

"Buffalo steak medium-rare?" the server asked, glancing around the table. Jeremy waved his hand and the waiter placed the steaming dish in front of him. Warren and Brent had ordered New York strips, and after setting everything down, the server hurried away.

The conversation flowed well while they ate, and as Scarlett began to relax and enjoy herself, the anger she'd felt at her friends earlier in the evening slowly vanished.

"How do you like the food?" Warren asked before he popped a morsel of steak into his mouth.

"It's so good. I can't believe I've never been here," Scarlett replied.

"This is the best barbecue I've had." Shelby licked her fingers. "Am I right?"

The group spent the next few minutes talking about the food, then changed the subject to best nightclubs in Pinewood Springs.

Warren leaned against Scarlett, his shoulder brushing against hers. "Do you want a bite?" He speared a morsel of steak and held it inches from her mouth. "It's real good and juicy," he said in a low voice.

"Thanks, but I'm pretty full," she replied.

"Just one little bite, beautiful."

Warren caught her eye, and she quickly looked down at her plate. She moved her fork around, pretending to be engrossed in her meal.

"Hey, there," a deep voice boomed.

She looked up, and for a second it didn't register that the muscular man standing by the table was the contractor working on the tennis house.

"Smokey—the dude working his ass off at your house." He leaned back on his heels.

"Right! Sorry, I ..." She waved her hand in the air toward him. "You just look different." Her gaze skimmed his leather vest. "Hi, how are you?"

He chuckled. "Better than you, lady."

"He thinks you're drunk," Warren whispered under his breath. "What a rude asshole."

Scarlett ignored the looks her friends were giving her as she engaged in small talk with Smokey.

"How do you like the food?" His eyes swept around the table as her friends mumbled praises of their meals.

"It's really good. I'll have to tell my parents about it," Scarlett said.

"Your dad comes here a lot," Smokey said, then pursed his lips together.

She widened her eyes. "I didn't know that. I wonder why he never suggested it to us."

He shrugged then looked toward the back of the room. "I gotta join my brothers."

She craned her neck and saw a table of about twenty men all wearing leather vests. "You have a big family."

Smokey burst out laughing and slapped his thigh a few times. "Fuckin' classic." He lifted his chin to her and sauntered away.

The back of his vest read *Insurgents* on the top and *Colorado* on the bottom; a skull that had blood dripping from it was in the middle with a pistol on each side.

"What a fucking lowlife," Warren said. Brent and Jeremy laughed as they glanced furtively at the retreating biker.

"Is that who's working at your house?" Kiara said.

"He's the contractor, and he's a nice guy." A spiral of tingling sensation rose from the pit of her stomach as she wondered if Shadow was one of the men at the table.

"What the fuck?" Warren swivel in his chair to face her. "Your dad hired a douche from an outlaw motorcycle club to work at your house?"

"He's in an outlaw club like the Hells Angels?" Daisy gasped, looking over her shoulder at him.

"The Insurgents. Didn't you see the patch on the back of his vest?" Brent asked.

Daisy looked at Scarlett. "I bet that dude who got in our face about the motorcycles is in the club. He was scary."

*Shadow's a biker in an outlaw club? This is like a movie. I don't even know what an outlaw club is all about.*

"I bet all the workers at your house are part of his damn club." Warren leaned in close to her. "I hope you're staying away from those criminals while they're on your property."

*Um … no.* Snippets of her time together with Shadow streaked through her mind.

"You are, right?" Warren nudged her with his elbow.

"They work all day," she replied. "Can you please pass the corn, Ashley?"

The conversation veered away from bikers and outlaws, and Scarlett was grateful for that. She had to have some time to digest what she'd just learned. Racking her brain, she remembered a couple of times when she saw Shadow wearing a leather vest. Scarlett had thought it was odd to wear it in the hot sun, but she hadn't paid much attention to it. The fact that he *might* be in that outlaw club frightened and excited her at the same time, and she didn't have a clue as to why she was feeling that way.

The room felt stuffy all of a sudden. Scarlett wiped her mouth, then folded the napkin and put it next to her plate. She pushed the chair back and rose to her feet.

"I'll be right back," she said.

"Are you going to the restroom? I'll go with you," Kiara said.

"Me too," Shelby added.

"I'm actually going outside to make a phone call—it's about the fundraiser." She fibbed. Without waiting for her friends' retorts, Scarlett scurried away from the table and crossed over to the lobby.

Sunlight spilled in, the minute she opened the ornately carved wooden door. Outside, she gulped in air like a drowning person who'd been washed ashore, then walked to the back of the restaurant. She gazed at the small ripples in the water being driven across the lake by a light breeze that carried the scent of sweet pine. Behind her she heard the crunch of footsteps, and she silently cursed Warren under her breath. *He just doesn't catch on!*

"It's a kickass view."

Scarlett whirled around and saw Shadow with a joint dangling from his lips, smoke curling up and biting his nostrils. He winked at her, drew in a deep breath, and walked toward her as he exhaled.

"I only came out for a smoke and look who I found." His gaze slowly skimmed over her.

Suddenly self-conscious, she folded her arms across her chest. "Did Smokey tell you I was out here?" she asked.

He shook his head *no* before exhaling. Spirals of smoke wisped upward, and she heard him mutter "Fuckin' bastard" as he ground the spent joint into the ground.

"The food is good here," she said, hoping to switch his focus off his friend.

"Yeah." He looked over her shoulder at the lake in the distance. "Have you ever been to Hanging Lake?"

"Yes, but"—she pointed to the crystalline water—"that's not Hanging Lake."

His gaze cut to hers. "I know. Have you ever gone swimming in it, under the waterfall?"

"Are we talking about Hanging Lake?" He nodded. "I used to go there with my parents when I was a kid, but I never went under the waterfall. My parents thought it was too dangerous." She dropped her arms to her sides. "It's been years since I've been there. It sounds like you like the place."

"I do. It's always been my go-to place when shit gets too crowded in my head." He crouched down and pulled on a blade of grass and put it between his teeth. "I like the outdoors."

"What kind of stuff do you have going on inside you?" she whispered.

"Memories and a whole lot of demons, baby." He grinned.

"I think we all have memories that aren't so wonderful, and there's a demon or two lurking inside me. No one's immune to them." She smiled.

"What're yours? Not wearing the right color nail polish with your outfit?"

She jerked back at his words as if he'd slapped her. "Do you think

I'm that petty and shallow?"

Shadow straightened up and rubbed his hand over his face. "I don't know much about you except that you give great head, feel good and tight around my cock, and have an exceptional pair of tits."

A brief flash of anger rankled over her skin, like goosebumps raised by frosty air. "Thanks for the sexual review." Bitterness punctuated her words.

He held up his hands. "Just telling it like it is."

She rolled her eyes and stepped back. Shaking her head, Scarlett held his gaze. "Everything you are is between your legs."

Taking a few steps toward her, he laughed, but she noticed the vein in his left temple twitching. Shadow stopped in front of her, and she turned away. He grabbed her face between his hands and tilted her face up toward him.

"I should just take off," she said.

"But you won't."

"I don't know why I let you talk to me like this."

He quirked his lips. "Don't you? It's called, *lust*, baby."

A heated flush crept up her neck and spread across her cheeks. She tried to pull away, but he pressed his thumbs against her cheeks, and she'd be damned if she told him it hurt.

"You're just—"

He let go of her face and pushed her against the wall of the restaurant with the length of his body. "Say it, baby." Grabbing her by the hips, he yanked her flush against him. "I'm common as fuckin' dirt, and you love it." He crushed his mouth on hers.

Her lips parted, letting him in, tasting the smokiness of whiskey on his tongue. She moaned and ran her hands down his back as his made their way under her skirt. It had been too long since they'd kissed, and she loved the wet tangle of tongues and the hard edge of his teeth on her lower lip.

He pulled away a bit and muttered "Fuck, babe" before he pressed his mouth back on hers. Heat flared at every pulse point and burned like a wildfire when he ground against her, making his dick rock hard through his jeans.

"Let's go somewhere," he whispered as he trailed light kisses along her jawline and down her neck. "Fuck, baby … you make me so damn hard." Shadow's warm fingers slid to the lace edge of her panties.

At that moment, Scarlett pushed him and scrambled away from his reach. Bewilderment skated across his face as he watched her walk away.

"What the *fuck*?"

Pausing, she spun around slightly and her lips turned up as she locked her gaze on his.

"Don't ever take me for granted, *baby*." Scarlett licked her lips, tossed her hair over her shoulder, and walked away as every part of her body pulsed with desire.

*How am I ever going to get him out of my system?*

She entered the restaurant and headed to her table.

# CHAPTER TEN

FORTY MEN FILLED the meeting room, some leaning against the concrete walls, some sitting on the floor with their knees bent in front of them, and others on metal chairs around the large mahogany table. Banger stood at the head while Hawk slouched down in his seat. A cacophony of cussing, fists pounding on the tables, and excited voices filled the room.

"There's no fuckin' way we're gonna let Skeet get away with this shit," Throttle said as he tipped the back of his chair against the wall. He waved his hand around the room. "We shoulda put a bullet in his head instead of giving him a beatdown last year."

Banger hit the gavel on the wood block. "It's what the club decided and what Metal wanted, so all this grumbling isn't doing a damn thing to help. Skeet's got shit for brains if he's aiming to take us on."

The men yelled their agreement amid guffaws and clapping. Hawk pushed back in his chair and slowly rose to his feet.

"Skeet's the new president of the Rising Order. He got a few of his buddies to oust Sniper from that position. We made a fuckin' mistake in not taking care of him after the situation with Tigger went down, but Skeet was a brother, and it's never easy to think a member will betray the brotherhood."

"He betrayed Metal by fuckin' his old lady." Bear shook his head. "Metal was too easy on her."

Animal nodded. "Bones and I were ready to haul her ass back to the club when we ran into Skeet and the skank last year, but Metal didn't want it. There's no way I would've been that forgiving."

"And the way she kept trying to convince us not to teach Skeet a lesson for fuckin' a brother's old lady was so damn annoying." Bones crossed his arms over his chest. "The only reason I didn't shut her up for good was outta respect for Metal's wishes. The brother's a real stand-up guy."

Metal was an older Insurgent who'd gone inactive when a slew of health problems forced him to retire from the club. His second wife, Thea, hadn't been too happy about being a caretaker at her young age. She was a little less than half of Metal's fifty years, and the thrill of being his old lady began to dissipate. Skeet was twenty-eight, rugged, and exuded all kinds of alpha-male sexiness, and soon the two were carrying on a torrid affair behind Metal's back.

The Insurgents MC had a rule that if any brother fucks another brother's old lady or girlfriend, that member would get a beatdown and be thrown out of the club. Of course there were exceptions, like in Wheelie and Sofia's case, but for the most part, the rule was taken seriously.

Skeet had left the club before Metal found out about the affair, and the ex-Insurgent weaseled himself into the Rising Order—a relatively new MC in Northern Colorado. Since Skeet had entered into that club, there had been rumblings over the MC grapevine that the Rising Order wanted to claim Colorado as their state—something the Insurgents would never allow. From their inception, Colorado had been Insurgents' territory and they'd go to war to defend their claim.

"I heard Twisted Kings wanna join forces with the Rising Assholes," Animal said as he pulled out a joint from his shirt pocket.

"They're wannabe outlaws. They think their shit doesn't stink because they got some affiliation with the Grim Henchmen in Oakland. What a bunch of weak-ass pussies," Throttle said.

"Panther told me even the Henchmen can't stand those fuckers," Jerry said. "Kylie and I went to San Diego for a vacation last week, and I met up with the brothers in the San Diego chapter. Scratch and Demon were fucking crazy at the club party." He laughed then stopped short.

Shadow glanced at Banger's stony face and chuckled. He and the other brothers had been taking bets for the last few years on when Banger was going to finally chill about his daughter being Jerry's old lady. Banger had calmed down a bit since the early years, but he still gave Jerry the evil eye whenever he talked about club parties or anything else the president didn't think was appropriate when it came to Kylie.

"Stupid assholes trying to play at running a one-percenter club can make a ton of fuckin' problems." Hawk rubbed his face. "Skeet's got some vendetta shit going on with us, so he can be dangerous. We'll watch it closely, but at the first signs of activity, we gotta shut it down."

"I have some buddies in independent clubs around the area up north who will keep me informed," Rock said.

"I bet the assholes will be at the Steamboat Springs bike rally in the fall," Cruiser said. "If they wanna start trouble, I'm all in for beating their asses. It's been kinda boring around here anyway."

The men laughed, some agreeing wholeheartedly with Cruiser.

"Get an old lady and a few kids and you won't have time to be bored," Hawk said, a smile tugging at his lips.

"That's okay, bro, I'll pass on that." Cruiser laughed.

"If they start shit at the rally, we'll kick their asses. It might be a good idea not to bring family to this one. I got a feeling shit may go down." Banger looked pointedly at Jerry. "I don't want any women or kids getting caught in the crossfire if things erupt."

Jerry nodded and looked away.

"What's going on with our real estate project in West Pinewood?" Helm asked.

Hawk's eyes narrowed into slits as he shook his head. "That Mansfield bitch is still causing all sorts of unnecessary headaches. I'm tempted to shut her up for good," he growled.

Smokey splayed his hands on the table and leaned forward. "Don't do anything to the uptight bitch until I finish the damn project at her house. I gotta get my full pay."

Hawk chuckled while nodding. "Just give me the word when you're done, and I'll make my move." He glanced over at the club's treasurer.

"You're up." He plopped down on the chair, and Hubcap stood up and walked to the head of the table.

Placing his hands behind his head, Shadow stretched his legs in front of him. Just the mention of the Mansfields had him thinking of Scarlett. They both seemed to be avoiding each other ever since that night at Big Rocky's Barbecue, but several times he'd caught a glimpse of her at the second-floor window before she quickly pulled out of sight behind her curtains. A smile ghosted across his lips as he recalled the few times when she hadn't turned away and their eyes had locked: the sexual current that passed between them just sizzled. Shadow licked his lips and shifted in the chair. *Damn. That woman gets me going like no other.*

When he'd bumped into her at the back of the restaurant the week before, Shadow was happier than he cared to admit, and when she gave him attitude, he wanted nothing more than to pull her against him. Just the feel of her lips on his made him hard as fuck, but he also wanted to get to know *her*. He knew her body and how to make her scream until she was hoarse, but he didn't know the person inside her very well. A night with Scarlett wrapped in his arms sounded pretty damn sweet, and waking up to her ass pressed snug against him would take it over the top.

Shadow glanced around the room to see if any of the members could read his pansy-ass thoughts, but no one looked his way, except for Smokey. Yeah … the dude knew Shadow had the hots for Scarlett in a bad way. He'd called him out on it several times but Shadow denied it, even though he knew Smokey didn't believe his BS for one second.

The truth was that Shadow had tried to put her out of his mind. He'd gone out of his way not to see her, but the attraction was too great, and it was something he'd never experience with any other chick before. He was drawn to Scarlett, mesmerized and captivated by her, and he had no damn idea how to get her out of his system … even if he'd wanted to.

"You gonna stick around?" Bones asked as the gavel hit the wood block.

"Is church over?" Shadow asked.

"Yeah, where have you been?" Bones replied.

Before he could answer, Smokey moved in closer. "I'm guessing buried in that cute Mansfield chick's pussy."

"Who's in who's pussy?" Rags asked as he sidled up to Shadow.

Shadow threw Smokey a dirty look. "He's just moving his lips."

"You gonna go fuck someone now?" Rags scratched his head.

"He's been doing it for the last half hour in his head." Smokey chuckled.

Shadow gave him the finger then fell in behind the other members as they filed out of the meeting room. He heard Rags still trying to figure out who Shadow was going to bang when he walked into the hallway.

The main room was bustling with activity as the prospects tried to keep up with serving the members their drinks. Shadow leaned against the bar and avoided looking at Smokey when he sauntered over to the counter. Shadow wanted to drink a few cold ones and then hit the road on his bike. The temperatures had dipped down a few degrees, and he longed for a ride around the mountain roads.

The phone vibrated in his back pocket just as he finished his beer. Glancing at the screen, he frowned when he didn't recognize the number.

"Yeah?"

"Hello, Shadow. Uh, this is Flo Karas. Remember me?"

The voice from his past startled him, hurling him to another time and place.

"Hello. Is this Shadow?" she asked, her voice sounding like she swallowed a handful of dirt.

He heard light crumpling noises, then a long inhale followed by an exhale. Her actions jarred loose an avalanche of memory: Flo sitting cross-legged on the faded couch in their trailer, firing up a cigarette with a lighter from her purse, and his mother smiling as she watched her friend.

"Shadow?"

The noise around him suddenly became deafening, and he cupped his hand over his other ear.

"Hang on a sec," he said as he crossed the room.

Once outside, he crouched down on his haunches and picked up a handful of dry pine needles. Spreading his fingers, they slipped through them and fell back down to the ground. Down past the trees, the Colorado River flowed like a stream of glass, glinting under the sunlight. Larkspur, fireweed, and columbine flowers lined the water's edge; the air was heavy with a honeyed scent, and the low-sounding hum of bees filled the hanging branches of pine trees.

"Did I lose you?" Flo coughed, a raspy, raw sound.

"I'm here. It's just been a fuckin' long time."

"I didn't even know you were in town. I thought you'd left years ago."

Shadow stood up and walked closer to the river, then, he bent down and picked up a flat, smooth stone, leaned forward, and skimmed it across the water. The rock bounced on top of the water in two or three spots, causing little splashes before it sank.

"Why're you calling after all this time?" He picked up a handful of pebbles then tossed them into the river, one by one.

"I meant to call you after everything calmed down, but I thought you'd left. No one knew where you went."

Shadow narrowed his eyes. "Who the hell is *no one*?"

Flo coughed again. "The cops."

"Is that how you got my number?"

"Yes, Detective McCue gave it to me. He seems like such a nice man. He said they're still investigating the death of your mother."

Shadow made a mental note to tear the damn badge a new asshole for giving out his number. Shadow had two phones: one for the club and very close friends, and the other for his business and acquaintances. *He* decided who got his number, not some fuckin' badge.

"So where did you end up staying after that night?" She stumbled on the words.

"Eli's parents took me in. You knew him."

"The clean-cut kid that never really fit with you? How's he doing?"

"Getting married."

"That's nice. What about you? Are you married?"

"Let's cut through the bullshit. Whaddaya want?"

The clink of metal brought back a memory of Flo's arms moving about and her many bangles jangling against each other while she told his mom a story about some guy at Satin Dolls. The story had made his mother laugh so hard that tears were streaming down her cheeks. A sliver of sadness stabbed his gut and brought him back to the present.

"I'm waiting," he grunted.

"Okay. I wanted to talk to you about Carmen's murder."

Blood froze in his veins. His pulse pounded in his ears. The pebbles in his hand fell to the ground.

"You still with me?"

Suddenly, his mouth felt like it was filled with sawdust. "Yeah," he croaked.

"I know some things about that night," she whispered.

After nearly fifteen years, Flo had come forward to tell him this now? *Fifteen years of fuckin' hell.* Fury-filled hatred coursed through him along with sadness and a slew of other emotions he had yet to comprehend.

"Why the fuck didn't you go to the police? What fuckin' game are you playing here?" He kicked the ground with his boots.

"I guess I shouldn't have called you," she said. "It's just that things are getting … well … they're getting out of control. I thought you should know some things in case anything ever happens to me."

"What the fuck are you talking about? Who's the bastard who murdered my mom?" He clenched his fist and swung at the air. "Tell me."

"Not on the phone. Can you come to my place?"

"When?"

"In two hours. I live at the Belvedere Condos on Larkspur Lane—1569 Larkspur Lane—to be exact. I'm on the top floor." Flo cleared her throat. "I have to go."

"Are you home now?" Shadow didn't want her to hang up—he didn't want to break the connection to his mother.

"I have to go," she whispered. "I'll see you in two hours."

The phone went dead, and he just stared at the dark screen trying to figure out what the hell had just happened. *Does Flo know who killed Ma? Why the fuck would she have waited so long to contact me?* The whole thing gave him an uneasy feeling. Why wouldn't his mom's friend have gone to the police with the information? *Maybe she's being threatened by the killer.* Shadow shook his head. *That doesn't explain the upscale address she just gave me.* He stared at the flowing river trying to make sense of the strange and unexpected call. *Or maybe she's got her own sugar daddy, but why call me then? She sounded anxious and … scared.* Then it hit him: maybe she'd seen something that night and had been blackmailing the killer all these years.

"That could explain how she can afford to live in such a rich part of town. I don't know what the fuck to think, but I'm sure Flo's running scared—something's spooked her and that's why she called me." He jammed his phone in the back pocket of his jeans and wiped his damp hands on the denim fabric. *Why the hell didn't she just tell me what she wanted on the phone? If she* does *know something about Ma's murder, how could she have kept this from me?* "Fuck!" He spat on the ground then turned around and made his way to the clubhouse.

SHADOW CIRCLED AROUND the area several times until he finally found a parking space a couple blocks from the Belvedere. He shoved his hands in the pockets of his jeans as he walked toward the building. It had been fifteen years since Shadow had last stomped through his old neighborhood. The area spurred memories that he preferred to keep buried deep inside him. When he passed by the Lanai Towers on the other side of the street, he was transported back to the night he'd pled with Detective McCue to let him go inside the building to see his mother, fearing and somehow knowing, she was the murdered victim the neighbors were whispering about.

Shadow stopped on the sidewalk and stared at the building. So much time had gone by, but the pain was still there, the recollection still raw. His mind pulled at the memory like a festered splinter. Fifteen years of gut-wrenching misery stemmed from that one fucking night. Anger rippled through Shadow so fiercely that his whole body shook. *If it takes me until the day I die, I'll find justice for you, Ma. Flo says she's got something to tell me, and when I find out who cut your life short, I'll strangle him with my fuckin' bare hands!*

The sound of a honking car broke into Shadow's thoughts; he dragged his gaze away and opened the glass door to Flo's building. The marble lobby smelled like the beach: briny and fresh. A man in his thirties, wearing a security uniform, looked up from behind the carved cherry-wood counter.

"May I help you?" he asked.

"I'm here to see Florence Karas," Shadow said. The simulated ocean scent made his eyes water.

The man's fingers flew over a keyboard, then he looked at the screen.

"Mr. Steve Basson?" the security officer inquired without looking up.

"Yeah."

The man held out his hand. "I'll need to see some identification."

Shadow slid his driver's license over to him and glanced around the lobby while the guy jotted down his information. There was no way Flo, who used to be broke all the time, came into money the legal way. *Maybe she won the lottery.* Shadow quirked his lips. *No fuckin' way.*

"Ms. Karas is on the top floor, first door to the right." He handed back Shadow's driver's license.

Shadow slipped it back into his wallet as he ambled toward the elevators. Soon he was in front of Flo's door, ringing the bell. No answer. He rang it again. Still nothing. Putting his ear to the door, he waited to hear some sounds coming from inside the condo. Nothing. He pulled back, blew out a breath, and looked at the time on his cell phone screen: 4:02. *Where the hell are you?* He rang the doorbell once more, then pounded on the door. Silence.

"This shit blows," he muttered under his breath as he took a bump key from his wallet. Shadow put on his riding gloves, turned the knob, and in less than thirty seconds, he was standing in Flo's foyer. The condo was pristine—nothing out of place—with lavish furnishings and a killer view. He crossed the room and stood in front of one of the floor-to-ceiling windows, his eyes focused on the Lanai Towers across the street.

Flo used to come often to visit, and his mother would make her famous vodka cocktails. The two women would talk and laugh for hours until they were both sloshed, then his mom would insist Flo crash in the guest room.

*"You're so lucky to have found a man to give you all this. One day I'm gonna be living like a queen. Mark my words, Carmen ... Someday we're gonna be neighbors."* Flo's raspy voice echoed through his brain as he watched people come in and out of the building he used to live in with his mother—the place where his mother could finally relax and just be happy.

"Fuck," he muttered under his breath as he turned away from the window. "You're living here now, and Ma is six fuckin' feet under. Where the hell are you, Flo?"

He walked from room to room, but she wasn't there. It was as quiet as a tomb in the condo. Figuring she was late, Shadow sank down on one of the couches facing away from the Lanai Towers, and stared out at the Rocky Mountains as he waited for his mother's friend to arrive. The seconds turned into minutes and he called her phone several times, but Flo never picked up.

His mom's friend had called him out of the blue and told him to meet her at four o'clock. It was now close to five and Flo wasn't answering her phone when she'd been downright insistent that she had to see him. Irritation niggled at the back of his brain. Something wasn't right.

Shadow pushed up from the couch and walked into the largest of the bedrooms and began to rifle through the drawers, careful to put everything back the way he found it. He went into a huge walk-in closet and looked around, still unsure of what he was searching for, until he came across a burgundy portfolio hidden behind several shoeboxes in the corner of the closet. He gripped it tightly, then walked into the bedroom.

There were pages filled with numbers, showing thousands of dollars in deposits each month for years on end, bolstering his presumption that Flo had been blackmailing the killer. His anger grew with each page he turned as he realized his mother's friend had kept justice from being served just so she could enjoy a rich lifestyle.

"Your dear *friend* made money off your murder, Ma," he whispered as his eyes scanned years of deposits.

Shadow closed the book and tucked it into the waistband of his jeans. He hung around for another fifteen minutes after calling Flo a few more times, and then he left. While he waited at the elevator, he took off his gloves and shoved them inside the pocket of his cut.

He stepped inside and kicked the door as it closed. Leaning back against the rail, he slowly blew out his breath in an effort to control his frustration. If he didn't keep it in check, he'd destroy the inside of the car.

The elevator *whirred* softly before stopping on the sixth floor. Shadow clenched his teeth and stayed pressed into the back corner, eyes downward. The doors opened and the scent of spiced vanilla filled the car. He saw the passenger's legs first: long, tanned, and toned sexy legs wearing heels. His eyes steadily traveled upward toward a sweet, rounded ass and glossy blonde hair that skimmed … *Damn.*

He took a few steps closer to her and could see his and Scarlett's reflection in the polished brass doors of the elevator. Their eyes met for a split second, then she spun around and faced him with a stunned look.

"What are you doing here?" she asked.

Reaching out, he stroked her cheek then caught a strand of her hair between his fingers and lightly tugged it. "I had an appointment with someone." He ran his gaze over her body, then fixed it on her face.

"What about you?"

"I'm checking out apartments." She stepped back.

"I'll be damned—the princess is stepping down from her ivory tower." He chuckled.

A line appeared between her brows. "Don't call me that—I don't like it *at all*."

Shadow drew her to him and nuzzled her neck. "I was just joking, darlin'." He rubbed his thumb across her lower lip. "You look beautiful."

Scarlett looped an arm around his neck and pressed her mouth to his, kissing him tenderly. "Thank you," she muttered against his lips.

He yanked her closer to him, then kissed her hungrily as if he'd been starving for her his whole life. Their tongues tangled, their bodies ground against each other, and his hands squeezed her perfect ass. Scarlett was the only thing that could push the dark memories away and calm the burning hatred that was always there bubbling away under the surface.

The elevator door chimed and Scarlett broke away from him, her fingers hurriedly smoothing down her hair. They began to part and Shadow watched their images spread out from the middle then disappear. Two older ladies stood aside as he grasped Scarlett's hand and exited the car.

"You need to sign out," the security guard said.

Shadow let go of her hand while she picked up a pen and then he followed suit before exiting the building. The heat was still pervasive, even though it was nearing five thirty.

Scarlett pointed at the Lanai Towers. "I saw two apartments over there. I really liked the one on the top floor."

He glanced at the building for the umpteenth time that day and shook his head. "If you end up living there, I won't be coming around."

"Why?" she asked, pulling on the shoulder strap of her purse.

He shrugged. "I got some bad memories with that place." Before she could reply, Shadow grabbed her arms and pulled her to him. "I need you." He kissed her gently.

Looking around, she pushed away then giggled. "Real romantic and smooth." She poked him lightly in the ribs.

Shadow shook his head and rubbed the back of his neck with one hand. "I don't mean like that—well … I do, but not right now." He glanced at the Lanai Towers. "I meant that I need a friend right now." Dragging his gaze away, he kicked at the sidewalk. "Fuck … I don't know … Just forget what I said."

Scarlett wrapped her arms around him, hugging him close. "I'm here for you," she whispered in his ear. "Do you want to go somewhere to get a drink?"

A quick shake of his head. "Not feeling that. I'd like to go to Crystal Lake."

A smile tugged at the corners of her kissable mouth. "Okay. Do you want to take your car or mine?" She ran her hands up and down his back.

"Mine, but the wheels are my Harley."

The smile faded away and a look of terror crossed over her face. He laughed and playfully smacked her ass.

"I'm guessing you've never been on a bike."

"Never," she mumbled.

"Then you're gonna love it. There's nothing like the feel of the wind all around you."

She glanced down at her sundress, waving her hand over it. "Can I go like *this*?"

"Yeah, but you'll have to tuck in the dress under your legs or you'll be flashing everyone." He chuckled when she gasped. "We'll be taking the back roads, so no worries—really. So what do you say?" There was nothing he needed more at that moment than Scarlett pressed behind him with the air wrapped around them. It was the salve that he craved to soothe the tension, the anger, and the sadness that coming to meet Flo had stirred up inside him.

"Okay," she replied after a long pause.

Relief spread through him and he hugged her tightly. "You're gonna love it. You probably should pull your hair back 'cause it's gonna be flying all around and in your face. I got a bandana if you need something." He tucked her hand in his, then they made their way to his motorcycle.

After folding his cut and putting it, the burgundy ledger, and her purse into one of the saddle bags, Shadow pointed out the parts of the bike that burned and pinched, then told her to keep her feet on the pegs at all times, hold on to his waist, and lean with him as they rode. Scarlett nodded at each instruction, then secured her hair in a low ponytail before scrambling on behind Shadow and wrapping her arms around him. When he felt her tits press up against his back, he looked over his shoulder and winked at her.

"Hang on, baby. Here we go."

He switched on the engine, then pulled away from the curb.

# CHAPTER ELEVEN

ADRENALINE SHOT THROUGH Scarlett at the roar of the engine, and she tightened her hold on Shadow as they rode down the street. At first she was terrified, but little by little elation overcame her fear, and she opened her eyes and saw the trees, buildings, and people whizz past her as they headed out of town.

When they reached the outskirts of the county, Scarlett pried her face away from Shadow's back and tipped her head back slightly, loving the way the wind whipped around her. *It feels like flying!* She'd been on this road many times, but on the back of the bike she could see everything more vividly. Holding on tighter, she watched pine and evergreen trees rush past. The streams that zigzagged through the valley looked like thin silver ribbons, and the wildflowers were a burst of kaleidoscopic color. It was awe-inspiring … and *freeing*. At that moment, she understood why Shadow loved to ride. Overcome with emotion, she kissed the back of his neck and then squeezed him tighter. He glanced over his shoulder and locked gazes with her for a split second, then he shifted his eyes back to the road.

Another motorcycle passed them in the opposite direction, and the biker lifted his hand in greeting. Shadow did the same, and a warm feeling spread through Scarlett. Since Warren had told her Smokey was in an outlaw motorcycle club, she couldn't get it out of her head, and had decided that maybe she should end her liaison with Shadow. Her parents would be flipped out enough if they just knew she was fucking one of the workers, but knowing he was a member of the Insurgents would throw all kinds of drama into the pot. So she'd tried real hard not to look at him while he was working or to bring cool drinks down to the construction zone, and she'd succeeded for the most part, but it had proven to be one of the worst weeks of her life. Then Scarlett bumped into him in the elevator and all her self-control, all her pats on the back for resisting him, crumbled the minute he took her into his arms.

*I'm crazy about him, and I don't care what* anyone *thinks. This is* my *life, dammit!* She snuggled her face against his white T-shirt and inhaled the scent of him: leather, soap, and his aftershave, which had a hint of darkness—something spicy yet dangerously seductive.

The bike veered to the right, and for about a mile they rumbled and bounced over a dirt road until Scarlett thought her teeth would shatter. Then the bike stopped and Shadow kicked the stand down, then he held out his hand to help her off the bike before he swung his leg over.

"That was fantastic!" She clapped her hands. "I felt like I was flying. It was so liberating." Scarlett looked at him and he gave her a soft smile.

Shadow leaned back on his heels, his intense gaze boring into her. For a long second a tenderness crossed over his face, then it was gone, and she wondered if she'd imagined it. Scarlett had never seen *that* look before and it made her feel all soft and mushy inside. The silence hanging between them magnified the cicada's group chorus. The smell of earthy, musty wilted green odors and the sweet fragrance of pine swirled around her. From the corner of her eye she could see butterflies flitting from flower to flower, their colorful wings outshining the hues of the mountain irises and columbines.

Scarlett ran her fingers through her windswept hair, pulling through the tangles.

"I guess you should've used my bandana to wrap it up."

His deep voice startled her, and she cut her gaze to him.

"I guess so," she said. "Are we going to the lake?"

"Yeah."

He walked over to Scarlett, then cupped her face and kissed her. It was a whisper-soft brush of his mouth, but she shivered at the contact. He threw her a wicked smile, then turned around and pulled out a blanket from a compartment on the back of the motorcycle. He clasped her hand and squeezed it. A small smile curved her mouth, and she leaned against him as they walked forward.

The sun bounced off the lake, making it look like molten silver. A large fish leapt through the air and landed back into the water, creating hundreds of ripples that milled out and scattered over the lake's surface.

"Let's sit here under the shade." Shadow opened the blanket and spread it out on the grass.

Scarlett sat down—legs crossed and each foot placed on the opposite thigh—and ran her hand over the soft cotton cover.

"It's been a long time since I came here," she said. "I forgot how beautiful it is."

"This and Hanging Lake are where I go when I need to get the fuck away." Shadow sank down next to her. "Not many people come here; it's not flashy enough for the tourists, which suits me just fine."

She smiled and gazed at the reflection of the mountains wavering on the water. "I can see why you come here—it's so peaceful. When things get too crazy, I love to swim. The water always relaxes me and takes me away."

He cocked his head and caught her gaze. "I didn't know that."

She pulled at the grass. "I didn't know about this." She waved her arm around. "I guess there's a lot we don't know about each other."

Shadow nodded, then gave her a small kiss on her cheek. "I think we should change that."

"Me too," she whispered.

The branches of the trees creaked in the soft wind.

"Can I ask you something?" she asked looking over at him.

He lifted his chin.

"Okay … uh … Are you in an outlaw club?"

"Yeah. Does that scare you?"

Shrugging, she pulled harder at the grass. "I don't know enough about those clubs to know if I should be or not."

"That's fair. My club is the Insurgents and we're a brotherhood, which means that we're not just a riding club—it's our way of life. I mean, we don't just put on leather and ride our bikes as a hobby." He rubbed his hand over his chin. "The brotherhood is us and we are the brotherhood."

"So, you're more involved with your club than the average biker?"

"I guess I'm not explaining this right. For me and the other members, we take the club, our loyalty to it and each other, and our bond to a life-and-death level. We step in front of a bullet for each other. There's a closeness among us that you don't even see in most families. We're united through the ride, the middle finger at society, and the respect we hold for our brothers. Being an Insurgent is a culture and a way of life. The freedom and excitement of that life are kickass."

His eyes sparkled as he spoke and she wanted to lean over and kiss him while running her hands through his thick black hair.

Shadow laughed. "Being an outlaw biker is not for the cowardly or the weak. It's hard for citizens to really *get it*, you know?" He brushed his knuckles over hand.

"Is that what I am? A citizen?"

"Yeah."

"Are the wives and girlfriends citizens too?"

"No—they're old ladies."

A lock of hair fell across his forehead, giving him an almost boyish look. She reached out and brushed it aside and didn't stop as she ran her hand through his hair, loving how soft it was—like silk beneath her fingertips.

"Do they like being called that?" she murmured.

"Yeah," he replied thickly, his heated gaze holding hers.

"Shadow," she whispered.

He moved closer to her then dipped his head down and covered her mouth with his. Scarlett stretched out her legs and let him gently push her all the way down on the blanket. She circled her arms around his neck and tugged him closer to her. His hands teased over her body, and hers slid under his shirt, skimming over his firm muscles. Scarlett felt the surge of wild passion only Shadow could stir in her.

She traced her fingers over his corded back as he pulled up the hem of her sundress. Arching her back, Shadow slipped the dress up and over Scarlett's head and hovered above her, capturing her eyes with his smoldering gray ones.

"Scarlett," he rasped before pressing his mouth on hers and kissing her passionately. Without breaking away, he had her cotton bra with the tiny daisies off in one fluid movement.

Cupping her breast in his hand, he pinched her nipple between two fingers even as his index finger stroked back and forth against the hard tip. Bolts of heat streaked through her, and she pressed against him.

"I missed you so much," he growled and leaned over her, his desire-filled eyes piercing into hers.

"Oh, Shadow. I almost died without your touch," she whispered close to his ear as she parted her legs.

His hand slid down and cupped her sex. "Fuckin' soaked, baby. I like that."

Her hips jerked and she cried out when he slid her panties down her legs then tossed them aside. Scarlett was completely naked and exposed, and she didn't give one crap if anyone was watching them, all she wanted was Shadow inside her. Now.

The sound of him unbuckling his belt and then unzipping his jeans was music to her ears, and she giggled and flushed from the anticipation of having him buried deep inside her. There was no doubt about it: Shadow was her drug, and like an addict, she always needed another fix.

"I want you right now," she said.

"Fuck, baby, I love hearing you say that." He kicked off his boots then pulled down his jeans and boxers until he stood naked in front of her.

Scarlett's eyes took all of him in, and she reached out and pulled him down to her. He chuckled at that. "Do you like what you see, baby?" His tongue slowly swiped across her lips.

"Oh yeah. You're just perfect," she whispered, tugging him closer before kissing him.

Shadow pulled up, knelt between her legs and spread them. Scarlett watched as he looked down at his hard dick while easing it into her. Then he grunted and pushed in hard, and she wrapped her legs around his waist and moved with him. Wild. Hard. And so very deep. She met his thrusts, scratched his back, screamed out while thrashing about. To be with Shadow and not have anyone around to hear them, unleashed a frenzied desire that Scarlett had kept cooped up inside her for far too long.

"Damn, baby, I love what you're giving me," he groaned as he kept pummeling in and out.

"Don't stop. Don't you dare stop!" she yelled.

"No fuckin' way, baby," he grunted.

Faster and faster. Deeper and deeper. Harder and harder. Sweat misted over their bodies, making them stick together in the warm evening. A jumble of emotion burned through her as she watched Shadow's face light up with fierce desire.

"You feel so fuckin' good," he growled.

The sound of his balls slapping against her ass drove her mad, and she tightened her hold on him, urging him even closer until they were fused together by their raw passion and lust.

"I'm so damn close, baby." He gritted his teeth.

"Me too." She gasped.

Shadow moved his hands under her hips and pounded wildly, and then a wave of ecstasy crashed over her; every nerve ending in her body was alive and vibrating.

He stiffened, then his body shook. "Scarlett … fuck, baby. Fuck," he grunted.

She felt his seed pour out in hot, dense ropes, and she clenched and unclenched around him, milking his dick for every last drop.

Stroking his damp skin, she smiled when he collapsed on top of her.

"Fuck, woman. What the hell are you doing to me?" he rasped before nuzzling her neck.

After a few minutes, he rolled away and drew her flush to him. She snuggled against his hard body and absentmindedly traced the lines of his tattoos.

"Did these hurt?" she asked.

"Not too much. You like them?" He kissed the top of her head.

"They're badass."

Shadow chuckled. "You like bad boys, huh?"

"I never thought I did until I met you. I usually go in for the suit-and-tie sort of guy, but then, you *were* wearing a jacket when I saw you at Brooke's party."

"And I hated it."

"Eli must be a very good friend for you to swap your jeans for dress pants." She gently poked him in the ribs.

For the space of a held breath there was silence. Then Shadow cleared his throat. "Yeah, Eli and me are real tight. We're more like family than friends … like cousins or something."

"So you two go way back?"

He interlocked her fingers with his. "Since we were kids."

The space between them had gone from light-hearted to somber, and Scarlett sensed that something sad and awful lingered in Shadow's past.

"I've been friends with Kiara since I was fourteen—she's my best friend. It's good to have someone that close to you who knew you when you were young."

"Like I said, Eli and me are tight, but the Insurgents are my family."

"It must be wonderful to belong to something like your club. I've always felt like a fish out of water my whole life."

"No fuckin' way. You've got everything, baby."

She tipped her head back and met his gaze. "Because my dad's rich?" She snorted. "You talk about 'citizens'"—she made air quotes with her hands—"not understanding your biker world, well, people who aren't rich don't get my world at all—and *it is* a different world. There are so many fucking rules I have to follow."

"Like what?"

She pushed up a bit. "Like which schools you can go to, what to wear, what to eat, *where* to eat, who to date … blah, blah blah. It's even worse if you're a woman. My only reason for being, according to my parents, is to marry and keep the fucking family line going. Who I marry is also decided based on a sound business decision." A warm flush started creeping up her neck, and she waved her hand to cool down her face.

"So, I'm your act of rebellion against your parents?" Shadow asked, a smirk pulling at his lips.

"Not really … at least not consciously—that was Marcelo." His brows raised slightly and she cocked her head to the side while looking at him. "I'd met him during my junior year of college when I studied abroad for one year in Rome. We had a fiery and romantic relationship, and he'd asked me to stay after my year was up. I'd fallen hopelessly in love with him, so I told my parents I wanted to finish out my studies in Rome and live there. They didn't agree with me, but I did it anyway."

"But it didn't work out?"

"No … it was a disaster after about three months. My dad cut the money flow, so I couldn't afford the tuition. Marcelo didn't think it was too much fun going to school full-time and working, and honestly, I was miserable. I came home with my pride wounded."

"I bet your dad had a field day with that."

"He never mentioned it. I just went back to my university and life went on. It changed me, though. It made me realize that I'm not a survivor. It was a somber experience."

Shadow grabbed her to him and nestled her head on his shoulder while he stroked her arm. "We're all survivors when we have to be. Staying in Rome wasn't your life or death moment. When *that* comes, you'll meet it head on. You're a lot stronger than you give yourself credit for."

"I don't know. I'm still living at home in a 1950s bubble."

"You're used to the pampered life, but if you want something bad enough, you'll do it even if you're scared."

Scarlett licked her lips and burrowed deeper into him. "I am scared," she whispered.

"Fear is good—without it, we get too fuckin' cocky and that's when life kicks us in the ass. The thing you gotta do is feel the fear, but do it anyway. Like you were looking at apartments today, but that doesn't mean shit until you take the first step—sign a lease."

"I know, but I don't even have a damn job."

"Your dad wouldn't go for you having your own place?"

"Nope—two sets of rules in my house—one for my brothers and one for me. I'm to get married and have babies and continue with my charity work—which I love doing, by the way."

"Then get a job. Hell, I could use some help at the warehouse. You wanna work for me?"

He laughed.

She looked up at him. "Warehouse? I thought you worked for Smokey."

"I'm just helping him out. I own several storage rentals and have an online business where I sell shit. I started the online business a year ago and it's really picking up now. I could use someone to help keep track of the inventory. I got a few guys working for me who pack the shelves, and prepare the stuff I sell for shipping, but I do all the books and shit myself too. I'm just saying …"

"That's so cool that you have your own business and own some property. I'll think about the offer, but I'd really like to work in marketing or public relations—that's what I studied in college."

"Then go for it. You must know a ton of people—ask around and make a case for yourself. Shit, baby, if you don't fight for *you*"—he lightly tapped his finger on her upper arm—"then no one's gonna do it."

Scarlett squeezed him and kissed his neck. "It sounds like you know this from experience."

"Damn straight," he said in a low voice.

A comfortable silence stretched between them as they lay intertwined on the blanket for a long while. The sounds of nature swirled around them, and Scarlett thought the soft rustling of branches sounded like trees whispering to each other.

"Let's take a dip in the lake," Shadow said, breaking the quietness. "I'll get another blanket from the saddle bag." He gently untangled her from him, then stood up.

Scarlett turned her head so she could watch the muscles in his delicious ass flex as he walked away. His butt was so nice and perfectly rounded that she wanted to chase after him, tackle him to the ground, and alternately squeeze and bite those muscular cheeks. *Yeah … a dip in the lake is definitely what I need to cool me down.* The truth was that she simply couldn't get enough of him. She just wanted to be in his presence: they didn't always need to have sex, or even talk, just as long as he was around her. That thought scared the hell out of Scarlett because she didn't want to give her heart to him only to have it broken. *I couldn't handle that.*

"Ready, baby?" His voice cut into her thoughts, and when she looked up at his grinning face, her insides melted.

Nodding, she ambled over to him.

The water was refreshingly cool and a wonderful juxtaposition to his hot kisses. After a half hour of fooling around, splashing each other, and laughing like a couple of demented hyenas, Shadow wrapped her in a large blanket, then led her back to where their clothes laid crumpled in a heap.

Scarlett slipped on her bra and panties, then tugged the sundress over her head. Shadow quickly dressed, then sank down.

"Come here," he said patting the empty space beside him.

She plopped down and he yanked her into his arms.

"You smell good," he said. "When do you gotta get back?"

"Not for a while. I thought we were just going to talk and not have sex. At least that's what you implied. You said you needed a friend."

He put a finger under her chin, tipped her head back, and kissed her. "Are you complaining?"

Twisting away, Scarlett sat in front of him. "Not at all. Do you do this with all your friends?" When the lines deepened on his forehead, she regretted asking the question.

Leaning back against the tree, he splayed his hands across his denim-clad thighs. "First of all, I can't keep my hands off of you. But second, I also wanted to share this place with you. You're the only chick I've ever brought here. I needed to be with you, that's all."

"I shouldn't have asked. I'm sorry."

"Don't be, and you have every right to ask. We got something going here, babe. I don't know what the fuck it is, but I do want you to know you're the only woman I'm fucking."

"That's good to know ... and so romantic." She laughed dryly. "I'm sure you have your pick of women."

"Easy pussy? For sure."

"Speaking of that, we didn't use protection. I was so caught up in the moment that I lost my head. Uh ... are you clean?"

"Yeah. I test a lot and I'm good. I'm guessing you're on birth control."

She nodded. "So you have a lot of women throwing themselves at you."

"It happens quite a bit, but I like what we have." Shadow winked at her.

"What do we have? A friends-with-benefits thing?"

"Not really. A couple of my buddies got something like that going, and both them and the women they're banging are fucking other people too." He quirked his lips and stared at her. "You fucking anyone else? What about that dude at Eli's party?"

"Warren?" She shook her head. "He's the one my parents, especially my dad, are chomping at the bit for me to marry."

"So are you still with him?"

"Would you be upset if I were?" she asked.

His nostrils flared as he breathed in and out noisily.

"I'm not. I was until I met you." She glanced down. "I know it sounds silly, because I didn't think I'd ever see you again, but after we hooked up, I felt so alive and ... daring." She looked up at him, surprised by the way his face had morphed from anger to gentleness so quickly. "The truth is that I haven't slept with Warren since then, but I haven't officially told him to fuck off."

"Hasn't he caught on that you don't want him?"

"Yes and no. He's persistent. I need to tell him it's over."

"Why haven't you? Are you playing both of us?" His words hit her in the gut.

"No! I'm just avoiding a lot of drama with my parents."

Shadow sighed loudly. "Babe, you gotta grow up sometime. Your parents aren't living your life, you are. Don't undersell it."

"You're right. I'll break it off with Warren for good. I just wasn't sure if you had someone in your life."

"Only you. And so you know—I don't share. You're with me or you're not."

"I'm with you," she whispered. "And you should know that I don't like sharing either."

"Then we don't have a problem, babe." Shadow reached into the pocket of his jeans and took out a joint and a lighter and then leaned forward to light it. He inhaled, and as he exhaled, he handed the joint to her.

After looking at it, Scarlett took a few short, quick puffs, then exhaled a plume of smoke and handed it back to Shadow. She pulled up her legs and rested her elbows on her knees as she watched him inhale deeply. When he stretched out his arm toward her, she shook her head, begging off another hit. Soon, he stamped the spent joint out on the ground.

"Are you an only child?" she asked.

A small pause, then, "Yeah."

"Do your parents live here?"

A longer pause. "They're dead."

*Okay … I wasn't expecting* that. "I'm sorry," she said. "It must be hard."

Shadow's face tightened, the carved planes hard and closed. "It's whatever." Something told her not to pursue the conversation any further. "So, are you gonna take the apartment?" he asked, changing the subject.

"I wasn't sure, but after all we've talked about, I'm going to do it. I have some money socked away." Scarlett didn't want to tell him that she had a very nice trust fund her paternal grandparents had left her. She never took from it, preferring to let it grow for the future.

"The one at the Belvedere?"

"I don't think so. The one I really liked was at Lanai Towers, but you told me you wouldn't come see me there. Do you want to talk about that?"

"No."

She caught the haunted look that flashed in his eyes. "Okay, but when you want to, I'm here. I'm a really good listener."

A smile ghosted his lips. "I'll remember that."

"The second contender is on Greenwood Boulevard. There's a top floor condo that has the most amazing view."

"Sounds great."

"It is. My friend Kiara absolutely loves it. I think you will too."

"Good to know since I'll be spending time with you at your place." He winked at her and she pushed forward and collapsed against him, peppering his throat, jaw, cheeks, and forehead with kisses. He laughed. "What the fuck did I say, baby?"

Then he caught her face between his hands and kissed her, fierce and deep, his tongue pushing inside, twining with hers. They clung to each other so tightly that two heartbeats became one as the rest of the world faded away, if only for a moment.

Her ringing phone brought Scarlett abruptly back to reality, and grumbling under her breath, she pulled away and dug it out of her pocket. Warren's name blinked across the screen, and she threw her phone across the blanket.

Shadow chuckled, then rose to his feet. "You ready to go?"

"Not really, but I guess we can't stay here forever." She took his hand and he helped her up.

They walked back, hand in hand, to the motorcycle—both of them lost in their thoughts.

As Scarlett held Shadow tightly over the bumpy roads, she leaned her face against his back. *I'm so falling for him. He wants us to be exclusive. If he only wanted to have sex, he wouldn't care, would he? Stop it. Just enjoy the moment. Stop analyzing every damn thing.*

When they got to the old highway, she relaxed a bit and enjoyed the landscape as it blurred past them.

By the time they returned to Pinewood Springs, the sky was a burnished copper, tinted with rose and dusky purple.

"Do you wanna go out to dinner on Friday?" he asked as he held open her car door.

"I'd love to."

"Have you been to Steelers?"

"No."

"Burgers are good—nachos are kickass."

"Sounds great. I can meet you there."

Shadow leaned against her. "No fuckin' way, baby. This is a date and I'm picking you up."

Scarlett swallowed hard, then nodded. "Okay. What time?"

"Does seven work?"

The image of her family's faces as she rode away on the back of a motorcycle while clinging to one of the workers flashed through her mind.

"That's perfect," she said.

He stepped back to let her slip inside the car, then bent down and kissed her hard and wet.

"I'll see you tomorrow at your house."

"I'm sure you'll need a lemonade break." She giggled.

"Fuck yeah—that's what I'm looking forward to, baby."

He closed the car door and she switched on the ignition and pulled away from the curb. Scarlett kept looking in her rearview mirror until she turned the corner and he disappeared from sight.

*He asked me on a date!* Excitement coursed through her, pushing away the fear that kept buzzing in her head like a pesky fly.

"It's about time I started living *my* life," she said out loud.

Switching on the CD player, she cranked up the volume and sang along with "We're Not Gonna Take It." The Twisted Sister song had suddenly become her new anthem, and Scarlett played it over and over until she pulled into the family's garage, switched off the engine, and went into the house.

# CHAPTER TWELVE

T HE THREE HIKERS huddled together, lines of fear etched on their faces. Detective McCue tipped his head in their direction as he plodded through the wooded area, cursing under his breath as numerous burs stuck to the bottom of his brown pants.

Ahead, yellow crime scene tape cordoned off a large area, and he saw his partner, Detective Ibuado, watching from the side as the crime techs did their job. The medical examiner stood by the body, head bent as McCue approached, only looking up when the detective stood next to him.

"What do we have here?"

Conrad Gaines, medical examiner for the past ten years, raked a hand over his face. "A woman in her late forties … maybe early fifties. Multiple stab wounds—at least forty or fifty, with a cluster of them in the right chest area. Some of the wounds passed completely through the victim's body. I could see the tendons on the arms, that's how deep they went."

A low whistle escaped through McCue's teeth. "Fuck. Sounds like it was personal."

"Yep—rage and deep-seated hatred would be my guess," Ibuado said as he walked up to the two men.

"Any ID on the victim?" McCue asked.

"Nope," his partner replied.

"Any signs of sexual assault?" he asked the ME.

"Her pants and underwear were pulled down, so maybe. I'll know when I do the autopsy." Gaines shook his head. "She died a horrific death. A blood-soaked rock was found near the body and the back of her head was bashed in, so I'd guess that's what dazed her, although there were a lot of defensive wounds. Our victim put up quite a struggle."

"But she lost. Fuck." McCue took out his pad and jotted down some notes. He was old-fashioned in that he still liked to hold a pen and write his thoughts and observations on paper. "Maybe she died of blunt trauma?"

Gaines shrugged. "It's hard to say. Any number of the wounds could've caused her death. I'll let you know as soon as I'm done with the examination." He slipped his hands into the front pockets of his pants. "I'm done here. I'll call you." He lifted his chin at McCue and Ibuado and walked away.

"Anything distinctive on her like a tattoo or some weird piercings that could help us ID her?" McCue asked.

Ibuado folded his arms across his chest. "Not that I could tell. Conrad will be able to give us more info once the body's cleaned up. She did have a lot of bracelets on both arms."

"Okay … I'm not too sure if that'll be helpful," McCue said as he wrote down that fact.

"I'm talking twenty or more thin ones on each arm. Not many women wear *that* many. Maybe we can release that fact to the press to help identify our Jane Doe."

McCue nodded and scratched the tip of his chin—a nervous habit he'd had ever since he could remember. "That may help. I'd think a woman who wears that many bracelets would do it most of the time, but then again, I'm not into women's fashions or what the hell they do with their accessories."

Ibuado chuckled. "With four daughters, a wife, and three sisters, I can tell you, a woman tends to dress a certain way, so I'd say our Jane Doe probably wore a lot of those things on her arms most, if not all, the time she went out. And when are you going to call Alma? She's been asking me that every day."

"I told you not to fix me up. One bad marriage is enough for a lifetime." McCue snapped the notebook shut.

"That was years ago, and Corinne was a nutcase. You can't like being alone all the time, dude. A man needs a family."

"I'm doing just fine on my own, and I'm too damn old to change diapers. I'm good, really. Tell Alma she can do a lot better than me."

"My cousin's not gonna give up that easily," Ibuado said.

"I told you not to play fucking Cupid. Now you have to deal with it," McCue said as he and his partner trekked back toward the hikers.

"Maybe she'd like Jarvis. He's kind of shy, but he seems solid. What do you think?"

"Go for it. Did you get a chance to talk to them?" He pointed toward the trio, who stood staring at the crime scene.

Ibuado shook his head. "Not yet. Brady said that they discovered the body, and he didn't get any vibe that they were involved in the murder."

"Okay—let's do this. I'll take the guy, you take the blonde woman, and"—he motioned to an officer to come over—"White can interview the redhead."

McCue's steps were heavy as he trudged over to the male witness, his mind still on the victim who'd been left like a piece of trash in the woods. The young man's face was pale and his body trembled slightly.

"I've never seen a dead body before." He folded his arms over his chest. "It was horrible ... just awful." The witness unfolded his arms and rubbed a hand over his face.

"I know it's quite a shock," McCue said as he took the notebook and pen out of his inside jacket pocket.

"I bet you're used to it ... I mean, you've seen a lot of bad stuff, huh?" Again, he folded his arms.

"You never get used to it." McCue held out his hand. "I'm Detective McCue, and I'm going to ask you some questions ..."

# Chapter Thirteen

"**D**ON'T YOU SMELL good?" Helm said when Shadow passed by. "Whatcha got going?"

"Like it's any of your fuckin' business," Shadow answered as he crossed over to the bar.

"Definitely aiming for citizen pussy," Blade said.

"No way would you give a shit how you smelled with the club girls," Buffalo added before he downed a shot of Jack.

"There's a reason you got your road name, dude. Just remember *that*." Shadow took a deep drink of beer.

Rags, Helm, and Blade guffawed.

"He got you bad, bro," Rags said, pointing at Buffalo, who perched on the stool glaring.

"I know I don't wanna smell like shit for any chick—even the club girls," Blade said as he leaned against the bar.

"Thanks, dude. I feel so much better now that I fuckin' know that." Buffalo slapped his hand on the counter and the prospect delivered another shot to him.

Helm and Rags busted out laughing and Shadow joined in with them. Glancing at the clock on the back wall, he guzzled the rest of his beer and took the keys out of the pocket of his black jeans.

"I'm outta here." Shadow jerked his chin at his friends as he ambled away. Before he could open the door, Smokey burst through it, smudges of dirt and grease on his face and hands.

"What happened to you?" Shadow asked.

"My Harley crapped out on me. I tried fixing it but couldn't get it to start, so I called Hawk, and it's at his shop now. I need to think about getting a new one—I think my baby's on her last lap."

"That sucks, but you had a lot of good rides on that one," Shadow replied.

"Yeah." Smokey's gaze skimmed over him and his nostrils twitched. "Why the fuck do you smell like you're planning on getting laid?"

Shadow heard laughter behind him and his muscles tensed. "Why the fuck are you all sniffing me? Don't you have any other shit to do to amuse you?" He pointed at the club women, who sat on the couch watching them in amusement. "They're the ones you should be smelling."

The men laughed harder and the club girls chuckled along with them.

"You're going out with that Mansfield chick, aren't you?" Smokey's brows knitted. "I told you to stay away from her until we're done with the damn job. Wet your dick with the club women."

"Take your own advice—you seem to need a good fuck right now." Shadow pushed past Smokey and stalked to his motorcycle.

When he arrived at Scarlett's house, she was standing outside the large wrought iron gates, looking sexy as hell in skinny jeans and snug crop top. She waved at him and the sliver of silky, smooth skin her top revealed teased him as she hurried toward the curb, her luscious hips swaying.

"Hi," she said, a smile inching across her lips. Her green eyes danced as they took him in so damn seductively. Scarlett reached out and stroked his jaw. "I like the scruff."

The way her fingertips slid over his face made his cock jolt. All she had to do was touch him and his body was on fire.

Every damn time.

"Get over here," he said, his voice low.

Scarlett looked over her shoulder then took a couple of steps toward him and started to climb on the back of the bike, but he grabbed hold of her wrist and yanked her to him.

Her eyes twinkled and those sexy fingers tunneled a path into his hair. "Your hair's messy from the ride," she said. "We better get going."

He pulled her in for a smoldering kiss. "You're killing me, baby," he rasped.

Pushing away, she glanced back at the gates and gripped his shoulder. "We need to leave."

Shadow glanced down and saw red-painted toes peeping out from her high-heeled sandals and groaned. The scent of spiced vanilla curled around him, and the way she tucked herself against him with those sensuous hands dipping dangerously close to his dick had him shifting uncomfortably before starting the engine.

By the time they arrived at Steelers, Shadow wanted to drag her off behind the bushes like some damn caveman. Looking at Scarlett, feeling her against him, and just being with her made him burn. Ignoring his aching dick, he helped her off the bike and led her inside.

Steelers was a restaurant and a bar frequented by bikers and citizens alike. It was known for its hot-and-spicy wings, colossal nachos, and low-priced drinks. It was also an Insurgents' favorite for family nights, which usually happened twice a month.

"Hi, Shadow." The hostess smiled, then looked Scarlett up and down before reverting her gaze back to him. "Booth or table?"

"Booth's good." He clasped Scarlett's hand and followed the hostess.

"I guess you do come here a lot," Scarlett said as she watched the young woman walk away.

Shadow leaned back against the dark green cushion. "The Insurgents have family nights here every month."

"What does that mean—family nights?"

"Brothers and their old ladies, but single guys go too. Sometimes the members bring their kids, but mostly it's for the adults. We normally have family cookouts at the club or at a park where we include the kids."

Scarlett settled back in the booth and smiled at him. "That sounds real nice."

"It is. I don't always go, but when I do, it's cool. I come here a lot with my buddies for lunch or a quick bite to eat. Next time I'll take you to Burgers & Beer Joint—great selection of brewed beers and killer burgers."

"I love that place! And you're so right about the hamburgers—the best in town. I don't really like beer, so I'll have to take your word on that."

"The club owns the place. They also own Big Rocky's Barbecue."

Her mouth dropped just a little and he wanted to lean over and slip his tongue inside.

"I didn't know that. I guess I just figured your club owned the stereotypical strip bar—not restaurants."

"We do own a strip bar—Dream House." He winked at her. "But we got some other businesses too. We're trying to build another strip mall that'll have businesses and apartments above."

"That sounds exciting. Where's it going to be?"

Shadow nodded at the waitress, who put down a shot of whiskey and a bottle of beer in front of him and a mango margarita in front of Scarlett. He took a sip of whiskey. "West Pinewood near Jackson Boulevard. We bought the land from your dad."

She lifted the glass to her mouth and with the tip of her tongue licked some of the sugar from the rim. Scarlett looked at him over her margarita.

"I didn't know that. I wonder if that's how he met Smokey." She took a sip then ran that damn tempting tongue over her lips.

Shadow leaned over and took the glass from her hands. A startled look crossed her face and she glanced at the drink.

"Is there something wrong with it?" Panic deepened the soft lines in her forehead. "Did you see a bug? Oh yuck … gross."

"There's no bug." He chuckled.

"What then?"

He slid his hand into her hair, the blonde strands tangled around his fingers as he cupped the back of her head and tugged her closer.

"This," he said in a low voice.

Then he took hungry possession of her mouth, devouring it with deep, sweeping strokes of his tongue. She tasted like tequila and sweet fruit, and he couldn't get enough of her. A low moan came through her lips and he swallowed it, loving the noises she made when he kissed her.

The waitress cleared her throat, and Scarlett pulled away and sank back into the booth's cushion. Shadow winked at her, then looked up at the server.

The young woman smiled weakly. "Sorry to interrupt, but I got your nachos." She put a heaping mound of tortilla chips and all the fixings in the middle of the table and then gave each of them a small plate. "Enjoy," she said before scurrying away.

Scarlett's eyes widened. "You weren't exaggerating when you said they're big." She picked up her fork and pushed her dish toward the appetizer. "I'm going for it."

Shadow laughed and scooped up a decent portion and put it on his plate. "Good, huh?" he asked as he watched her eat.

"Super good. I can't believe my friends and I have never been here. We go out to eat a lot, so I'm surprised we missed this place. I'll have to tell them about it." She popped another chip in her mouth. "I still can't believe your club bought the land from my dad. That's cool. How's the building going?"

"We've run into a few snags, but nothing we can't conquer." For a split second, Shadow contemplated telling her that her bitch mom was causing all sorts of fucking problems, but he decided against it, not wanting to upset her or cause any more of a rift between the two of them.

"Can I ask you a question?" she said, breaking into his musings.

He glanced up. "You don't have to ask me for permission. If you wanna know something, just ask me, babe. I'll try and answer the best I can, but if your questions are about club business, then you're not gonna get shit outta me." Shadow poured some salsa over his nachos.

Nodding, she wiped the corners of her mouth with a napkin. "Okay. Is Shadow your *real* name? I know you guys have road names, so I was wondering if it's yours."

"Road names. I'm impressed, baby. You've been doing some home-work." He winked at her and she blushed, and damn if that wasn't the cutest thing he'd ever seen. *She's just too fuckin' irresistible.*

"I've read up a bit on the whole biker thingy. Some of the clubs are real bad—like the Hells Angels and Mongols."

"Yeah … well, we're not exactly choirboys. I'll just leave it at that. And my real name is Steve, but I've been using the moniker Shadow since I was a teen."

"Where did you get the name from?"

"My mom used to call me her shadow." A quizzical expression spread across her face. He took a deep breath then exhaled. "I'd try and be around all the time when my fuckin' dad would use my mom as a punching bag." He shrugged, his gaze darting away from her sympathet-ic one. "I liked the name, so I started using it." He picked up the bottle of beer and took a long gulp.

"Did your mom start calling you that too?"

"Yep. So are you gonna order something more?" A lame question, but he didn't want her to start asking questions about his mother or his sonofabitch father. He didn't need those memories to come out. Not tonight.

As if understanding, Scarlett didn't miss a beat. "I'm thinking to order a cheese enchilada. Are they good?"

"Totally Americanized, but they're decent. In my opinion, the best Mexican restaurant in town is El Tecolote. That place rules."

A huge grin broke over her lips. "That's my favorite place for Mexi-can food. I go there all the time."

"Me too. I'm surprised we never ran into each other."

"We probably did, but we didn't know each other so …" She brought the margarita to her mouth.

Shadow watched as her lips hugged the glass. *Get a fuckin' grip. I'm acting like a damn lovesick pussy. Shit … this woman just gets to me. Real bad.* She put the glass down and did that shit with her tongue skimming over her lips again. *Dammit.*

"Believe me, darlin', I would've noticed you if I'd seen you at El Tecolote," he said.

She locked her gaze on his. "I'd have noticed you too," she whispered, leaning forward.

"Fuck, baby."

Their mouths met in the middle, crushing and twisting together. She parted her lips and he slipped his tongue inside, probing and teasing then entwining with hers in a passionate dance.

"Scarlett, what the fuck are you doing?" A man's voice cut through their desire.

She broke away and looked up, and Shadow watched her flushed face quickly drain of color. He snapped his eyes to the guy and recognized him as the asshole who he'd thrown out of Dream House for disrespecting Honeysuckle. Behind him was the dude Shadow had found in the parking lot that night with the hooker. Shadow smirked and rested back on the cushion.

Disgust crept across the preppy-looking guy's face as he glared at Shadow and then at Scarlett. "*This*"—he waved his hand at Shadow—"is why you've been avoiding me? So you're slumming it now?"

Anger rose in Shadow like a tide, but he sat still, eyes narrowed, smirk still front and center.

"Warren, please go away."

"I'm sure your dad doesn't know about this. And your mom? What the hell's the matter with you? You're supposed to pay the help, not fuck them." Warren gripped the table and pushed it, making the glasses and plates rattle.

Shadow slid out of the booth. "The lady told you to go away, but you're still here. Now I'm telling you to get the fuck outta here."

"Let's go," Warren's friend said from behind him.

"Listen to Jonah, Warren," Scarlett said.

"I'm not going anywhere until I find out what the fuck's going on."

She picked up a glass of water and Shadow noticed her hand trembling, which fueled the anger inside him even more.

He bumped against Warren. Hard. Then he threw him a death glare. "If you can't figure it out, then you're dumber than I thought you were, asshole. I'm not telling you to get out again."

"Please go—you're causing a scene. We'll talk later," Scarlett said softly.

"Talk about what? That you're fucking a lowlife biker? Scum of the earth? Talk about falling so low that—"

Anger came boiling up out of Shadow, burning hot and white, and his fist landed on the side of Warren's jaw with so much force that it knocked the jerk to the ground. Without any hesitation, Shadow was on top of him, pummeling the asshole with both fists, in the face, the chest, the belly while the downed man tried to fend off the blows.

"Stop, Shadow. Stop!" Scarlett yelled. Then a gut-wrenching sob hit his ears, and he suddenly halted.

Shadow jumped up and wiped the sweat off his forehead with the back of his arm, then slid back into the booth. Max, the manager, came over to the table and glanced over at Warren, who was slowly rising to his feet, then to Shadow.

"You got this taken care of?" he asked.

Shadow lifted his chin. "Yeah."

Max nodded, then turned to Warren and Jonah. "Go on to your table ... or get out."

Warren wiped the blood from the corner of his mouth with the back of his hand. He jerked his head toward Shadow. "This animal attacked me and you're going to throw *me* out?"

Max shook his head. "Only if you keep bothering my customers. Lori got you a table, so go to it." He crossed his body-builder arms in front of his broad chest.

"I wouldn't stay another second in this dump." Warren looked at Jonah. "Let's go to the club. I've got to take a shower to get rid of the stench of the common class." He stepped back then glared at Scarlett. "I'm not done with you—you're not going to make a fool of me."

"You already beat her to that, asswipe," Shadow growled as he started to stand up from the table.

"You'll find out," he said to Scarlett, his words dripping in disgust. He stalked away, and he and Jonah stormed out of Steelers.

"For having to put up with *that*, I'll send you a round of drinks," Max said as he sauntered away.

For a long while Scarlett stared out the window, not even casting a glance at him. Shadow fought the impulse to get up and sit next to her and wrap her in his arms. Instead, he simply watched her for several minutes, then reached over and covered her hand with his. After he laced their fingers together, she gave him a brief sidelong gaze but went back to staring out into the distance.

"I lost my head, but the jerk had it coming to him by the way he was disrespecting you." His voice came out gruffer than he'd intended.

"Is that the way you handle conflict—just punch your way through it?" Scarlett didn't look at him.

"If it's necessary, then … yeah. I don't go around smashing anyone who pisses me off, but he was outta line. I warned him … He knew the consequences."

"This is the first time I've witness a fight. I've seen them in movies, but I've never seen one up close. It was … disturbing."

*Shit! Why the hell did that fucker have to show up?* "Fighting's been a part of my life since I can remember. I gotta admit that I don't under-stand where you're coming from, but I'm gonna try."

A small smile flitted across those soft lips he loved to kiss. Scarlett swiveled in place and met his eyes. "My background never included physical violence. I was never spanked as a child, and my dad would never dream of raising a hand to my mother. Fistfights and such are just not part of my world, so I'm not used to it and"—she stared at him for a second, then averted her gaze downward to her plate—"I don't want to be." She grew silent, fidgeting with her fork.

Sighing, Shadow pressed his lips together and leaned back in the booth. "I get what you're saying—we come from different backgrounds. Yours was calm and civilized, and mine was a damn minefield most of the time." He tipped his head and downed the rest of his beer. "My old man loved beating on me and my mom, and when I was old enough to fight back, I used my fists to get my way or to have people listen to me. As alien as it is to you, it's common to me. It's just how I grew up. We didn't live in pretty neighborhoods until my mom got mixed up with some rich fucker. He's the one who moved us to the Lanai Towers. Yeah … we were bought and paid for." Bile rose up in the back of his throat and he swallowed it down.

Squeezing his fingers lightly, Scarlett looked up at him, those beautiful eyes laced with sympathy and concern. Not anything he wanted or needed.

"Who was your mother's … boyfriend?"

"You mean sugar daddy, right? I mean, that's what he was—an older man who lavished his younger woman with an expensive apartment and a healthy stipend. There's no doubt he was married, and my mom believed his 'getting a divorced bullshit.' I even warned her to be careful so her wouldn't break her heart."

"It sounds like she was really in love with him," she said, her voice soft.

"She liked him—appreciated what he did for us … but love? Nah. She sold herself for the only person she loved unconditionally—*me*." Shadow turned away and looked at the jagged mountain peaks, wishing he could jump on his bike and ride hard and fast into nothingness.

Scarlett drew his hand to her mouth and kissed it. "Your mother sounds like she was quite a woman."

"She was." The raw ache inside him twisted brutally.

"My mother's love has always been conditional at best." Her voice trembled slightly.

Shadow pushed aside the pain and laced her fingers with his. "I was lucky. So … are we good here? What do you need from me right now?" He stroked her knuckles with his thumb.

"To hold me," she whispered.

In less than a heartbeat, Shadow was at her side, drawing her into his arms. Scarlett tilted her face toward him, and dipping his head down, he pressed his mouth to hers and kissed her gently.

"We got differences, babe, but we can either work with those or not," he said against her lips.

"I know. What … uh … do you want to do?" she whispered.

Shadow laid her head on his shoulder as the question echoed in his mind. What the hell did he want? The truth was that he'd never felt this way with any other woman, but he wasn't sure if Scarlett was on the same page. Warren had been surprised to see her with him and that pissed Shadow off a bit. Hadn't Scarlett said she was going to tell the jerk it was over? *She obviously didn't say shit. Is she playing both of us?* But in his heart, he didn't really believe that. When they were together, Scarlett was with him all the way; unless she was a cold-hearted manipulator, he didn't think she could fake the warmth and passion that emanated from her every time they were with each other.

"It isn't a trick question," she said.

Her voice brought him out of his thoughts, and when he looked down at her, tenderness and *love* shone in her eyes, and a pink flush accented her chin and cheeks. A crazy mix of emotions tore through him—an alchemy of possessiveness, tenderness, and something else that made him uncomfortable. Shadow's world had crashed the night he'd lost his mother, and since that moment, he'd put up barriers around his heart … his feelings. Scarlett was weakening those barricades, and she threatened to knock them down, but he wasn't ready to let them go … he wasn't ready to open his heart all the way.

"We're just getting to know each other. Let's just roll with that," Shadow said.

Scarlett broke away from his embrace and scooted away until she plastered herself against the wall. "That's a noncommittal answer." A dry laugh fell from her lips.

"That's the best one I've got right now," he replied as he slid out of the booth and resumed his seat across from her.

The waitress came over to the booth.

"Who gets the enchilada?" she asked.

Shadow pointed at Scarlett. The server set the plate down in front of her.

"And the steak sandwich must be for you," she said, putting it down in front of him. "Anything else?"

Shadow shook his head as he reached for the steak sauce, and she glanced down at her food. She ate in silence, the only sound coming from her fork scraping the plate softly.

"I want you to know that you're the only woman who has stirred some feelings inside me." He took a bite of his sandwich and chewed while thinking about what he was going to say next. "What I know is, that I like you, a lot, and I want to keep seeing you. I got some dark shit from my past eating away at me most of the time, but when I'm with you, I feel good … happy. I just don't know if I can give you what you deserve. Until I can get straight with my past, I don't know if I can let …" Shadow didn't finish the sentence because he didn't want to admit to Scarlett that he was already falling for her and it scared the hell out of him. The thought of losing her made him resist opening his heart to her.

Scarlett met his gaze for a moment and then looked down at her plate.

"Okay … I'll considered myself warned." She smiled weakly, then took a bite of her dinner.

Shadow squirted ketchup on his fries then sprinkled a generous amount of salt on top of them. "Did you decide to get the apartment?" he asked.

"I did. I wished you could've seen it."

"The pictures you sent me looked totally cool. It's the right decision." He popped some fries into his mouth.

"I told my dad that I decided to move. He wasn't too happy about it, but he understood. My mom has been trying to guilt me over it, but I've made up my mind. I'm going to sign the lease tomorrow morning."

"Do you think that jerk's gonna tell your parents about seeing us?"

"No, but he'll tell his father, who will then tell my dad. I should be moved out before the fireworks go off."

"What's going to happen when they go off?" He sucked in a breath.

"A lot of threatening to cut me off." She laughed. "It worked years ago when I tried to stand my ground and stay in Italy, but this time I have some money and I'm going to get a job."

"Can you handle the deep freeze your parents will put you in?"

"If you're with me, I can handle anything." The corners of her mouth turned up.

He exhaled slowly as a relieved feeling washed over him. *I'm in so fuckin' deep.* "I'm here for you. When are you moving in?"

"This Saturday. My dad's going to New York City on business and my mom's going with him to do some shopping. They leave tomorrow morning."

"I can help you—I'll get some of my buddies to help out too."

"I doubt if they'll want to spend their Saturday moving my crap. I don't have that much, but even so …"

"If I ask them, they'll do it—we help each other out. Although, I'm not gonna say they won't grumble about it." Shadow took the last bite of his sandwich.

"It's wonderful to have such good friends. I know I can count on a few of my close ones too. Tell the guys I'll have pizza and beer."

Shadow laughed. "Then, for sure they'll come without bitchin'. Hell, they'll do just about anything for pizza and beer."

Laughing, she reached over and grasped his hand. "You're too funny." Her green eyes sparkled like a forest stream in the morning sun. "I like spending time with you."

"That's good to know since I plan on seeing a lot more of you." He glanced at her empty plate. "Are you ready to go?"

"Uh … yeah." A flash of disappointment flickered on her face.

"I thought we'd go for a ride."

Beaming, she nodded. "I'd love to go for another ride."

"Cool. Riding a bike at night is completely different than during the day." Shadow waved his hand, gesturing to the waitress for the bill. "I enjoy the isolation of riding at night. Without the chaos of daytime traffic, I can really focus on the ride. There's nothing better than a night sky studded with stars and a bright moon shining down on the mountain tops and evergreens." He paused as the images filled his mind. "And the lakes and streams look like glittering pools of silver. It's the best—fuckin' awesome."

"That's so beautiful. You make it sound exciting and special, but I have to say, I'm a bit scared. It's so dark out and I worry if cars will be able to see us."

Shadow picked up the bill and scanned it. "You'll be with me, so don't worry. I'm not one of those crazy fucks who ride the way they do during the day. We'll be on the back roads so there won't be many cars, if any. The biggest thing with night riding is that visibility is down and deer and coyotes dash across the road. I'm experienced, so all you gotta do is trust me, hold on tight, and enjoy the view." He placed the money in the bill plate, slid out of the booth, then gripped Scarlett's hand and she followed suit.

Soon, the warm night air swirled around them as Shadow rode around curves until he finally stopped at Inspiration Point—one of the highest points near the town. It offered a great view of the town, and from the high vantage point, the vista to the northwest was spectacular: layered scenery of the mountains and fields.

"I love it up here," Scarlett said. She whirled around as if trying to take in the different views all at once.

"It's kickass," Shadow agreed as he took out a Navajo print blanket from one of the saddle bags. "I love coming up here—it's not far from town, but you feel like you're a million miles away." He put his arm around Scarlett and led her to a grassy area then spread out the blanket.

"I've never been here before, and it's so close to Pinewood Springs," she said as she sat down next to him.

"You've lived a sheltered life, baby. I used to come up here with Eli and some other buddies to drink beer and smoke pot when we were in high school. Even then, I appreciated the strength and wonder of the universe."

"Did Eli and your other friends feel the same way?" She leaned her head against his shoulder.

Shadow laughed. "Fuck no. They just came here to booze and smoke without getting caught. The badges hardly patrol this area."

He lay down, taking Scarlett with him, then hovering over her, he kissed her deeply, enjoying the feel of her soft body pressed against his.

The breeze blew warm around them and carried the aroma of pine trees and fragrant wildflowers. The solemn hooting of an owl in a nearby tree and the distant rush of waterfalls echoed through the valley.

Shadow rolled on his back, tucked her into the curve of his arm, and held her close. Scarlett snuggled her face into his chest, draping an arm across his waist.

"It's so beautiful here," she murmured.

"Yeah." He stroked her hair with his hand, kissing the top of her head.

Against a perfect black velvet, the stars hung above them as if strung in the air by invisible thread.

"I like being here with you," he whispered. She was so soft against him, and she smelled incredible. *Damn.* He let his hand drift down to her tit, but she gently pushed it away then burrowed closer to him.

"Can you just hold me?" she said.

"If that's what you want," he replied.

"I just want to absorb all this with you. Does that make sense?"

"Uh-huh." And it did, even as it blew his mind.

They lay in silence gazing up at the starry sky. When was the last time he'd held a woman without fucking her? *Never. Damn …*

Clutching her tight in his arms under the nighttime sky was all right. No … it was …

*Perfect.*

# CHAPTER FOURTEEN

"I LOVE YOUR place," Kiara said as she looked around the room.

"Thanks," Scarlett replied. "What I love the most about my condo, besides the fact that it's all mine, is all the light."

"I agree—the wall of windows is stunning." Kiara picked up her glass and took a sip. "You make a mean sangria. It's so perfect for such a hot day." She groaned and fell back against the floral couch cushion. "When is it going to get cooler?"

"I know—too damn hot this summer. Thankfully, fall is not too far away." Scarlett picked up her wineglass.

"Oh … isn't that awful what happened to Warren? He looks terrible—like something out of a scary movie."

Scarlett stiffened, then slowly put the glass back on the coffee table. "What happened to him?"

"How could you not know? When he was water-skiing last week, he fell in the lake and one of the skis landed right on his face." Her friend visibly shivered. "Ouch—I can't imagine how painful that must've been. I can't believe he didn't tell you. I bumped into him at the grocery store and he seemed embarrassed by the whole thing. Silly, huh?"

"Yeah," Scarlett said as guilt wove through her. *I wish Shadow would've let me handle the situation without resorting to using his fists on Warren's face, but … Warren was being an ass, and Shadow did warn him.*

"So I guess Warren's been laying low since the accident." Kiara picked up a piece of cheese, stacked it on a wheat cracker, then popped it into her mouth.

"I haven't spoken to him in a while. We're not with each other anymore." Scarlett looked away to avoid seeing the pained look on her friend's face.

"Oh, Scarlett. I wish you would reconsider. I thought you two made a great couple."

"Appearances are deceiving." She inhaled deeply and exhaled slowly. "I was never in love with him, and I doubt that he was in love with me. It seemed like we were together to please our parents and that never works out. Anyway, I'm seeing someone else."

Kiara's hand froze in midair. "Who?"

"You don't know him," she replied as she watched her friend stuff another cheese and cracker into her mouth. "My parents don't know … *yet*."

Kiara's eyes twinkled. "He must be someone who'll meet your parents disapproval. Tell me his name—I might know him."

"Believe me—you don't, and my parents are going to flip out." Scarlett crossed her legs. "His name is Shadow—it's sort of his nickname. I mean … his birth name is Steve, but he's gone by Shadow ever since he was in high school."

Her friend nodded before taking another drink of wine. "Okay—a bit strange, but okay. What does he do? Where did he go to college?"

Scarlett licked her lips. "He's from here and he never went to college. He runs an online business and owns some storage rentals, and I met him at Brooke's party."

"When? I don't remember you telling me about meeting someone that night. Wait … you were with Warren that night." She laughed and shook her head. "You're bad."

"I didn't think I'd ever see him again, but then he ended up being one of the guys working on the tennis house, and the rest is history."

Kiara's eyes widened. "You're with one of the workers?" She clapped her hands. "Your parents are going to shit a brick. I have to hand it to you—when you fuck up, you go all out. Remember Marcello?"

"Yeah, but this is different—I'm older and I'm keeping my feelings in check with Shadow." *I'm such a liar.*

"And how does *Shadow*—it sounds so weird to call someone that—

feel about you?"

Scarlett picked up her glass, leaned back in the cushy chair, and took a drink. "I know he likes me a lot, but I also know he's confused and scared shitless about his feelings for me."

"That sounds promising." Kiara smiled.

"It is, because he's done things with me that he's never done with any other woman. He's taken me to places that are special to him and shared them with me. We go out to dinner, we went to a movie the other night, we watch the stars, swim in the lake, and go on long rides on his motorcycle."

"*You* on a motorcycle? I can't believe it."

"The first time I climbed on behind him, I wondered if I was insane, and now I can't imagine not riding. It's so much fun—so freeing and exhilarating. And the best part of all is that I get to hold him tight."

After a short pause, Kiara slumped back. "You've fallen for him." She put her hand up, cutting Scarlett's protestations off. "Don't deny it … not to me. I know you, remember?"

She quirked her lips. Yes, Kiara knew her, sometimes better than Scarlett knew herself. "I didn't want to," she whispered. "I fought it, but …"

In the beginning she knew she should've walked away from Shadow, but the excitement and the rush of being with him had made it impossible for her to give him up. She craved him, and after she had her fix, she always wanted more. As she'd gotten to know Shadow, his humor, his quiet strength, and his tenderness captivated her in ways no other man ever had. Scarlett's insatiable appetite for him wasn't just for the sex, but for the whole confusing mix of physical and emotional feelings. And now, not having him in her life was not an option.

"He must really be something," Kiara said.

"He is." Scarlett covered her face with her hands. "I'm toast, aren't I?"

"With your family … yes, but with him? I guess it depends if he's in love with you. If so, then you're lucky as hell. We only have one life, so why not be happy? I'm just mad at you for keeping him a secret for so long."

"I didn't mean to. I really didn't think it would go anywhere past a summer fling, but I should've told you. I guess I thought you'd disapprove. I didn't want to hear what I'd been telling myself over and over—that I was crazy to be involved with him."

"Do you still tell yourself that?"

Scarlett shook her head. "Not anymore. I'm just letting myself live in the moment and be happy."

"I want to meet him. I bet he's gorgeous. Does he have tattoos?"

"Yes … He's so sexy and buffed and hot. I still melt every time I see him. It's like I'm thirteen all over again and just discovering guys."

"Let's go on a double date this weekend," Kiara said.

"Do you think Conrad would be cool with that? He and Warren are on the same soccer team."

Kiara laughed. "Conrad can't stand Warren—he thinks he's an arrogant blowhard."

"I didn't know that." She giggled. "You and Conrad have been spending a lot of time together since you guys started dating a few weeks ago."

"He's awfully sweet. Time will tell if he's my Prince Charming."

"Every time I've seen him at the club, he can't stop talking about you. I hope it works out for you guys." Scarlett knew how anxious her friend was to settle down and have her own home and family.

"We'll see. How do you like your job?"

"So far I love it, but it's only been three days," Scarlett said. "I've always loved the history and Victorian architecture of the Palace Hotel, so to be working there now as a public relations assistant is just amazing."

"Maybe a full-time slot will open up soon."

"I'm good with working part-time because I still want to stay active in the Sheridan Center for Children. I've been asked to join the board, and I'm seriously considering it."

"That's great." Kiara snatched another cracker and nibbled on it. "Hey"—she snapped her fingers—"why don't you bring Shadow to the pool party?"

"I'm not sure if he'd want to go." The thought of her friends possibly judging and ostracizing him tugged at her heart.

"Ask him, then you'll have your answer. He has to know your world, right?"

"Right," she replied with a bit of hesitation. "But … there's something I haven't told you about Shadow. He's … uh, a member of the Insurgents."

Kiara blinked several times. "The outlaw biker gang?" Scarlett nodded. "What the hell? Are you crazy?"

"I think I am, but his club isn't a part of my life, you know?" As a matter of fact, Shadow rarely talked about the club, and he never introduced her to any of his friends or brought her to the clubhouse.

"It's totally a part of his life—it *is* his life. Check out some of the documentaries about outlaw clubs on YouTube—pretty scary stuff."

"I've watched a ton of them. I don't know why, but it doesn't freak me out," Scarlett said. "I guess it's because I know him."

Kiara nodded. "I get that, but be careful. Anyway, you should still think about asking him to Daisy's pool party."

"We'll see." She put her empty glass down on the table. "I wish Shadow would open up more. I think something bad happened in his past, but every time I get close to asking him, he changes the subject. I think it has something to do with the death of his parents."

"He's an orphan?"

"He told me his parents are both dead. I know he doesn't have good memories of his father, but he adored his mother. I can tell by the way he talks about her and the look he gets in his eyes—so full of love and adoration. What I'm not sure about is how they died. I've pieced together that he was younger when his dad died and in high school when he lost his mother. I wish he trusted me enough to share his past."

"Maybe it's too painful for him and he'd rather not talk about it," her friend said.

"I know, but it's eating at him, and I know he'd feel better if shared it with me."

"Give him some time."

Scarlett smiled. "You know me—I want everything right now."

"Some things never change." Her friend joked. "So when's the dining room set coming in?"

"Not for another month. It's all handcrafted so that in itself is definitely worth the wait." Scarlett rose to her feet and collected the empty glasses. "Do you want some more sangria?"

"I'm good, thanks. Do you feel like going out to eat?"

"Totally. I haven't finished unpacking the kitchen, and I'm not in the mood to cook. Where do you want to go? I'm up for everything but barbecue."

"What about Little Pepina's? I'm craving shrimp fettuccine Alfredo."

"That does sound good—I'm in."

Kiara stood up. "I'm going to freshen up." She ambled toward the guest bathroom.

Scarlett went into the kitchen to put the cheese and crackers away and wash the glasses. As she was drying them, her phone rang.

"Hello?"

"Hi, darlin'."

Her insides fluttered, the butterflies loose and twirling by just the sound of his voice.

"Hey," she replied.

"Whatcha up to?"

"Kiara is here and we're going to Little Pepina's for dinner. What about you?"

"Not much—just got back from a ride with Smokey and some other brothers."

"Where did you guys go?"

"Ghost Pass. We had some chow at the roadhouse on the top of the mountain."

Shivers ran up her back as she listened to him talk. *I don't think I'd recover if he broke my heart.* "You'll have to take me there."

"We'll go, but it's a hairpin ride for sure. We can take the highway, but then, that's no fun." His soft, deep chuckle hit her right between the legs, and she bit the left corner of her lower lip as she shifted from one foot to the other.

"Are you ready? I'm starving," Kiara said as she walked into the family room.

Holding her finger up, Scarlett mouthed, "One minute."

"What time are you gonna be home?" he asked.

"In about three hours—we like to talk." She giggled.

"I'll be waiting for you in front of your building. You've been on my mind all day, baby."

"Maybe we can watch a movie. I can make popcorn—I did manage to take some pots out of the boxes." She giggled again.

"We can do that, too, but first I'm gonna pleasure you real good. I got an ache that only you can ease."

*Oh God.* "I'll eat fast—make it two and a half hours."

Shadow chuckled.

"I better go," she whispered. "Kiara looks like she's going to die of starvation."

"I wouldn't want to be responsible for that."

Scarlett heard the smile in his voice.

"I'll see you later," she said. In the background she heard a woman squealing with laugher. "Where are you?"

"At the clubhouse."

"Is there a party going on?"

"There's always a party going on."

"I don't know if I like that." A small frown settled between her brows.

"My party's gonna start when I have you in my arms, darlin'."

She relaxed against the counter and looked out at the traffic below. "I can't wait," she said.

"Scarlett ..." Kiara called.

"Coming," she answered. "I better go."

"Have a good dinner, babe."

She switched off the kitchen light, then picked up her purse from the chair. "Let's go"

Kiara bounced over to the front door, and soon the two women were making their way to the restaurant. A thrill of excitement raced through Scarlett at the prospect of seeing Shadow that night. Just thinking of him made her burn with arousal.

She shook her head to scatter the naughty thoughts of what she would do with him later on. It was too late though, they were already there; *he* was always on her mind.

*Kiara's right—I've fallen for him. Hard. Too hard.*

It was rash and dangerous, and she wasn't sure about the depth of Shadow's feelings for her. Nevertheless, Scarlett was caught up in how good and wonderful it felt to be near him ... lost in it, really, and she knew one thing: she never wanted it to end.

Gasping, she covered her mouth and stopped in her tracks. *I'm so in love with him!*

"What's wrong?" Kiara looked over her shoulder, her hand on the door handle of the restaurant.

"Uh ... I think I forgot my wallet." *Liar!*

Her friend laughed. "No reason to freak out—I can spot you, silly." She opened the door and walked inside.

*What if he doesn't love me? He practically told me he couldn't love anyone. How did you let this happen?*

The love she felt for Shadow was deep and euphoric, but it also made her jittery. It was like falling in love for the very first time, and she wanted to tell him in the worst way, yet she wouldn't. Scarlett was afraid to hear his answer or, even worse, the silence before the dreaded hemming and hawing as he tried to come up with a reason for not loving her back.

*I've got to stop getting ahead of myself. I'm happy and that's all that counts.*

Poking her head out the door, Kiara said, "Hurry up—they have a table for us."

"I'm coming," Scarlett replied, picking up her pace. The smell of garlic and basil wafted through the open door. *Focus on the present and don't overthink the future.*

At dinner she'd have a glass of Chianti, a plate of pasta, and a good time with her best friend. Then she'd spend the night with Shadow—the man who'd captured her heart.

Smiling, she reached for a breadstick and nibbled on it as she looked at the menu.

# CHAPTER FIFTEEN

DETECTIVE MCCUE LOOKED up from the file he was reading and lifted his chin at his partner as he walked into the office.

"It's hotter than Hades out there," Ibuado said as he plucked a few tissues from the chevron-designed box on the corner of McCue's desk. He wiped the sweat from his forehead, then pulled out a few more and ran them over his black matted hair.

"There're bottles of tea in the fridge," the detective said to his partner as he opened a desk drawer and pulled out another file. "Our Jane Doe's got a name," he added while thumbing through the papers in the open folder.

"We got a hit on her fingerprints?" Ibuado asked, walking to the mini-fridge. He bent down and grabbed a bottle of tea, then opened it and downed half the contents before running the cold surface over his forehead, face, and neck.

"Better now?" McCue asked as he watched in amusement.

"Yeah. When the hell is this heat going to break?" Ibuado bent down and took out another bottle, then he crossed the room and sank into one of the chairs in front of McCue's desk.

"Doesn't seem like it's going to any time soon." He scanned the information from NCIC. "*Florence Karas* is the name of our Jane Doe."

"What did she do to have the honor of being in the criminal database?"

"She was popped years ago for hooking on Penn Street, but what I find real interesting is that she stripped at Satin Dolls around the same time our cold case victim Carmen Basson worked there."

Ibuado tossed the empty bottle into the trash. "Coincidence?"

"I don't like coincidences. Our former Jane Doe had a condo in the Belvedere." The detective nodded at his partner's low whistle. "Yeah … Where the hell does a stripper, who was also turning tricks, get that kind of money to buy a condo in the one of the ritziest parts of town?"

"Maybe she had the same sugar daddy as Carmen Basson."

"Another coincidence that I don't like." McCue pulled out an envelope and waved it in front of him. "A signed search warrant for Florence Karas's condo."

"I just cooled off," Ibuado said as he rose to his feet.

"And I just got an AC flush for my car. Now it's like the damn North Pole in there." McCue grabbed his notebook. "My gut's telling me Karas's murder is somehow related to Basson's."

"Mine too. After we finish with the search, let's pay a visit to Satin Dolls."

"Great minds think alike," McCue said, walking into the elevator.

He put on his sunglasses and pushed open the door, sucking in his breath as a blast of scorching heat rolled over him. He slipped off his sports jacket, draped it over his shoulder, and he and his partner made their way to the parking lot.

For the next three hours, the detectives and several police officers combed through Florence Karas's condominium, bagging items, shuffling through papers, and rifling through drawers.

"We found a calendar planner in one of the dresser drawers under a stack of papers and books," one of the officers said as he handed a magenta-pink book to McCue.

The detective took it in his gloved hands and thumbed through the pages. From the coroner's report, he knew the victim had been dead for a couple of days, so he searched the day planner hoping to glean some clues. A couple of days before the body was discovered, he saw a handwritten notation: *Shadow at 4:00 p.m.*

"Well I'll be damned," he muttered under his breath. He opened a plastic bag and dropped the planner in it, then he sealed it and handed it to one of the techs who whisked it away. The detective then took out his phone and called Carly Leight—one of his favorite prosecutors.

"Is it hot enough for you, McCue?" Carly joked.

"Not quite." He chuckled. "I wanted to let you know that we got a name for our Jane Doe—Florence Karas. I'm at her place now."

"Finding anything helpful?" she asked.

"Yeah. How's the search warrant for the victim's phone records going?"

"It's in front of Judge Romero right now. I don't think it'll be a problem to get it signed. I'll dash over there and amend Jane Doe to our victim's name. I'll call you the minute I have the signed warrant in my hands."

"Thanks, Carly—I owe you."

"Maybe that drink that you keep promising me?" A soft laugh. "Now let me get off the phone so I can get over to Romero's chambers."

McCue shoved the phone into his pocket. Questions raced through his mind about the connection between Florence Karas and Shadow. *Why the hell was he meeting her? Never once in the investigation did her name come up. Why didn't he ever mention her to me?* He doubted that the outlaw biker would be forthcoming with much information, but he'd give it his best shot. The case of Shadow's mother haunted him, and he was determined to solve it at all costs.

With a sigh, the detective picked up a box that had been under the bed and began to sift through it.

# Chapter Sixteen

WARREN PERCHED ON the edge of the leather wingback chair, watching his father's face morph into a mask of rage. He'd witnessed that more times than he could remember throughout his lifetime. Whenever Warren hadn't done well on a test, received less than an *A* in his classes, or won a soccer game, his father's rage boiled over. It'd seemed that no matter what Warren did, his father wasn't quite satisfied.

Now Warren had lost Scarlett to a fucking outlaw biker, and in all fairness, he didn't blame his father for being livid. Who loses their girlfriend to an Insurgent? *A loser, that's who.* It wasn't that he was in love with Scarlett, but that his pride had been wounded and the dirty lowlife had humiliated him in public *and* in front of her. Anger streaked through him as he remembered the incident. *And the damn bitch just sat there with him. She didn't even bother to follow me out. Fucking cunt.*

"Why the hell didn't you propose to her before she got bored of your sorry ass?" His father's voice sliced through Warren's thoughts.

"I was going to, but I didn't think she was ready."

"Ready? What the fuck does that mean?" Red blotches covered his dad's face like a checkerboard.

"I felt that we needed to get closer. I was working on it when …" his voice trailed off. There was no need to retell the story of his ultimate shame.

"Working on it, my ass. *You're* the one in charge, not that bitch. You've always been weak—just like your mother. Weakness can be sniffed out a mile away, and people don't respect it—they trample on it. I tried to teach you that, boy." The desk shook under the force of his father's fist.

"I can't make Scarlett or any other woman fall in love with me," he said between clenched teeth.

"What the fuck does love got to do with it? I asked you to be a man for one fucking time in your life and you failed me miserably. We *need* the Mansfield fortune. I explained that to you and you said you understood. Now you've gone and lost her to this"—he waved his hand frenetically in the air—"asshole in a biker gang. I always thought you were a dumbass, but I gave you the benefit of the doubt. Now I know I was right!"

When Bruce Huntington yelled, people listened, and Warren was no exception: he felt like he was back in grade school, awaiting punishment from the father he loved but could never please.

"Can't you just sell the land to Mr. Mansfield?"

Bruce slammed back against the chair, a loud, frustrated sigh pushing through his thick lips. "I can, but that'll barely pay off the loan. What about all this?" Again his hand waved wildly around. "This lifestyle that you and your mom have grown to love. It ain't cheap to have it, boy. Not. At. All. George and I had it all planned out—you'd marry his daughter, he'd get the land he wanted for a good price, he'd give you an executive job at his real estate firm, and he'd throw in a big bonus for me for arranging to have our two families merge. On paper I still look damn good, but it's nothing but a damn paper house. The plan was perfect, and now it's fucked up."

"I didn't do anything. I've been wining and dining that frigid bitch for almost a year. I've put up with her boring talk on politics and literature, and hung out with her friends. Can I help it if she's a fucking psycho?"

His dad ran his narrowed eyes over him. "Maybe you don't fuck so good."

Warren clenched his fists and bolted from the chair. "Shut your fucking mouth, old man."

Bruce smirked. "Go ahead and slug me. I know you want to do it.

Come on, belt me." He turned his face so his jaw was in perfect view of his son. "You're mad as hell at me—hit me."

Warren's nostrils flared as he panted, his body rigid as a board. He wanted to smash his father's face, hear the bones crunch, see the blood flow, and get rid of that damn smug look once and for all.

Several seconds lapsed and the anger slowly quelled as Warren slinked back down in the chair and sat with his shoulders hunched and his head hung down.

"I'd have respected you more if you would've decked me," Bruce grumbled. "Does George know about his daughter's whoring?"

"I don't think so." He kept his eyes fixed on a piece of lint on the Karastan rug.

"Once he does, he'll break it up for sure."

"I wouldn't be so sure about that. Mr. Mansfield roars like a lion a lot, but he's got a soft spot for Scarlett even though she denies it."

Bruce threw his head back and a deep laugh rumbled from his chest. "He's not going to let his pretty, sweet daughter bring scum of the earth to his home. And Pamela won't allow that at all." He chuckled. "You can't accuse her of having a soft spot. She's not weak like you or your mother—she's one of the strong ones, and if I have to make her my ally against George, I will. I'm not losing this deal. You say the fucker's in the Insurgents?"

Warren glanced over at a large twelfth-century samurai sword hanging on the wall beside the fireplace. How he wished he had the guts to run that sword through his father's heart, but he didn't … he wouldn't survive one day in prison. His gaze cut over to Bruce's, and he nodded.

"That's tricky, but we can figure it out. Do you know which one of the pieces of shit he is?

"Scarlett called him 'Shadow.'"

His father's face grew taut and he gripped the bottle of scotch on the side table and poured a healthy dose of it into the cut crystal tumbler. Warren watched as the old man drained the glass.

"He comes from trash. His mom was a stripper who thought she could wash the dirt from her by trying to move into our world." Bruce brought the glass to his mouth and threw back another shot of scotch.

"How do you know that?"

"I know a lot of things." His dad tilted his head back and stared vacantly at the ceiling.

"I can't believe you even know the asshole." Warren crossed his legs then uncrossed them.

After a few awkward minutes, his father said in a low voice, "I'll take care of this, but you're going to help." Then his cold hazel eyes locked on Warren. "And this time, you're going to do exactly what I tell you. Understand, boy?"

Nodding, he pushed away the anger sizzling inside him.

"Now fetch me the brandy, and I'll tell you what I got in mind."

Warren pushed up from the chair and shuffled over to the wet bar to grab two snifters and the decanter. If only he had money of his own—a trust fund like Scarlett. *That bitch is causing me all sorts of problems. Fuck her!* He should be at the Lakeside Inn having a fun time with that floozy he'd picked up at the dive bar a couple of weeks ago. As long as he lavished compliments on her and a few bucks, she didn't care that his face was still bruised.

"Hurry it up—we got business to go over," his dad barked.

Gritting his teeth, Warren slowly walked over to his father.

# Chapter Seventeen

S HADOW LOCKED THE door to the small warehouse he rented and slowly walked toward his motorcycle as he scanned the parking lot. Since the day before, he realized someone was following him. He hadn't actually seen anyone, but he sensed it: eyes watching him, scoping him out, perhaps even measuring him as a target. But now, as his gaze focused on the oak and pine trees surrounding the building and asphalt lot, he saw nothing.

Another person would chide himself for being paranoid, but Shadow had more than a decade's worth of experience living as a one-percenter. Being an Insurgent, he'd learned to notice minutiae details—to be hyperaware of his surroundings at all times—and his gut had picked up on something that had triggered alarms in his head. He knew better than to ignore them.

Without breaking his stride, Shadow put on his sunglasses, swung his leg over the bike, and turned on the engine. Not wanting to tip anyone off that he was on to them, he used his peripheral vision to check out any movement. Nothing. He gripped the handle bars, shifted, then took off, quickly blending into traffic on Main Street.

Instead of taking his usual route home, Shadow weaved in and out of traffic, purposely staying on crowded streets, and then he caught a glimpse of a small black car with tinted windows—maybe a Corolla—darting between cars behind him. Three automobiles separated him from his pursuer. *Gotcha, asshole.* Shadow turned down a narrow side street and pulled into an alley behind Shave Time—a barbershop that sold electric and stick razors. He parked his bike, and instead of going into the shop, he crossed the small lot and hid in the adjacent doorway of a used book store and waited.

Less than a minute passed when Shadow spotted the black car pass by the alley several times before it turned in slowly and cruised past the barbershop's back lot. The Toyota Corolla pulled into the vacuum repair's lot, which was four shops down, then a man wearing a pair of tan Dockers and a brown Polo shirt slid out. The guy looked to be in his mid-thirties and was of medium height, shaved head, and burly shoulders. He tugged at the waistband of his pants then quickly strode toward the barbershop.

Reaching under his cut, Shadow pulled his gun from his back holster and slipped it into his waistband as he quietly stepped out from the doorway and waited for his prey. The man walked by without even a sidelong glance, his whole focus appeared to be on Shadow's bike and the barbershop, where he seemed to think the biker was inside.

As silent and agile as a cougar, Shadow fell in behind him, and the stalker hadn't noticed until the biker's arm wrapped around the man's neck from his rear, and a startled cry rang out. Shadow kicked the back of the guy's knees, knocking him off his feet and onto the hot, hard concrete. He slammed a boot on the back of the stalker's neck, then crouched down low and pushed the gun into his back.

"Why the fuck are you following me?" he growled.

The man groaned.

"You got less than a second to take, then I'm putting a bullet in you." Shadow dug the gun further into the man's lower back.

"I'm a private investigator," the man said, his voice strained.

"So-*the-fuck*-what," Shadow gritted out.

"I was hired to get information on you—that's all." Another groan escaped through his swelling lips.

Shadow patted him down in the back then yanked him around and checked to see if he was carrying a weapon. Nothing. He pulled the guy up by the front of his shirt and dragged him into a narrow passageway between the two stores, and then slammed him against the wall.

"Who hired you, and you don't wanna give me that privacy bullshit because I'm ready to end your life here and now."

Beads of perspiration trickled down the man's face, mixing in with dirt, gravel, and blood.

"Please … I just stake out people for my clients. I usually do affairs for divorces and stuff."

"Stop stalling, fucker! Who the hell hired you?" Shadow pulled him forward then slammed him back against the wall so his head *thumped* dully against the bricks. "Last chance."

"Pamela and George Mansfield. I met with Mrs. Mansfield because her husband was too busy, but they wanted to know about you."

"Like what?" His grip tightened on the man's shirt.

"Who you are, where you come from, if you're married, how many women you have … just the usual stuff. They said they were looking out for their daughter."

*Yeah … I bet they are. Fuckin' sonsofbitches.* "You started yesterday, right?"

"Yes. I really didn't want to do it, especially after I found out you were a member of the Insurgents, but the money was real good. I got a wife, two kids, and another one on the way."

"I don't give a fuck about your life."

"It's nothing personal—just business."

"I know." Shadow rifled through the man's pockets with his free hand and pulled out a wallet. He flipped it open and saw a picture of two small girls in frilly dresses, beaming and sitting on either side of a woman with long brown hair. The other side of the wallet carried a badge that read *Private Investigator* on the top and *Charlie Bowen* under it. He held it in front of Bowen's face. "These badges are illegal," he said. "Did you get this shit online?"

"Yeah … it helps with my ordinary cases."

"I bet it does." Shadow shoved it back in Charlie's pocket. "What shit did you dig up on me?"

"Not too much. I just started yesterday. I got your real name—Steve Basson—and that you've been in the Insurgents for a while—it's damn near impossible to get any intel on your club."

"It fuckin' better be or we're screwing up big time."

A small smile ghosted the investigator's lips. "I just found out basic things like your age, where you went to high school, if you had any arrests—that sort of stuff."

"And my parents, right?" Tightness spread through his body and his jaw clenched.

"Yes. That stuff's in the records."

"Did you turn over that shit to the Mansfields?"

"Not yet—they already know you're in the Insurgents, but that's all they know." Sweat dripped into his eyes and he blinked.

Shadow let go of Bowen and he watched as the PI wiped his face with the front of his shirt.

"You're not gonna give them shit, got it?"

Bowen looked up at him. "They gave me a thousand-dollar retainer that my wife and I have pretty much used up."

"How much for the whole job?" Shadow kept his gun on the private investigator.

"Another thousand—so two in total."

"Fuckin' cheapskates," Shadow muttered under his breath.

"Everything that I have is in the public records. You're from here, so learning your real name wasn't hard. There's no way I can pay them back."

Shadow watched the man with the broad shoulders crumple before him. "Just give them the record shit, but nothing about my mom, you got that? If they wanna find out more about me, they can check the fuckin' records themselves. Rich sonsofbitches."

"I remember when your mother was killed. Awful stuff," Charlie said in a low voice. "For what it's worth, I'm sorry."

Shadow narrowed his eyes. "Don't think I won't hesitate to put a bullet through you or slit your throat."

The private eye sighed. "I don't."

"Forget about me and I'll forget about you." Shadow placed the gun near Bowen's head. "And you definitely want me to forget-the-fuck about you."

"I'll tell them it's gotten too dangerous with you being in the club." Charlie looked down at the ground. "I wouldn't be lying."

"If you get into my business again, I'll kill your picture-perfect family, and I won't blink an eye in doing so." Shadow watched as surprise and fear inched across the investigator's face. "Just remember *that*. You want to stay under the radar with me and my club."

"I … uh … I don't want any trouble from you guys."

"Then stay smart." Shadow placed his gun in his waist then grabbed Bowen's shirt and threw him down on the ground, kicking him sharply in the side. The private eye let out a low groan, and Shadow landed another blow to the guy before walking back to his Harley.

The bike roared to life, and a moment later, Shadow sped away like a bullet from a gun. Anger burned through him—a molten rage threatening to overflow. He gripped the handlebars tightly, his knuckles white with strain. It took all of his steely discipline to keep from going to the Mansfield house and confronting Scarlett's fucking parents. Instead, he took a sharp left and headed to Grove Valley—a ride that always helped to clear his head and calm the rage.

An hour later, Shadow sauntered into the clubhouse and noticed the badges, McCue and Ibuado, seated at a table. Several members leaned against the bar, their lips pressed into a thin line, their faces taut, giving the two badges the evil eye while the club girls gaped at them from the sectional sofa on the other side of the room.

Shadow lifted his chin at McCue when the detective rose to his feet.

"How are you?" the badge asked.

"Good." Shadow motioned to Skinless to bring him a beer. In less than a second, the prospect handed him a bottle and hurried back to the bar.

"Is there somewhere we can go to talk?" McCue asked as he watched Shadow take a swig of beer.

"I'm good here." Shadow pulled the chair out from the table, then raised one leg and placed his foot on the seat.

McCue glanced around the room, then shrugged. "Okay," he said as he took out a notepad and pen from an inner pocket of his jacket and eased his body back into the chair.

Shadow put the empty beer bottle on the table, then leaned forward and rested his forearms on his thighs to meet the badge's eyes. "What're you doing here?"

"Do you know Florence Karas?" McCue asked.

A slight pause—Shadow wasn't expecting *that* question. "Yeah ... why?"

"How do you know her?" The fuckin' badge scribbled something in his damn notebook.

"She lived in our shithole trailer park. What's this all about?" *Someone offed her. McCue wouldn't be asking me these shit questions if he knew who. Fuck, these damn badges are incompetent.*

"How well did your mom know her?"

"What the fuck is this all about? Quit playing this damn cat-and-mouse game. She worked at the same strip joint as my mom. They were friends. End of fuckin' story." Shadow straightened up and pushed the chair over.

Ibuado's hand flew inside his jacket, and McCue sat motionless, staring at the biker.

"Just spit it out. Fuck!"

"When's the last time you saw Florence Karas?" McCue asked in an even tone.

"I haven't seen her in years. Not since the murder." *This fucker found something that links me to that greedy bitch.* "She called me up out of the fuckin' blue a couple of weeks ago and said she wanted to see me. We made plans to meet at her condo, but she never showed up. Are you gonna tell me why she didn't keep the appointment, or am I supposed to guess?" His eyes narrowed.

"She's been murdered."

"It's time you left," Hawk said as he slipped beside Shadow. "This shit's over. Now."

Shadow shook his head. "It's cool, bro."

"You accusing him?" Hawk's voice dripped ice.

The badge slowly stood up. "Just asking questions, that's all."

Ibuado cleared his throat. "We got a dead woman and we need to talk to everyone who knew her. Basic investigating—the same shit you'd do if you were in our place."

Tension crackled in the air, and both McCue and Ibuado, one hand resting on their side holsters, stepped back from Hawk and Shadow.

"Did she tell you why she wanted to meet up with you?" McCue asked.

Shadow could feel the anger emanating from Hawk. "No."

"You didn't ask?" Ibuado said.

"No."

"So, a friend of your mom's who you haven't spoken to in fifteen years calls you out of the blue, and you don't even ask her why she wants to get together with you?"

"That's right." Shadow stood with his feet planted wide, arms crossed over his chest, and his brow furrowed.

"You're done," Hawk growled to the two badges.

McCue nodded and snapped shut that damn notebook. Shadow didn't break eye contact with him. "You know," the detective said, "Florence Karas' murder may be linked to your mother's death. Whether you believe it or not, I want to bring your mother's killer to justice." He slipped the notepad and pen inside his jacket. "We're on the same side with this one, Shadow … We always have been."

The two badges walked backward until they hit the front door, then they turned around and left the room.

Hawk clasped his hand on Shadow's shoulder. "Did that woman know something about your mom's murder?" he asked, concern lacing his voice.

"Yeah, but she wouldn't tell me shit. I found a ledger in her place, showing years of deposits into her bank account. The bitch made money off my mom's murder." A streak of white-hot anger shot through him.

"Fuck, dude. That's tough. Sounds like the bitch got what she deserved," Hawk said.

"When she called me, she was running scared." Shadow slammed his fist on the table then kicked over another chair. "I was so fuckin' close to finding out who killed my mom. Dammit!"

"Give me the ledger—I'll see what I can find out," Hawk said.

"We'll do what we can, bro," Animal said as he approached them.

"Count me in too," Helm added.

"And me." Bones walked up to Shadow and bumped fists with him.

"I got your back, bro—you know that." Smokey pulled him into a bear hug. "You've been denied justice far too long, and now we got something to go on."

Banger walked over and locked eyes with Shadow. "Rock told me what's going on. You know we'll fight and stand by you, no matter what, brother."

Shadow nodded, then bumped fists with his president and his other brothers. Pride swelled inside him and a deep sense of comfort spread through him. For years people had pitied him because he'd lost both his parents. They'd tell him what a shame it was to have lost his family. McCue had been telling him that for years, but what citizens didn't understand was that he had the best family in the world—the Insurgents. And those people who said that a person couldn't choose his family didn't have a fucking clue what the meaning of brotherhood meant.

"You need a good blowjob, dude, and a shot of Jack," Bones said. "Rusty, Skinless, get the drinks flowing, and Brandi … get your ass over here—my brother needs some attention."

Shadow accepted the shots gladly, but the only lips he wanted wrapped around his cock were those of his sweet Scarlett, so he steered Brandi in Blade's direction while he and several of the other members talked about motorcycles.

The phone vibrated in his back pocket and he snatched it out and looked at the screen. His face broke into a grin when he saw the number.

"Hey, babe," he said.

"How are you?" Her voice lilted through the phone.

"Good. How was work?" Music and loud voices filled the room, and Shadow squeezed the cell hard against his ear.

"Great—I really love my job!"

He smiled at her exuberance. "That's good, babe."

"Are you busy tonight?"

"With you."

A small giggle. "I was hoping you were coming over. What time?"

He threw back the rest of his whiskey. "What works for you?"

"Now?"

Her answer made his dick twitch. "I'm on my way."

"I'll be waiting," she whispered.

Shadow pushed away from the bar, telling his buddies that he had something to do, then he raced outside and hopped on his bike.

On his way to Scarlett's building, he turned onto Larkspur Lane and slowed down when he passed the Lanai Towers and the Belvedere. A thread of sadness and regret wove through him as he thought of Flo. His mother had really liked that boisterous, gaudy woman, and Shadow had to admit that he'd loved seeing the two of them together, laughing and talking into the late hours of the night. When Flo had called, a part of him wanted to see her because she was a direct link to his mother, but he was angry that she betrayed his mother by keeping the identity of the killer a secret just so she could profit from it. In any case, he hadn't wanted Flo to die, and her murder angered and saddened him.

A horn honked behind him and Shadow rolled on the throttle, raising the speed of the bike. Two streets over, and he was pulling up to the curb in front of Scarlett's building. Sensing someone looking at him, Shadow glanced across the street and saw Warren glaring at him as the jerk opened the door to a red sports car then slid in. There was another guy in the passenger's seat, but Shadow couldn't make out his features.

"What the fuck's he doing here?" he muttered.

Then he heard the squealing of tires as the sports car pulled out of the parking space and sped away. Shadow hurried into the building, stopping only to sign the register book with the front assistant after scanning the sheet to see if the asshole's name was on it. It wasn't. By the time he got off on the top floor, his nerves were so tight, they felt like they'd snap at any second. He turned the doorknob and it opened, and the aroma of banana-nut bread wafted out into the hall.

"Hey, babe, I'm here," he said, closing the door behind him. "It's not safe to leave your door unlocked, no matter where you live." He walked into the living room and slipped off his cut, carefully placing it on the back of a chair.

"The front desk called me when you got into the elevator."

The scent of her perfume curled around him in a seductive embrace. Shadow turned around and hissed in a breath. "Fuck, baby," he rasped as lust slammed into him with the force of a two-ton truck.

Scarlett wore a black teddy that hugged her delicious curves in all the right places as her golden hair fell in soft waves over her shoulders. The sheer cups, lace bodice, and open crotch left just enough to the imagination to make his cock punch against his jeans.

"Turn around," he growled.

Scarlett slowly spun around, then looked over her shoulder and smiled at him, a wicked glint sparking in her eyes.

"You're killing me, darlin'." He took in the thin piece of fabric between the rounded cheeks of her luscious, naked ass. *So fucking beautiful. So damn tempting.* He wanted to squeeze and spank and bite those delectable cheeks—hard. Hard enough to brand her, leaving no doubt that she was his. *All mine.* "I can't fuckin' wait to unwrap you," he said, walking toward her.

She turned around and Shadow snagged an arm around her waist, drawing her close to him. "I've got a real burn for you, woman," he whispered in her ear.

"I'm so crazy about you," she said, wriggling against him, rubbing her hand over his throbbing dick.

Groaning, his fingers dug into her silky smooth ass cheeks while his mouth devoured hers, as their tongues twisted, breaths mingled, and teeth clashed. Shadow walked them backward toward the couch until her legs bumped against it. He angled her back onto the cushions then broke away; kicking off his boots and unbuckling his belt, his gaze fixed on her pink pussy peeking out at him.

The heat in Scarlett's eyes as she watched him tear his clothes off almost made him jump on top of her and bury his hard-as-steel dick deep inside her, but Shadow wanted to take his time and tease her until she begged to be fucked.

He dropped to his knees near her feet then slowly nipped and licked the inside of her right leg, stroking her other leg with his hand. He felt Scarlett shiver under his touch as her skin pebbled beneath his lips.

"Shadow." She sighed and held her arms stretched out, reaching for him.

Capturing her green gaze, he ran his index finger through her slit, groaning when her slick juices covered it. "So fuckin' wet ... dripping," he murmured as he lowered his head. With two fingers, he opened the folds, exposing her glistening clit. "So beautiful." He stroked her smooth lips then pushed his finger inside her body, sliding in as deep as his knuckle, and then he stopped. Scarlett panted. Leaning over, he untied the front of her teddy and captured her pretty pink nipple between his teeth while he moved slowly in and out of her.

"Oh, fuck, Shadow," she said in a ragged breath.

"You like that, baby? You feel so fuckin' hot and tight, I can't wait to shove my cock in you and fuck you good and hard." He trailed his mouth down her body until he reached her sweetness. "You taste real fine," he said as he swept his tongue from her clit to her heated wetness. He pulled out his finger then thrust his tongue inside her, pushing in and pulling out in quick succession.

"Shit." Scarlett moaned and grabbed fistfuls of his hair.

His thumb moved round and round her clit as he plunged in and out of her until she cried out, her head thrashing about as he felt her whole body shudder.

Scarlett opened her eyes and they locked onto his. He leaned back and slid his finger into his mouth, licking her juices off of it. "I like that," he said, smiling at her widened gaze.

"How does it taste?" she whispered, a pink streak brushing across her cheeks.

"Fuckin' awesome." Shadow bent over and dipped his head down, capturing her mouth. "Taste yourself, baby," he said against her lips.

Her arms circled around his neck and she yanked him closer.

"Do you like your sweetness?"

"It tastes different—tangy and a little sweet. Kind of like a sweet and sour salad dressing. I don't know." The pink blush deepened and she buried her head in the crook of his neck.

"You're so fuckin' adorable." He lifted her face up then covered it in feathery-light kisses. "Did you buy your sexy outfit for me?"

She nodded.

"I love that, baby." He fused his lips on hers and they kissed passionately. "You know what I want?" She shook her head. "I want you to ride me so I can see those gorgeous tits swaying as you bounce up and down on my cock." Shadow pulled up, taking her with him, his gaze never leaving hers. He slowly took off the lingerie, nipping and kissing his way down her body until she stood before him, beautifully naked. They kissed again, then Shadow held her hand and helped her straddle him after he lay back on the couch cushions.

Scarlett's hair brushed across his chest as she bent down, and he grabbed one of her swaying tits and squeezed it hard, eliciting a cry from her. Pulling her closer to him, he lifted his head and sucked one of her hardening nipples into his mouth while he rolled the other one between his thumb and middle finger. Moaning, she raised slightly, and fire roared through his veins when her wet pussy brushed back and forth over the tip of his throbbing cock.

"I need you, darlin," he rasped, then gripped her hips and eased inside her, inch by inch, as their eyes locked. The intensity of being with

Scarlett jolted his senses like a power surge, and it made him groan.

She bent down, then kissed him and said, "Let me do it," and raked her nails down his chest. "Just enjoy the view and the ride."

Then she took him in—all of him—inside her. Her hot walls molded around his cock, and it felt so damn good. Wanting to be closer to her, to feel her tits against him, he sat up and buried his face in them.

"Ride me good, baby," he growled against her soft skin before he caught one of her nipples between his teeth. He sucked hard, loving how she moaned and threw her head back as she kept riding him. Moving his hands down her body, they settled on her ass, and he squeezed it tightly as he rocked his hips so she could take him in deeper. Shadow loved the way her pussy pulsed around his cock, her juices covering him and dripping down his balls. He raised his hand and landed a slap on her ass.

"It feels so good." Scarlett moaned over and over.

Her tits jiggled in front of his face as she rode him fast, and he thrust from below, going deeper. When their eyes met, he saw the wildness and pleasure on her face, and the pressure in his balls escalated.

"I'm coming." Her voice was soft, yet ragged.

Then her pussy started to pulsate around him and she moaned savagely, clawing at his chest.

"You're mine, woman. All mine." Shadow grunted as the base of his spine tightened. He gripped her harder—wanting her delicate flesh to bear his mark—then he exploded, pouring his seed deep inside her, filling her.

*Sex with her is incredible.* But it wasn't just the sex, it was everything. It was all Scarlett. She made him want to be a one-woman man—for the first time ever.

Shadow eased Scarlett off of him, then cocooned her in his arms, never wanting to let her go.

# CHAPTER EIGHTEEN

S LIVERS OF SUMMER'S morning sunlight filtered through the wooden slats, casting thin yellow strips across the hardwood floor like threads of gold. Scarlett rolled over on her side and smiled. *I love waking up next to him.* Propping up on her elbow, she stared at Shadow, the man who had taken possession of her heart.

"Do you know how much I love you?" she whispered in a barely audible voice.

Shadow looked so peaceful—the dark look that crossed his face more often than not was gone. A small snore made her smile, especially when his lips turned up slightly as if a pleasant dream was playing in the theater of his mind. And those lips ... they had kissed every inch of her body. A flutter of arousal landed between her legs at the memory of their night together. They'd spent most of it making love, talking, and laughing. At one point, he'd confided in Scarlett that he had more in common with her than he'd ever had with any woman. Hearing him say those words had made her insides melt. Scarlett understood exactly what he was saying because she felt the same way: Shadow was her soulmate. It was funny because she always thought the whole "soulmate" thing was a lot of bunk. She'd roll her eyes while reading articles about it in her many women's magazines, and when some of her friends referred to their boyfriends as "the one," Scarlett would bite her inner cheek to keep from laughing out loud.

*And now look at me. I guess what they say about karma is true.* Warmth and tenderness spread through her as she softly ran her fingers down his corded arm, loving how the dark hairs stood on end. Yes ... there was such a powerful and electrifying connection to him that it took her breath away. The night before and earlier that morning, Shadow had told her she was all his, and she kept replaying the words over and over in her head, her body tingling each and every time.

Scarlett leaned closer to him. *Yours—how wonderful. And you are all mine. Do you love me too and are afraid to say it? What dark secrets are you keeping buried inside you?*

She watched him sleep, his eyelids fluttering, then Shadow opened his eyes and smiled drowsily as she looked down at him.

"How long have you been checking me out, babe?" he asked, tugging at a few strands of her hair.

"Not too long," she said, running a finger along his jaw. "You looked so peaceful and content that I couldn't help but watch you."

"I was dreamin' about you, darlin'."

"Sweet or nasty?" she murmured.

"Both," he said, pulling her down on top of him.

Without a pause, their mouths joined, passionately exploring each other as their hands touched everywhere. Combined moans of pleasure filled the room as she lost herself in his touch, his scent—*his everything*.

An hour later, naked and sated, they lay tangled together in each other's arms.

"What're you doing today?" she asked, her fingertips dancing in small circles against his skin.

"I gotta go to the warehouse. A big shipment came in so I have to catalogue and list it. Do you work today?" He raked his hand through her hair, then kissed the top of her head.

"Not today. My mom wants to meet me at the club later this afternoon. I'm dreading that. I'd like to see your warehouse and what you do."

"Yeah? That's cool. You can follow me there. I should probably get going in a bit." He tipped her head back and brushed a light kiss against her mouth. "I don't want to leave, baby."

"Me neither," she said as a low growl grumbled from her stomach. She giggled. "I guess my stomach has other ideas. Are you hungry too?"

"I could go for some chow."

Scarlett kissed him quickly before pulling away. "I'll whip up some breakfast, then we can go. I can't wait to see you at your job." She scrambled off the mattress and shuffled to the bathroom to get ready.

After showering and dressing, Scarlett took out apple-smoked bacon from the refrigerator along with two decent-sized potatoes, a small white onion, and a green chile pepper. She opened a cupboard and grabbed two frying pans and a grater, then set to work on making breakfast.

By the time Shadow walked into the kitchen, the small table was set, orange juice filled two glasses, and the bacon and hash browns were heaped on two small platters. A small plate held several slices of buttered toast.

"I've got fresh coffee to wake us both up," she said, pouring the dark liquid into the mugs.

"Last night was fuckin' incredible," he said, then gave her a wink. He blew into his mug then took a sip. "*You* were fuckin' awesome."

"Well, I can't complain about you either." She teased him as she slid into the chair.

"And you never will." Shadow picked up a piece of bacon and took a bite.

"Someone's a little cocky." She brought the glass of juice to her lips.

"Not cocky, darlin', just confident." He shoved the rest of the strip into his mouth.

Laughing, she reached over and patted his hand. "And you have every reason to be." Scarlett leaned over and kissed him, then fell back against the chair. The smoky taste of bacon lingered on her lips and she licked them, loving the way Shadow watched her every movement.

"You keep that up, and we're gonna be fucking on this table." He picked up a piece of toast. "Now that I think of it, we need to do that."

"We have to save something for later, right?"

Their fingertips brushed, and as he moved toward her, the sound of her phone broke through the moment.

"Let it go," he said, his voice thick.

"You'll never make it to the warehouse," she whispered before sliding from the chair.

"True …" He sat back and bit into the toast.

"It's my mom." She groaned after looking down at the screen.

"What does she want?"

"Wait a sec." Scarlett skimmed the text. "Just confirming our late afternoon tea. My mom's obsessed with having teatime in the afternoon. It's kind of annoying."

"Are her people from England or something?"

"Not at all. She's got some French and German in her. My mom never talks about her background. She was an only child, and after her parents died when she was real young, she was brought up by a great-aunt. Anyway, she thinks having teatime makes her classy or something. It's kind of strange."

"Do your parents know about us?"

"I'm betting that they do and that's why my mom wants to meet with me. At least we'll be at the club. My mother would rather die than cause a public scene."

Shadow nodded. "I need to talk to your parents."

Panic shot through her. "No, you don't. What the hell are you thinking?"

"That I'm not a fuckin' pussy, and I'm not gonna hide behind you. I'm a man and I need to tell them how it is between us."

"I appreciate your gallantry, but trust me, it's better if I talk to them."

"I don't like it." Shadow stood and took his plate to the sink.

"Let me soften them up first, then you can meet them, okay?" She cleared off the table. "Promise me?"

"Again … I don't like it. I'll play by your rules for a little while, but *I am* going to talk to them." He slipped his arm around Scarlett's waist and drew her back against him. "We're in this for the long haul."

Happiness spread through her. "We are," she murmured, resting her head against his chest.

"Then I gotta meet your folks and let them know that I'm not going anywhere." Shadow kissed the side of her face.

"I agree, but after I talk to them. After all, I *do* know my mom and dad. You'll get your chance." She craned her neck and looked up at him. Shadow pressed his mouth on hers and they kissed like they had all the time in the world. Finally Scarlett broke away. "We better get going."

He swatted her butt, then helped her load the dishwasher before they gathered their things and walked out of the condo.

PINEWOOD COUNTRY CLUB was one of the oldest and most exclusive clubs in the area, and the Maroon Grille offered the members a warm, comfortable place to meet throughout the day for meals and conversation. The high ceilings and table linen gave it an air of elegance, whereas the stone fireplace and western paintings lent a casual and family-friendly feel to the restaurant. Beyond the dining area's huge picture windows, an impressive golf course lay amid mountain peaks, making the view one of the best in the county.

Scarlett stirred her frozen daquiri with a red straw and looked up as her mother pulled out the chair opposite her.

"Sorry I'm late. Your father's meeting went longer than he thought." Pamela Mansfield waved the waiter over and ordered an Arnold Palmer with a shot of gin in it. "Have you been here long?"

Her mom looked cool and collected in a simple peach cotton shift; a strand of pearls rested just below the scoop neckline.

"I've been here for about fifteen minutes," Scarlett replied. "Is your car in the shop?"

Pamela's eyes widened slightly. "No, why?"

"Dad's at the club too?" Her mouth went dry and her stomach clenched.

"Yes, he's meeting Bruce and Alan to play golf. He'll be here in a minute." Her mother smiled at the waiter when he placed the drink in front of her.

"Are you ready to order?" he asked.

Pamela glanced over at Scarlett and she nodded.

"I'll have the shrimp cocktail," she said, even though her appetite had disappeared. How she wished she were back at the warehouse with Shadow. She had to admit it was a real turn-on watching him at work. He was so in charge, so confident, so sexy. *I'm proud of him for being an entrepreneur.* But of course, it fit his personality. The way she figured it: Shadow was better on his own because the rebel in him wouldn't make it one day with an employer calling all the shots.

"Scarlett, are you listening to me?" Irritation tinged her mother's voice.

"Oh, sorry, I was thinking about something. What did you say?"

Her mother looked pointedly at her. "Something or *someone*?"

*Here we go …* "What were you talking about?"

"I was asking if you've seen Warren. His dad said he's here with some friends having lunch." Pamela looked around the room. "He must be eating at the Cabana Café."

Scarlett picked up the bread basket in the middle of the table. "Do you want a piece?"

"No, and you shouldn't either—all those empty carbs go straight to a woman's stomach or hips, or in the case of Adele Semper—her belly and behind."

Choosing the largest slice, she put it on her bread dish, then slathered butter all over it before taking a large bite. "I didn't see Warren and I don't care if I do. I've told you that I'm not seeing him anymore."

"We'll talk about that when your father gets here."

"It doesn't matter if Dad is here or not, I'm never going back to Warren. Let's just talk about the elephant in the room—Shadow. I'm dating him and have no intention of stopping." Scarlett took another bite of her bread.

Her mother took several large gulps of her drink, then leaned forward in the chair, her eyes narrowed. "You will *not* disgrace your family this way. You will not humiliate your father *or* me by your selfish and childish behavior," she said in a voice that could cut glass.

"You act like I'm doing all this on purpose, Mom. I'm in love with Shadow—it's that simple."

Pamela clenched her hands into fists. "Of course a spoiled brat would think it's so simple. For once in your life, think about someone other than yourself."

"I've been thinking about the family my whole life," Scarlett said, her voice rising. A few people glanced over at the table, and she took a deep breath and exhaled. "I went to the schools you and Dad wanted, came back to Pinewood Springs after college even though I wanted to live in Boston, played the good daughter for all the charitable fundraisers you roped me into, *and* dated Warren for much longer than I wanted to because of you and Dad. And *I'm* the selfish one?" She tossed her head back and let out a dry laugh. "I've decided to live *my* life, Mom."

"Are you finished?" her mother asked. "Your gang member boyfriend has already begun influencing you in a bad way." Pamela rested against the chair. "It's really not very becoming, Scarlett. Not. At. All."

"Shrimp cocktail?" the waiter asked, his eyes avoiding both of them.

"For me, thank you," Scarlett said.

"And the Brie en Croute is for you," he said placing the dish in front of her mother. "Would either of you like another drink?"

Scarlett shook her head while her mother nodded hers.

"Another Arnold Palmer coming up with a shot of gin," he said.

"Make it a double shot," her mother said as she picked up her fork and knife.

The server bowed his head then walked away.

Before she could squeeze the wedge of lemon over the shrimp, Scarlett's phone vibrated in her pocket. After fishing it out, she glanced at the screen and a small thrill of pleasure coursed through her. *Shadow.*

**Shadow:** *Hey, babe. How's it going?*

**Scarlett:** *Like most of my times with my mom—crappy. She says ur a bad influence on me.*

**Shadow:** *Me a bad influence? No fuckin' way!*

**Scarlett:** *Ur getting blamed for my attitude. :)*

**Shadow:** *Fuck, baby, u've had an attitude since I met u. ;)*

"Please put the phone away. It's rude," her mother said as she placed a piece of the gooey cheese on a slice of French bread.

**Scarlett:** *I have to go.*

**Shadow:** *Want to go for a ride? 5:30?*

**Scarlett:** *Yes!!! Meet u at my place. Bye.*

She slid the phone back into her pocket and then speared a shrimp with her fork and put it into her mouth.

"There's your father," Pamela said, her eyes brightening.

"Goody," she said under her breath.

"My two favorite girls," her dad said. He bent down and brushed his lips across her mother's cheek.

"Where's Bruce?" Pamela asked.

"He's having a drink with Warren and a few of his friends. I'm going to meet up with him and Alan soon." He looked up at Scarlett. "How's my little girl doing?"

"Just fine," she said as she stabbed another shrimp and popped it in her mouth.

"I'll have a whiskey on ice," he said to the waiter.

George Mansfield was larger than life, and when he entered a room, his presence commanded attention. He was so unlike her mother, who preferred to stay behind the scenes, thus allowing Scarlett's dad to shine. Since she was a child, Scarlett remembered her mother telling her that a man needed to feel important, his ego to be constantly stroked, and it was up to the woman in his life to do so. She watched as Mother now withdrew to the background and her dad took the stage—front and center.

"How's that job of yours going?" He tore off a hunk of French bread, then reached for the butter.

"It's great—I really love it." She ignored her mother's almost inaudible snort.

"It's good to work. It makes a person feel useful and alive." His jowls jiggled as he chewed the piece of bread.

"I think fundraising is more work than going to an office," her mother said, but her dad glanced at his phone instead of acknowledging her comment.

"Do you want the rest of my shrimp, Dad?" Scarlett pushed the large cocktail glass toward him.

"Are you sure you don't want it?" he asked, already dipping one of the jumbo shrimp in the red sauce.

"I'm not very hungry," she answered. A finger of nausea poked her stomach. Any moment now, the lion would begin to roar. The suspense of *when* played havoc with her nerves.

"You need to eat more—you look like you lost weight. Do you need a cook?" He squirted lemon over the food.

She laughed, the tension easing up a bit. "I can manage to cook, Dad. I'm actually pretty good at it."

George stopped for a moment, looked his daughter in the eyes, then resumed eating. "I didn't know that. You'll have to invite your mother and me over for dinner one night."

"We still haven't seen your place," her mother said, bitterness lacing her voice.

"I didn't think you wanted to. I mean, you haven't called me since I moved."

"Your mom's just upset because she misses you." George wiped his hands with a napkin.

*That's hard to believe.* "It's whatever, Dad. I'd love to have you"—she glanced at her mother sideways—"and Mom over some night. I'll call you and we can set a date."

"Here come Bruce and Warren," her mother said, looking over Scarlett's shoulder and waving her hand briskly.

Scarlett, staring down at the crumbs of bread on the white tablecloth, groaned inwardly. *Can this fucking lunch get any worse?*

"Pamela, you look as lovely as ever," Bruce said. "Have you forgotten about our golf game?" he said to George.

"How've you been, Scarlett?" Warren said as he crouched down on his haunches.

"Fine, thanks. You?" She glanced at him quickly.

"Good. Work has been real busy." He paused, then said, "I heard you're working now. That's great. Do you like it?"

"I do." She shifted in her seat.

"Maybe we could meet for lunch sometime. My office is just a block away from the Palace."

Scarlett was acutely aware that even though her dad, mom, and Mr. Huntington were talking, their ears were on the stilted conversation she and Warren were having.

"How about next Tuesday? I could come by the hotel and we can have some lunch."

"Tuesday doesn't work." All of a sudden the room grew very stuffy and small, and everyone started to blur into caricatures of themselves. It was like she was in one of those abstract paintings she'd seen at the Museum of Contemporary Art in Denver that past spring.

"Wednesday or Thursday is good for me too."

She pushed away from the table and rose to her feet. "None of those days work. I have to go," she mumbled.

"You're not leaving?" her mother asked.

Her lips tipped up, and she nodded. "I have an appointment." Scarlett grabbed her purse and slung the strap over her shoulder, her gaze cutting to her father. "I'll call you, Dad."

Her heels clattered on the wood floor as she headed out of the restaurant.

Not wanting to run the risk of her mother, or even worse—Warren, coming after her, she snagged the keys from the valet and hurried to her car. Once there was distance between the club and herself, Scarlett finally started to relax.

Stopped at a red light, she pulled out her phone and tapped in

Shadow's number.

"Hey, baby. I was just ready to text you again to see how things were going. You've been on my mind." His warm-as-whiskey voice soothed her frazzled nerves.

"I just left. The worst thing was that my dad didn't say a word about it, but the issue was there—crackling between us and bubbling under the surface. Then, Warren and his dad came by, and I just had to get out of there. It seemed like they were ready to gang up on me or something. I don't know—I just *had* to get away."

When a horn honked behind Scarlett, she glanced up at the green light, then stepped on the gas pedal, turned right, and then made another immediate right into Clermont Park.

"Hang on," she said to Shadow as she pulled into a space shaded by the large branches of a sprawling oak tree.

"What're you doing?" he asked, his voice tinged with concern.

"I just pulled over, that's all."

"Where are you?"

"Clermont Park. I miss you."

"Me too, baby. It sounds like you left that fuckin' lunch just in time. I'm with you—they were gonna gang up on you. You don't deserve that shit. I'm sorry as fuck that I wasn't there to hold you in my arms while I set everyone straight."

Warmth spread through her as she switched off the engine. "I love having you in my corner."

"I'll always have your back, darlin'. *Always.*"

His words caused a tiny blip of her heartbeat, and a knot formed in her throat. In the space of a held breath, there was silence. Then, she whispered, "You're the best."

"Just telling like it is." Shadow cleared his throat. "You need a ride so damn bad. I'll meet you in front of your building in fifteen minutes."

"I thought you were working until five."

"I was, but I can come in earlier tomorrow." As if anticipating her protest, he added, "And don't argue with me. Fifteen minutes. See you then, babe."

Scarlett put the phone on the passenger seat, turned the ignition, and headed to her place; she wanted to change from heels to flats and swap sunglasses. Just the thought of fresh air rushing past her, the feeling of flying, and her arms wrapping around Shadow made her press harder on the accelerator.

When Shadow was talking on the phone, it was as if his heart touched her, and she could feel his affection ... his *love* pouring through and filling her. The things Shadow did for her spoke volumes about his feelings for her. Even though Scarlett craved to hear those three short words—*I love you*—she knew how hard it was for Shadow to say them. Something had hurt him badly in the past, enough to keep his rational mind in constant battle with his heart. But at the end of the day, the words didn't really matter, it was the way he treated her, looked at her, kissed her, and made her feel safe and adored without conditions.

Scarlett pulled into the underground garage of her building, then after parking in her space, she rushed over to the elevator and went upstairs to quickly get changed.

SHE WAS WAITING downstairs, leaning against the marble column when she heard the roar of Shadow's bike. Excitement shivered down her spine as she walked over to the curbside grass.

The bright sunlight cast a blue sheen to the wind-blown mess of Shadow's black hair as he approached her. The yellow metallic motorcycle gleamed under the late afternoon rays, and Scarlett noticed a few people stopping on the street to stare as Shadow pulled to the curb.

Scarlett didn't move, instead, she sucked in a deep breath and took him in. He lifted his sunglasses off his face and slipped them into the front of a white T-shirt that tugged at his solid chest. Ribbons of hair fell casually into eyes that were the color of gathering storm clouds. Shadow's gaze seared hers with a glowing intensity, and a flow of tingles rushed to her core.

She walked toward him, their eyes still locked on to each other's.

When she stopped near the motorcycle, he reached out and yanked her to him, then kissed her deeply. At that moment, nothing mattered but Shadow and how incredible it was to kiss him, to be near him, to be a part of his life.

"Ready," he said against her ear.

"Ready," she replied. She gripped his shoulder and swung her leg over the leather seat, then looped her arms around his taut waist. The rumbling purr of the motor turned to a roar as the bike pulled out into the street, weaved in and out of traffic, and rolled through a couple of stop signs. The wind whipped through her hair, the bike vibrated between her thighs, and the events at the club soon became a blur once they were on a narrow two-lane highway taking them away from Pinewood Springs. With her body pressed to his, Scarlett could feel Shadow's back muscles flex against her chest as she leaned with him then came back to center when he did. With each bike ride, she became more familiar and comfortable with his movements; it was like dancing with a partner, only much more exhilarating and freeing.

"Faster!" she yelled.

Shadow glanced back at her, grinning. "Hold on," he said before the wind carried away his words.

She tightened her hold as he opened the bike and they surged around twists in the road. Laughing, she tilted her head back and watched the clouds scuttle across the sky; it felt like if she reached out she could touch them.

All too soon, the bike slowed down before turning into a parking lot in front of a small eatery. Scarlett kissed Shadow on the back of the neck before sliding off the bike.

"That was exactly what I needed," she said.

"It's the best way to get rid of all the shit bouncing around inside your head." He tugged her to him and dipped his head down. "I like the way you feel pressed against me on the back of my bike." He rubbed his thumb over her bottom lip.

His breath fluttered warm over her face, and she tipped up her mouth. And then they were kissing. She looped her arms around his neck, and he lifted her up a bit onto her tiptoes, their lips never breaking contact. The space around them evaporated, and for a moment, everything in her world was just perfect; sneaking around and dating Shadow seemed worth the struggle, worth the tension with her parents and the whispered gossip behind her back.

"You don't know how much I—" But his lips smothered her words as he deepened the kiss.

A short while later, Shadow's hand slipped down to squeeze her behind, then he playfully smacked it.

"Let's go inside, babe," he said, snaking an arm around her shoulders.

"Okay." She leaned her head against him as they crossed the lot and went into the restaurant.

The place was packed and noisy, and Scarlett clung on to Shadow's arm like a vise as he weaved them through the labyrinth of people. They walked straight out of the roadhouse to the back patio, and he stopped at a table next to a railing in the corner. The rush of the Colorado River echoed through the valley, and she held on to the wood bannister and looked down at the clear water as it wended its way between the wildflower-dotted sloping banks.

"The water is lower than usual," she said, pushing away from the edge and joining him at the table.

"It's because we haven't had any rain for the past couple of months," he said.

"It's strange not to have our usual afternoon thunderstorms. I heard on the news last week that it's been one of the hottest summers on record. That's crazy, huh?"

"Yeah, well, I won't go into my theory about that."

"Let me guess—conspiracy all the way." Scarlett poked his upper arm lightly.

He laughed. "You know me." He held up his middle finger. "To the establishment."

"The true rebel." She squeezed his bicep. "That's one of the things I like about you."

Shadow swiveled in the wrought iron chair, an amused smirk playing across his lips. "There are more things?"

She nodded. "A lot ... Like how you listen to me go on about my friends or my family when they piss me off, even though I know you think I'm overreacting ... or how you laugh at my lame attempts to be funny or the way you hold me and tell me that you have my back ... and so many other things."

He looked away, his gaze fixed on the vista of mountains and evergreens.

*Oh shit. I gushed too much. He's feeling pressured, like he has to say something back about me.* She cleared her throat, but before she could say anything, his eyes shifted back to hers. She bit the inside of her cheek and her heart squeezed: lurking in his stormy orbs was pain. *Did I cause that?*

"My mother was murdered. Stabbed—it was brutal," he said, both anger and sadness in his voice.

Shock swept through Scarlett as a rush of tears welled her eyes. She reached out and stroked his arm as she took in a heart-jolting breath. "I'm so sorry. I ... don't know what to say. How horrible."

A small shrug, then a quick shake of his head. "There's nothing to say—I just wanted to tell you."

A silence stretched between them, and her mind whirled with a slew of questions that she wanted to ask Shadow but didn't.

"Sorry for the delay," a perky waitress with large breasts encased in a tight top said as she put down two glasses of water, plates, and cutlery wrapped in napkins on the table. "Do you want something to drink?"

"Coors on tap," Shadow said.

"Uh ... I don't know. Do you have mango margaritas?"

The waitress looked over her shoulder at the inside of the restaurant. "Nope—just the regular and strawberry."

"I'll take a strawberry one—frozen, please."

"Be right back," she said, then scurried away.

"This is a popular biker place," he said.

"Is that why the waitress is showing off her assets in a big way?"

He laughed. "Yeah—the bigger the tits, the better the tip."

There was another pocket of silence, only broken by the clink of glasses as another server put their drinks down on the table.

"Meghan's busy with two large parties inside, so I'm helping out." The cute brunette, who was also very well-endowed, smiled and took out a pad and pencil. "Do you know what you want?"

Shadow glanced at Scarlett. "Do you wanna share some nachos?"

The earnest expression on his face made her smile, and Scarlett nodded even though she had no appetite.

"Supreme or regular?" the waitress asked.

"Whatever you want," Scarlett said when he looked over at her.

"Supreme."

"Okay." The brunette slipped the notepad into the pocket of the red apron she wore around her waist.

"It seems like the two of us and that other couple are the only ones crazy enough to be sitting out here in the heat," Scarlett said as she watched the server hurry over to a table on the other side of the patio.

"Is it too hot for you? We can go inside," Shadow said as he started to pushed the chair back.

"No … I love it out here. It's quiet and beautifully serene. I can't believe how many small out-of-the-way places you know of to stop in for some food and drinks."

"It comes from years of exploring on my bike."

Scarlett sucked in a deep breath, then let it out. "Do you want to talk about it?" she asked softly.

"No … I just wanted to tell you."

"Okay, but can I ask a couple of questions?" She shook her head. "Forget what I just said. I shouldn't have asked that."

Shadow tucked her hand in his and locked his eyes on hers. "It's okay. You should ask me about anything, except club business. What do you wanna know?"

"Are you sure you're okay with this ... that it isn't too painful?" She pressed her lips together.

"Yeah—go ahead." He picked up the glass and took a gulp of beer.

"How old were you when your mother was killed?"

"Fifteen." Another gulp of beer.

Playing with the small red straw that came with her drink, Scarlett dipped her head down and took a small sip. "Did you know the person who did it?"

A long pause, then she saw his jaw tighten and the veins in his left temple bulge. "It was her fuckin' sugar daddy," he gritted out.

"How horrible. I wonder if my parents knew him or if I know the name."

"He's from here, but that's all I know about the sonofabitch. The damn badges never caught the fucker."

In that instant, Scarlett understood the darkness that engulfed him. *How terrible it must be to know the man who murdered your mother is still free and enjoying life.*

"The asshole probably skipped town. I'll find him—I won't rest until I do."

"You never met him."

Shadow gripped his glass of beer, then brought it to his mouth. Looking over the rim at her, he said, "No—my mom wanted it that way. I should've tried to find out who the fucker was, but I respected her wishes. Fuck!" He slammed the glass back on the table without taking a drink.

"Here you go," a tall and skinny man said as he placed a platter in the middle of the table. "And here are some extra napkins. Enjoy."

"The nachos here are pretty good," Shadow said as he unwrapped his cutlery.

"Nachos, wings, and barbecue are your favorites. Oh ... and steak. I can't forget that." She smiled even though her heart was breaking for him.

"Steak … the way you grill it with those peppers and eggplant is way better than any restaurant." He put a healthy portion of stuffed chips on a plate and gave it to her.

Looking down at it, her stomach churned. "I'll have to pick up some steaks to grill for this weekend. Are you free on Sunday?"

He laughed. "I'm planning on spending the weekend with you, babe, so … yeah, I'm free."

"I wish it were already Friday." She leaned against him and he turned and brushed his lips across hers before he popped in a bite of food.

"I just want to tell you that I'm so sorry you had to grow up without your parents. I remember you told me your dad had died when you were young."

"Yeah—some guy slit his throat in a bar fight, and it was the best news I ever got in my life." He chewed for several seconds. "It may sound shocking, but the man was a useless piece of shit who treated my mom like utter dirt and got his kicks beating the shit outta her and me. Believe me—I didn't shed any tears when he got wasted."

Scarlett scraped most of the toppings off a chip, then picked it up and nibbled on it. "I'm not very hungry," she said in response to his bemused look.

"You feeling okay?"

"Yes." She put the half-eaten chip back on the plate and placed her hand on Shadow's shoulder and gripped it. "Thank you for trusting me enough to tell me about your mother. Losing your mom like that and not having justice for her death can really eat you alive, so I just want you to know I'm here for you if you ever want to talk."

Shadow nodded and scooped up several more chips with his fork.

Resting back against the chair, Scarlett sipped her margarita as she watched Shadow eat. That first time she'd seen him at Brooke's engagement party, her lust and rebellious streak drove her to him. It was only supposed to have been a hookup for that moment in time. Scarlett shook her head, a smile whispering across her lips. Shadow was the last man she ever thought she'd be in a relationship with, but he just swept her off her feet when she least expected it. He challenged the way she was raised, the rules of her world, and she couldn't imagine her life without him. Scarlett loved him so completely, and she wanted to calm the storms inside him from his mangled past and hold and comfort the little boy in him that was still in so much pain after all these years.

The late afternoon sun filtered through the thin fabric of the overhead umbrella and danced on her skin. As Shadow put his knife and fork on the empty platter, the clink of utensils startled Scarlett from her musings.

"You're a million miles away, baby," he said, crumpling his napkin into a ball.

"Just enjoying being with you."

Shadow leaned over and snaked an arm around her shoulders, then pulled her against him. "We're good together."

It was a simple statement filled with so much meaning. She cocked her head and looked up at him. "We are."

Cupping her chin with his hand, he bent down and kissed her.

Scarlett wanted to tell him that she loved him with a fire that could never be extinguished, but she held back, afraid to break the intimate thread connecting them at that moment.

The skinny guy came back and cleared off the table, and Shadow broke away from her as he took out his wallet and placed a couple of bills on the table.

"I'll be right back with your change," the server said.

"I'm good." The legs of Shadow's chair squeaked against the wooden floor as he pushed away from the table.

"Thanks, man." The waiter balanced the dishes and glasses on the tray in his right hand and walked away.

"I wonder if he'll split the tip with the other two."

"He will 'cause he knows they'll beat the shit outta him if he doesn't." Shadow chuckled and placed his hand on the small of her back as they walked through the noisy restaurant.

"Are you going to stay the night?" she asked when they stopped in front of his motorcycle.

"Yeah." He took out his sunglasses and put them on. "The sun at this time of day's brutal when you're riding to the west."

Nodding, she slid her hand into her pocket and pulled out a pair of Christian Dior shades. As she put them on, Shadow stepped closer then leaned in, his nose against her hair, his lips touching the shell of her ear.

"I love you, woman," he whispered.

Heat flushed to her face as a million butterflies exploded inside her. She wanted to break out in song and dance around the parking lot. Hearing him say those three words took her by surprise in the best possible way. Knowing they loved each other meant that no matter how complicated everything was, no matter how tough their journey ahead might be, they were in it together. *Together!* She melted inside and a warm throb rose through her.

"I love you so much." She buried her face in his neck, then kissed him hard.

"Scarlett," he growled, gripping the sides of her face with his strong fingers. "Fuck, darlin'."

Then, she tipped her head back, and Shadow claimed her mouth, swallowing her small moans. The kiss was possessive, passionate, and full of love, and they clung to each other, fused together as one.

When he finally broke away, Scarlett had to hold on to his arm for fear of falling: he was her rock in a sometimes swaying world.

He tweaked her nose, then swung his leg over the bike and started the engine before she climbed on behind him. He made a smooth half circle then sped out of the lot. As they rode along the silvery river, happiness filled every inch of her, and she held him tight and pressed close against his warm body.

# CHAPTER NINETEEN

S HADOW SAT IN one of the chairs in front of his president's desk, staring out the window while he waited for Banger to finish a conversation on the phone. Part of him wondered why he'd been summoned to his office, and he racked his brain trying to figure out if he fucked something up at the dispensary or Dream House the last time he'd worked at those businesses.

"I got a phone call yesterday evening," Banger said as he slid his phone into the inner pocket of his cut. "Got any idea who it was from?" The president shifted in his chair, the springs squeaking as he tipped back.

"No," Shadow said. "Why don't you just tell me."

"Pamela Mansfield. You know who she is, right?" Banger scowled. "Yeah, of course you do—you're fucking her daughter."

Anger streaked through Shadow, and he jumped to his feet with his hands clenched in fists, resting against his thighs. "My personal life isn't club business," he growled.

"It is when it fucks up a club project like the building on the west side of town."

"Bullshit! That tight-ass bitch has been fighting the club for months—way before I met Scarlett."

"Sit the fuck down," Banger snapped, and Shadow sank back into the chair. "She called to propose a truce—we get our building without any more BS and you stop fucking her daughter." The president shrugged. "Seems reasonable to me, especially since we're losing thousands of dollars on this project being held up because of that *tight ass.*"

"I'm not gonna stop seeing Scarlett. I can't believe you'd even *talk* to that stuck-up rich bitch, let alone *agree* with her." He smoldered with resentment.

"Get another chick—if you want a rich one, ask Eli—he's marrying one. No reason to fuck the club over just 'cause this woman's wetting your cock. Plenty of pussy around to do that. Hell, we got nine club girls willing to do that, and I hear we may be adding one or two more."

"Scarlett's not just another pussy." His jaw tightened as he bit back the words *you asshole.*

Banger leaned forward and the springs of his chair creaked loudly. "You got something going on with this citizen besides having a good time?"

Locking his gaze on his president's, Shadow pumped his legs out in front of him. "Yeah."

For a short pause the only sound in the room was their breathing, then a loud guffaw erupted from Banger, his mouth splitting into a wide grin.

"Well, I'll be damned," he said, shaking his head. "You're like Hawk—you like them rich women." The president's blue eyes crinkled at the edges like candy wrappers.

Shadow crossed his legs at the ankle. "So tell the bitch to go fuck herself. She's been trying to break the two of us up since she found out about us."

"I bet she has. I just never thought you'd go for a woman like—"

"Like *what?*" His body stiffened.

"Whoa … calm the fuck down. I was gonna say *her,* meaning rich and high society. I know you've got a problem with rich folks. Just took me by surprise, that's all. At first I didn't even believe the bitch when she called, but Smokey told me you'd been having a fling with the daughter for a while." Banger shook his head again. "I just can't believe it."

"Scarlett's different from the others in that world. Anyway, you can't judge a person by the social class they belong to. Look at Cara and Hawk."

Banger held his hands up. "You don't need to convince me of anything. You're the one that's gonna have to go through a minefield, what with her being the daughter of George Mansfield and all. I guess you must think she's worth it."

*Worth it?* Hell, Scarlett was the only woman who satisfied him in a way no other woman ever had or ever could. She was the blowtorch that had melted away the steel around his heart, then filled in all the dark places. She made him all kinds of crazy in the best damn way. But there was no way in hell he was going to tell Banger any of that.

"She is," Shadow answered in a low voice.

Banger rubbed his hands over his face, then looked over at him. "You gonna have a problem if we gotta do some strong persuasion to get the old bitch off our backs?"

"Not at all—it's club business."

"Okay then, I'll tell this *Pamela tight-ass Mansfield* to go to hell."

The corners of his mouth twitched as Shadow lifted his chin at the president.

"Hawk wanted to talk to you about that ledger you found at that woman's house. I'll text him to come in here 'cause I wanna hear what he has to say. We gotta find this fucker to give you peace of mind and let your mama rest."

"Yeah." Shadow's chest tightened. "I'm closer than those damn badges ever were."

There was a rap on the door and then it swung open, and Hawk pumped his fist in the air at Banger and Shadow.

"Turns out that lover boy here has the hots for *Miss Mansfield*, so I'm gonna tell her bitch mom to fuck off," Banger said.

Hawk's brows raised slightly as he looked at Shadow. "No shit. You got a bumpy road ahead of you, dude. Cara's dad has done some legal stuff for George Mansfield. She told me that Mansfield likes to play dirty—so watch your back."

"Yeah. So what did you find out about Flo and all those deposits?"

"It was what you thought—she was blackmailing someone. I pulled the records on her condo, and she purchased it fourteen years ago."

"A year after my mom's murder," he said under his breath.

"It was a cash purchase. She'd been getting greedier over the last two years, asking for more and more—at least that's what the ledger shows. The deposits were made by her into three different bank accounts—two in town and one in Denver. The bad news is that there's no notes or anything about who was giving her the money, but I'd say the person or persons paying her every month lived in town. Sometimes there was more than one deposit a month, especially in the last two years. She had to have been meeting up with the killer to get the money. I checked with the post office, and your mom's friend never had a PO box."

"It's not believable that the killer would've sent all that money to her by mail," Shadow said. "Maybe the money was wired to her and she picked it up."

"Not for the kind of money she was getting. It started out at about five grand a month, but your friend kept raising it each year, right up until this past year when forty grand was her monthly take," Hawk said as he took out three joints from the pocket of his cut. "Her greed got her killed."

Shadow took the joint from the vice president and held it between his thumb and index finger. "Flo must've gotten the vibe that the killer was sick of paying her demands. She was definitely running scared. She should've told me who killed my mom that day on the phone. After living off my mom's death, she fuckin' owed that to me." He placed the joint between his lips and lit it.

"I'm still trying to figure it out, bro. I'll keep digging to see if I can find a loose strand. The killer was a very rich man—he's paid a fortune to your mom's friend over all these years—well over several million bucks," Hawk said.

"Did anyone besides this Flo woman know you were meeting up with her?" Banger asked after he blew out a stream of smoke.

"I don't think so, but the killer may have gotten it out of her before he offed her." Shadow inhaled deeply, held it for a second, then exhaled, watching the smoke rise toward the ceiling.

"Be extra vigilant," Hawk said. "I know this fucker's still in Pinewood Springs. I just feel it, you know?"

"I do too—I always have. Every time Scarlett talks about her upcoming fundraiser and all the donors, I can't help wondering, *Is this guy the one, or is it that one? ...* It's driving me fuckin' nuts." He slammed his fist on his thigh.

"I don't blame you, but you gotta stay focused and put up a barrier between your emotions and finding this bastard, otherwise you'll jeopardize your safety," Banger said.

"I know, but sometimes it's damn hard." Shadow stubbed out the joint. "Thanks, dude," he said to Hawk as he pushed up from the chair. "I owe you. Next time we go out for chow, it's on me."

"Sounds good, bro." Hawk bumped fists with him.

"We done here?" he asked Banger and the president nodded. Shadow lifted his chin then walked out of the room.

"Did Banger kick your horny ass?" Smokey asked the minute Shadow walked into the main room.

"Nah, but he's ready to kick that Mansfield bitch's ass." He pulled out a chair and sat down.

"He seemed pretty pissed at you for fucking the bitch's daughter," Smokey said.

"Yeah, but he's cool now. I might as well tell you that Scarlett is my woman, so respect that *and* her."

"Sure, dude. You must like complications in your life. Tangling with George Mansfield is demanding trouble." Smokey shook his head, then picked up his sandwich.

Once a brother declared a woman as his girlfriend or old lady, the members shifted their focus. They accepted and respected that she was their brother's woman.

"I'm glad we finished the project at Mansfield's house," Smokey said. "I bet if he'd known what had been going on while we were there, he would've pulled the plug."

"I would've made up the difference," Shadow replied as he picked up the shot of Jack the prospect gave him.

"The next six weeks we're inside with big-ass fans while we work. The heat's gotta break soon—we're already in August."

"I'm just glad that most of my jobs are inside air conditioned homes," Animal said as he put the plate down on the table and sat in a chair.

"You're not working today?" Smokey asked.

"I was in the area and thought I'd stop by for lunch. I talked to Chains last night and he said that he and a bunch of other Night Rebels are gonna be at the rally next month."

"That's cool. I haven't seen Chains in quite a while. How's he doing?" Shadow asked.

"Good." Animal cut into his burrito. "Do you have any faucets at the warehouse?"

Shadow nodded. "Just standard ones."

"I'll come by later this afternoon to check them out. I'm gonna need four of them. I expect you to give me a good price." He chuckled.

"Only the best for my brothers. I'm gonna head out now, but I'll see you later on." Shadow rose to his feet and took his keys out of the back pocket of his jeans.

"You want to join Bones, Helm, Hubcap, and me for a ride? We're going to Lakeview, grab some barbecue at Fat Daddy's Smokehouse then ride back," Smokey said.

"Sounds tempting, but I have to catch up on some work, then I've gotta be somewhere. Let's plan on a long ride next week. Later." Shadow turned around and walked out of the club.

The birds chirping in the trees were soon drowned out by the low rumble of his motorcycle. The bike's wheels crunched on the gravel as he rode off the lot. The road to town was quiet, and Shadow veered off to the north and took a shortcut to the warehouse. He parked his Harley, then welcomed the cool air inside the building as he headed to his office down the hall.

An hour into listing items on his online store, several raps on the door broke his concentration, and Shadow glanced over. "Come in."

The door swung open and a man, who Scarlett bore a striking resemblance to, loomed in the doorframe. Fine lines creased his face, and his thick blond hair was short and graying at the temples. The man wore an expensive light gray suit, a crisp white shirt, and a purple paisley tie, and the gold watch on his left wrist gleamed under the recessed lighting. For an older man he was quite fit: trim, broad shoulders, and muscular. He was tall and looked like he might have played college football back in the day. Dark green eyes bore into Shadow's with fierce intensity.

"So you're the man who's been fooling around with my daughter and creating all the ruckus in my household," George Mansfield said.

Shadow didn't say a word or move a muscle, he just sat there stony-faced, watching Scarlett's father walk over to the desk and settle into the black vinyl chair in front of it.

"Your name's Shadow, right?" His voice was gruff and impatient.

"You know that. Let's cut through the bullshit."

A deep laugh rumbled from his chest. "I like a man who gets down to business." Mansfield leaned forward. "Stay the fuck away from my daughter. There's no in-between here. I know your type, and Scarlett's fool enough to think you're serious, but I know you're just having some fun."

"You don't know shit," Shadow said, his gaze never wavering.

"I know you belong to that damn outlaw club. You think I want my daughter mixed up with a hoodlum? Don't fucking underestimate me. This thing with Scarlett stops ... *Now*." His meaty fist pounded the desk, knocking over a cup of pens.

Raw anger shot through Shadow, but he held it in check, the face of his woman playing through his mind. *Scarlett wouldn't like it if I beat the shit outta her old man, but he's itching for it in the worst way.*

George sat back in the chair, his gaze piercing. Shadow drummed his fingers on the steel desk then pressed his lips together.

"You had your say, now get the hell out of my office." Ice dripped from every word.

Scarlett's father didn't respond, instead, he just sat there staring at him. For a nanosecond, Shadow saw something in the old man's eyes that startled, angered, and confused him all at the same time. He couldn't pinpoint what it was, but it felt familiar and strangely unfamiliar at once.

Shadow cleared his throat. "I have work to do and you've taken up enough of my time. What Scarlett and I do is *our* business. I respect that you're her father, but you don't call the shots anymore—she's all grown up and living *her* life."

"This isn't just about you and her. What you're doing is affecting a lot of people."

"Then they need to get a fuckin' life and stay out of ours." Shadow stood up from his chair. "I'm gonna ask you one last time to leave."

"Or what? You're nothing but a goddamn thug. I can imagine what your …" Mansfield's voice trailed away.

His blood turned cold. "My *what*?" Shadow took a few steps toward the older man. His pulse pounded so loudly in his ears that he could barely make out the words spilling from George Mansfield's mouth.

"*Parents* is what I was going to say." The man's voice became clearer as Shadow pushed down his emotions.

"What?" Shadow asked.

"I can imagine what your parents would think about you being an Insurgent." George darted his eyes away from Shadow's.

"Did you know them … my mother?" Shadow asked, his voice low.

Mansfield fixed his gaze on him. "No."

"But you know my parents are dead. I'll bet Charlie Bowen told you." Shadow smirked when Scarlett's father's eyes widened slightly. "Yeah—I made him real fast. If you wanted to know about me, you should've asked *me*—not hire some fuckin' private investigator. You wasted your money."

"I figured that out when Bowen made up some BS excuse why he couldn't finish the job. What did you do—threaten him? That's something your club does routinely, isn't it?" He rubbed his hand over his chin. "Charlie told me about your folks, and I remembered it, so that's why I didn't finish the sentence. I thought it was in poor taste for me to bring up your deceased parents." Mansfield pushed up from the chair. "Anyway, this"—he waved a hand between him and Shadow— "isn't about any of that. I don't want you seeing my daughter any-more—plain and simple. You got her all mixed up, and she has a very nice young man who wants to marry her."

"Warren?" Shadow snorted. "A real good catch."

The door opened and Animal popped his head inside. "Sorry, I didn't know you were busy. I'll ask Scott to show me those faucets."

"No, come on in," Shadow said, narrowing his eyes at Mansfield. "We're done."

"I don't plan to let this go," Scarlett's dad said as he walked out of the room.

"Who was that?" Animal asked.

"Scarlett's old man. He came by to tell me to stay away from his daughter."

"And you're gonna listen, right?" Animal busted out laughing, and Shadow joined in as he strode over to the window.

He watched George Mansfield drive off in a black Cadillac. "There was something odd about him."

"Whaddaya mean?" Animal went over to the small fridge and took out a can of Coke, then popped the top.

"I don't know. He kept staring at me, but not like he was trying to intimidate me or act tough. It was like something was there—then it wasn't. I can't explain it. For a split second, I wondered if he was the man my mom was seeing."

Animal started coughing and choking. "You think Scarlett's dad killed your mom? Fuck, dude, that's just ... I don't know. It's fuckin' weird."

Shadow scrubbed his face with his fist. "I know. I just got that stab in the gut, but then it passed real quick. I don't know ... It was just the way he kept looking at me."

"Maybe he's bi and wants a piece of your ass." Animal laughed.

Shadow punched him in the arm, then shook his head. "Forget I said anything. I'm just pissed as hell that he came over here to tell me to stay away from Scarlett. We're not in fuckin' high school."

"You shoulda kicked him in the ass and sent him packin'." Animal tossed the empty can in the trash.

"I would've, but I didn't think Scarlett would appreciate me beating up her dad." Shadow walked out of the room.

"Yeah—chicks are funny about that, although I think Olivia would love it if I punched her dad in the face a few times." Animal chuckled.

"But she doesn't get along with her dad. Scarlett's daddy's girl—even though she'd never admit to it." He opened a door and they entered a large room. Rows of shelves with products on them lined the center of the room and the walls. "The faucets are nice, and I can give you a rock bottom price on the four of them."

"Sounds like we've got a deal," Animal said as he followed Shadow to the back of the room.

The rest of the afternoon flew past, and by six o'clock Shadow was ready to pack it in. As he was closing the browser on the computer, the phone rang and a grin spread over his face when he saw Scarlett's name on the screen.

"Hey, babe."

"Hi. Are you still at work?"

"Just heading out. Are you at home?"

"I just got in. I had a great day at work."

"So you're liking your job?"

"I love it. I'm hoping I can transition to full-time when a spot opens up."

"If you want it bad enough, it'll happen."

"I would make a lot more money. How was your day?"

"Interesting." Shadow decided he'd tell her about her dad's visit when they were together. "Are you up for El Tecolote? I got a hankering for their smothered green chile tacos."

"That sounds so good. I'm starving."

Shadow locked the outside door and strode over to his Harley. "Me too. I'll be there in fifteen."

"Come on up because I want to change out of my work clothes."

"See you soon."

He slid the phone into the pocket of his cut, then got on his bike and took off toward Scarlett's place.

When she opened the door, he swept her up in his arms and kissed her passionately.

"I missed you, darlin'," he whispered against her lips, walking her backward into the condo. The fruity scent of her shampoo filled his nostrils, and he inhaled deeply. "You smell good."

"Shadow," she sighed, leaning into him.

Her nipples were hard against the thin fabric of her top, and he groaned and rubbed against her.

"Fuck, darlin'." He gently took her earlobe between his teeth, nipping it.

Scarlett audibly sucked in a breath. Her hand on his bicep curled into the fabric of his T-shirt, drawing him even closer.

He trailed kisses down her neck and then over the top of her shoulder and back along the curve toward her ear, and with each of Scarlett's moans and whimpers, Shadow's cock ached for release. He buried his hand in her hair and pulled her in so tight that it was like they were fused together. Then he slowly inched his mouth over to hers and kissed her over and over again. Quick kisses. Long, slow kisses. Gentle lip brushes. Tiny nips and passionate caresses.

Shadow pulled back a bit and ran the back of his fingers over the side of her face. Scarlett's eyes were heated with desire, yet soft with arousal, and damn, she was beautiful.

"Scarlett," he growled, then his mouth came to hers again, hard and demanding.

She clawed at his back, tongues meshed together, groans bounced off the walls.

"Shadow," she moaned.

"Fuck, baby," he rasped as he broke away and yanked her shirt over her shoulders. His mouth fused to hers again, then tore down her throat and over her tits as his teeth nipped and his hands squeezed—possessing, bruising as they moved over her body.

Scarlett grabbed at his T-shirt, and he moved back a bit to let her push it up and run her fingers over his muscles and down to the waistband of his jeans. He pressed his hard cock against her, loving the way she moaned in frustration as she tried to undo the belt buckle.

Then Shadow slid his hands under her skirt and jerked her panties down, and her head fell back on a sharp cry.

"I need you," he said as he whirled her around and slammed her against the wall. He threw her lacy underwear on the ground, pulled down his boxers and jeans, then unclasped the front of her bra and sucked one of her hard nipples in his mouth while he tweaked the other with his fingers.

"Oh God," she said, gripping his shoulders.

Unable to hold out anymore, Shadow lifted her up and her legs curled tightly around him. He grabbed her ass with one hand and shoved into her.

"Fuck," he grunted.

"Feels so good," she panted. "I want it hard and fast."

"You got it, baby." Shadow's hands squeezed her ass cheeks.

He pulled out then thrust into her, her back against the wall, their mouths connected, and her heels digging into his back as he banged her exactly how she wanted it.

"So fuckin' good," he rasped as he pushed hard and deeper.

"I'm close, Shadow."

Their voices filled the foyer, and Scarlett screamed out his name. And then all the tension in his balls released into a quick burst of intense pleasure shooting through his dick.

"Scarlett ... fuck!"

They clung to each other like a vise, their orgasms washing over them. Then they slid to the floor, panting in each other's ears, their bodies sated.

After the wave of rapture faded, he smothered her face with kisses and then helped her up before pulling up his jeans and buckling his belt.

"Let me go freshen up before we go." Scarlett brushed her lips across his, and he lightly swatted her behind as she bent down to retrieve her panties.

"Love your ass, babe." He winked at her and watched her rounded cheeks jiggle as she walked toward the bedroom.

Shadow strode into the living room and over to the wall of windows. Warmth spread through him as he gazed at the purple-edged clouds stretched across a glowing, burnished copper sky that highlighted the mountain tops.

*My woman's in my heart.* Scarlett had come into his life, burning brighter than the evening sky, catching his soul on fire. He chuckled. *And I never saw it coming.*

"Ready?" Scarlett's body pressed against his back, the scent of her wafting around him. She stood on her tiptoes and kissed the back of his neck tenderly. "I'm starving."

Shadow turned around and brushed his lips against hers. "Let's go."

"Okay, but I wanted to give this to you." She pressed a key into the palm of his hand. "It's to the condo."

For a long pause, he stared at the shiny gold-toned key as a mixture of emotions coursed through him: love, pride, surprise, and happiness. *She trusts me completely, and there's no fuckin' way I'll ever let her down.*

"Are you okay with having it?" Trepidation crept into her voice.

He hugged Scarlett and kissed the side of her head, pressing his face in her hair.

"I'm more than okay with it," he murmured.

After a few seconds, Shadow broke away and tucked her hand into his.

"I love you," she said, leaning against him.

"Me too, woman."

Scarlett closed the door behind them, and they walked hand-in-hand to the elevator.

# CHAPTER TWENTY

URSING UNDER HER breath, Scarlett zigzagged her vehicle through traffic with one foot on the accelerator and one hand on the horn. Tour buses packed with people hanging out the windows and taking pictures crawled through the streets.

"Take a picture of a tree because you don't have any where you're from. So fucking ridiculous!" she griped out loud as she blared the horn at a group of pedestrians ready to cross against the light.

The tires of the Mercedes squealed as she rounded the corner too fast. Deep breaths and a death grip on the steering wheel didn't do much to extinguish the burning anger with her dad. That morning, before Shadow had left for work, he'd told her about her dad coming by the warehouse the day before. At first she couldn't believe it, and then the anger began to build until it bubbled over well after Shadow had left. What her dad did was out of control. *I'm a grown woman. I'm so damn sick of being told what to do. It's my life.* She slammed the heel of her hand against the steering wheel and winced as pain shot up her forearm.

It wasn't that Scarlett thought her parents would accept Shadow, it was just that she'd hoped they'd at least *respect* her decision. *Dad is such a bully.* A smile tugged at her lips when she pictured Shadow telling her father to leave. *I guess you've met your match, Dad.*

When the Mercedes slowed down, Scarlett pressed the remote and the tall iron gates swung open; she drove through and headed up the driveway toward the five-car garage. She knew her mom was at a charity event with several of her friends, thus the reason Scarlett picked this moment to confront her dad. He refused to go to the majority of the charity fundraisers to which her mother was invited, opting to only attend the black tie events on Saturday nights. He blamed his busy work schedule as the reason he begged off most of the time, but Scarlett suspected that her dad preferred the company of other women to that of her mother. From what she had witnessed over the years, her parents' marriage seemed to be one of convenience more than of love and companionship.

Just short of running the Mercedes into the wall, Scarlett stormed out of the car and into the house. She rushed past Clara and Jane with a mere wave of her hand and a quick "Hello" and crossed through the massive dining room until she arrived at her father's office. The carved cherry wood door was cracked open a sliver, and Scarlett was just ready to charge through when she heard the voice of Warren's father.

*What the hell is Mr. Huntington doing over here?* Her parents weren't good friends with the family even though they constantly told Scarlett how wonderful the Huntingtons were and how lucky she was that Warren was interested in her. It had grated on her nerves most of the time and made her want to gag whenever they started the whole "Warren is such a nice man" broken record.

"I'm asking you again, George—what the fuck are you going to do about this?" Bruce Huntington's voice boomed.

"I'm trying to make the young man understand how foolish the situation is since Scarlett is hellbent on carrying out her rebellion." Her dad's voice sounded frustrated … and tired, a string of guilt pulled at her heart.

"That's not good enough. This lowlife biker is seeing dollar signs, so he's not going to just walk away. You have to fight insolence with a strong and heavy hand."

There was a long pause followed by the sound of ice cubes clinking against glass. She imagined her dad pouring his favorite whiskey into the tumbler, then taking a long drink. The *thump* of the glass meant it hit either the wood desk or the end table, if they were seated next to the fireplace.

"Seems like your boy couldn't keep my daughter interested. It's a phase she's going through and it'll pass. I'm a patient man when I have to be," her dad said.

"Patient my ass! And Warren did everything a gentleman should do with a woman. He can't help it if Scarlett likes trash. You and I had a deal, George. I can't wait any longer."

*A deal? I* knew *it! Dad and Mr. Huntington were using me and Warren as bargaining chips in their damn merger.* Heat rushed to her face and she pressed her hands lightly against her warm cheeks.

"I still want to develop the area, Bruce. I'm not reneging on the deal to buy your land. It's pretty obvious that Scarlett doesn't want your son. Her hooking up with this biker is my problem, not yours."

"The deal was that they would marry," Bruce Huntington said in a low voice. "Warren needs to marry Scarlett, and you need to make sure that happens."

There was a loud, deep laugh. "Your son doesn't need to do shit. I just said that Scarlett isn't fancying Warren—it happens. We can draw up the papers this week for the land sale."

*The initial bargain was for me to marry Warren for a land deal. How cold can you get?*

"I want them married—that was what we agreed on." Ice dripped from Bruce's words.

"It didn't work out. I'm not going to make my daughter marry someone she doesn't want. If you don't wish to sell the land, that's another thing. I'd like it, but I also have my eye on some other properties in the area."

"No … I still want to sell the land." Panic laced Huntington's voice. "I'll take care of this dirtbag—don't you worry about that."

Scarlett put her hand over her mouth to keep a gasp from escaping.

"Just let it be, Bruce."

"When someone fucks with *me* and my son, it becomes *my* problem. You should be enraged by this shit."

Unable to contain herself anymore, Scarlett pushed open the door and stalked into the room, her eyes narrowing as she glanced at her dad, then at Warren's father.

"And what *shit* are you talking about?" Satisfaction wove through her when she scanned both of their startled faces. "If you're talking about Shadow and me, Mr. Huntington, then I have to say that it's none of your business what I do or whom I date." A flash of anger rankled over her skin, like goosebumps raised by frigid air.

"Scarlett, what do you mean by bursting in here? We're having a private conversation." A frown pinched a space between her dad's brows as he turned the crystal tumbler around in his hand.

"A conversation about *me.*"

With a huff, Bruce Huntington pushed up from the leather wing-back chair, threw her a dirty look, then shook his head. "Manners are lost on the young today." He picked up a brown leather briefcase. "We'll be in touch, George." Not even deigning a glance in her direction, he marched out of the study.

"Good riddance," Scarlett muttered, then sank down in a chair opposite her dad. "I don't appreciate you going to Shadow's warehouse yesterday. If you have something to say, then tell *me*, not him." She folded her arms across her chest.

"You won't listen to sense, so I thought he would, but he's just as hardheaded as you are."

"I intend to stay that way. I love him, Dad. There … I said it."

George jerked his head back. "Love? That'll get you far. Marriage is hard, and in a couple of years that love you talk about will fade—and coming from the same background and understanding the elite society in which we live, that'll keep you together. You need a foundation."

Scarlett's hands fell down to her lap. "First of all, I'm talking about dating him, not marrying him. I'm only twenty-five, and I have a job I'd like to turn into a career. Besides, Shadow and I do have things in common." She laced her fingers together. "He's the one for me," she whispered.

"*The one*," her dad scoffed. "What the hell does that mean?"

"It means that I'm in love with him and I'd do anything for him. It's that simple and that perfect."

"You know your mother's sick about this." Her dad poured some more whiskey into the glass.

"She'll survive—she always does. She'll find some more charities to keep her busy."

"Don't talk disrespectfully about your mother. She loves you and wants the best for you."

"I don't think so," she said in a low voice. "Mom wants the best for *her*. Everything revolves around her."

Her dad brought the drink to his mouth.

"Why did you and Mom marry? The last time I saw any affection between the two of you was when I was a kid. Did you two ever love each other, or was your marriage one of convenience?"

George looked hard at her over the rim of the tumbler as he drained the last drop of whiskey.

"You young people think you invented love. How naïve and childish. There are all kinds of love … and affection. You don't have a damn clue. Your mother and I have a quiet understanding—a bond. We've been together for a long time. Enough said about that."

Scarlett wanted to ask him how he thinks her mother feels when he's with other women, but she held her tongue and glanced over at the window instead. Outside, glittering water danced from the mouths of several stone lions perched around the edge of a large fountain, creating mini rainbows of brilliant prismatic hues.

"I'm not going to break up with him," she whispered. Leather squeaked as her dad shifted in his chair.

"I know. Just promise me you won't rush into anything until you get to know him better."

Glancing at him, she nodded. "That's fair. Mom will be mad that you're not reading me the riot act or cutting me off."

A slow, tired smile whispered across his lips. "Would either of that do any good?"

"No," she replied.

"Then why go through the motions? You might not believe this, but I want what's best for you. That's why I thought Warren would've made a good husband."

"There was nothing sincere about the way you were shoving him down my throat. I can't believe that you used me as a damn bargaining chip with that loathsome Mr. Huntington. Way to go, *Dad*."

"It wasn't like that." He held his hand up in front of his face. "Let me finish. Yes, I would've received a bargain price on Huntington's land if you and Warren married, but I really thought the two of you were perfect for each other. He comes from the right background, has a good career … good schooling. What parent wouldn't want someone like that for their daughter? None—that's who."

"Warren didn't make me happy, and Shadow does."

"For now."

"This isn't just a crush or an infatuation kind of love. My heart hurts just thinking of my life without the joy he brings. That's the kind of love it is."

"When everything is great, that works. But life is full of ups and downs, of past events we wish we could change. Life can be wonderful and cruel, and I've always wanted to give you the world—to protect you from all the ugly bullshit. I feel like I've failed you."

In that moment, for the first time in her life, Scarlett saw her father as just a man and not as the domineering patriarch of the family.

Her heart squeezed. A lump filled her throat. "You haven't failed me," she murmured. Scarlett stood up and went over to her father. "I've always thought I disappointed *you*."

George shook his head. "I'm sorry I gave you that impression. You never knew your grandfather, but there was never any pleasing my dad. No matter how hard I tried, it was never good enough. I guess I was the same with you and your brothers."

"You've never talked about your childhood or your dad."

"Because it was a hard one, one I wanted to forget, but it stays here"—he tapped the side of his head—"forever."

She perched on the arm of his chair, then planted a kiss on the top of his head. He looked up and tweaked her chin, then poured another splash of liquor in the glass. They sat like that for a long time, their silence speaking louder than words, and then Scarlett rose to her feet.

"I have some errands to do," she said.

A slight nod of his head.

"So … I'll see you around." She walked toward the door.

"When do you work next week?"

Scarlett looked over her shoulder at her father. "Tuesday … why?"

"Do you want to meet for lunch at Barney's?"

"Okay," she replied, fighting a smile from spreading across her face. She wasn't sure if she could trust this newest gesture of friendship and … *love? Maybe, but I—we have to take baby steps.*

"Good. I'll meet you there at one." He threw back his glass.

"All right. I guess I'll see you then. Oh … Dad?"

George looked over at her, his brows raised slightly. "Yes?"

"Do you think Mr. Huntington will hurt Shadow?" The worry of something happening to him sliced through her and jabbed into her gut.

"He's more talk than anything. Bruce is mad because he's broke. He thought that if Warren married you, Bruce would reap the benefits. He doesn't know that I was planning to have his son sign a prenuptial agreement."

Scarlett chuckled. "You really are looking out for me."

"Always, and don't you forget it."

She smiled. "But you don't think Shadow's in danger?"

George rubbed a hand over his face. "I can't say for sure—money makes people do stupid things, but you should warn Shadow just in case."

The smile faded and concern lined her face. *If something happens to Shadow, I'll never forgive myself. He may be in danger because of me.*

"And don't go blaming yourself for this. I suspect that Shadow knows how to take care of himself just fine."

The grandfather clock in the corner chimed, and Scarlett knew her mother would be returning to the house soon. Not wanting to bump into her mom, she fumbled for the keys in the pocket of her sundress and glanced over at her dad.

"I'll see you."

"Next Tuesday," he said.

"Right. Bye."

She hurried to the garage and slipped inside her car. When she'd first arrived, Scarlett had been prepared to do battle with her father, but now it seemed as though the two of them had an unspoken truce.

Scarlett passed her mother, who didn't appear to have noticed her, while on the road not too far from her house. She let out a relieved breath. That night she'd make Shadow one of his favorite foods: grilled steak with mushrooms sautéed in butter and white wine. A warm, fuzzy feeling engulfed her when she thought of him. Each day, each hour, Scarlett fell deeper in love with him. Shadow was her safe place—she could turn to him regardless of her mood or situation. She felt completely at ease with him, and that had never happened to her with any other man before.

The car sped up as Scarlett made her way to the grocery store. She wanted to do a quick shopping before heading home to start dinner. She couldn't wait to see him that night. It seemed like they missed each other whenever they weren't together, but they were also cool to let each have their space. Shadow liked to hang with his friends and go out riding with the guys, and she loved meeting up with her friends for drinks and a good meal.

"I'm so in love with you," she said, smiling.

And there was no way in hell Scarlett would let anyone or anything get between her and her man.

Once she parked, Scarlett slipped out of the car, grabbed a cart, and hurried into the store as thoughts of spending a romantic evening with him played in her mind.

# Chapter Twenty-One

"WHEN ARE WE gonna meet this woman who's been occupying most of your time?" Helm asked as he took a joint out from his pocket.

"I don't know," Shadow grunted, leaning back in the white wicker chair.

"How do you like these big-ass cushions the club girls bought?" Bones jerked his chin toward the one behind Shadow's back.

"They're pretty comfortable. The print is gaudy as all hell—neon pink flamingos and huge-ass flowers? Give me a fuckin' break." Shadow stretched out his legs while putting his hands behind his head.

Bones chuckled. "I'm glad I'm not the only one who thinks they're fuckin' ugly."

"I'm not crazy 'bout them either, but there's no damn way I'm telling the girls that." Helm placed the joint between his lips, cupped his hand, and lit it.

"They tried, but I gotta say the cushions are comfortable. Way better than the thin ones we had before," Shadow said.

"So are you living with this girl you're dating?" Helm asked.

"No, we just hang out a lot," Shadow said. A lot meant that he spent four to five nights a week, at Scarlett's condo. He had to admit that he thought maybe they'd get sick of each other by now, but as time had gone by, he'd wanted to be with her even more. It was a totally new experience for him, but then he'd never been in love before. It was mind blowing, exhilarating, and fucking scary all mixed together, but it felt good … perfect even.

"Whatcha thinking about? Your forehead's all scrunched up like you're figuring out some hard calculation or some shit like that." Bones propped a leg up on the ottoman that matched the garish cushions on the patio furniture.

"I suck at math," Helm added, stubbing out his joint on the bottom of his shoe.

"I was just using that as an example." Bones rolled his eyes.

"And I was just saying that numbers and I don't mix. I can't even begin to figure out those fuckin' word problems about some kid having six apples, then another having ten oranges … fuck, man."

Bones leaned forward a bit, the muscles in his face tightening. "What the hell are you talking about?"

Shadow busted out laughing. "You guys are like some damn skit on Comedy Central."

A mask of confusion spread over Helm's face. "You're gonna try out for Comedy Central? I thought we were talking about the kids and the fruit and how many the other kid has. When Animal helps Lucy with that shit, it hurts my brain. Fuck."

Bones clenched his hands into fists, then unclenched them. "I was never talking about math or apples or whatever the fuck you're saying. That joint you smoked must've had a strong-as-hell strain."

"Huh?" Helm said as he rested his head on the back of the chair and closed his eyes. His legs were crossed, and his left leg began to rock back and forth to the music from inside the clubhouse.

Bones cut his gaze to Shadow. "I don't even remember what the fuck I was saying in the first place."

"Something about math calculations." A grin pulled up on his lips.

"Don't you go starting that shit up. We finally got *him* to shut the fuck up." Bones raked his fingers through his hair. "I wonder where he got the stuff."

"Probably from that new strain our dispensary produced. Hawk said it was kickass. I guess he was right." Shadow chuckled. "I haven't tried it yet."

"Yeah, well, I was just getting ready to punch him to shut him up."

Bones reached over and grabbed a can of beer. "Shit—it's warm as piss." He craned his neck, attempting to look around the doorframe into the club. Then he put two fingers to his mouth and whistled. "Wendy! Get out here!"

A curvy brunette in a tight-fitting T-shirt dress sashayed toward them. Her blue eyes danced as she sized up Bones and Shadow.

"What do you boys want?" The tip of tongue slowly skimmed her top lip.

"Fuck," Bones muttered under his breath.

"Can you bring us two cans of beer." Shadow picked up the one Bones put back on the tabletop. "This one's warm."

"Sure. I don't know how you guys can stand it out here in the heat." She glanced up at the ceiling and pointed at the twirling fan. "That's just moving the hot air around. I'd be melting sitting here."

"I wouldn't mind seeing your luscious body gleaming in sweat, sweetheart," Bones said.

Wendy laughed. "I wouldn't mind seeing yours either. We could slide and slither against each other."

"That's an image that's making my cock wake up." Bones chuckled low in his throat.

Wendy giggled, and her long nails, painted a hot pink, thrummed against the back of one of the wicker chairs.

"When it's ready, come find me." She winked, flipping her silky hair over her shoulder.

Wendy bent down low to pick up the beer can from the table, the angle offering the men a generous view of her cleavage.

"Fuck, you're killing me," Bones muttered.

"Do you want anything else, Shadow?" The club girl jiggled her big tits before straightening back up.

"Just the beer. Thanks."

"Okay." Another wink then she walked away, her rounded hips swaying slightly.

"Damn," Bones said. "How the fuck can you give up the variety, dude?"

"Been there and done that more times than I can count." Shadow shifted in his chair; he didn't like talking about his feelings for Scarlett to his buddies.

"What's up with him?" Smokey asked, pointing to Helm, whose leg still rocked back and forth.

"He tried the new stuff we're producing," Shadow replied.

Smokey guffawed. "That's some strong shit. I smoked some last night in my room, and I was chair-locked for hours."

"The club should make a shitload of money on it." Shadow glanced down at his phone.

"That's what Banger and Hawk are banking on." Smokey plopped down on a chair next to Bones.

Shadow nodded while opening the text.

**Scarlett:** *Everything ok?*

Shadow scrubbed his face with his free hand. When his woman had told him about Warren's dad threatening to hurt him, Shadow thought it was adorable as fuck that Scarlett worried and fussed over him. But now, five days and counting, her concern had started griping his ass.

**Shadow:** *I'm fine, babe. U don't need to worry.*

**Scarlett:** *I'm not. Just asking. What're u doing?*

**Shadow:** *Sitting with Smokey & Bones. We're watching a stoned-as-fuck Helm.*

**Scarlett:** *Sounds stimulating. Hehe.*

**Shadow:** *How was ur lunch with ur dad?*

**Scarlett:** *Good. He didn't raise his voice once or bring u up. Wonder what he's got up his sleeve.*

**Shadow:** *Maybe nothing. Don't worry so much.*

"Here you are." Wendy rubbed her ample chest against his arm as she set the beer can in front of him."

Shadow glanced up. "Thanks."

"I brought you some mixed nuts because I know how much you like them." She threw him a warm smile.

"Thanks again." He looked back down at the phone.

*Scarlett: I can't help it. With my dad it's definitely the calm b4 the storm.*

*Shadow: Whatever your family or that fuck Huntington dishes out, we can handle. How's work?*

*Scarlett: Good. R u coming over tonight? I hope so.*

He looked up from the phone.

"Are we still going for a ride this evening?" he asked Smokey.

"Yeah. Chas, Axe, Cruiser, Blade, Animal, and Wheelie are gonna join us."

"I'm getting in on that too," Bones said as he stood up. "But first I got some pussy I need to eat."

Shadow and Smokey chuckled as Bones scurried after Wendy.

"He left his beer, so it's mine now," Smokey said, popping the top.

The phone vibrated against his thigh as Shadow took a long pull of his drink.

"You talkin' to Scarlett? I'm surprised her old man hasn't hired someone to take you out, dude." Smokey scooped up a handful of nuts and popped some in his mouth.

"Believe me—my guard's up just for that."

He checked out the latest text his woman sent.

*Scarlett: R u there?*

*Shadow: Sorry, babe. Talkin' with Smokey. Tonight I'll be over at around 9. Some buddies and me are going for a ride and some chow.*

*Scarlett: That'll be fun. I'll call Kiara and Ashley & see if they can do dinner.*

*Shadow: Then I'll see you at 9.*

*Scarlett:* Can't wait. Oh, I bought something.

Before he could respond, the phone vibrated again, then there was a picture of Scarlett wearing an ultra-sexy red lace teddy with peek-a-boo cut-outs over her tits that left little to the imagination. Another picture came through showing her sweet rounded ass in a thong. Shifting in the chair, he tried to relieve the pressure when his cock stirred. *Down, boy. Smokey'll have a heyday with this, and we don't fuckin' want that.*

*Scarlett:* Do u like it?

*Shadow:* Yeah—if I was there, I'd have u flat on your desk pounding into ur sweet, wet pussy. Fuck—u got me going now, and Smokey's here.

*Scarlett:* Sorry.

*Shadow:* No you're not. U like teasing me …

For the rest of the time until he saw Scarlett, all he'd see was the picture of her in that skimpy teddy in his mind.

*Scarlett:* U know me too well. I have to go. xoxo

*Shadow:* For that you're gonna get a good spanking.

Again he squirmed in the chair, ignoring Smokey's stare.

*Scarlett:* I can't wait. I love when u spank me.

"Fuck," he muttered under his breath.

*Scarlett:* I have to go. My boss is going to be here any minute.

*Shadow:* See u tonight. Love you, woman.

*Scarlett:* I love you too. And by the way, I took the pics b4 I went to work this am. xxxxx…

Shadow put the phone down on the table, then he picked out the cashews in the bowl and tossed a few into his mouth.

"You done sexting?" Smokey said.

He jerked his head back. "Fuck off."

"I'm pretty sure that's what you wanna do." Smokey chortled. "So where should we eat tonight? Axe, Chas, Wheelie, and Cruiser want Mexican so we can go to Rosarita's in Crystal Grove, or we can get some thick steaks at Choppers in Estes Valley."

"Choppers is my vote," Shadow said, glad that the conversation was steering him away from the pictures Scarlett had sent him. But the minute he thought about them, his dick stirred again. He just had to focus on the road, his brothers, and the food. *Simple. But I can't wait to unpeel that sexy outfit from Scarlett's body, piece by piece. Aw shit … there I go again.*

"Okay, Choppers it is." Smokey wiped his hands on his jeans. "You ready to rock 'n roll, or do you need a moment, bro?" His gaze fixed on Shadow's crotch.

"Shut the fuck up." Shadow jumped up from his chair. "Let's get going. I'm itching to get on the open road."

Smokey nodded, then pointed at Helm. "He was supposed to go with us, but I guarantee he'll be in the same spot when we get back."

Shadow laughed as he dug out the keys to his Harley from his pocket. He threw the cans of beer in the recycle bin, then walked down the steps onto the lawn, the soles of his boots crunching over patches of brown, dying grass.

"This damn heat's killing everything," Smokey said as he came up beside Shadow.

Up ahead, he saw the other riders waiting by their bikes under the large oak tree at the far end of the parking lot, and he picked up his pace, each footstep scattering small rocks and gravel across the asphalt. Smokey and Shadow bumped fists with the other brothers, then went over to their Harleys and jumped on.

The motorcycles roared out of the lot, kicking up dust and shattering the late afternoon stillness. Shadow was in the middle of the line next to Wheelie, and the warm summer air rushing around him felt damn good. And as he passed sheep grazing in fields on the left and a group of horseback riders following a trail along the river on the right, all thoughts vanished from his brain. Shadow relaxed as he became one with the ride, peace and a feeling of invincibility descending upon him. *That* is what he and his brothers lived for.

THE TRAFFIC LIGHT suspended on a span wire across Main Street changed from yellow to red, and he braked then stopped. Shadow ran his gaze up and down the deserted rows of storefronts and businesses, and he glanced at the time on his phone: 11:49 p.m. There were no pedestrians; the only signs of life were a truck and a few cars. Tall metal streetlights spaced evenly on both sides of the road threw pools of yellow onto the sidewalks. On weeknights, Main Street was empty after ten o'clock, even during tourist season.

All the action was centered a few blocks over on Spruce and Maple, where bars, nightclubs, and restaurants lined each side of the roads.

The light turned green and Shadow rode until darkened buildings gave way to rows of houses with large front lawns. Lights from windows and porches cast yellow streaks over shrubs and trellises. A canopy of stars brightened the dark, moonless night.

When Shadow turned on Scarlett's street, a surge of excitement rushed through him. He couldn't wait to hold her soft body close to him and kiss her deeply. Shadow had texted her when he left the clubhouse to tell her he was on his way so she had time to slip into that sexy teddy that had been on his mind since Scarlett had texted him the picture of her wearing it. All through dinner at Choppers, he kept sneaking peeks at it. If it were up to him, Shadow would've hauled ass back to Pinewood Springs three hours before, but when they got back to the clubhouse, there were several members from one of the Insurgents' chapter clubs there. It would've been disrespectful to the visiting brothers if he didn't stick around, so he did until he couldn't stand being away from Scarlett for one more minute.

Most of the windows in the apartment buildings were dark, and the street had an eerie stillness about it. Stopping at a light, Shadow caught the flicker of a shadow in the corner of his eye and turned to see … nothing there. He rubbed a hand over his eyes. *I could've sworn I saw someone. Shit … I stared at the damn computer too long today doing inventory.*

Shadow pulled through the intersection, then he saw it again—a wisp of brightness that faded away all at once. He slowed down. *What the fuck?* The night breeze sighed and the trees whispered. Shaking his head, he shifted gears and picked up his speed when he caught a flutter of swift movement off to his right side behind the cluster of shrubs. Shadow hesitated, sensing something, but it was too late. He saw a figure dash out of the trees toward him. Shadow revved higher, but his peripheral vision picked up something flying in the air, and he turned his bike sharply, trying to avoid the object from hitting him. *Clang!* The sound of metal slamming against metal vibrated through him.

"Fuck!" he cried as he was bucked off his motorcycle. Shadow slammed into the side of the road and tumbled a few times. "Shit!" Streaks of pure adrenaline pushed him up on his feet, running and looking for his bike. The Harley was still rolling, and before Shadow could reach it, it crashed into a parked car, then fell on its side. Pain reverberated through his back, hands, and left arm as he ran over to his downed motorcycle.

A couple in a minivan pulled over, exited their vehicle and hurried to him.

"Are you all right?" The fine lines in the man's face deepened with concern.

"Yeah—I just need to find the fucker who did this," Shadow growled.

"We saw the guys come out from behind the tree and throw something at your bike," the woman who was with the older man said.

"Did you get a good look at their faces?" Shadow asked as he looked down at his shredded gloves. Blood oozed from between the tears.

When she shook her head, gray curls brushed across her forehead. "Not really. It was too dark. We'll call an ambulance for you."

"I don't need one." Shadow glared at the torn sleeve of his leather jacket. His left arm felt like molten lava had been poured onto it. He slipped the jacket off and surveyed the road rash. *That's gonna be sore for a while.* He could see patches of gravel imbedded in his skin. *When I find the fuckers who did this, I'm gonna make them pay.* Fury burned through him as he walked back to the area where he wiped out.

"My wife's right—you should go to the hospital." The man called out after him.

In the middle of the road, a twenty-inch tire iron lay on the asphalt. Shadow grimaced when he bent down to pick it up. *I'm gonna beat the shit outta the fuckers with this!* Strewn around the area were bits and pieces of his cell phone and sunglasses.

"Do you need us to do anything?" the woman asked as she walked toward him.

"Yeah. I need to borrow your phone—mine's busted up." Shadow gazed down the road again, then over to the right from where the men had approached. "Did you see where the fuckers went?"

"They took off running past that building"—the man pointed to Scarlett's place—"then they got inside a car. It looked like a Mercedes or BMW."

"Color?" The rage inside him intensified.

"Not sure—rust or brown maybe."

"No, Jim, it was burgundy, or it could've been red. It's dark out so the color could be off, but it's in the red family for sure," the woman said.

"Great, thanks." Shadow took the phone she offered to him.

"We should call the police. This was a criminal act—an assault," Jim said, anger punctuating his voice.

"No badges," Shadow said as he plugged in Smokey's number.

"You don't want them to get away with this," the woman said.

"Lynn, leave it alone. If he doesn't want the police involved it's his business." The man came over to her and held her hand.

Shadow nodded at them. "I appreciate your help, but I'll take care of this in my own way. There's no fuckin' way I'm letting those bastards get away with what they did," he said turning his back and walking away, out of hearing distance.

"Hello?" Suspicion laced Smokey's voice.

"Hey, it's me. My phone got busted because some fuckers threw a tire iron at my bike."

"What the fuck?" Anger replaced wariness. "Do you know who the assholes are?"

"I got an idea."

"Did you get hurt?"

"Not really. Road rash—the shit that happens when you wipe out. I'm just glad I wasn't going too fast. I knew something was off. Fuck! I should've gone by my gut."

"I'll get some of the brothers to come with me. Where are you?"

"I'm at 1238 Greenwood Boulevard. A couple stopped to help me out—I'm using the woman's phone."

"How's your bike?"

"It doesn't look so good. It crashed into a parked car. That's gonna be a fuckin' pain in the ass. I'll leave a note and have them call me at work. I'm so fuckin' pissed!"

"You got every right to be. I'm pissed too. Okay—so we're on our way. In a while, dude."

Shadow glanced over at the couple. "I need to make one more call," he said in a loud voice. They nodded and he tapped in Scarlett's number.

"Hello?" Her voice softened his rage a little.

"Hey, darlin'," he replied.

"Why are you calling me from a different number?"

"I'm using someone's phone. I got into an accident." He heard her gasp. "Don't freak out, babe. I'm all right."

"Are you sure? Oh God, I can't believe this. Where are you?"

"I'm sure. I'm near your building."

"I'm coming down now," she said, worry coating her voice.

"You don't have to. I can come up as soon as Smokey and some of the other brothers get here."

"I'm already pushing the button on the elevator."

"Turn to your right when you get outta the building—you'll see me."

"Okay. The connection is crapping out since I'm in the elevator. I'll be …"

Scarlett sounded like she was talking underwater, so he hung up then cleared both her number and Smokey's from the woman's phone. He'd tell Scarlett some punks threw the tire iron because he didn't want her to worry or talk him out of exacting vengeance.

The pain seared through him as he walked over to the woman.

"Thanks," he said, handing it back to her.

"Did you call someone to come get you?" Lynn asked as she slipped the phone into her purse.

"Yeah. Do you have a piece of paper and a pen?"

Nodding she fished around in her purse.

"Do you have a way to get your motorcycle to a shop?" Jim asked.

"My buddies are coming and will help take care of things." Shadow took the paper and pen from Lynn and wrote a quick note and then walked over to the car that his bike crashed into and left the folded paper under the windshield wiper.

"I still worry that you may be hurt. I used to be a nurse and there are different degrees of road rash. It looks like you have some debris in your arm, probably in your hands too. You have to get that cleaned out. You don't want to get an infection. You really should go to the ER," Lynn said.

"I've wiped out before so I know what to do. Anyway, I got a friend who's a doctor and he'll check me out."

"We'll stay with you until your friends get here," Jim said.

"That's not necessary. They'll be—"

"Oh, baby."

Shadow turned around and saw Scarlett running over to him. He noticed her face blanch after she looked at his motorcycle beside the parked car. She came up to him and threw her arms around his neck.

"Fuck," he gritted.

Scarlett jumped back. "Did I hurt you?" She glanced at his arm and her lips trembled. "You're injured!" Then her gaze fixed on his gloves. "There's blood. Take your gloves off." She reached out to help him, but he shook his head and unfurled the gloves from his throbbing hands.

"Jim, go get that towel in the back seat," Lynn said.

"What happened?" Scarlett asked as she placed her hand on his shoulder. "How can I help you?"

"The guys will be here soon. I gotta go to the clubhouse to get cleaned up."

"Two men threw *that*"—Lynn pointed to the tire iron tucked into Shadow's waistband—"at him. My husband and I saw them. We couldn't believe anyone would do that. The world is getting crazier by the day."

One of Scarlett's hands flew to face, covering her mouth. "That's horrible." She cut her gaze to Shadow. "Did you know them?"

"No."

"I wonder if Bruce Huntington had anything to do with this. Remember what I told you I overheard? I can't believe he'd do it—that would be too terrible."

"Probably just some punks who thought it was funny." He stepped closer to her.

"Funny?" Her green eyes flashed. "You could've been killed!"

"Yeah, but I wasn't. When you ride a bike, you know shit can happen."

"But this was intentional, not just an accident. There's a big difference. How can you be so flippant about this?"

Shadow was right in front of her now. "Because I don't want my rage over this to get outta control. Now give me a kiss, darlin'."

The corners of her mouth tugged up, and she leaned closer to him. "I don't want to hurt you," she whispered.

"My lips are just fine." He lowered his head and pressed his mouth to hers.

"Here's the towel," Jim said.

Scarlett broke away from the kiss and took it from Jim.

"Apply pressure to his palms to stop the bleeding," Lynn said. "If it doesn't stop in about ten minutes, then he *has* to get to the hospital."

"She's fuckin' obsessed with dragging my ass to that damn place," Shadow muttered.

Scarlett pressed the towel against his skin. "She's just being nice and helpful," she whispered.

He hissed at the sizzle of pain that shot through his hands.

"I'm sorry," she said.

She push down harder on the wounds, sending another wave of pain searing through his nerve endings.

*Fuck!*

"Are you doing okay?" Scarlett glanced up at him.

"Yeah," he gritted between his teeth.

A low rumble in the distance built to a roar as six motorcycles rolled up the street. A brown pickup truck followed behind then pulled up beside Shadow.

Smokey glanced at the couple then at Scarlett before resting his gaze on Shadow. "Where's your bike?"

"It's over here," Jim said before Shadow could answer.

Smokey shifted his gaze back to Shadow. "Who's he?"

"He and his wife pulled over to help me."

"Oh yeah, you used their phone." Smokey rode forward, then switched off the engine and exited the truck.

"What the fuck, dude?" Helm said as he came over with Bones and Cruiser following behind. "Smokey said some fuckers threw an iron at you."

"They're fuckin' dead when we find them," Cruiser said, then snapped his mouth shut when he noticed the couple behind Shadow.

"These people helped me out," he said in a loud voice so all the brothers could hear lest they reveal more than they wanted the citizens to hear.

"That's cool," Bones said. "So your bike's pretty fucked up?"

Shadow lifted one shoulder. "I don't know. I'm hoping it's an easy fix."

"I'll take it over to Hawk's shop. Banger's having Doc meet us at the clubhouse," Smokey said.

"I'm so glad you're seeing a doctor," Lynn said.

"Yeah. So, thanks again. You can go now—we got things under control." Shadow saw the way Jim was checking out the brothers and staring at the rockers on the back of their cuts.

"Let's go, Lynn." Jim turned to him. "I hope you feel better soon."

"Thanks, man." Shadow watched as Jim talked into Lynn's ear as they walked back to their minivan. Several times, she looked over her shoulders with widened eyes, then went back to listening to her husband.

"We'll talk about what happened when we get to the club. There's no way those fuckers are getting away with what they did to you," Hubcap said, his hands clenching into fists.

"There are security cameras in front of all these buildings. Maybe you can get the footage," Scarlett said.

Hubcap whipped his head around to gape at Scarlett as if realizing for the first time a woman was in their midst. Surprise etched across his face, and he glanced over at Shadow, giving him a *what-the-hell* look.

"This is my woman," Shadow said as he hooked his good arm around her shoulder and pulled her to his side.

"Oh," Hubcap answered, his gaze still fixed on her.

"If the cameras are live or close circuit, Hawk can get into them." Shadow kissed the side of his woman's head. "Thanks, babe, for that information."

"You ready to go?" Smokey asked.

"Yeah." He looked down and caught her gaze. "You don't need to come, baby."

"I want to." Her eyes shimmered and she blinked rapidly.

Warmth spread through him, and at that moment, he never thought he could love a woman as completely as he did Scarlett.

"Then come on." He brushed his lips across hers and led her to the truck.

The truck rolled down the old highway, and every bump it hit felt like a fireball exploded inside him. The bleeding had stopped on his palms and on portions of his left arm, which was a good sign, because it meant the cuts weren't too deep. Chances were that he'd suffered second-degree road rash since there was debris embedded in his skin.

"When we get to the clubhouse, you need to stay in the main room at one of the tables. I'll tell the others that you're with me, so they won't be messing with you. We got some guys from another chapter there, but I'll have one of the prospects watch over you."

"You're sort of scaring me," she said.

"The outlaw world is different. It's a male-oriented world, and the women who hang at the club during non-family times are viewed as fair game." He sucked in a breath.

"Now you're freaking me out. Can't I be with you?"

"Doc's gonna have to clean me up. I got some gravel and shit lodged into some of my wounds. It's not gonna be pretty."

Scarlett bumped lightly against him. "Are you afraid I'll tease you about whining?" She joked.

He laughed. "There's no fuckin' way you or anyone else is gonna hear me whine. If that ever happens, just shoot me."

"Ditto," Smokey said, catching Shadow's eyes in the rearview mirror.

She let out a small giggle that sounded like windchimes blowing in a light breeze. "You're such a macho man."

He pivoted to her and dipped his head. "And you love it, baby." Shadow captured her lips.

For the rest of the drive Scarlett sat close to him, her head on his shoulder, as he stared out the window at the blurred shapes that raced by them.

*Once I'm patched up, those fuckers better watch out. I think I'll pay Charlie Bowen a visit to see what he knows about tonight. My gut's telling me he does.*

He leaned his head back against the seat and closed his eyes, letting the hum of the motor lull him to sleep.

# CHAPTER TWENTY-TWO

SCARLETT SAT AT one of the tables, nursing a bourbon and water, pretending that she was cool with everything that was going on around her. It was bad enough that a good majority of the men leered at her as if she were a deer surrounded by a pride of lions, but it was all the copulating in plain sight that had her looking down at the table and stirring her drink like it was never going to mix.

"Did you want something to eat?"

Scarlett glanced up and saw a pretty woman with auburn hair and blue eyes standing at the table.

"No, thank you," she replied as she brought the drink to her lips and took a small sip; the alcohol was now watery since the ice cubes had melted.

"You're Scarlett—Shadow's woman, right?" The woman pulled out a chair and sat down. "I'm Kristy." She smiled broadly.

"Nice to meet you." Scarlett tried to keep her eyes away from the woman's skimpy top that did little to cover her large breasts.

"You look like you needed a friend. You had that deer-caught-in-the-headlights look." Kristy laughed. "I guess the club comes off as being over the top if you're not used to it."

"A little bit. Who is your boyfriend? I don't know any of the other members except for Smokey."

"I heard he did some work at your house."

"My parents' house, and he did a real good job. Is Smokey your boyfriend?"

Kristy burst out laughing. "No way. I can't see Smokey being *any* woman's boyfriend. I'm a club girl, so I'm not attached to any one member."

Scarlett took another gulp of her drink, wishing the prospect—*what was his name*—would add another shot of bourbon. In her research of one-percent MCs, she stumbled across the club girls. Some of the articles referred to them as *club whores, mamas,* and even *sheep.* She couldn't even begin to understand what would attract a woman to choose a life as the club's chattel, banging any man who wanted or demanded it. She shuddered at the idea of it.

"I gotta admit I never thought Shadow would settle down. He's broken a few hearts around here."

"Really? I thought club women didn't get attached to the men."

Kristy shook her head. "Of course we do—we're women, you know? Some of us have our favorites, others just go in for the fun and never anything beyond that. I had it bad for Hawk—the VP—and I still have a soft spot for him." She leaned in close. "Don't tell anyone that, okay? I must be more tipsy than I thought. I can't believe I told you that."

"Is Hawk here tonight? I've heard Shadow speak about him a lot."

"He rarely comes to parties now that he's hitched with three kids. He got himself a rich one too. Do you know her?"

"Who?"

"Cara something. She's a lawyer." The lines around Kristy's mouth deepened when she frowned.

"*Cara Minelli*? I definitely know her—she's on my committee for the Sheridan Center gala. *She's* married to a biker? I never knew that. She's older than I am so we never hung out. I'm just sort of shocked."

"So was I when he hooked up with her. I was his favorite." Kristy blinked several times. "Brandi and me have been here the longest. These young sluts coming in think they're the shit. I can out-fuck any of them—hands down." She hiccupped, then giggled. "I can't believe I'm telling you all this shit. Fuck … I must be wasted."

"Radar's looking for you, Kristy. Go find him," Smokey said.

Scarlett looked behind her shoulder and smiled at him. "How's Shadow?"

"Good. He wanted me to get you."

She leapt out of the chair. "I've been so worried about him. What did the doctor say?"

"You can ask him." Smokey spun around and strode away.

"Nice talking with you," Scarlett said to Kristy, who was busy pulling down her top. Since Smokey was tall and had long legs, she had to practically run to keep up with him.

Shadow's room was small but very neat, which pleased her immensely. His furniture consisted of a desk, chair, double bed, nightstand, chest of drawers, and what looked like a recliner. A table lamp sat on the nightstand, and a floor lamp stood next to the recliner. The walls were bare, but the top of his dresser had several framed photographs of a woman, who Scarlett guessed was his mother. She wanted to pick them up to get a better look, but several men were crowded around the room, and she didn't want to draw attention to herself.

"Baby," Shadow said. A grin graced his face. He reached out his hand and she noticed it was bandaged.

Scarlett walked over and sat at the edge of the bed. "Are you feeling better?" she asked, bending down. "You scared the hell out of me," she whispered before pressing her lips to his.

"It wasn't my idea to do that. I had a whole different plan for tonight. You know I can't get that picture you texted me outta my mind," he said, his voice low.

"I'm wearing it under my sundress. I slipped this dress on real fast as soon as you told me what happened." She smothered his face with tiny kisses. "When you're feeling better, we'll have some fun."

"My arm and hands are messed up, not my cock, baby." He swiped his tongue over her lips.

All of a sudden Scarlett remembered the other men in the room, and she felt the heat rising to her face as she sat up straight.

"What did the doctor say?"

"What I thought—second-degree road rash. I just gotta change the bandages, put on some antibiotic cream, and some other shit. Been there, done that."

The other men in the room chuckled as they nodded.

In that moment, she realized how dangerous riding a motorcycle could be, and she shivered.

"Are you cold?" Shadow asked.

"No. It just dawned on me how dangerous riding can be."

"Don't go getting all bent outta shape and start worrying about me all the time. We all know the risks of riding, but it's worth it. Besides, I'm a skilled and good rider, *this* is on account of those fuckers."

"I know, it's just—"

"It's nothing, darlin'. Don't blow this outta proportion." He tugged on the ends of her hair.

She bit the corner of her bottom lip and tilted her head. "I won't. How's your pain?"

"Gone—amazing what pain pills and a good joint can do." Shadow chuckled, and the men in the room joined in.

"Aren't you going to introduce me to your friends?" Scarlett asked.

"If you want, sure." He pointed at each man. "This is Helm, Cruiser, Blade, Bones, Hubcap, Puck, and you know Smokey." He winked at her. "And this is Scarlett."

"Nice to meet all of you," she said, smiling.

The men grunted something inaudible, then focused their attention back to him.

"If you don't need anything, bro, I'm gonna head out," Helm said.

Shadow ran his bandaged hand down her arm. "I'm good."

"Okay, I'll catch you tomorrow so we can discuss things." Smokey lifted his chin then walked toward the door.

The rest of the men either raised their fists in the air or lifted their chins before leaving the room.

When the door closed, Shadow pulled her down on top of him, then kissed her deeply. "I'm so fuckin' pissed our night was ruined," he said against her lips.

"I'm so fucking pissed that those two delinquents hurt you," she replied before kissing him again.

She pulled back and lightly ran her fingers over his face. "I about died when you told me that you had an accident. I never want to lose you. I couldn't bear it." Her voice hitched.

"Come on … where's my strong woman? I'm not going anywhere, babe. I saw those fuckers, so I swerved my bike to avoid a worse accident. I'll always be here."

"I'm going to hold you to that," she whispered.

"You do that, darlin'," he said thickly.

Pushing up, she looked at him and noticed his lids were heavy. She raked her fingers through his hair. "I think the pain pills are making you sleepy."

"Yeah—I'm so damn tired."

"Then sleep. I'm staying with you."

"Love you," he mumbled then his eyes shut and his lips parted slightly.

Scarlett dipped her head down and kissed his forehead. "Love you too, baby," she whispered. She watched him as he slept, loving the way he looked so serene. Shadow was nothing like the other men she'd known, who told lies and exaggerated tales in the name of supposed love. She huffed. No … Shadow was the real deal, and she'd almost lost him that night. *Okay, I'm being overly dramatic, but he* did *get hurt, and what if another car had been driving up the street and hit him.* There was an ache in Scarlett's chest and her eyes stung with tears. *I need to stop this now. He's safe—that's all that matters. But what if—* She shook her head vigorously. *No. Stop it.* A small snore stopped her thoughts, and she smiled and brushed a kiss over his cheek then stood up.

Scarlett switched off the lamp on the nightstand, then walked over to the large window and pulled down the blinds. She shuffled over to the dresser and opened the top drawer, looking for a T-shirt to wear to bed. It was then that she remembered the framed pictures, and she slowly picked up them up and went over to the floor lamp and switched it.

The first photograph showed a young lady of about eighteen years, holding an infant who had black hair. *That's Shadow—I'm sure of it.* Scarlett ran her finger over his picture. *He's adorable. And his mother is so young. She probably got pregnant in high school. She's beautiful.* The woman's sparkling eyes and dark hair looked very much like Shadow's. Two of the other three pictures were of his mother, only at different ages: maybe twenty-three or twenty-four, the other around thirty. The last photograph was of Shadow—she recognized him right away—when he was about fourteen or maybe fifteen. He was tall, and Scarlett could see that his arms were toned and even muscular back then, although not like they were now. A badass vibe emanated from Shadow by the way he stood, cocked his head, and snarled his lips. His mother had her arm around him, and her face was glowing with happiness and love. *She was so young, and he was too young to lose his mom.*

The tip of her index finger traced over both Shadow and his mother as sadness filled her. "I wish I could've met you," she whispered to his mother. "You raised an amazing son."

The bed creaked and Scarlett froze as her gaze flew to that side of the room. Shadow had turned on his good side, and the sheet had fallen away, exposing all the bandages running up and down his left arm. She tiptoed to the dresser and put the frames back on top of it, then rummaged through his drawer to find one of his undershirts.

After she had splashed some water on her face and changed into Shadow's T-shirt, she padded over to the bed and pulled the sheet over him before slipping in beside him. She listened to him breathe for a long time, the images of his mother and a teenaged Shadow floating through her mind.

Slivers of moonlight filtered through the blinds, looking like thin fingers, and Scarlett watched as they wavered on the wheat-colored carpet and across the bed until sleep tugged at her lids. She finally gave in to the stillness, to his low and deep breathing, and to the murmuring chants of the whip-poor-wills.

SCARLETT AWOKE TO soft sheets and the morning sunlight seeping in through the slatted blinds. She rubbed her eyes with her knuckles then slowly turned on her side and propped herself up on her elbow. Shadow lay on his back sleeping, and she touched him lightly, careful not to wake him up. Her fingertips ran over the muscles of his chest, and the bones of his ribs and hips. Shadow moved slightly and a small groan slipped from his lips, and she froze. Looking at his scraped arm and hands, Scarlett wished she could kiss away the pain and make it all better like her father used to do when she was a kid and had roughed up her knees after falling from her bicycle.

After a few seconds, his breathing was even and steady, and her hands continued to explore his warm, manly body. She pulled down the sheet gingerly and stared at his erection pointing upward at the ceiling. Scarlett put her hand to his groin and grasped his dick and lightly trailed her fingertips up and down his tight, thick shaft. Again Shadow stirred and she pulled her hand away.

"Don't stop now, baby," he rasped.

She looked up and met his heated gaze and gave him a wicked smile.

Shadow pushed himself up then collapsed back down. "Fuck!" he yelled as sweat poured down his face.

Scarlett bolted to a sitting position and ran the back of her hand over his face. "Let me get you your pain pills, baby."

"I'm okay."

"You're not and stop acting like something's wrong with you because it hurts." She rolled out of bed and went over to the nightstand and opened the prescription bottle. The night before she'd put two bottles of water next to him in case he needed a drink during the night. She poured some in a glass and helped him up a bit as he downed the two pills. He flopped back down on the mattress, a scowl creasing his brows and forehead.

"It's okay," she said. "I can help you change your bandages and put the lotion over them. I read somewhere that if you put petroleum jelly over the lotion, it'll keep the gauze from sticking to your skin when you change out the bandages."

A smile whispered across his lips as he stared at her. "Doc told me that too." A grimace played across his face as he gripped her wrist. "You can help me out later. Right now I need your lips wrapped around my cock."

Shaking her head, Scarlett climbed back onto the bed. "Are you sure I won't hurt you?"

"No way. I need you bad, darlin'."

"Do you, now?" she asked, raking her nails up and down his chest.

"Yeah," he replied thickly.

"That's good to know because I need you too, baby." She replaced her fingers with her tongue as she moved lower toward his dick.

"Fuck," he grunted.

Circling his inner thighs, she lightly brushed his tight balls with her fingertips, her gaze fixed on his smoldering one. Scarlett slowly stuck out her tongue a little then, using the tip of it, she moved it up and down his dick in small circular motions.

"Damn, baby," he groaned, his gaze still locked on hers.

Opening her mouth wide, she took him all in, and his briny taste lingered on her tongue. She felt his legs tremble under her touch and she sucked him hungrily, his grunts and groans driving her wild with desire. When she licked and sucked gently on his balls, she felt them tighten and she knew he was close.

"I want you to ride me, darlin'. Hard and fast."

"Are you sure you'll be okay? I don't want—"

"Just fuckin' do it, babe."

Scarlett pulled up and wiped her mouth before she straddled him, her knees on either side of his hips.

"You look fuckin' hot wearing my T-shirt," he rasped. "Now, take it off. I want to see your tits bounce."

She slipped it off and he whistled, low and deep.

"Fuckin' gorgeous. I love the pink color of your nipples. Now bend down and bring those babies to my mouth so I can suck them."

Scarlett carefully scooted up a bit then lowered her breasts toward Shadow's face. The second they were within reach, he cupped each tit, massaging them while his thumbs stroked her beaded buds.

Throwing her head back, her back arching, she moaned. "That feels so damn good. You made me so hot." She reached down and gripped his dick then slid it back and forth between her pulsing folds. "Do you feel how wet you make me?" she breathed.

A broad smile spread over his face. "Does your pussy want some loving?"

"From you—always." She bent down and kissed him deeply then lifted up on her haunches and hovered over his hard dick. Slowly, she descended, his smooth head poking through her glossy slit.

"That feels so good," she groaned.

Shadow placed his hands on her hips and his fingers dug into her soft flesh.

"Your hands, baby."

"Fuck that," he grunted as he rocked his hips upward, shoving more of his cock inside her. "Take all of me into your sweet heat."

Thrusting his pelvis up and toward her while she pushed down and back, they ground in tandem, each grunting and moaning as their excitement escalated. Fingering her hot button as she bumped and ground against him, her heated wetness clutched and squeezed him.

Then he stiffened.

"Fuck, Scarlett," he growled. As his warm seed filled her, a pulsing pleasure ripped through her body and she writhed and quaked above him.

"Oh, Shadow, oh …."

"Damn … it's so good with you. Fuck."

Bending over, Scarlett peppered his faces with feathery kisses before pressing her mouth against his in a deep kiss. Then she rolled over and slumped next to him and put her arm across his flat belly. They lay together for a long while then Scarlett rolled away and rose to her feet.

"You definitely need to have your bandages changed. I'll go get the stuff."

Scarlett disappeared into the bathroom then opened the medicine chest and took out a roll of gauze, a jar of Vaseline, some medical adhesive tape, and a tube of antibiotic cream. She washed her hands then with her hands full, she padded over to the bed.

"Let me help you sit up," she said.

"I can do it on my own."

Ignoring what he said, she helped him sit back against the headboard.

"Thanks," he grumbled.

Scarlett kissed the top of his head then shuffled back to the bathroom to retrieve a bar of soap, several warm washcloths, and a couple of towels. She knew how hard it was on him to have her see him so vulnerable, and she wished she could make Shadow understand that it was okay … that she didn't view him as weak because he needed her help. He was so used to being tough and keeping a stiff upper lip ever since he'd been a kid, that he probably didn't understand how to sit back and let her help him.

"Here we go." Scarlett perched on the edge of the bed. Shadow stared straight ahead as if purposely avoiding her stare. *That's okay, but I'm not going to back down. I'm going to help you.*

She ran one of the washcloths over his shoulders and chest.

"What the fuck?" he said.

"I'm giving you a quick sponge bath before putting on a fresh dressing."

"I don't need you to do that. I'm not a fuckin' wimp."

"I didn't say you were," she replied, washing his private parts and legs. "I want to do this. Please let me."

"Whatever." His jaw clenched and his lips formed a hard thin line as he burned a hole into the wall in front of them.

After she dried him off, Scarlett bit the inside of her cheek as she slowly took off the bandages and cleaned the wounds. They looked awful but she couldn't let him know how affected she was by all of it.

"How long did the doctor tell you it'd take to heal?"

"Two weeks. It's not that big of a deal." Shadow still avoided her gaze.

"It is if you get an infection."

For the next several minutes, she chatted brightly about this and that while he remained stoic.

"That's it," she said, standing up. Scarlett took the supplies and walked toward the bathroom. "Do you happen to have an extra toothbrush?" she asked, pausing for a moment.

"Bottom drawer of the dresser."

"Great. I'm guessing you have to change the bandages twice a day."

"Yeah," he grunted.

"I'm going to wash up."

An hour later, Shadow sat at a table with Helm, Cruiser, and another guy Scarlett didn't know, chomping on a turkey and swiss sandwich she'd made for him in the club's kitchen. Earlier, when she'd been slathering mayo on two slices of wheat bread, a few of the club girls came into the kitchen and tried to stare her down, but Scarlett had just hummed softly and finished making her man's lunch. A few tortilla chips, a scoop of potato salad, two pickle spears, and a peeled orange had completed the plate. Then Scarlett brushed past by a bleached blonde woman with green tipped talons who'd tried to block her way out of the kitchen.

"Bitch," the woman gritted.

Scarlett threw the witch one of the smiles she'd learned in etiquette school back when she was in third grade, and then walked out. She wasn't sure what it was about the smile—soft, not too wide, and refined—that pissed people off, but it always came through for her whenever anyone gave her shit and she didn't want to deal with them.

On a chair next to Shadow, Scarlett stole one of the orange slices off his plate and took a bite. The sweet juices ran down her chin and she grabbed a napkin and wiped them away. Shadow glanced at her sideways for a second then went back to lamenting with his friends over what had happened to his motorcycle. There was never a mention about what had happened to *him*, just his bike. *Shadow's right—this is a different world.*

A tall good-looking man with black hair pulled back in a ponytail and deep blue eyes came over to the table and placed a hand on Shadow's shoulder.

"How're you doing, bro?"

"Sore as fuck, but okay."

"Good."

"Did you get a chance to check out my bike?" Trepidation laced his voice.

"Yeah, and I can save it. It's messed up pretty good, but the engine's sound. Any idea who the fuck did this to you?"

Shadow's shoulders slumped down as he visibly relaxed. "Awesome news about my bike. When's it gonna be ready?"

"A week, ten days max."

"Cool. I'm not sure who the fuckers were. There're cameras up and down that street 'cause it's in the rich part of town."

"Smokey told me. I'll see what I can do."

As the men spoke, Scarlett looked harder at the tall man talking to them and she noticed his leather vest had the title *Vice President*.

"You're Hawk," she blurted out, remembering Kristy had told her Hawk was the vice president of the club.

Everyone at the table stopped talking and fixed their eyes on her. The vice president glared at her, a deep frown embedded across his forehead.

"I know your wife, Cara. She's on my committee for the Sheridan Center gala. She's awesome. Her dad has done some legal work for my dad's real estate company."

"Who the *fuck* are you and why the *hell* are you talking to me?" Hawk folded his arms across his muscular chest.

*What's his damn problem?* "I told you—I know Cara. Cara Minelli's your wife, right?" *Maybe Kristy was bullshitting so I'd make a fool of myself. These women around here can't be trusted.*

"So you know my old lady. That doesn't answer why you're talking to me." He glanced around the table. "Who does this woman belong to?"

"Me," Shadow said. He put his sore hand on top of her thigh as if to shush her, but there was no way in hell *that* was going to happen.

Scarlett sat up straighter in the chair as irritation pricked at her skin. "I don't *belong* to anyone since I'm not a piece of property. I'm with Shadow—he's my boyfriend. Besides, I was just asking a question so there's no reason to be so rude."

The room grew quiet like a tomb, and the tension in the room was as oppressive as the heat outside.

"Set your woman straight if she wants to ever come back to the club," Hawk said to Shadow as he turned away, dismissing her. "I'll let you know what comes up with the cameras and we'll go from there."

"Sounds good." Shadow said but there was an edge to his voice.

*Is Shadow seriously mad at* me? *After this jerk was so damn rude?*

"Later," Hawk said as he squeezed Shadow's shoulder and walked out of the room.

"What the hell is—"

Shadow threw her a death glare and she clamped her mouth shut. For the next hour, Scarlett fumed while he and his friends talked about motorcycles. She glanced at her phone and saw Kiara had sent her a text inviting her to join the group—Ashley, Daisy, and Shelby—for dinner at the club. She looked over at Shadow then back at the message. At that moment Scarlett wanted to tell Kiara she'd be there, tell Shadow and his club to fuck off, and get the hell out of there. *But I don't have a car.* Yeah … that would definitely thwart her dramatic exit. *Shit. I doubt Lyft would come here to pick me up.* She giggled at the thought of it then slid out of her chair.

"Where're you going?" Shadow asked.

"I need some fresh air," she replied curtly before turning on her heels and stalking away.

The sound of the river beckoned her and she followed it around the back of the property. Scarlett saw a doe across the way near the edge of the water, and nearly hidden behind it were two white-spotted fawns. Afraid she'd frighten them away, Scarlett stopped in her tracks and watched them, marveling at the beauty that surrounded such a misogynistic club.

"Are you okay, Scarlett?" Shadow asked.

Without turning around she replied, "Not really."

"What's wrong?" He stood beside her, the tips of his scrapped fingers running over her bare arm.

"You just sat there letting that asshole speak to me that way," she said, her voice rising in anger.

The doe raised its head and stared at them from across the river. Sensing no danger, the deer lowered its head back to the water.

"It doesn't work that way. Hawk's the VP." Shadow quirked his lips.

"That's the best you can give me?" She shook her head. "Unbelievable."

"It's the way our world works, babe. I should've explained things to you before you came to the club, but last night I wasn't in a real good way. I always thought I'd prepare you before I brought you to see where I live and hang out."

"So rudeness to women is part of your world?"

"Not really. It's just that the club is *ours*. What I mean by that is it belongs to the men, not the women. The women aren't members of the Insurgents only the men. So the women are there by invitation of the members." He cleared his throat. "They're in the background, so to speak."

"What does that have to do with Hawk being rude to me?" She sank down on the grass, and pulled on several of the blades.

Shadow sat down next to her. "There are rules like in any club, and a certain protocol that has to be followed. One of the rules is that no woman—even the old ladies—can ever just jump into a conversation or ask questions of a member they don't know. The thing is you aren't wearing my property patch so—"

"*Property* patch?"

"Let me finish. The property patch brings respect with it. The club members respect the woman who wears it and she's accepted into the fold. It doesn't mean she's a club member, but she's part of the club family. Wearing a property patch is actually an honor, and it's a big deal. Other bikers won't mess with a woman wearing the patch, and the property thing is like a ring for citizens—it binds the couple together. Am I making sense?"

"I guess. So if I had this patch, Hawk wouldn't have jumped down my throat?"

He shook his head. "Not exactly. The rules still apply and the old ladies can't interrupt their men, butt into conversations, or argue with a member if they don't agree with what he's saying to his one of his brothers." Shadow shrugged. "It's just the way it is."

Scarlett stretched her legs out and leaned back on her hands. "It's just so alien to me. I read about the whole property thing but I didn't think it still went on. Does Cara wear that rude guy's patch?"

"Yeah, and believe me, she's got more power than Hawk will ever admit to." Shadow chuckled.

"Maybe I should talk to her about all this," she said.

Shadow's eyes lit up. "That's a great idea. She's been with Hawk for years and she's the second in command of the old ladies. Belle—that's Banger's woman—is first since she's the president's old lady then comes Cara. She's a perfect one to talk to, and she comes from your same background."

"I guess."

"What you gotta understand, and I know it'll take some getting used to, is that the club is not a lifestyle, it's a way of life. That's all I can say. The way you jumped into our conversation and talked to Hawk was viewed as disrespectful, and respect is everything to us. If you were at family night and Hawk and Cara were standing together talking and you came over, he'd have been totally cool."

"So what you're telling me is that the old ladies are basically second-class citizens. I find it hard to swallow that my boobs automatically render my intellect inferior to a person with a dick and a three-piece patch."

For a long pause Shadow didn't say anything and Scarlett thought she may have gone too far, but she was pissed and still stinging about Hawk's abruptness and Shadow's acquiescence to the whole ordeal. Then he laughed so loud that the doe jerked and ran away, the fawns following close behind.

"Fuck, babe. I love the way you just tell it like you see it. Most women would be kissing my ass right now because they'd be afraid they may be banned from the club. Not you."

"I'm not most women," she said glancing sideways at him.

"No you're not and that's what drew me in. You're different in all sorts of ways, yet we got stuff in common. Look, what we do away from the club is our own business. I'll always treat you right."

She pushed up then turned to him, her hands resting on top of his thighs. "I never said you wouldn't. I love you and I want to try and understand the world in which you live, but you have to respect that this is hard for me to wrap my head around. You have to get that I may not agree with all this."

His face grew somber. "If you can't accept my world then that's gonna be a big problem because it's a part of me. As times goes on, it'll get easier … that is if you want to give it a try."

Scarlett leaned forward and kissed him gently on the lips. "My love for you isn't conditional. Of course I'll accept your world, but it doesn't mean I have to agree with the way the club views women."

He put his arm around her and drew her closer. "That's fair, but it isn't this constant tug-of-war between the sexes. The men respect their old ladies to the *nth* degree, and they'd do anything for them. It's just that the club belongs to the brothers and club business stays inside the club." He kissed her softly. "That's the way it is in a nutshell, darlin'."

Scarlett let her head rest against his shoulder while she digested everything he'd said.

A comfortable silence stretched between them as they sat together listening to the rush of the river, the birds singing, and the tree branches rustling.

"Thank you," Shadow said, his voice low.

"For what?" she asked.

"For helping me out this morning."

Scarlett's heart swelled—not just because of his words, but because she knew how hard it was for him to say them.

"You're welcome," she replied.

Scarlett took out her phone and sent a message to Kiara telling her she couldn't make it to dinner that night. Then she nestled against him with a smile, resting her head on his chest and listened to his beating heart.

And, at that moment, life was perfect.

# Chapter Twenty-Three

*Three weeks later*

A FEW STARS freckled the inky black night, and Shadow stood in a darkened corner, waiting.

The alley behind the building was lined with empty crates and dumpsters that reeked of rotting food. Tall weeds and clumps of grass grew from the cracked asphalt of the lot.

The sound of a door slamming shut and the tapping of heels on pavement drew him out of the shadows and toward the burly man who was walking with his head down across the tarmac. The jangle of keys echoed eerily in the deserted parking lot, and Charlie Bowen, as if sensing Shadow's presence, paused at his car and looked over his shoulder. Shadow took a few steps back into obscurity, avoiding the only light in the lot: a dim spotlight focused on the alley. From Charlie's small, jerky movements, Shadow knew fear was creeping up his spine, and just as the private investigator opened his car door, Shadow was beside him.

Charlie cried out, the keys dropping from his hands with a *clunk* as he turned around, his eyes widened in fear.

"How are you, Charlie?" Shadow asked, his voice low.

"Fuck, you startled me." A sheen of sweat glistened across his face. "I'm good."

"So you decided to come out of hiding?" Shadow wedged himself between the open car door and Charlie.

"Hiding?" A nervous laugh. "Why would I be hiding? I just took my family on a vacation before the summer ends. We went to Gunnison. It was so much cooler there. Did some fishing, hiking—"

"Cut the shit—I don't want your fuckin' itinerary. I want you to tell me what you know about someone throwing a tire iron at my bike."

"Why would I know about *that*?"

Shadow laughed dryly. "Because my gut tells me you do."

The footage Hawk was able to pull from the security cameras was grainy at best, and the two fuckers had their sweatshirt hoods pulled down low over their faces. The license plate of the two-door Mercedes sports car was illegible, but from the physical characteristics Shadow, Hawk, Banger, and Smokey could see, the guys were not old men, and the car was a convertible.

"I didn't do anything." Charlie ran his hand over his face. "I swear."

"Were you asked to?"

Charlie shuffled a foot across the gravel, eyes darting everywhere, but avoiding any eye contact with Shadow. "I don't want any trouble."

He was on Charlie like a shot, grabbing the front of his shirt, then lifting him on his toes, his face only inches from the private eye's.

"This is your *only* chance to tell me the fuckin' truth."

"Okay … okay. I was asked to do it, but I said no. He offered me a ton of money, but I refused it, then I cut out of town. You can check. The night it happened, I wasn't here, I was in Gunnison with my family."

Shadow pushed Charlie back hard, and the burly man slammed against the opened car door.

"Did that fucker Mansfield try to pay you to do it?"

Charlie Bowen's head shook vigorously. "No, it wasn't Mansfield. It was Bruce Huntington. He said something about ridding the town of scum like you. He was angry about you screwing something up between his son and Mr. Mansfield's daughter."

Rage swirled inside him like a tornado, and he clenched his scarred hands into fists as he tried to control his emotions.

"Did he say anything else?"

Charlie looked away, a pained expression spreading across his face.

"Spill it—tell me what the fuck he said."

Bowen's shoulders slumped, and stress showed on his face from the frown lines between his brows to the flat line of his lips.

"He mentioned your … uh … mother." He said the last word so low Shadow could barely hear him.

"My mother?" The rage turned white hot and burned through every nerve in his body.

"Yeah. He said he knew her and she …" his voice trailed off, and his gaze caught Shadow's. "I don't want any trouble. I didn't say this shit. I'm just repeating what he told me. I just do family problems like cheating spouses and—"

"What the fuck did he say?" He struggled to keep his tone steady and calm as liquid fury rushed through his veins.

"That she deserved exactly what she got," Charlie whispered. "I don't believe that at all. What happened to your mother was—"

Shadow stepped back from the car, his head throbbing as thoughts twirled in his brain like a spinning top. *The sonofabitch knew my mom. He* was *her sugar daddy. He* fuckin' killed her.

"What's the fucker's address?"

"He lives in Pinewood Estates. I don't know his exact address. I swear. He came to my office."

"If I find out you're double-crossing me—you're fuckin' dead."

"I'm not. Please don't tell him you got the information from me. I just want to go back to my ordinary life and easy cases and—"

Shadow glared at him. "Shut the fuck up about that. If you're telling me the truth, you won't have any trouble with me or the Insurgents."

"I *am* telling you the truth—I swear it. I wouldn't fuck you over. Do you think I'm stupid or something?"

Shadow stared hard at Charlie, who was sweating profusely, and looked like he was ready to pass out. "Get the fuck outta here," he growled, and the private investigator quickly slid into the driver's seat and slammed the door. Shadow heard the *click* of the automatic locks before the engine started and Charlie Bowen sped out of the lot.

For a long while Shadow stood rooted to the spot, staring into the darkness. A red tabby cat leapt up on the dumpster and rummaged through it, then, it looked over in Shadow's direction, froze for a second until it jumped off the edge and ran away, vanishing into the darkness. He let out a breath he didn't even know he'd been holding and took out his phone. His first thought was to call Scarlett and ask for the address of Bruce *fucking* Huntington, but he didn't want to involve her in this, so he called Smokey instead.

"I found out who tried to kill me—the same fucker who killed my mom." His jaw tightened along with his chest.

"What the fuck, bro? Who?"

"Huntington—but there's no damn way that old man was the one in the video camera. It must've been his pussy son and a friend. The fucker was my mom's sugar daddy. Fuck!" He hated how his voice hitched, and he bit his inner cheek hard, hoping the pain would push away his emotions. He had to be clear and level-headed; otherwise, he'd fuck up and that's the last thing he wanted to do. Killing Huntington and his fuckin' son had to be done with calculated precision. No bodies or evidence would ever be found—the Insurgents would make sure of that.

"Where are you? I'm coming now. Don't do anything stupid, man. We gotta take care of this in the right way."

"I know, but I wanna kill the bastard with the same mercy he gave my mom. Fuck, this is hard. I've waited all these years and the sonofabitch was under my nose the whole time. *Fuck!*"

"Cool down, bro. I know this is difficult, but we gotta be smart. I'm gonna call Hawk and Banger. I'm walking outta the clubhouse now. Are you at Scarlett's?"

"Nah—I'm in the lot behind the First Union Building."

"Stay tight."

Shadow leaned back on his boots and tried to put a shield between his thoughts and what needed to be done, but threads of memories kept weaving through his mind. Shadow's cell phone rang out from inside his jeans pocket, and he hurried to retrieve it. He glanced at the screen and saw it was Hawk.

"Yo," he said.

"How're you doing? Smokey told me what's going on. Finding out about your mom must be fuckin' rough."

The support of his brothers cocooned around him like a warm blanket. "It is, but I'm dealing with it. Thanks."

"Yeah, you gotta get your head on straight with this one, even though it's harder than shit. Emotions have no place when exacting revenge. If you don't think you can keep it in check, we'll take care of the asshole for you."

"I'll be okay."

"I located the fucker's address, and I also called Banger. He's calling an emergency church tomorrow so we can decide how we're gonna proceed. There's no fuckin' way this asshole's getting away with what he's done to you or your mom."

"I'll finally give my mom the justice she deserves. Those fuckin' badges have had all these years and manpower to find this sonofabitch, and they're still clueless."

"Maybe they were getting paid off. I don't trust the damn Establishment," Hawk said.

The sound of loud cams had Shadow walking over to the alley and looking down it. He saw a single headlight approaching.

"Smokey's here," he said.

"I'll let you go. I'll see you at church tomorrow. Stay strong, bro."

Shadow jammed the phone back in his pocket and lifted his chin at Smokey when he turned into the lot.

"I called Hawk," Smokey said, straddling his bike.

"I know—I just talked to him. Banger's calling an emergency church tomorrow."

"How're you holding up?"

Shadow shrugged. "Okay. I'm trying to push the past to the dark corners of my mind and just focus on what needs to be done. Right now it's running about fifty-fifty."

"You need to smoke some weed, get fuckin' drunk, and let Tania give you one of her stellar blowjobs, dude," Smokey said.

"I'll go along with the weed and getting wasted, but the only chick I want near my cock is my woman."

"Are you gonna stay with her tonight?"

"I don't want to involve her in this, and she'll know I'm upset. It's best if I go back to the clubhouse tonight."

"Let's get going. Where's your bike?"

"I parked it in the next lot."

"I'll wait, then we can ride back together," Smokey said.

Shadow crossed the lot, then went on to the one next door, and a few minutes later, he and Smokey were riding side by side on the old highway toward the Insurgent's clubhouse.

The loud rock music, the bear hugs from the members when Shadow walked in, the soft looks the club women threw his way, and the nonstop shots of whiskey were exactly what he needed that night. His brothers were there for him, offering him support, loyalty, and camaraderie, and Shadow would've done the exact same thing if one of the other members was hurting. The brotherhood was surrounded by a circle so strong that each member could confidently depend on it.

At some point—Shadow had no idea when—he'd managed to stagger up the stairs to his room. He flopped down on the bed and his head sank into the pillow. The room spun around, and he kept his eyes open until dark oblivion finally arrived.

SHADOW SAT ON the metal chair, his elbows propped on the wooden table, holding his throbbing head between his hands. Animal slid a bottle of water in front of him, and Shadow just looked at it, then groaned inwardly. It was like a damn freight train was running right through the middle of his head.

The gavel hit the wood block and vibrated through his bones, sparking his nerves and settling behind his aching lids.

"Church is in order," Banger said. "By now, you all know why I called this emergency church. Our brother here"—he pointed to Shadow, who nodded feebly—"needs us to help get justice, which the fuckin' badges haven't been able to do. He's been waiting fifteen years to exact vengeance on the fucker who killed his mama and that day has come."

The roar of the members was like nails pounding into his head. Shadow forced himself to lean back in the chair and lift his fist in the air.

"As a bonus, we know who tried to kill our brother here, and it turns out it was the same fucker."

"His pussy son," Shadow grunted. His throat was dry as sand, and his damn head felt like jackhammers were drilling into it.

"A family who stays together, dies together," Helm said, and the members busted out laughing.

"When are we gonna string these fuckers up?" Smokey asked.

"Hawk's working on that with Rock, Jax, Buffalo, and Puck." Banger turned to the vice president. "You wanna take it from here?"

Hawk stood up, placed his foot on the chair rung, and leaned forward. "I've located the sonofabitch's house and business. I also got the address of where the pansy-ass son lives and works. We gotta tread real careful with these fuckers because of who they are. These assholes got some clout in the community, but the old man is also on the verge of bankruptcy." Hawk glanced over to Shadow. "That's why he was pissed about you stealing the Mansfield woman away from his wimpy son. Anyway, neither of the fuckers is in town right now. It seems that they left right after Shadow went down. We gotta find out who else was with the bastard son when the iron was thrown at our brother."

"Maybe it was the old man," Throttle said.

Hawk shook his head. "I've looked at those images until I can't see straight, and it looks like the fuckers were younger—definitely not in their early sixties."

"So when are we gonna teach them not to mess with an Insurgent?" Blade asked.

"When they get back. I'm gonna need each of you to sign up for stakeout duty. I want two or three checking on each of the fucker's residences."

"Someone should watch out for Shadow. I don't trust that the private investigator kept his mouth shut. There's too much money he can make for selling information," Animal said.

"And if this Huntington asshole gets wind that Shadow knows he killed his mom, the fucker will go after him," Helm added.

"I don't need a damn babysitter! What the fuck? I can take care of myself," Shadow scoffed.

Several of the brothers voiced their objections to Shadow's statement, and when he jumped up to his feet, he crumpled just as fast back down on the seat as a wave of nausea hit him.

Another bang of the gavel against the block.

"Calm the fuck down! All of you!" Banger yelled. "*I'll* decide what's necessary." He glared at Shadow.

"I'm not gonna stand for it," Shadow mumbled. "I'm not some pussy."

"No one's saying you are. It's just a precaution. I'd order it for any of the members. You still got your balls—no worries there." Banger folded his arms over his chest and held Shadow's stormy gaze.

"Anyway, we're just in the talking stages about it," Hawk said, but Shadow caught the look the vice president and the president exchanged, and Shadow *knew* he'd be getting a damn babysitter assigned to him.

"So, are we all on this?" Banger asked.

Shadow's chest swelled with pride as a resounding "Yea" reverberated around the room.

"Good. We'll call another church once the details are ironed out and the fuckers are back in town. They can't stay away forever," Banger said.

"And if they do, we'll track them down. There's no way they're getting away with this." Throttle tipped his chair back, his nostrils flaring.

Hawk nodded. "Agreed."

"If there's nothing else, then we'll call it a wrap." Banger dropped the gavel down for the third time.

The scrape of chairs, the thud of boots, and the chatter of voices filled the room as the members filed out and made their way to the main room. Not moving an inch, Shadow fixed his gaze on Hawk and Banger, waiting until the place emptied.

"I don't want anyone watching out for me," he said.

"Noted," Hawk replied without looking up from a clipboard.

"I'm serious." Shadow pressed his fingers to his temples.

Hawk glanced up. "I know. You had your say, now shut the fuck up about it."

A frustrated sigh escaped from the back of his throat, but Hawk and Banger didn't look his way. They huddled together talking in low voices. The table groaned when Shadow slammed his fist on it, then stormed out of the room and walked down the hall to the patio. He wanted to be alone, and his stomach twisted at the thought of alcohol. His boots clumped on the grass and then the dirt as he trekked over to the river. Kneeling down at the river's edge, he cupped his hands and splashed the cool water on his face several times. Shadow sat back on the sun-warmed grass and watched the mists from the river eddying around the banks. A small shoal of minnows darted in the water, their shiny blue scales glittering in the sunlight.

The sound of his phone's ringtone startled him and seemed out of place among the stillness of the landscape. Shadow glanced at the screen and the corners of his mouth turned up.

"Hey, baby," he said.

"Hi. I just wanted to hear your voice," Scarlett said.

"Yours is just what I needed right now."

"What're you doing?"

"Hanging out back by the river. I tied a few on pretty good last night, so my head is a fuckin' mess."

She chuckled. "What was the occasion?"

"We never need one at the club."

"Are you too hungover to have dinner at my place? I'm grilling steaks, onions, and red peppers."

"I'll be there, babe. I thought we'd go for a bike ride tomorrow after work. There's a rock festival in Silverton that I'd like to take you to."

"That sounds great, but I can't go. I'm sorry, but I have a committee meeting for the upcoming gala. We'll be going over the programs, addressing all the invitations, and a bunch of other things. I'd love it if you were at my place when I got home, though."

He chuckled. "You can count on that."

"Hmm …"

"You at work?"

"Yes, but I'm leaving pretty soon. You can come by at any time."

"I'll be there in an hour, darlin'."

"I can't wait to see you," she whispered. "Bye."

Shadow put the phone down on the grass and looked back at the river. Part of him was still in disbelief that he'd found his mother's murderer after all this time. Then all at once, an overwhelming urge to have his mother next to him grabbed hold of him like a vise.

"You'd really like Scarlett, Mom. She's a good woman," he said out loud. A strange idea then popped into his head. "Did you bring her to me? That would be something you'd do. She's the type of girl I know you'd want for me to settle down with."

Shadow tilted his head back and squinted. White clouds scuttled across the cornflower blue sky; several birds circled and dipped in the great expanse as if in a graceful dance. After a long while, he rose to his feet and walked up the small incline, then entered the club and made his way to his room and changed his clothes.

An hour later he had Scarlett in his arms, their lips fused in a fiery kiss. Her moans and small whimpers fueled Shadow's constant desire for her, and he scooped her up in his arms and walked slowly to the bedroom.

# Chapter Twenty-Four

THE GOLDEN ORANGE and smoky purple streaks melted into gray under the moonlight. Shadow glanced out the window while he massaged the ache in the back of his neck. He'd been bent over the computer for most of the day, and his dry eyes and aching neck were the result of no breaks. Whenever he got involved in something, time would rush by without him noticing it.

He looked over at the wall clock: 7:15 p.m. Scarlett had texted him over an hour ago, saying she would be home later than she'd thought. Shadow planned to make her his signature dish: shrimp scampi. It was a favorite of his mother's and whenever shrimp had gone on sale, she'd snatch it up. His mom had often told him that if he learned to cook only one dish, it had to be shrimp scampi, and so she'd taught him how to do so.

Shadow had gone to the grocery store before coming in to work, and now he walked over to the small fridge and took out the bag of shrimp, a container of basil, and a bottle of white wine imported from France. He locked the office door, then set the alarm before exiting the warehouse. Glancing around, he didn't spot any of the brothers or prospects and wondered if Hawk and Banger had reconsidered having someone watch over him. Since the whole babysitting shit had come up a couple days before, Shadow hadn't noticed anyone tailing him.

The only sounds came from the silhouettes of trees, their branches swaying in the wind of a newly silver sky, and the soft scampering of a nocturnal animal taking cover in the bushes.

He crossed the lot, put the groceries and wine in the saddle bags, then jumped on his bike and headed over to Scarlett's. That night, he wanted to pamper her, to give her the princess treatment, then after dinner he'd put aside his gentlemanly ways and bang her good and hard—just the way she loved it.

Shadow parked in front of her building and lifted his chin at the desk attendant as he walked over to the elevators. Scarlett had put his name on the list as a permanent guest so he didn't have to keep signing in and showing his damn driver's license.

Shadow looked at his reflection in the mirrored elevator doors: a bottle of wine in one hand, a couple of bags of groceries in the other. If anyone would've told him two months ago that he'd be making dinner for a woman he *loved*, Shadow would've punched them out. He shook his head and chuckled, then stepped out when the doors opened on Scarlett's floor.

He unlocked the door and entered the condo. It was quiet except for the low hum of some of the kitchen appliances. When Shadow walked into the living room, he saw the silhouette of a woman sitting in one of the overstuffed chairs.

"Hey, baby," he said. "I guess you finished sooner than you thought. Why the hell are you sitting in the dark?" He felt around on the wall and found a light switch.

After he flipped it on, Shadow widened his eyes in surprise as his gaze fell on Scarlett's mother, sitting with her legs crossed on one of Scarlett's favorite chairs.

"What the fuck are *you* doing here?" he growled as he took a few steps forward.

Pamela laughed dryly. "No 'Hello, Mrs. Mansfield'? I can't believe my daughter is involved with such a Neanderthal."

Shadow walked away and into the kitchen.

"You haven't answered my question as to why you're here," he said, putting the groceries into the refrigerator.

"I wanted to speak to Scarlett since she makes it a point to come by the house whenever I'm not there."

"That should tell you she doesn't want to see you. Did you bribe the attendant to get inside?" He took out a box of linguine from the pantry and set it on the counter. The last thing he wanted was for his woman to be upset, so he had to get her bitch mom to leave.

"Scarlett has always been a very spoiled and silly girl."

"Your daughter and I love each other, and I told your husband the same thing." Shadow pulled out the pasta pot and filled it with water.

"*Love*," she scoffed. "What you are talking about is desire—just brutal desire."

"Call it whatever the fuck you want, but I don't want you upsetting my woman tonight."

Pamela snorted. "*Your woman*. What a perfectly crass thing to say." A small pause. "You're white trash."

"Damn straight I am, lady." He slammed the filled pot on the stove. *This is getting old.*

"The thought of you pawing my daughter makes me sick to my stomach."

"Then don't think about it." Shadow leaned against the quartz counter, his jaw clenching so tightly he thought it might break. "You've said your shit, now get out."

"If you think I'm going to allow you to ruin the Mansfield name, you've underestimated me."

Shadow marched back into the living room.

"I have worked hard to be in the position I'm in, and I'm not letting some lowlife come into *my* family and take it all away. I know what it means to be poor, to live among trash, and I worked my ass off to make sure I'd *never* go back there again. So don't even think for one second that my husband or I will accept you. How much do you want to stay away from Scarlett?"

Raw anger shot through him. "You think this is about money?"

Pamela lifted her chin arrogantly. "Isn't everything?"

"I don't need your fuckin' money."

Her upper lip curled in disdain. "*Everyone* can be bought." She lifted her hand and two gold bracelets jangled as she smoothed her hair.

Then a quick tiny glimmer drew his attention to her throat and the necklace that fell just at her collarbone. His heart pounded in his ears as the image of his mother wearing the silver necklace with the red coral and turquoise pendant burned in his brain. He'd given it to his mother and it was the one thing that couldn't be located after her murder. And now Pamela Mansfield had his mother's prized possession around *her* neck.

"Where the fuck did you get *that*?" he growled, stalking toward her.

"Where the *fuck* do you think?" A smug smile twisted her lips. "Don't come any closer." Scarlett's mother reached into her purse, took out a gun, and pointed it at him.

Rooted to the spot, his gaze took in the .22 caliber, then cut to the bangles on her arm. "Flo's, I'm guessing." It felt like cotton was stuffed into his mouth, but he wouldn't let this bitch know she'd thrown him for a major loop. *Scarlett's mom murdered Ma? Is she covering up for her husband? Huntington. Are they fucking each other. Dammit. I didn't expect this.* He moved his arm, reaching slowly behind him for his .38 special.

"Keep your hands where I can see them," she ordered.

"Who gave you that necklace?"

"Your mother—well, technically she didn't *give* it to me. I took it." A broad smile cracked her face.

A guttural growl vibrated in the back of his throat.

"This entire situation is distasteful and ironic. I thought I was done with your family when I punished your mother for fucking my husband, but now you're humping my daughter. You're just like your white-trash mother."

*Scarlett's dad was my mom's sugar daddy? What the fuck?*

"You're too proud, too macho to even blink an eye, but you must be exploding inside. My husband is like all men—a dirty, vile pig. Since he makes my skin crawl, I looked the other way when he sought physical enjoyment with other women. It worked between us—I kept a good home, raised the children, and did all the social things a wealthy wife is supposed to do. He provided very well for me all these years. Then he met your mother at that strip club she worked at. I never thought that would be a problem, but the stupid old fart fell in love with her." Pamela laughed heartily.

"You're a fuckin' bitch," he grunted.

"And you're going to join your slutty mother. She was taking my husband away from me. What woman goes out with a married man who has three children? She was breaking up our home."

"Your respectable husband told her he was getting a divorce. I knew something was up with him. I should've taken care of it long ago."

"But you didn't, so I had to step in. I didn't want to be the divorced woman in town who everyone pitied and spoke about in hushed voices behind my back. Your mother was a threat to my marriage, my way of life … my *survival*. I had no choice—it was either her or me. You should know about that. You're in that criminal club. I'm sure you've killed for survival." Another dry laugh. "You see … you and I are not all that different."

Shadow forced himself to stay where he was rather than to rush the bitch. He had no doubt that she knew how to use the gun in her hands. And with the short distance between them, being shot by a .22 could kill him, or do some serious damage.

"Does *he* know you murdered my mom?" *I wanna wrap my hands around her fuckin' neck and squeeze the life outta her. She needs to suffer like Ma did.*

"No. The only one who knew was that nosy and greedy friend of hers—Flo. She came by to talk to your mom that night and caught me leaving the apartment covered in blood. I should've killed her right then and there, but I panicked and fled." She shook her head. "A stupid mistake that cost me millions and a lot of unnecessary stress. And she kept getting greedier."

"So you offed her."

"You have such a way with words." Another large smile.

Shadow glanced at the glowing numbers on the microwave and realized that Scarlett could be home at any moment. There was no way he could risk this crazy bitch hurting his woman. He'd have to rush her—there was no other option.

"Bruce Huntington told me about your mother and George. I'll always be indebted to him for that because I doubt if I would've ever found out until it was too late. He was taken with your mother, too, but she rebuffed all his advances. Anyway, now you've come around and screwed up all the plans I had for Scarlett and Warren. I promised Bruce I would make it happen."

"So he knew you killed my mom?"

Pamela shrugged. "I never told him, but he may have figured it out. Who knows?" A short pause. "And now it's your turn. You should've stayed away from Scarlett. You're a good-looking man, and I'm sure your motorcycle and leather jacket gets you plenty of women. You shouldn't have infiltrated my family."

Then a series of raps on the door diverted Pamela's attention for a nanosecond, but it was enough time for Shadow to move to the side and jump over to her. He felt the bullet when it hit. It was like a metal rod tapping the inner side of his left wrist.

"You fuckin' cunt!" Shadow grabbed the gun and pistol whipped her repeatedly.

Just then, Smokey and Helm broke through the front door—ripping it completely off its frame. The sound of wood cracking and splintering filled Shadow's ears, but his rage boiled over and he kept beating his mother's killer over and over again, his arms still flailing after Smokey and Helm pulled him away.

"She killed my mother. That fuckin' bitch destroyed my mother's life. My life! I'm gonna make her pay!"

Smokey held him tight but Shadow kicked and cussed even though his wrist hurt like hell and blood was dripping on Scarlett's pristine marble floor.

"Call Doc," Smokey said to Helm. "Get him over here stat. Then go find a towel so we can stop the bleeding."

Shadow jerked away from his friend's grip. "I wanna kill her," he said, looking at Pamela, who was slumped over and not moving.

"You may have already done that," Smokey said as he went over and took her pulse. He shook his head. "Nah, she's still alive. Lemme call Banger and see what he wants us to do."

Shadow stalked over to the murderer and ripped his mother's necklace off Pamela's neck. A low moan escaped her lips and her lids fluttered open. He stared at her dilated pupils as she groaned softly while holding her head.

"Tell Banger the bitch's got a concussion."

"I'm so dizzy," she whined.

"Life's a bitch," Shadow replied, glaring at her.

"Here," Helm said, handing him a large towel.

Shadow wrapped it tightly around his wrist then pulled out his phone with his other hand and called Scarlett. He had to make sure she didn't come to the condo; he couldn't let her see what was going on.

"Hi, Shadow. I'm just leaving now." Her voice sounded like a ray of light in the middle of all the darkness.

"Hey. I'm gonna ask you to do something and I can't tell you why. You're just gonna have to trust me and do what I say."

"You're scaring me. What's wrong?"

"You need to go to your parents' house. Don't come here."

"Why?"

A sharp, narrow fingernail of irritation scratched along his spine. "I just told you that I can't tell you. Trust me, okay?"

After a moment of hesitation, he heard her breathe quickly. "Okay. You'll call me, right?"

Relief washed over him. "I'll call you, but be patient if you don't hear from me for a while. It doesn't mean I won't call you. Love you, babe." *But your mother destroyed my life fifteen years ago.*

"I love you too. Please stay safe. I'll wait for your call."

Shadow saw Doc rush into the condo.

"I gotta go, Scarlett. I'll talk to you later." He shoved the phone in his jeans pocket and walked over to Doc.

"What happened?" Doc asked him.

"The bitch shot me."

Doc darted his eyes from Shadow to Pamela then back to Shadow. "Sit down and let me take a look." He unwrapped the blood-soaked towel.

"If it wasn't for Smokey and Helm, things would've turned out differently. They were the distraction I needed."

"We were your 'babysitters' tonight," Helm said, clasping Shadow's shoulder.

Smokey strode over and bent down on his haunches next to Shadow. "Banger's calling Chief Landon. It was self-defense."

"Actually, it was," Shadow said. His gaze locked with the bitch's. "It was a matter of *survival*."

Smokey scratched his chin. "Yeah … stick with that. The cunt came after you, shot you, and you had to hit her 'cause she kept coming at you. She was so fuckin' crazed, beating her was the only way to get her off you."

"That's the way it happened," Shadow said without breaking eye contact with her.

"I have to get the bullet out," Doc said. "Let's go to my office so I can take an x-ray to see what's going on inside. It doesn't look like any tendons were damaged, but I want to be sure, and I have to see about the bone."

"Fuck," Shadow muttered. "I gotta wait for the fuckin' badges."

"They're on their way up." Helm stood by the floor-to-ceiling windows.

Detectives McCue and Ibuado walked in and rushed over to Shadow.

"What happened here?" McCue asked, his eyes shifting from Shadow to Pamela.

"This crazy bitch murdered my mother. She killed Flo too. She's wearing her bracelets, and the cunt had this on around her neck." He handed over the necklace to the cop. "I gave that to my mom years ago."

McCue nodded. "I remember it was the only thing missing."

The paramedics transferred Pamela to a stretcher, then wheeled her out. Two uniformed badges followed behind them.

"Landon said it was self-defense. She shot you?" McCue asked.

"Damn straight. She's a fuckin' psycho bitch."

"Okay." He wrote some stuff in a notepad.

Doc cleared his throat. "Shadow needs immediate attention."

The detective nodded. "Go ahead. I know where to find you to get your statement."

When Shadow stood up, he swayed on his feet. Smokey and Helm rushed over and each wrapped an arm around him, holding him steady as they slowly walked out of the condo.

"You just do what Doc says," Helm said. "I called some of the brothers and we'll put a new door in. You better have your woman stay with you at the clubhouse until we get her place cleaned up."

"Yeah," Shadow muttered. *What the fuck am I going to do with Scarlett? I need to talk to her dad. What a fuckin' mess.*

And in the middle of it was the two of them.

The problem was—Shadow didn't know if their love was enough to pull them through this chaos.

# CHAPTER TWENTY-FIVE

I T WAS THE pain that woke him—that and the chirping birds. Shadow opened his eyes and saw the first beams of sunlight piercing through the blinds. He pushed up with his right hand and sat on the edge of the bed, blinking and wiping the sleep from the corners of his eyes. Spotting the bottle of water on the nightstand, Shadow grabbed it and took a long drink. The events of the last week played in his mind, as they always did when he was awake.

Pamela Mansfield, charged with two counts of first-degree murder and a slew of other charges, sat in a jail cell. The police department determined Shadow had acted in self-defense, thus declining to charge him with assault. The *Pinewood Springs Tribune* ran a front-page story on the cold case murder, and the scandal was a major topic of discussion at the Pinewood Country Club.

Since his mother's death, Shadow had been so convinced it was the rich man in his mom's life who had murdered her that he'd never once entertained the possibility that a scorned woman could have been responsible for committing such a heinous act.

And that woman was Scarlett's mother.

*Scarlett. Fuck.* Shadow knew that she was in a world of hurt, and he wasn't helping by distancing himself from her, but he needed to make sense of everything that had happened before they could go back to where they were. *Maybe we never can. Maybe everything is too damn broken.* He scrubbed his face with his hand then rose to his feet and headed to the bathroom.

An hour later, Shadow sat in front of the wrought-iron gates at Scarlett's parents' house. When she'd texted him the day before, Scarlett had told him she was staying with her father for a while. He hadn't seen her since the day after the revelation when he'd told Scarlett what had happened. The extent of their relationship after that had consisted of texts and a few phone calls. Scarlett had told him she wanted to give him the space and time he needed, but Shadow knew his distance was breaking her heart—he heard it in her voice.

He picked up his cell and opened the photo app, then scrolled down to a bunch of pictures that captured every aspect of Scarlett: sexy, silly, and happy, as well as few of them together. Shadow stared at the photos for a long time before tapping in her number. On the second ring, Scarlett picked up.

"How are you?" she asked.

"All right."

"How's your wrist doing?"

"It's getting better. I hate having to drive a cage, but it's only for a few more weeks." He picked up the thermos of coffee and took a sip.

"That's not too bad, but it probably seems like years to you. I know how much you love riding."

There was an exaggerated cheerfulness in her voice, and it was obvious she was trying way too damn hard to act like everything was normal when it just wasn't.

"How are you doing?" he asked.

"Taking it day by day." A small sigh. "Are we ever going to see each other again?" Her words were laced with apprehension.

Sucking in a deep breath, Shadow slowly let it out. "I'm in front of your gate."

"You are?" Her tone was guarded but happy.

"Yeah."

"Do you want me to open it?"

"Not really."

"Oh. Then what?" The anxiety and fear had crept back in.

"Nothing. I'm just here, that's all."

A second of quiet.

"I really miss you ... *us*. I know everything has been thrown off kilter. I can't even make sense of it, so I can only imagine how devastating and surreal this is for you." The slight hitch in her voice made his chest tighten. "But I want to see you." Another pause. "Don't you want to see me too?" she whispered.

*Want to see her?* Hell, he wanted to hold her in his arms again, have his mouth on hers, tell her he loved her, then apologize for his coldness—but Shadow didn't respond.

A few sniffles. "I better get going."

"Is your dad there?"

"Yes. He really wants to talk to you."

"I have nothing to say to him." Shadow reached over to the glove box and pulled out a baggie. He took out a rolling paper, filled it with weed, and shaped the joint with his fingers as the phone sat in the console on the speaker.

"I wish you would," she said tentatively.

After rolling the joint, he put it between his lips, and lit the end. He inhaled deeply and blew out a plume of smoke.

"I bet the marijuana helps with your pain."

"And a lot of other things." Another inhalation.

The sound of Scarlett clearing her throat rasped through the phone.

"My dad told me about everything. He said that ... umm ... he loved your mom very much."

Shadow stubbed out the joint with two fingers, then put it back into the baggie for later.

"What the fuck do you want me to say to that?" he said, slamming the glove box shut.

"I just wanted you to know. I guess I shouldn't have said anything. I'm sorry."

"You have nothing to be sorry about. I've always said you can say whatever to me."

Then Shadow heard the metal gate clang, and he jerked his head up. And there she was: radiant and smiling, golden hair falling past her shoulders, captivating green eyes. Other than a light pink shine glossing her lips, she wore no makeup. A purple sundress hugged all Scarlett's curves, and her slender arms folded across her chest as she approached the car. His heart raced and his breathing quickened. *She's fuckin' beautiful.*

Scarlett opened the door and slipped inside, then swiveled toward him, her gaze holding his.

"I thought it would be easier to talk in person," she said softly.

The phone fell from the console and he cursed as he bent down to retrieve it.

"Are you mad that I'm here?"

Spiced vanilla swirled around him, waking up his dick and playing havoc with his emotions.

"No."

She lightly caressed his forearm, then leaned over and brushed her fingers over the bandages on his wrist and his arm. Her touch was so damn soft, so *perfect.*

"Do you still love me?" she whispered, pulling her hand away.

"Yeah," he said quickly.

"That's good," she muttered.

Shadow tucked her hand in his and squeezed it. "All of this feels like some fuckin' B-rated movie. I don't know …"

"I'm sorry for what my family did to you. I'm in shock over it, really. I can't believe my mother could do something like that. She's always been cold and distant, but …" her voice trailed away.

"This isn't your fault, and it isn't mine either. We were just kids put in the middle of our parents' bullshit." Shadow pivoted in his seat so that he faced her. "But sometimes … no, a lot of times, I blame myself. If only I could've made more money, my mom wouldn't have had to hook up with a rich man … your dad," he said.

"You were a teenager. How much money could you have made? You've carried the blame for your mother's death since it happened. I don't think she would've wanted that. The one to blame is my mother.

She murdered yours. I can't believe it or get past it. My family has caused you so much pain. How can you ever look at me again without thinking about all of this?" She pulled her hand away and looked down.

For a long minute Shadow watched her, then he reached over and brushed the long, wavy strands of hair over her shoulder. She looked up and a ghost of a smile whispered across her lips.

"When I look at you, I see a beautiful, sexy woman. I don't see the ugliness of your mother or the lies of your father. This isn't about you."

"Then, why are you pushing away from me?"

Shadow shook his head while he raised one of his shoulders. "I don't know."

"Do you want us to go our separate ways? It'll be hard, but being in limbo like this is worse." She turned her head and looked straight ahead.

The thought of Scarlett not being a part of his life, of never seeing her again, ripped a hole in his chest. "You're the only thing that's grounding me. I've just needed some time by myself."

"I understand that," she said, her eyes shimmering. "I just want to know that we're okay. I can't stand the thought of you not being in my life."

Shadow leaned over and pressed his lips to hers, then broke away. "Baby, you've changed my life in ways I never thought anything or anyone could, and I want you on the back of my bike."

Scarlett flung her arms around him and pulled him closer. "I want that too."

She swept her mouth against his, and he wrapped his arms around her. It felt so good to hold her, to kiss her, to breathe in her scent. Grief and anger had made him lose his head and push her away. He pulled away slightly. "I should've reached out to you instead of trying to figure it all on my own," he said before kissing her again.

"Just know I'm here for you no matter what," she whispered across his lips.

They kissed, touched, and held each other through the constant *whirr* of lawn mowers from neighboring houses, the screams of children riding bikes up and down the street, and the barks of dogs as their owners walked them on the sidewalks. And they would've stayed that way except for the incessant vibration of Shadow's phone against the dashboard.

"Hey," he said.

"The fuckers are back in town. Banger's called an emergency church in one hour," Smokey said. "Are you at the warehouse?"

"I'm not. I'll see you in an hour. Thanks for letting me know." He put the phone in the console.

"When will I see you again?" Scarlett smoothed the wrinkles from her dress.

"I may have something to do tonight. I'll call you, though. How long are you staying with your dad?"

"I don't know. He's awfully shaken up about all of this."

Shadow's eyes narrowed. "Yeah … well."

She looked at him quickly, then cut her gaze back to her dress. "Anyway, I could never go back to my condo. I've decided to sell it. I'll stay with my dad for a while." Scarlett leaned her head against the head-rest. "What a fucking mess this is. I hope my mom does the right thing and pleads guilty. I can't even imagine how horrible it would be for you to go to the trial."

"Yeah—the best would be a plea deal."

"I still can't believe this is all happening. I keep thinking I'm in a dream and that I'll wake up soon. How the hell could my mom do something as horrible as that?"

Shadow drew her to him and wrapped his arm around her. "Jealousy and fear are a lethal combination." He kissed the top of her head. "I'll call you."

"Promise?"

"Yeah." He kissed the tip of her nose, then moved away from her.

Scarlett climbed out of the car, and she was still standing on the sidewalk watching him when he turned the corner.

Instead of going to the clubhouse right away, Shadow stopped off at the grocery store, bought a bouquet of roses, and then proceeded through the business district as he headed to Mountain Crest Cemetery. It'd been a long time since he'd visited his mother's grave, but Shadow had the strong urge to go.

Driving through the entrance, he saw the office and pulled into the lot; he didn't remember where the location of the gravesite was. Several minutes later, he drove slowly past mausoleums and tombstones until he saw marker 157.

Shadow grabbed the bouquet and slid out of the car, then walked across the grass until he reached a small rose-colored granite gravestone set flush to the ground. It read *Carmen Basson - Beloved Mother* on top with the dates of her birth and death on the bottom. He knelt on one knee and pulled the weeds away from the border of the stone, then stood up and stared down at it.

A gentle breeze whistled through the pine trees that dotted the manicured grounds, and wildflowers perfumed the early afternoon air. The wind sounded like ghostly voices calling back and forth through the treetops.

"Hey, Ma," he said, his voice low. "I brought you some flowers."

Shadow ripped off the plastic wrapper and tissue paper, then stooped down and put the red roses on the grave.

"You got your justice now." He brushed his fingers against the cool granite and closed his eyes, letting memories of him and his mother flood through his mind. Then he slowly straightened up. "Fuck … I miss you." He tapped his hand against his chest. "You're always in here," he whispered before turning away and walking back to the car.

When Shadow arrived at the clubhouse, there was a tense excitement in the air, and he followed the members to the meeting room.

Banger was at the head of the table with Hawk by his side, and the gavel didn't hit the wood block until the room grew quiet.

"The fuckers are back in town," Banger said.

"Probably think they're safe since that bitch got arrested," Throttle said.

"They think we're stupid enough to believe that *she* was behind the tire iron bullshit," Rock added.

"They don't know the Insurgents," Bones said.

"They will now!" Chas shouted and the room exploded with cheers, whistles, and fists on the table.

A proud smile lit up Banger's face, and Shadow felt very lucky to be part of the Insurgents brotherhood. He tipped his chair until it back hit the wall and waited for the noise to die down before he spoke.

"I'm fuckin' honored to call all of you my brothers. It's been a tough week, but it would've been even harder if I didn't have the brotherhood."

"We got your back, bro," Helm said as the others voiced their agreement.

"And I got yours," Shadow said.

The gavel hit the block again.

"Now that you pussies had your fuckin' Dr. Phil moment, let's get back to being men," Banger growled, but there was a twinkle in his eye, and his mouth twitched as though he was fighting a smile.

"Since we know that the old fucker didn't murder Shadow's mom, our plans of doing him in may change," Hawk said.

"We should kill him for what he did," Buffalo said.

Hawk looked at Shadow. "It's your call, bro."

"The old fucker's on the verge of losing all his land and money. I'd rather have him alive when that happens," Shadow said.

"Serves the old fart right," Helm said.

"So a beatdown for his pussy son and his friend, who I found out is Jonah Rollins," Hawk said.

"I know that asshole," Shadow said. "He was the one in Dream House's parking lot with the hooker a while back. The jerk just hasn't learned his lesson."

"He will tonight." Axe laughed.

"I bet it was Warren who threw the iron at me. That Jonah wimp doesn't have the balls."

"It doesn't matter *who* did it, they'll both get the shit kicked outta them," Rock said.

"And the old man?" Shadow asked.

"We'll rough him up, then destroy his hundred-thousand-dollar car," Hawk replied.

The membership cheered and banged their fists on the table, and Hawk reclined against the wall, a huge grin plastered on his face.

Shadow knew that destroying the jerk's car would be the best retribution for a superficial asshole on the cusp of filing for bankruptcy.

"When are we doing this?" Shadow yelled above the noise.

Banger held out his hands, gesturing the men to quiet down.

"Some of us will go to the old man's house and teach him a lesson, and the others will straighten out the spoiled fuckers," Hawk replied. "Which group do you wanna be with?"

"Kick the spoiled fuckers' asses," he answered.

"Those assholes will be at their club for a party tonight. We'll stake them out, then follow and let the group that'll be stationed at each of their houses know they're on the way. Then we'll ambush them. It's pretty simple." Hawk grabbed the bottle of beer on the table and brought it to his mouth.

"Child's play," Rock said.

"Like taking candy from a fuckin' baby," Animal added and several members guffawed.

"Rock and I will make sure the alarm system is disengaged at the old man's house before we teach him his lesson. We'll meet at ten and go from there. Any questions?" Hawk asked.

After a round of questions and answers, church was adjourned. Not all of the members were participating in the night's activities—namely, Banger and Jax, who had obligations with their families.

The members went into the main room to have a couple of drinks, play some pool, and have fun with the club girls. Shadow downed a shot of whiskey before going up to his room. He needed some quiet time to think over what Scarlett had told him about her dad loving his mother.

He couldn't help but think that George Mansfield was the one who was ultimately responsible for his mother's murder. If he would've told his mom in the beginning that he was with solidly married instead of leading her on to believe that he was going to divorce his wife, things may have turned out very differently.

"Fuck!" he shouted while he banged the side of his head with his fist. Shadow was sick and tired of thinking about it, and if he had his way, he'd just put George out of his mind and move on. But Scarlett loved her dad and he would always be in her life. *I'm gonna have to confront him. I have to do this for her.* Satisfied for the moment that he had at least made a decision, he took out his phone and texted her a quick message, telling her he was tied up but they could have dinner the following night. He kicked off his boots, then lay down on the bed and flung his arm over his eyes.

SHADOW, QUICKLY BUT quietly, sprinted behind Warren's parked car, crouching low so the asshole wouldn't see him in the rearview mirror. Rock had scrambled the security cameras a few seconds before he, Helm, Axe, and Cruiser entered the garage. Four of the other brothers were lying in wait for Jonah at his apartment.

The jangle of keys hitting the pavement told Shadow that the asshole had opened the car door. A few cuss words echoed in the underground parking lot, then Warren bent down and picked up the keys, and staggered away from the car. Like a flash of lightning, Shadow intercepted him, and Warren bumped into his strong chest.

"What the fuck?" Warren slurred as he looked up.

The annoyed look on the jerk's face was quickly replaced by fear.

"What are you doing here?" he asked, swaying in place.

Shadow could smell the alcohol on his breath. "We got a score to settle, motherfucker."

"I don't know what you're talking about." All of a sudden Warren seemed to have sobered up.

"Yeah, you do. The more you bullshit me, the harder I punch." Without warning, he sank his fist in Warren's belly.

The man's hands clutched his stomach as he bent over. "Is this about Scarlett?" he gasped, trying to catch his breath. "I'm over her. We're good, bro."

Anger flooded his veins. "I'm not your *bro*, asshole." Shadow threw a quick punch that connected square with Warren's jaw.

The asshole stumbled backward. "Fuck! What's your problem?"

"Fuck … I don't know." Another punch to the man's face. "I guess I don't like shit thrown at me and my bike. I'm funny that way." Several more quick, hard jabs to Warren's face. Sizzling pain radiated from Shadow's injured wrist, but he ignored it.

"I don't know what you're talking about. Whatever happened to you, I swear it wasn't me."

"Wrong, fucker. It *was* you!" He then delivered blow upon blow to Warren's ribs, belly, and back up to his face. Satisfaction spread through him when he heard the crunch of bones shattering.

Warren's hand flew to his nose. "Shit! You broke my nose."

"That's not all I'm gonna break," Shadow growled.

"You've made a mistake. Really, I don't—" The asshole stopped short and his eyes widened with fear as they landed on Axe, Helm, and Cruiser who came up behind Shadow then circled around Warren.

"Do you wanna rethink what you were saying?" Axe asked, his hands clenched.

"Okay, guys. Okay. Just don't kill me. I have money in my wallet and you can have my car. Just—"

"We don't want shit from you!" Rage filled Helm's voice.

"What then?" Warren's eyes darted around the parking lot as if trying to find a means of escape.

"The truth," Shadow said calmly.

The other three bikers stepped closer to Warren.

"It was my dad's idea. I didn't want to do it. He was obsessed with Scarlett and me hooking up. I told him I didn't want any part of his plan."

"Who threw the tire iron?" Shadow asked.

"Jonah," he said quickly.

Shadow shook his head. "Wrong fuckin' answer." He struck another blow.

"Fuck!" Warren rubbed his chest. "I'm telling you the truth."

"That's funny 'cause your pussy friend's saying it was you," Cruiser said.

"What?" Warren gasped.

"That's right, asshole. Your buddy's having the same conversation with some of our friends. It's like we're all just having a party." Axe laughed.

"He's lying. He did it." Warren shook his head. "I wouldn't have done something like that."

"That's *exactly* what a pussy like you would do." Shadow looked at the other bikers. "Can you believe this fucker gave up his dad"—he snapped his fingers in front of Warren's face—"just like that."

"Loyalty isn't something you're good with, is it, asshole?" Helm smacked Warren in the back of the head.

"Since I don't know for sure which one of you fuckers did it, I'll hold you both responsible." Shadow reached behind him and took the tire iron from the waistband of his jeans.

Sweat dotted Warren's hairline. "No, please. I didn't do it."

"Shut the fuck up!" Cruiser yelled.

"Let's get this shit over," Shadow said, gripping the metal rod.

Axe, Helm, and Cruiser grabbed Warren and held him still while Shadow swung hard against Warren's legs. The cracking of bones blended with Warren's cries. The three bikers released their hold on him and he fell to the ground, groaning and writhing.

"Time to get the hell out of here," Cruiser said.

Shadow bent down on his haunches next to the asshole. "Payback's a fuckin' bitch, isn't it?" Then he stood up and tucked the weapon back in his waistband.

The men hurried out of the garage and blended into the night as they made their way to Helm's SUV parked four blocks away. Axe sent a text to Rock so he could unscramble the security cameras, then the men settled into the vehicle and drove back to the clubhouse.

By the time the other bikers returned, Shadow was on his third shot of whiskey. The mission was a success: the two fuckers had broken legs, and the old man would sport a black eye and some bruises in the morning, and his car was primed for scrap metal.

Justice had been served. Outlaw bikers took the adage "An eye for an eye" literally. If someone messed with one of them, that person messed with the whole club. Retaliation was the answer to a wrong done to a brother.

It was *their* world and *their* rules.

Nothing else mattered.

# Chapter Twenty-Six

*Two weeks later*

SCARLETT SAT IN the family room waiting for Shadow to come over, fearing that he'd change his mind. A big part of her understood his reluctance, but if the two of them had any chance of a happy life together, Shadow had to talk to her dad about everything in the past.

Scarlett jumped when the doorbell rang. She hurried down the hall and yanked the door open. Shadow stood on the front porch in his tight blue jeans, white T-shirt, and black leather vest. He flicked his dark hair off his tanned face and lifted his chin.

"Hey," he said.

"Hey." She let out a breath before throwing her arms around his neck and pressing her lips to his, her tongue darting into his mouth as she sank against him.

"Now that's what I like," he murmured, his hands gripping her behind. Then he crushed Scarlett to him, and their lips fused in a fierce and wild kiss.

She clung to Shadow as arousal surged through her senses, screaming for him to take it further. One of his hands moved from her bottom and skimmed past her hips and side, and then molded over her breast, his fingers flicking over her nipple through the soft cotton of her tank top. Each tug at her breast brought a moan to her lips.

"I need you so bad," she softly said.

A hard pinch on her hard bud made her cry out in pain and desire, then he kissed her gently. A lazy smile flitted over his lips as his thumb stroked her cheekbone.

"You are my sweet woman," he murmured.

He tweaked her nose then gave her a soft peck on the lips. Scarlett missed his warmth almost immediately as he took a step back from her.

"I gotta go in and talk to your old man, but I'd rather drag you down to the tennis house."

Scarlett nodded, brushing the strands of hair sticking to her forehead. "Me too, but I don't want my dad to come out there and catch us. God, I would totally feel like I was in high school if that happened." She giggled.

Shadow swatted her behind, then stood to the side, gesturing her to go inside the house. They walked in silence down the hallway to her father's den. When she knocked on the door, her dad's deep voice boomed, "Come in."

"Good luck," she said to Shadow as she turned the knob.

"I want you with me," he said.

Her brows raised slightly. "Are you sure? I mean this is sort of private, right?"

While shaking his head, he grasped her hands. "We're a team, baby, and you're part of my life."

Her heart fluttered and she leaned against him. "I'll go in with you," she whispered.

"Come in!" her dad bellowed.

"Showtime," she said, opening the door.

Surprise flashed across George Mansfield's face when she and Shadow walked in. He picked up a brandy snifter, took a sip, then motioned for them to sit down on the small leather couch across from him.

For a long moment silence filled the room, then Shadow broke it.

"So you were my mom's sugar daddy," he said. Bitterness dripped from his words, and she ached for him.

The facial muscles in her father's face tightened, and his fingers whitened around the glass in his hand. "I was *never* her sugar daddy. I loved Carmen with all my heart."

"Bullshit," Shadow said.

"You don't know shit. I knew your mother for a long time. I used to see her at the grocery store, the post office, and at the hardware store." He chuckled, and his features softened with the memory of Shadow's mother. "I helped her pick out a lot of items for do-it-yourself projects that never got done. We had a weekly meeting at the hardware store, and I'd help her figure out what she needed for the endless projects she wanted to do."

"I never knew that. I always wondered why we had so many damn screws and tools around the house," Shadow said, a hint of surprise lacing his voice.

"I think we both knew they were just excuses to meet up with each other. We graduated to having a cup of coffee every now and then, and each time we met up, I became more enthralled with Carmen. I loved hearing her laugh. She had the most wonderful way of creating sunlight wherever she went. I loved that about her."

In that moment her father was back in the past, talking not to Shadow but to Carmen, to their memories—to their love.

"Then Bruce took me to this strip club—Satin Dolls, and I was shocked to see Carmen on stage. She never once mentioned to me that she was a dancer. I hated that she had to earn a living that way." George then looked at Shadow. "She worked hard to give you the life she thought you deserved. She was a wonderful mother."

"I know," Shadow whispered, and Scarlett placed her hand on his and squeezed it lightly.

"Carmen talked about you all the time. You were her reason for living." He took another sip of brandy. "So different from Pamela," he muttered, the words barely audible.

Scarlett's heart went out to her father. *How terrible it must've been to be in a loveless marriage for all these years. I wonder if Mom ever loved any of us. Is she even capable of loving anyone but herself?*

"That night at Satin Dolls, Carmen was so embarrassed to see me that she acted like she didn't know me. Even had the sleazy manager threaten to throw me out if I kept bothering her. For several weeks, she didn't show up to the hardware store, then I went back to the strip bar to find her. She cried when I told her I thought she was a wonderful and loving mother. I told her it didn't matter what she did. And that's when she agreed to go out with me on a proper date." He chuckled softly.

"You shouldn't have told my mom that you were in the process of getting a divorce when you had no fuckin' intention of doing that." Shadow glowered.

George nodded. "You're right, but I was afraid she wouldn't give us a chance, and by the time we went out on the date, I was already in love with her. But not telling her in the beginning was selfish. I take responsibility for that."

"If you'd been honest, she'd be alive now." Anger punctuated his words.

"Maybe, maybe not. Your mother loved me too." Her dad's gaze bored into each of them. "And as you know, love is pretty damn powerful. It makes people do all sorts of things they swore they would never do."

Scarlett felt Shadow tense and she patted his hand gently.

"Even so, you owed her that," he gritted out.

Her dad nodded. "In the beginning, yes, but after she admitted that she loved me, too, I told her the truth, and asked her to marry me. You see, by that time, I had decided to file for divorce."

Shock vibrated through Scarlett, but she kept quiet. *He was going to leave Mom and us?*

"I don't fuckin' believe you."

"It's the way it was. Carmen was mad that I lied about my true marital situation when we first started going out, but she forgave me. We were in love. Anyway, Carmen told me she'd think about it, but I never got the answer …" her dad's voice trailed away.

"You've known all along I was Carmen's son," Shadow said.

"I knew the day I came to your office. You bear a striking resemblance to her. She talked about you all the time, but she never wanted me to meet you until things were permanent between us."

"You're a fuckin' hypocrite," Shadow growled. "You tried to break up Scarlett and me, yet you lied and fucked my mom over big time."

"I loved your mother! And you're a member of an outlaw club. Do you think your mom would like that? I don't." George's face was red, his anger visibly rising.

"She'd have supported me. Anyway, that's not any of your fuckin' business." Shadow rose to his feet. "I'm done with this."

Scarlett followed suit and stood up. "Dad, you and I can talk later. I just want you to know that I love Shadow and I'm not leaving him. You can accept it or not."

Her dad looked at her over the rim of the snifter. "You're grown up now, and you have to make your own decisions. I still don't think this relationship is going to work, but you'll have to find that out for yourself."

"At least ours isn't built on a pack of fuckin' lies," Shadow said as he walked toward the door.

"I'll talk to you later." She went over to her dad and rubbed her hand over his head. "Are you okay?"

He craned his neck and caught her gaze. "I'm fine." He gripped her arm lightly. "Thanks for asking, honey."

She smiled softly then walked out of the room, hurrying to catch up with Shadow who was barreling down the hallway to the front door. He jerked it open just as she came up behind him.

"Slow down," she said, grabbing his arm.

He stopped in his tracks. "Your dad's full of shit!"

"I know you're angry, but I don't think he was lying about how he felt about your mom."

"She never would've broken up a family. She had values, principles. I know she would've turned him down."

"I'm sure you're right—you knew your mother better than anyone. It's just that you should feel some comfort in knowing that your mother was happy and had a man who loved her very much," she said.

"I guess," he grumbled.

"Can you forgive him? It's important to *our* relationship that you can do that because he's my dad, and he's not going anywhere. He'll always be a part of my life."

Shadow embraced her, and she pressed close to him, loving his scent and the warmth of his body as his arms held her tight.

"I know you love your dad, but I'm gonna be honest here. I can't forgive him right now. It'll take time—how much? Fuck, I don't know. That's all I can give you right now."

Scarlett tipped her head back. "I'll take it." Then they kissed, and she knew deep in her heart that everything would be just fine.

A FEW DAYS later, Scarlett sat at one of the picnic tables under a white canopy stretched over the yard and secured on each end of the chain-link fence. Several children ran around the area squealing as they tried to catch iridescent bubbles coming from a machine that sat on the corner of one of the tables.

"Here you go, babe," Shadow said as he handed her a bottle of water and a glass of white wine. He'd explained that on family days at the club, wine was on the bar menu, otherwise, it never graced its shelves during club parties.

"Thanks," she said, scooting down a bit to give him some room to sit by her.

"Who do these kids belong to?" She took a sip of her drink.

"The dark-haired girl with the braids is Lucy—Animal and Olivia's daughter. The blonde cohort is Paisley, and she's Cheri and Jax's daughter. Hope is the smaller girl with the yellow top, and she's Addie and Chas's girl, and the little one with the long wavy hair filled with bows is Isa—Cara and Hawk's daughter."

"That's Cara's little girl? She's so cute. Where is Cara?"

"Inside helping Belle and the other old ladies with the food."

"Should I be in there helping too? I feel rude by just sitting here doing nothing."

Shadow wrapped his arm around her. "You're doing something—

you're keeping me company." He kissed her softly, his light scruff scratching again her cheek.

Then several boys ran into the yard, screaming and jumping on the picnic tables.

"Get the fuck off of those!" a deep voice boomed.

Scarlett turned her head and saw Hawk stalking toward three boys, his face glowering.

"Uh-oh, I wouldn't want to be them," she said, shivering slightly.

Shadow laughed. "Hawk's bark is worse than his bite when it comes to the kids."

The three boys immediately jumped off the tables and stood in a line, their small bodies shifting from one foot to another.

"Braxton, you know better than that! You want me to call your dad out here, Harley? What about you, James? You guys could split your damn heads open. Next time you pull that stupid shit, it'll be the end of playing for a while. Got it?"

Each of the boys nodded, their eyes still cast downward.

"Okay. Don't piss me off again."

The boys raced away, and Hawk walked toward Scarlett and Shadow.

"Oh God. He's coming over here and he's mad as hell."

Shadow chortled. "Relax, babe."

"Hey," Hawk said, lifting his chin at Shadow then at her.

"Hi," she replied tentatively.

"Cara will be out in a minute. She's looking forward to seeing you." Hawk smiled, then brought the bottle of beer to his mouth.

Slowly her muscles loosened. "I can't wait to see her either."

Then Shadow and Hawk began talking about motorcycles, and she leaned against him and let her mind drift. Classic rock songs softly played on four speakers hooked up to the fence. Strings of unlit hanging lanterns swayed gently in the warm breeze, yellow and white checked oilcloths covered the tables, and a solid yellow one covered a long table against the fence.

The aroma of fried chicken and tangy barbecue wafted throughout the yard as several women walked toward the buffet table carrying large pots and platters.

Hawk glanced over his shoulder. "I'm gonna help the women," he said then sauntered away.

"I should help too," Scarlett said as she started to get up, but Shadow held her down.

"The old ladies' men will help them. There's a system to this, babe." He nuzzled his face against her neck. "After dinner, we can go for a walk by the river."

Goosebumps pebbled her skin at the touch of his scratchy face. "Just a walk?" She teased, squeezing his upper thigh.

"I do have something more in mind," he whispered into her ear before nibbling her earlobe.

Scarlett wiggled, then pushed him gently away. "The kids," she said, tipping her head in their direction.

He laughed, then stood up and held out his hand. "The food's on. Let's go eat."

She took Shadow's hand after she pulled down her skirt when she stood up. "Where are Smokey and your other friends?"

"They went on a bike ride. Sometimes the single brothers show up for family times and sometimes they don't. It depends what they got going on."

"And the women in the club?"

"The club girls? No fuckin' way. Family times are for members and old ladies only."

"*Tsk, tsk,*" Scarlett clucked her tongue and shook her head.

"It's the way it goes, babe." He brushed his lips across hers and led her to the buffet table.

Scarlett looked around for Cara, and when she saw her tying one of the bows in Isa's hair, she smiled. *Someday, I'd love to have a baby with Shadow.*

As if sensing someone was looking at her, Cara straightened up and turned around. When she met Scarlett's gaze, she smiled warmly and walked over to her.

"Hawk told me you were dating Shadow," she said as she hugged Scarlett. "I've been meaning to talk to you about it, but I missed the last two committee meetings."

"I want to talk to you about it too, and about all of *this*." Scarlett waved her hand in a circle. "Is it hard to be a part of this life?" she whispered.

"Sometimes, but the rewards of being with your man make it all worth it. Yeah … we need to talk." Cara laughed. "How about lunch next Wednesday? We could meet somewhere downtown near where you work."

"Wednesday's my day off. How about at the club?"

"That'd be great. I haven't been there all summer." Cara stepped closer to Scarlett. "I'm so sorry about what happened to your mother. My heart goes out to you. My parents were saddened to hear the news as well," she said close to her ear.

"I appreciate that. I'd be lying if I didn't say it hasn't been hard and heart wrenching, but I've got Shadow, and some great friends who haven't abandoned me like some others did. And I still have my dad and brothers. We'll manage to get through it."

"If you need anything, just let me know." Cara patted her hand.

"Mama, Daddy won't let me sit by Harley," a small boy with a mop of dark hair said.

Cara looked down and smiled. "If Daddy says no, then it's no. He wants you to eat and not fool around during the meal." She ran her fingers through the young boy's hair and he scowled. "This is my son Braxton."

"Hi." Scarlett smiled. "I saw your daughter—she's precious."

"Thank you. I have another son, Neo. He's fourteen months. Hawk's got him."

Shadow nudged her. "Did you want to eat or talk 'cause you're holding up the line."

Scarlett and Cara both laughed, then Cara said, "You have to love these guys, right? I'll call you so we can firm up next Wednesday." She then scurried away.

After a delicious meal, Scarlett insisted on helping to clean up over Shadow's protests, and thirty minutes later he came into the kitchen, gave her a dish towel, and told her to wipe off her hands because it was time for their walk.

The other old ladies assured her they could finish up, and she folded an apron Belle had given her and ambled out with her man.

The clean, pungent smell of the woods swirled around them as they followed the edge of the river toward a small cabin.

"Are we still on Insurgents' property?" she asked.

"Yeah. We got acres of land. We also got several cabins scattered around the area. They're places to go if a brother wants some time alone."

"It's so beautiful and serene. It feels like we're a million miles from any civilization."

"I come out here a lot to clear my head, especially in the winter months when the roads are iced up and it isn't safe to ride."

The cabin was one large room that housed a small kitchen and one bathroom. A stone fireplace was the focal point of the room. The furnishings were simple: two couches, one recliner, a coffee table, two end tables with lamps, and a rug with geometric designs on it.

Shadow walked to the refrigerator in the kitchen and pulled out a can of beer. "That's all we got in here except for water and some Coke."

"Water's good," she said as she sank down on the couch cushions.

"Here you go," he said, handing the bottle of water to her then joining her on the couch. "How did you like spending some time with the brothers and their families?"

"It was great. I don't know what I expected, but it wasn't *that*. The women are all so different and nice. And the guys acted like I was a person today, even Hawk."

Shadow bumped against her. "See, I told you."

"You were right." She took a drink of water, then put it down on the end table beside her.

"Do you think you could be a part of my world?"

"Aren't I already?"

"Sorta, but I mean, belong to it like Cara, Belle, and the other old ladies."

"Yeah, I think so. I mean, I love you, and if you can rent a tuxedo and wear it to the gala next week, then I certainly can don leather and hang out with your friends."

"And understand that I can't tell you shit about club business and that the club will come first a lot of times?"

"The club business absolutely, the coming first rubs me the wrong way. I want to be first in your life."

"You are and always will be in my heart, but I'll want to hang with my brothers and go to rallies and poker runs and to some of the parties … or just go for a ride and a beer."

"If you're loyal to me, I have no problem with any of that."

"I'll always be loyal to you. I don't go in for cheating, no matter what. I'm not your dad," he said.

Scarlett winced at the reference to her dad, but chose to ignore it. "Then we won't have a problem. If you want to be with your friends sometimes, you have to understand that I, too, will want to hang out with my friends, which might mean going to happy hour once in a while."

A low growl rumbled from his chest. "I'm not liking that."

"Fair is fair. If you want me to trust you, then you have to trust me too."

"I do—it's the other guys I don't trust."

"But I'd be the one in control. Anyway, I probably won't go at all, but if I do, I don't want you getting mad."

"Yeah, and I probably won't go to very many club parties. I basically want to spend time with you."

"Same here. We should do things together. Why are we talking about all this? Are you giving me some sort of test?" She laughed. "Did I pass?"

"You passed, darlin'." Shadow drew her close to him. "You wanna be my old lady?"

Her heart skipped a beat. "Is that a proposal in the biker world?"

"Sometimes it's like a citizen's proposal, and sometimes it means to stay together without making anything legal."

"How do you mean it?" She held her breath.

"Like a citizen." He pulled out a small box from the inner pocket of his cut. "Marry me, baby."

A heartbeat passed, then she held the box in her trembling hands and opened it. A large diamond solitaire glittered in the early evening light.

"It's gorgeous," she muttered. Tears blurred her eyes and happiness burst inside her like a fireworks display.

Shadow took the box from her, then slipped the ring on her fourth finger. "I love you, darlin'."

"I love you too." She wiped her eyes. "I'd be honored to be your old lady. I'll be the best one I can be."

"That's all I need to hear." He clasped her against him, then kissed her passionately.

Burning desire consumed her: searing flames that melted her bones and scorched her skin. Scarlett shoved his shirt up, then broke away from him and smothered his chest with hard kisses and light bites. He groaned and the small sound sent a shockwave of need down to the very base of her toes.

"You're so fuckin' sexy," he rasped as he pushed her down on the couch, then peeled off her clothes. "You complete me like nothing ever has in my life." He bent his head down and captured her lips. After a few moments, he shed his clothes and boots, then hovered over her.

"I need you," she whispered, spreading her legs wide.

"You want it bad." Shadow chuckled, the vibration tickling her stomach as he slid his tongue further down her body. "We got time, darlin', and I want to enjoy every inch of you."

Scarlett writhed and moaned, arching into him as she pushed his head down lower.

"I'm gonna get there all in good time." He winked at her, then trailed his mouth back up her body. He lingered on her breasts, nipping and sucking on her hard nipples, then he devoured her mouth, kissing her deep and rough and hard. She relished the feel of Shadow's bare skin against hers, the deep murmurs of his voice in her ear, the touch of his lips on her naked skin.

Then her eyes caught the glint of her diamond and a love so profound seized every part of her, and she held him tight.

"We're going to spend the rest of our lives together," she whispered.

"That's right, baby. You've got a lifetime of me lovin' you."

Then his lips trailed down her throat, and he slowly kissed and licked her body, working his way down to her sweet hot spot.

It was in that moment of desire and anticipation that she realized she had found her home, and it was safely in his arms.

Make sure you sign up for my newsletter so you can keep up with my new releases, special sales, free short stories, and other treats only available to newsletter readers. When you sign up, you will receive a FREE hot and steamy novella. Sign up at: http://eepurl.com/bACCL1.

Find all my books at: amazon.com/author/chiahwilder

I love hearing from my readers. You can email me at chiahwilder@gmail.com.

Visit me on facebook at facebook.com/AuthorChiahWilder
Visit me on twitter at twitter.com/chiah_wilder
Visit me on Instagram at instagram.com/chiah803

# Notes from Chiah

As always, I have a team behind me making sure I shine and continue on my writing journey. It is their support, encouragement, and dedication that pushes me further in my writing journey. And then, it is my wonderful readers who have supported me, laughed, cried, and understood how these outlaw men live and love in their dark and gritty world. Without you—the readers—an author's words are just letters on a page. The emotions you take away from the words breathe life into the story.

**Thank you** to my amazing Personal Assistant Natalie Weston. I don't know what I'd do without you. Seriously, I'd be lost without you. You keep me organized and on track. I so appreciate that! Your patience, calmness, and insights are always appreciated. Thank you for stepping in when I'm holed up tapping away on the computer, oblivious to the world. You make my writing journey that much smoother. Thank you for ALWAYS being there for me! I'm so lucky you're on my team!

**Thank you** to my editor Lisa Cullinan, for all your insightful edits and making my story a better one. This book was down to the wire and I so appreciate your flexibility in working with this book. Your edits and insights always make my books rock and shine! As always, a HUGE thank you for your patience and flexibility with accepting my book in pieces. I never could have hit the Publish button without you. You're the best!

**Thank you** to my wonderful beta readers Natalie Weston, Maryann Becker, Sera Lavish, and Christina Spence. You rock! Your enthusiasm and suggestions for Shadow's Surrender: Insurgents MC were spot on and helped me to put out a stronger, cleaner novel.

**Thank you** to the bloggers for your support in reading my book, sharing it, reviewing it, and getting my name out there. I so appreciate all your efforts. You all are so invaluable. I hope you know that. Without you, the indie author would be lost.

**Thank you** ARC readers you have helped make all my books so much stronger. I appreciate the effort and time you put in to reading, reviewing, and getting the word out about the books. I don't know what I'd do without you. I feel so lucky to have you behind me.

**Thank you** to my Street Team. Thanks for your input, your support, and your hard work. I appreciate you more than you know. A HUGE hug to all of you!

**Thank you** to Carrie from Cheeky Covers. You are amazing! I can always count on you. You are the calm to my storm. You totally rock, and I love your artistic vision.

**Thank you** to my proofers who worked hard to get my novel back to me so I could hit the publish button on time. There are no words to describe how touched and grateful I am for your dedication and support. Also much thanks for your insight re: plot and characterization. I definitely took heed, and it made my story flow that much better.

**Thank you** to Ena and Amanda with Enticing Journeys Promotions who have helped garner attention for and visibility to the Insurgents MC series. Couldn't do it without you!

**Thank you** to my awesome formatter, Paul Salvette at Beebee Books. You make my books look stellar. I appreciate how professional you are and how quickly you return my books to me. A huge thank you for doing rush orders and always returning a formatted book of which I am proud. Kudos!

**Thank you** to the readers who continue to support me and read my books. Without you, none of this would be possible. I appreciate your comments and reviews on my books, and I'm dedicated to giving you the best story that I can. I'm always thrilled when you enjoy a book as much as I have in writing it. You definitely make the hours of typing on the computer and the frustrations that come with the territory of writing books so worth it.

And a special thanks to every reader who has been with me since "Hawk's Property." Your support, loyalty, and dedication to my stories touch me in so many ways. You enable me to tell my stories, and I am forever grateful to you.

You all make it possible for writers to write because without you reading the books, we wouldn't exist. Thank you, thank you! ♥

## Shadow's Surrender: Insurgents Motorcycle Club (Book 14)

Dear Readers,

Thank you for reading my book. I hope you enjoyed it as much as I enjoyed writing Shadow and Scarlett's story. This gritty and rough motorcycle club has a lot more to say, so I hope you will look for the upcoming books in the series. Romance makes life so much more colorful, and a rough, sexy bad boy makes life a whole lot more interesting.

If you enjoyed the book, please consider leaving a review on Amazon. I read all of them and appreciate the time taken out of busy schedules to do that.

I love hearing from my fans, so if you have any comments or questions, please email me at chiahwilder@gmail.com or visit my facebook page.

To receive a **free copy of my novella**, *Summer Heat*, and to hear of **new releases**, **special sales**, **free short stories**, and **ARC opportunities**, please sign up for my **Newsletter** at http://eepurl.com/bACCL1.

Happy Reading,

Chiah

# CHAINS: Night Rebels MC
## Coming November 2019

**He didn't know he needed her until she came into his life.**

Chains is a **Night Rebel,** one of the **largest MCs in Southern Colorado**. Powerful Harleys, stiff drinks, and club girls are his idea of the good life.

He swore off relationships years ago when he caught his old lady and his buddy sharing some fun time between *his* sheets. Now bitterness is his companion.

The only women in his life are the club girls who know the score: fun without commitment. He likes it that way—he's better off alone.

Then he meets *her* at the veterinary clinic and everything changes. **Sexy curves that spark his libido,** and the **darkest, most soulful eyes** that penetrate the emptiness inside him.

Autumn Stanford has worked hard to build her veterinary practice, and at thirty-one years old, she finally has it all: career, money, a fiancé. She should be busting with joy, but she's not—something's missing.

When the rugged biker brings his dog to her clinic, she is taken in by his **good looks and muscular build.**

**An undeniable desire sizzles between them.**

But there is one small problem: Autumn is engaged to Chains' brother.

All of a sudden, Chains' world turns upside down, and he questions everything he thought he knew about his family.

Autumn is caught in the **crossfire of grudges and family secrets**. And when a secret of her own comes out, will Chains be able to stand by her or will he reject her like his brother did?

**The Night Rebels MC series are standalone romance novels. This is Chains' story. This book contains violence, abuse, strong language, and steamy/graphic sexual scenes. It describes the life and actions of an outlaw motorcycle club. HEA. No cliffhangers.**

# Other Books by Chiah Wilder

### Insurgent MC Series:

Hawk's Property

Jax's Dilemma

Chas's Fervor

Axe's Fall

Banger's Ride

Jerry's Passion

Throttle's Seduction

Rock's Redemption

An Insurgent's Wedding

Outlaw Xmas

Wheelie's Challenge

Christmas Wish

Animal's Reformation

Insurgents MC Romance Series: Insurgents Motorcycle Club Box Set
(Books 1 – 4)

Insurgents MC Romance Series: Insurgents Motorcycle Club Box Set
(Books 5 – 8)

### Night Rebels MC Series:

STEEL

MUERTO

DIABLO

GOLDIE

PACO

SANGRE

ARMY

Night Rebels MC Romance Series: Night Rebels Motorcycle Club
Box Set (Book 1 – 4)

## Nomad Biker Romance Series:

Forgiveness
Retribution

## Steamy Contemporary Romance:

My Sexy Boss

Find all my books at: amazon.com/author/chiahwilder

I love hearing from my readers. You can email me at chiahwilder@gmail.com.

Sign up for my newsletter to receive a FREE Novella, updates on new books, special sales, free short stories, and ARC opportunities at http://eepurl.com/bACCL1.

Visit me on facebook at facebook.com/AuthorChiahWilder
Visit me on twitter at twitter.com/chiah_wilder
Visit me on Instagram at instagram.com/chiah803

CPSIA information can be obtained
at www.ICGtesting.com
Printed in the USA
LVHW021202071019
633402LV00001B/210/P